## PRAISE FOR *THE DEEPEST BLUE*

"Fans will be eager to reenter Renthia and discover another queen."

—*Booklist* (starred review)

"This intriguing dive into the powers that attempt to control Renthia yields an action-packed fantasy."

—*Library Journal*

"*The Deepest Blue* is an excellent stand-alone story that will have you looking at the ocean in a whole new light, and one I highly recommend."

—Lightspeed Magazine

## PRAISE FOR THE QUEENS OF RENTHIA

"Durst is an expert world-builder and has crafted an enthralling tale."

—*Washington Post*

"Durst knows how to move her audience and rattle the earth."

—Tor.com

## PRAISE FOR *THE QUEEN OF BLOOD*

"A truly wonderful fantasy novel that doubles as an allegory for our own earthly struggle between Man and Nature. Filled with fresh ideas and excitement, told with verve and heart, this book deserves a wide readership, and I think it will find one."

—Terry Brooks, *New York Times* bestselling author

"Thrilling—heartrending—enchanting—absolutely un-put-down-able!"

—Tamora Pierce, *New York Times* bestselling author

# THE DEEPEST BLUE

BY SARAH BETH DURST

*The Deepest Blue*

**THE QUEENS OF RENTHIA**
*The Queen of Blood*
*The Reluctant Queen*
*The Queen of Sorrow*

# THE
# DEEPEST
# BLUE

TALES OF RENTHIA

# SARAH BETH DURST

HARPER Voyager
*An Imprint of HarperCollinsPublishers*

HarperCollins books may be purchased for educational, business, or sales promotional use. For information, please email the Special Markets Department at SPsales@harpercollins.com.

Harper Voyager and design are trademarks of HarperCollins Publishers LLC.

A hardcover edition of this book was published in 2019 by Harper Voyager, an imprint of HarperCollin Publishers.

FIRST HARPER VOYAGER PAPERBACK EDITION PUBLISHED 2020.

Designed by Paula Russell Szafranski
Maps by Ashley P. Halsey
Title spread art © Rich Carey/Shutterstock, Inc.
Chapter opener art © Creaby 0/Shutterstock, Inc.; © fatproject/Shutterstock, Inc.

Library of Congress Cataloging-in-Publication Data has been applied for.

ISBN 978-0-06-295541-8

20 21 22 23 24  LSC  10 9 8 7 6 5 4 3 2 1

*For the Kolkos:*
*Nan, Ira,*
*Valerie, Matthew, Rafi,*
*Allen, and Lauren*

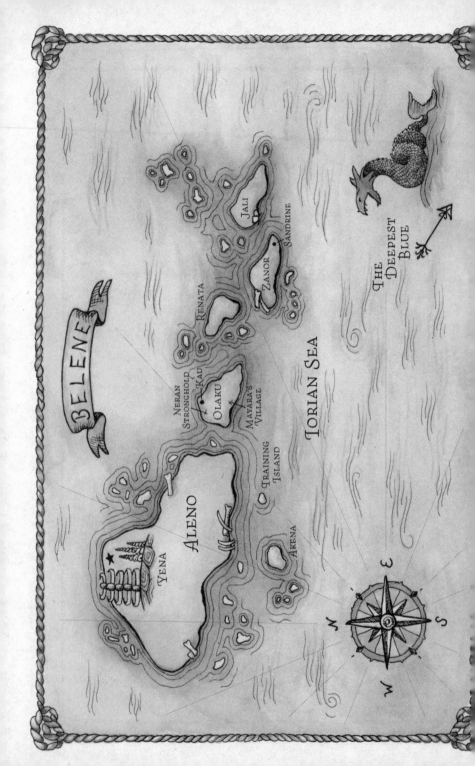

# THE DEEPEST BLUE

# CHAPTER ONE

*Death is blue.*
*Black blue, churned by storms,*
*Green blue, stained by kelp,*
*Pale blue, bleached by sun,*
*The turquoise blue of the sea's shallows,*
*And the deepest blue of its depths.*

On the dawn of her wedding day, Mayara knotted her diving belt around her waist and climbed the skull of a long-dead sea monster. At the top, she straddled the eye socket and looked down. Below, far below, the ancient skull was cracked, and within the fissure was a deep pool of water so still that it looked like glass. She imagined it would shatter when she dived into it.

*Breathe,* she told herself. *Just breathe.*

She'd never done this dive before. It was known to be one of the trickiest on all the islands of Belene. But today was special.

*Today I marry my best friend. It's the perfect day to defy death.*

Or, as she used to say when her sister ran off to try a new dive, to dramatically meet it.

She eyed the barnacle-encrusted rocks far below, on the edges of the fissure. So easy to die: impaled on the rocks, neck broken, body sliced. So hard to live: one opening, just a little wider than a vertical human body. You had to hit it just right, perfectly straight, arms in front of you, pressed against your ears.

*I can do it,* she thought. *I will* do it.

She'd told no one where she was going, especially Kelo, though she knew he'd guess. He knew her better than anyone. At dawn, she'd slipped out her window and run up the winding path. The seagulls were already awake, cawing over the fish in the shallows. A few clamdiggers were on the beach, bent over their shovels, and the grandmothers—the eldest villagers— were already at the end of the rock jetties with their favorite fishing rods. None of them had paid any attention to Mayara. They were used to her sprinting out of the village at odd hours, clutching her diving belt with its assortment of knives and pouches, whenever the urge to dive struck her.

But today's dive wasn't a whim. She'd planned this, in honor of her sister. Exactly eight years ago today, when Mayara was eleven and Elorna was sixteen, Elorna had done this very dive. She'd come back exhilarated, with her pouches full of abalone, and woken up Mayara by emptying her pouches onto Mayara's bed.

*My quilt stank like fish for a week.* But Elorna had been so excited, and Mayara had been so happy that her beloved sister had come to her first, bypassing their parents, her friends, every- one, to share the moment with Mayara.

"It's so peaceful down there," Elorna had said. "Like every- thing that ever upset you has drifted away, and there's no past and future. Only the blue, all around you."

"Death is blue," Mayara had said automatically. It was an islander saying.

Elorna had laughed. "I'll tell you a little secret: death can't catch you if you *chase* death. While it looks for you here"— she tapped Mayara's nose—"you'll really be *here*." She grabbed Mayara's hand and yanked her out of the house.

Yelping, Mayara stumbled along behind her. "Elorna, I'm

not dressed! And that doesn't make sense. If you chase death, you're just more likely to die."

But Elorna had only laughed again and kept running, dragging her little sister with her through the still-asleep village, all the way to the shore and straight into the shallows. Without releasing Mayara's hand, she'd pulled her into the ocean, and they'd plunged into the breaking waves together.

It was one of Mayara's favorite memories.

If Elorna were here today, on Mayara's wedding day, she'd have woken Mayara early and dragged her off on some adventure: climbing to the top of a cliff or discovering a new secret alcove. Or they'd have swum out to one of the rocks in the bay to watch the sea spirits at sunrise. Or "borrowed" a boat and dared the dangers of the reef.

But Elorna wasn't here.

*And so I'll dive.*

*I have to live enough for both of us now.*

Mayara breathed deeply, then exhaled, pushing all the air out of her lungs. She inhaled one more time, then gasped like a fish on land in order to suck in extra puffs to fill both her lungs to capacity. When her lungs were so stuffed she felt as if they would burst, she leaped up and out, bent in half, then kicked her legs behind her.

Straight as an arrow, she sliced through the air. She felt the wind in her face, heard its shriek, and saw the sliver of blue straight below her. Arms straight over her head, she pressed her palms together as if in prayer.

And then she pierced the water.

Silence filled her instantly. Beautiful silence. It wrapped her in its embrace. She kicked her feet together, propelling herself deeper. Her eyes stung from the salty water, but she kept them open, as she'd learned to do as a baby. Murky blueness was all around, and she felt as if it had erased the entire world.

For the first thirty seconds, she felt like an invader, forcing herself through the water.

In the next thirty seconds, she felt her body rebel, her lungs burning, her muscles shaking, as every bit of her body told her she didn't belong. She needed air!

But she went deeper.

Then the shaking pain receded, replaced by a calmness.

It was a calmness only the deep divers ever experienced, and with it came the feeling of becoming one with the water, as if Mayara belonged here in this airless world.

The best divers on the islands could dive on one breath for eleven minutes.

Mayara had trained hard to withstand eight minutes, a full minute longer than Elorna had ever achieved. She loosened one of the straps on her belt and unhooked one of her knives. Giving another powerful kick, she propelled herself down toward the rocks below.

Few had harvested here, and the abalone were thickly clustered. She chose the largest. Gliding toward them, trying not to alarm them and cause them to cling harder, Mayara deftly slid her blade between the sea snail's muscly foot and the rock. She tucked the creature into a pouch and went for a second one that looked to be the size of her father's shoe. She could fit only one in each pouch, they were so big. She saved the last pouch for sea urchins, filling it with the spiky creatures, working quickly but smoothly so as not to disturb the water.

She judged she'd reached six minutes.

Her thoughts already felt sluggish. She couldn't remember why she was here, why she'd decided to gather these poor creatures, or even what they were called. Silver fish flitted past her, and she saw a brilliant purple fish dart into an orange anemone. The colors were vivid and cloudy simultaneously. . . .

It was time to return to the surface. She performed a graceful half-somersault and kicked upward. Behind her, the fish scattered in her wake. She swam up, bending her body fluidly as if she were a dolphin.

Above, she saw a glow—the sun warming the surface, but in the shape of a crescent moon, the fissure she'd dived into. She aimed for it. Her lungs were hurting now, and black spots began to dot her vision. She wondered if she'd miscalculated. She thought she knew exactly what she could handle.

A trickle of fear slid into her.

Ruthlessly, she quenched it. Fear could kill you faster than anything else down here. She had to stay calm, conserve every last molecule of oxygen in her body. She'd reach the surface soon. She hadn't dived *that* far.

Had she?

The glow intensified until soon it was all she could see. Her lungs were near bursting . . . and then *she* burst out of the water. *Breathe!* She sucked in air, and it hurt as she filled—

She sensed the water spirit in her mind, like a too-sharp tickle inside her skull, only a split second before its jaws clamped onto her leg. It yanked her down before she could finish her breath. Mayara swallowed water instead. Flailing, she fought to reach the surface again. She kicked the spirit, and it released.

Aiming for the glow, she erupted out of the water once more, this time coughing and spitting. She inhaled deeply, banishing the black spots. Her limbs quit trembling.

From the surface, she couldn't see the water spirit. She knew it was still down there—she felt its nearness clawing at her mind. She couldn't give it a chance to grab her again.

Inhaling once more, she propelled herself back under. She spun in the water, searching for the spirit, and saw it: vaguely humanlike, it was the size of a two-year-old child but as thin as an old woman who cannot eat anymore. Its skin was gray like a shark's, and it had three rows of sharp teeth. Its all-black eyes were fixed on Mayara.

Knife out, Mayara kicked her feet, aiming for the spirit even as it swam at her.

*I'm chasing death now.*

She sliced with her knife, but the spirit pivoted faster than she'd expected and let out a keening shriek that pierced through the water, echoing.

*Oh no you don't. No calling for friends.* She stabbed fast, aiming not for the spirit's heart this time but for its throat. She felt the blade nick the soft, wet flesh. A cloud of red puffed around her hand.

The spirit clapped its clawed fingers over its throat and then spurted backward. She hadn't killed it, but it was hurt enough to retreat.

Mayara hadn't been fast enough, though.

A larger water spirit—this one shaped like a squid and as milky white as a pearl—was darting through the water toward her. It had heard the childlike spirit's cry, either through the water or in its mind.

She tried to outswim it, aiming for the fissure, but it wrapped its tentacles around her waist, pulling her under. She jammed her knife into one of the tentacles. Blood stained the water, but the spirit didn't loosen its grip.

*No! I am not dying today!*

Yanking the blade out, she stabbed again and again, but still the spirit pulled her deeper. Her lungs ached, her head spun, and blackness filled her vision. She heard her sister's voice in her head: *Mayara, don't do it. Promise me you won't.*

*But, Elorna, no one will know!*

*You know that's not true. They'll know. They can sense it when you use your power. It draws them like sharks to chum. You'll make it a hundred times worse.*

*What's a hundred times worse than dead?*

*I don't want to find out, my little minnow.*

*Are you afraid? Elorna, you aren't afraid of anything.*

*I'm not afraid for me; I'm afraid for you.*

But she knew as she thought it that it was a lie. Mayara was afraid for herself too. The blackness was almost complete. In seconds, she'd lose consciousness. And Kelo would never see her again. He'd wake alone on their wedding day, he'd complete the dress he was making for her—the one he refused to show to anyone, not until it was ready—and then she'd never come. Her parents would lose a second daughter. Her mother rarely left their house as it was, and her father wouldn't touch his boat, saying it was cursed with bad luck, ever since Elorna died so far from home. It rotted in the harbor. How much more would they fall apart if she died today? Mayara knew what Elorna had meant when she'd said she was more afraid for her. Because more than being afraid for herself . . .

*I'm afraid for* them. *Forgive me, Elorna.*

Mayara then reached with her mind—clumsily, due to her lack of experience—toward the squidlike water spirit. *Release me,* she ordered. She pushed the thought directly into the spirit, as if she were plunging a knife into the spirit's mind. She'd never done it before, not intentionally, but Elorna had described how it felt, like a shout but silent. It sounded impossible . . . but it worked.

The tentacles unwound, and the spirit retreated.

Looking up, Mayara saw the glow of the sun in the fissure. But it was too far. She was too deep now. *I'm not going to make it.*

*I'm sorry.*

She heard a high-pitched giggle—the child-shaped spirit. Its throat may have been torn by her knife, but she still heard the giggle in her mind. The sound felt like claws scraping inside her skull.

Mayara aimed her thoughts at the spirit and shouted silently, *Give me your air!*

Compelled, it swam toward her.

*Air—now!*

The spirit clamped onto her, its tiny arms wrapping around her torso. It pressed its face against hers and exhaled. Manipulating the water as if it were fabric, the spirit created a bubble around Mayara's head. It filled the bubble with air pulled from the water.

Mayara breathed.

Holding on to the spirit as if hugging it, Mayara kicked her legs and swam upward. The air pocket came with them.

She broke through the surface. Releasing the spirit, she ordered, *Go!*

With another horrible high-pitched giggle, it sank back under the surface. Mayara swam for the rocks and hauled herself out of the water. She collapsed on her back, her head resting against a mound of seaweed, and stared at the sky as she breathed in the sweet, plentiful air.

Her leg, where the spirit had bitten her, began to throb. She held up one arm and examined it. She had the barest blush of a bruise where the tentacles had squeezed her. *That will be magnificent in a few hours.* Worse, at some point in the fight, she'd lost her favorite knife. She'd probably left it embedded in the squidlike spirit.

"Ow," she said out loud. Her voice cracked.

She closed her eyes and let herself unceremoniously pass out.

WHEN SHE REGAINED CONSCIOUSNESS, HER FIANCÉ, KELO, WAS there, quietly dabbing her wounds with a salve. He was intent on his work and hadn't noticed she'd awoken. She studied him in silence for a moment.

He was undoubtedly handsome. Mayara's cousin Ilia had once declared that he was the most delicious-looking man in Belene, and Mayara was positive it wasn't an exaggeration, though she admitted to being biased. His hair was so black that it was nearly blue, his arms and chest were muscled from lugging rock back and forth across his studio, and his dark bronze skin was smooth and perfect. But as nice as all that was, it wasn't what drew Mayara to him.

*It's this. The fact that he isn't yelling at me for being stupid, when I richly deserve it.*

"Do I want to ask what happened?" Even Kelo's voice was beautiful.

She tried to decide what to tell him. Ultimately, she chose the truth. "I did Elorna's dive," Mayara said. "And then it got complicated."

"It always seems to. But you're alive." He kissed her forehead. "That's what matters."

But it wasn't all that mattered. She'd broken a promise to her sister and used her power. She hadn't broken her greater promise, though: no one in the village knew she'd used it, and they wouldn't know.

And maybe that was enough.

Because that was what had happened to Elorna. She'd used her power in front of the village, word had spread, and the queen had heard.

And that had led to Elorna's death.

Only Kelo and Mayara's parents knew that Mayara, like Elorna before her, could sense and control the spirits that plagued Renthia. And even telling him had been tough; it had pretty much been the moment she realized she loved him and trusted him with her heart . . . and life. Still, she felt it necessary to say, carefully, "If anyone asks what happened . . . I'm going to have to lie." She knew he'd read between the lines to see the truth.

"No one will ask," Kelo said confidently. "You'll look too radiant. Can you stand?" He helped her to her feet. She expected pain when she put weight on her leg, but none came—Kelo must have brought a strong salve. She wondered how he knew she'd need that.

*Because he knows me,* she thought wryly.

He looked up at the top of the skull. She did as well and noticed a rope dangling—that was how Kelo must have gotten down.

"Can you climb?" he asked.

Eyeing the top of the skull, she thought it seemed much farther up than when she'd dived. "Sure." Gripping the rope, she began to climb. He followed.

She tried not to think about what had just happened: how she'd used her power, how she'd hallucinated Elorna's voice, how she'd nearly died. And for what? A few abalone?

*No,* she realized firmly, *that's not why I did it.*

Ever since Elorna died on Akena Island three years ago, Mayara had been determined—in addition to living her own life—to live the life her sister had striven for, to try to experience the things that Elorna would have wanted to experience. It was the best way she could think of to honor her.

Besides, Kelo was going to love the shells! She could tell by the weight of the pouches that she'd harvested massive ones.

Next time she did this dive, she'd remember to keep her senses open for spirits. Perhaps bring a fishing spear. She'd done successful dives with spears before, even though it made things a bit more difficult. But it would be worth the extra challenge in order to have that kind of defense. She'd had her knives, but they hadn't been much use against the squid spirit. . . .

*Wait . . .*

"Next *time*"?

Reaching the top of the skull, she flopped over the edge and rolled onto her back. She then started laughing. She wasn't even sure *why* she was laughing. Just that the sky looked so beautiful and blue. And she had seaweed stuck in her hair. And it was her and Kelo's wedding day, and she was alive. Alive!

Kelo hoisted himself up on top of the skull beside her. He lay down next to her and waited for her to calm down. "Any interest in telling me what happened during your near-death experience?" he asked blandly.

"You want so badly to yell at me, don't you?" She knew he wouldn't, though.

"You are who you are," Kelo said. "I'm not marrying you in hopes of changing you. I'm marrying you because I love you, all of you, even the parts of you that make bad decisions."

Mayara sobered, suddenly not feeling like laughing at all anymore. "I used my power," she said softly, though there was no one nearby to hear. Even the gulls were too far above them. She knew he'd guessed already from her hint, but she didn't want any secrets between them.

"That wasn't the bad decision." Always calm, Kelo seemed unruffled by her confession. She loved that about him. "That kept you alive. No, the bad decision was your equipment. Next time, you should bring your spear."

She sat up. "Exactly what I was thinking!"

He sat up too and grinned at her. Leaning over, he cupped her face in his hands and kissed her. She kissed him back with every bit of breath she had.

When they came up for air, Mayara rested her forehead against his.

"Do you think you can avoid any death-defying activities for the rest of the day?" Kelo asked, a plaintive note in his voice. "It is kind of a special day."

"You know I'd do anything for you," Mayara said, then kissed him again before grinning and adding, "But no promises."

# CHAPTER TWO

Mayara let Kelo blindfold her. She felt him knot the cloth, pressing her wet hair closer to her scalp, and then she felt a feather-light kiss on her neck.

"All dark?" he asked, his breath warm on her ear.

She grinned. "All dark."

He kissed her—and the surprise of it thrilled Mayara—then led her by the hand, and she followed, shuffling her feet forward to feel the rocks. She knew the path to his studio by heart—up along a rib bone of an ancient leviathan, high above their village, across and up from the ceremonial plaza and the storm-shelter caves. She felt through her sandals when the rocks shifted to broken shells. "Stop here," he said.

She waited, listening while he opened the door; then he guided her over the threshold. She breathed in the familiar smell: the salty tang of seaweed, the sweet scent of hibiscus, and the mellowness of a whale-fat candle. Chimes tinkled as a breeze blew in through the open doorway behind her. She felt herself smiling, even though she hadn't seen anything yet.

"Ready?" he asked.

He sounded adorably anxious, as if he was unsure whether she'd love it or not. She already knew she'd love it, whatever it looked like. She always did, with everything he made.

She felt his fingers in her wet hair again, and the knot loosened.

He removed the blindfold. "Look."

Kelo's studio was her favorite place on the island. All the tables and shelves were stuffed with piles of driftwood, baskets of abalone and conch shells, and jars of pebbles that gleamed like tiny moons—nearly all of it collected by Mayara. Kelo's finished art hung on the walls and from the ceiling rafters. Her favorites were the wind chimes and the pendants that dangled in the windows, catching the twinkling sunlight.

As wonderful as it looked, his art was also designed to repel spirits—his work was a mix of beauty and necessity. *Rather like Kelo himself,* she thought, and smiled. Because of the nature of his art, his work fetched a pretty price at markets in the nearby villages—he was one of the best charmworkers around. No spirit would enter a house that was decorated with Kelo's charms.

His life's work, he often said, was to make people feel both protected and loved.

Mayara knew that from experience.

She saw he had a pile of new charms on a nearby worktable: driftwood carved into the shape of tiny animals and then inlaid with mother-of-pearl. He made those to dangle over cribs, to ward spirits away from newborns. "Is that for my cousin?" she asked. Her cousin Helia was expecting her third child, and she'd been pestering Kelo for a new mobile. She claimed she shouldn't have to pay, since they were "all nearly family"—conveniently forgetting that if Kelo didn't charge any of Mayara's very large, very extended family, he'd be working for free for half the village. *I'll talk to her again,* Mayara thought. She didn't want anyone taking advantage of her almost-husband.

With a fond sigh at her lack of focus, Kelo cupped Mayara's cheeks and turned her head toward the eastern window. Glowing in the morning sun was her surprise.

Her wedding dress.

It was ready.

And it was perfect.

He'd taken her grandmother's simple wrap dress and, without destroying its simplicity, sewn a mosaic of mother-of-pearl into the fabric so that the entire garment shimmered as if it had been dipped in the light of a moon rainbow. Mayara felt tears prick her eyes.

She'd never cried over a dress before. Or even cared about what she wore, so long as she could swim and climb in it. But this . . . He must have spent hours and hours on it, sewing on each tiny shard.

"Do you like it?" he asked.

She gave him a look.

He laughed. "You love it."

"And you." Throwing her arms around his neck, she kissed him. He kissed her back, and she began to slide out of her diving gear. As she loosened the straps of her top, she heard a whistle then a shout from the path.

"Mayara! Kelo!" It was her aunt Beila, her mother's sister. Mayara's mother had four sisters and two brothers, and Beila was both the eldest and the loudest. She wouldn't object to Mayara and Kelo "playing" while they were supposed to be preparing for the wedding, but she would make plenty of embarrassing recommendations. *Really rather avoid that*, Mayara thought.

Quickly, Mayara retied her straps. "Later," she promised Kelo.

He hurried to the door. "It's your aunts."

"I know. I heard . . . Wait, did you say 'aunts,' as in . . . ?"

He nodded soberly. "All of them."

"Can I hide?" She eyed the worktables. If she tucked herself into a far corner . . .

Kelo's lips twitched. He was laughing at her. "You wouldn't leave me alone with them, would you? That would be cruel."

"Maybe I'm a cruel and terrible person, and you just never noticed." She backed up to one of the tables, then had a better idea. *I could leap out a window. Back into the sea. Take my chances with the spirits. . . .*

Unfortunately, Kelo had the idea first. He catapulted himself out the window, calling, "You're a beautiful and brave person!" over his shoulder. And then she heard: "Freedom!"

"You—"

Cutting herself off, she plastered a smile on her face as her four aunts barreled through the door into Kelo's studio. Shrieking like gulls, they swarmed her, wishing her a happy wedding day, fussing over her bruises and injuries, gushing over all the preparations for the celebration, chiding her for not being dressed yet, exclaiming over the beauty of said dress . . . until Mayara's head began to ache.

"Don't look so pained, my dear," Eyara, one of her aunts, said, patting her shoulder. She was Mother's youngest sister, and she was clearly enjoying Mayara's discomfort. Last year she'd had to suffer through the village's excitement over her own much-anticipated wedding. "You know you love us."

"Of course I do," Mayara said. *Just maybe not all at once.*

But Mayara didn't have much choice. Before she could object, her aunts stripped off her swim clothes, bathed her with the traditional perfumed sponge, and dressed her in the mother-of-pearl dress. Two of them were brushing her hair at once, often bumping into each other and accidentally—or not—yanking her hair, while the others cleared space on one of Kelo's worktables and laid out a tea set.

The traditional wedding-day tea was supposed to be between mother and child, but Mother hadn't come with her sisters. Mayara felt her heart lurch. Mother had barely left their house since Elorna's death, only coming out when Papa coaxed her with the promise of a perfect sunset. *Mother can't resist a perfect sunset.*

But she could resist her own daughter.

For the second time that day, tears almost came as Mayara realized she'd be sharing the tea with her aunts instead of with her mother. She'd hoped that today would be different. . . .

*It is different. It's special. And Mother will join me . . . when she can.*

Until then, Mayara wasn't going to let anything mar the new, wonderful memories she was making today. She was going to treasure every second of specialness.

She walked across the studio in the mother-of-pearl dress. It clinked as she moved so that she sounded as if she herself were one of Kelo's wind chimes. Sitting, she poured the tea for herself and her aunts and then sweetened it with spoonfuls of rare sugar.

Aunt Beila said kindly, "You know your mother wanted . . ."

"It's all right," Mayara said, willing herself to believe it. "As Aunt Eyara said, I love you all, and I am honored to share this moment with you."

Her aunts all sighed happily at that.

Each of them raised a teacup. Aunt Beila began: "May the warmth of this tea keep you safe from the bitter wind."

Aunt Leera: "May the sweetness of this tea keep you full of joy."

Aunt Gelna: "May the bitterness comfort you in times of pain and sorrow."

Aunt Eyara: "May the . . . Oh drat, I've forgotten." She improvised. "May your tea taste good, your life be long, and your marriage even longer." She then chugged a great gulp of the sugared tea.

Laughing, Mayara drank too, as did the rest of her aunts.

And then they all bustled her out the door to her wedding.

ONE SIDE EFFECT OF HAVING A LOT OF AUNTS AND UNCLES: MAYARA also had a *lot* of cousins. Eighteen of them, and that wasn't counting her cousins' children. And absolutely all of them seemed to be determined to make Mayara and Kelo's wedding into the most celebrated event on the island, or even all of Belene.

Maybe all of Renthia.

*It's just one day,* she thought as she watched everyone scurry around the wedding site. They looked like hermit crabs on a beach, scuttling back and forth across the sand. Three cousins were wrestling a table piled high with cooked shrimp and clams. Another cousin was plucking petals from a barrel of flowers so that guests could toss them into the wind—a good-luck tradition. Yet more cousins were tying firemoss lanterns to posts so that dancing could continue long after the sun went down. Everyone seemed obsessed with making sure every detail was perfect. Which made her stare at them in wonder.

*Because I don't care whether today is perfect. I care about all the days that come* after.

*And I care about getting some of those shrimp. . . .*

She caught one of her cousins by the arm. "Ilia—"

"Oh, you look gorgeous!" Ilia squealed. "Kelo is brilliant!"

"Yes, I know—can you snag me some of those shrimp before Uncle Imer spots them?" Mayara nodded at the shrimp table. Uncle Imer was well known for his ability to consume shellfish at an impressive rate.

"Can't, Mayara, sorry! Grandmama told me to wake the drummers. She wants them to start early so we can dance before the ceremony begins."

"But they're supposed to play all night. If you wake them now—"

"Do *you* want to argue with her?"

Mayara winced. She would cheerfully dive into the narrow crevice from that morning all day, but even she knew better than to argue with Grandmama. Standing on tiptoes, she spotted the formidable matriarch, the self-appointed leader of the village grandmothers, in the center of the ceremony site. She was seated so regally on a kelp-green chair that she may as well have been sitting on a throne. Though too far away to hear,

Mayara could still tell her grandmother was barking out orders to all her progeny—and anyone else who accidentally wandered within range.

"Is it too late to go back to Kelo's studio?" Mayara asked Aunt Eyara, who was still beside her. The other aunts had fanned out, immersing themselves in the fray, when all Mayara wanted to do was turn tail and flee. *And Kelo thinks I'm brave. Clearly I'm not.* Being the center of so much attention was more unnerving than facing down a spirit underwater. She didn't think of herself as superstitious, but she felt like she was tempting luck. "Or I could just take a nice nap in one of the storm-shelter caves. . . ."

Aunt Eyara chuckled. "You know what they say: Marriage is for the bride and groom; weddings are for the family. All the family, even those of us you don't like. Come on, Mayara, you know you'd do anything to be with Kelo—I've seen the way you are with him. Being the star of the best party ever thrown is not such a terrible price to pay for a lifetime of joy and happiness." She laughed even louder at that, then *firmly* ushered Mayara forward into the chaos.

Mayara spotted Kelo through the crowd. *Ha!* He hadn't escaped after all—he was with his parents and had been roped into stringing charms along the cliff wall. Their wedding site was a stone plaza built on a cliff that had once been part of a leviathan's sternum, not far from Kelo's studio. Over the centuries, the ancient rib cage had filled in with dirt and rock. On top of it, the islanders had built the plaza as a place to hold celebrations and ceremonies, and they'd surrounded it with a hip-high stone wall to keep anyone from falling off the edge. It jutted out above the village and boasted views to the south and the west.

The plaza had always been a part of life. She had played here. Had seen other family married here. Had snuck out at night to meet Kelo here for a different kind of play. As much as she wanted to run away, she knew she was exactly where she wanted to be too.

Mayara weaved her way through friends, neighbors, and cousins until she reached Kelo and his parents. Kelo was the only child of two only children, so he wasn't related to nearly as many of the guests as she was. *Lucky,* she thought. But even in her thoughts, she didn't mean it. She loved her huge, crazy family.

Kelo's mother embraced her, while his father nodded approval at her dress.

"Kelo, it's a masterpiece," his father proclaimed.

"*She's* a masterpiece," Kelo replied.

Mayara rolled her eyes. "You two rehearsed that, didn't you?"

"Only once or twice," Kelo admitted. "Did you like it?"

She was about to answer when an odd jerking movement in the clouds on the horizon caught her eye. Stepping up to the wall, she stared out across the ocean toward a cluster of gray and blue clouds. Making a comforting sound, Kelo's mother said, "Not to worry. The storm is a long way out. You'll be good and married before it reaches the islands."

But Mayara continued to stare at the distant clouds. She thought she'd seen . . . But the clouds were behaving normally now, with no twitches or sudden un-cloud-like movements. *I must have imagined it.*

She forced herself to turn back to Kelo and the preparations. Across the plaza, the drummers began to play, and a few of her younger cousins and neighbors started to dance, romping in a circle. She smiled at them, and they waved at her.

*Don't worry about the storm,* she told herself. *You aren't sugar in tea. You won't melt in a little rain.* She just hoped rain was all it was.

It was a perfect sunset.

All the clouds on the horizon had shifted, as if Mayara's relatives had bargained with the storm to dissipate so that Mayara's mother would come see her daughter's wedding.

Mayara, in her nacre dress, stood with Kelo on a raised

platform by the stone wall. His parents were behind him, on the ground, each holding symbols of health and happiness: a knot of seaweed for health and a ripe coconut for happiness. Her parents, with Mother leaning heavily on Papa's arm, were behind Mayara, with symbols of long life and protection from pain and sorrow: a piece of driftwood and a sliver of fossilized bone from an ancient water spirit.

Rose and orange from the setting sun soaked into the stones of the plaza and were reflected in the water in the sea beyond. Mayara gazed into Kelo's eyes and wished she could preserve this moment forever.

"You live in my heart," Kelo said.

"You live in mine," Mayara replied.

"Our souls are one."

"Our souls are two, made one." She'd heard these words at every village wedding, and she'd known that someday she and Kelo would be standing here, on the cliff above the village, with the sea and the sunset and everyone they loved as their witnesses. In fact, she'd known since she was six years old. Kelo claimed he'd known since he was three. Everyone always oohed and aahed when he said that, until she pointed out that at three, he'd also thought he was going to marry his father's boat, his favorite chicken, and a bowl of clam soup. "Always, I will—"

She saw it again, out of the corner of her eye, a twitch in the clouds on the horizon. She turned her head to see that the ocean looked darker. Clouds had blown in front of the setting sun, blocking some of its light. *That was quick.*

Unsettled, Mayara continued. "Always, I will share my days and my nights, my hopes and my dreams . . ." Her attention drifted again as she felt whispers inside her head. Wordless, the whispers scratched at her. She strained to hear them.

A worried frown crossing his face—he'd clearly noticed her distraction—Kelo picked up the traditional words. "Always, I will share my fears and my sorrows, never to walk alone."

The words passed through her mind, but something else dominated her thoughts now.

It felt like a spirit. But she'd never sensed one like this. . . . It sounded like . . . *It sounds like* many *spirits, all jumbled up.* She again looked at the clouds. They were moving fast now, across the ocean, and the waves were breaking in front of them.

*It's nothing,* she told herself. *I'm imagining it. Just bad weather.*

It had to be, because she'd never been able to hear any of the wild ocean spirits while she was on shore, and the heirs kept the so-called tame spirits away from the villages.

*It's an ordinary storm. And it's too far away to worry about.* Kelo's mother had said it wouldn't arrive until later, and she was never wrong in her predictions. The fishermen often charted their routes based on her readings of the sky.

Mayara dragged her mind back into the moment, and she again gazed into Kelo's eyes. *This* was all she had to worry about. Not messing up the final words of the ceremony in front of everyone she knew. "Together, forever, we will sail the seas of life."

"Together, forever, I pledge myself to you," Kelo said.

"And I to you."

As their families and everyone in their village cheered, Mayara and Kelo kissed. Then they turned, hand in hand, their backs to the sea and the storm. Grinning broadly, Kelo waved at the crowd. "Hey, we did it! It's time to eat and dance!"

The cheering was even louder.

Kelo jumped off the platform and held out his arms. Smiling back at him, Mayara jumped, and he caught her and twirled her in a circle before setting her down. The drummers began to play again. Soon Mayara and Kelo spun apart—each of them greeting their guests and accepting their congratulations.

Papa kissed Mayara's forehead. "You know I wish you—"

Mother laid her hand on Papa's elbow, stopping him. Her face was pale, and she had dark circles under her eyes. Mayara was certain she was going to say she had to leave the celebration early—that all of this made her think too much about Elorna, how Elorna had never had a chance to fall in love and marry, how this only reminded her of what they'd all lost—but Mother didn't say that. Instead she managed a small smile. It looked foreign on her face, as if her lips had forgotten they could curve, but it was undoubtedly a smile. "We both wish you every happiness, Mayara."

Mayara felt a lump in her throat and blinked back tears that suddenly sprang into her eyes. She loved them both so very much. *I am the luckiest woman in the world.* "Thank you, Mother." She hugged her. "And you, Papa." She hugged him too.

When she released them, she felt it again—this time louder, the voices of wild spirits pounding in her head. She couldn't ignore it or pretend she'd imagined it. Keeping a smile on her face, Mayara pushed past her parents, only half paying attention to other well-wishers, as she maneuvered through the crowd to the cliff wall.

She looked out at the horizon.

The horizon was gone, swallowed completely by the storm clouds.

*It's not an ordinary storm.*

And it wasn't coming slowly. It was flying over the sea, unnaturally fast. The voices in her head . . . They were from *within* the storm. "It's coming for us," Mayara breathed. She stumbled backward, away from the cliff wall, and turned to face her family, her friends, and her neighbors—everyone she knew and loved.

"Spirit storm!" she screamed.

# CHAPTER THREE

Long ago, Renthia was only four countries: the forests of Aratay, the mountains of Semo, the farmlands of Chell, and the glaciers of Elhim. Their queens tamed the spirits of the land—the spirits of earth, tree, air, water, fire, and ice—by bonding with them, and humankind flourished within their borders.

But there are no borders in the ever-moving sea. And so the wild, unclaimed spirits that lived in the Iorian Sea attacked the land, killing with their teeth and their waves, until the queens united and drove them back, slaying many and forcing the worst and largest of the monsters into an uneasy slumber many fathoms below, in a region of sea known in stories and songs as "the Deepest Blue."

The islands of Belene were formed from the bones of the giant spirits the queens killed, as a barrier to protect the mainland from the krakens and sea dragons and other leviathans.

For generations, each queen of Belene has been ever-vigilant, using all her power to keep the largest of the leviathans asleep and relying on the heirs to protect the islanders from the rest. Whenever wild spirits seek to attack the islands, the queen senses their approach and dispatches her heirs to repel them.

Except when she doesn't.

MAYARA FELT THE STORM IN HER BONES. IT HURT, THE SAME WAY IT hurt when she dived deep without a proper breath, as if her body wanted to tear itself apart from the inside, as if her skin didn't fit, as if her blood were boiling.

First, it was wind.

Screaming as it came, it flew across the sea and onto the shore. It bent the trees until they bowed, their tips touching the sand. It tore at the houses, ripping the shutters from their windows and the clay tiles from their roofs.

Second, it was waves.

Rising up in massive swells, the waves slammed into the island, flooding the homes that were closest to shore, destroying gardens and drowning livestock.

Third, it was monsters.

The wild spirits rode in on the wind and the waves. Most were water spirits, though a few were air. Some looked like winged eels, others were humanlike but with claws and shark teeth, and one was a dragonlike sea serpent.

All were deadly.

"Get back! Into the caves!" Papa was yelling. He, along with others possessed of booming voices, were herding the villagers back from the cliff wall. A few of the more foolhardy tried to run toward the path down to the village to protect their homes, but they were intercepted by their neighbors.

They cursed their neighbors now but would—hopefully— thank them later.

Little kids were scooped up by anyone who could carry them. The elderly were carried too—one woman on Uncle Imer's back, another by a fisherwoman who regularly hauled nets into boats, another by two of Mayara's cousins.

Grabbing Kelo's hand, Mayara ran for the storm-shelter caves. Rain was already pelting the plaza. Hard rain that hit as if it were pebbles. She shielded her eyes with her hand so she could see where she was running.

At the mouth of the cave, Papa stopped her. "Did you see your mother?" He had to shout to be heard over the wind.

Mayara shook her head. "I thought she was with you!"

But no. She wasn't.

*By the spirits . . .*

She let go of Kelo's hand.

"Mayara, it's not safe!" Kelo cried. "You have to get in the cave!"

But Mayara was already plunging back through the rain, which was falling in diagonal sheets so thick it felt like buckets of water being dumped on her head.

She could barely see more than a few feet in front of her. The wind and waves were so loud that she couldn't tell who was screaming: the weather, the spirits, or her people. "Mother! Where are you?"

She heard a giggle in her head, razor sharp.

She veered left, away from where she sensed the spirit to be, and pressed forward a step at a time. She knew where Mother had been, near the ceremony platform, and she knew loosely which direction it was in, even if she couldn't see it.

Something swept past her, grazing her arm, and she bit back a cry. *If I can't see them, they can't see me.* She didn't know if that was true, though. The wild spirits had created this storm. Surely they could navigate through it.

Keeping silent, Mayara pushed on, until at last she saw a shape, a human figure.

She forded through the rain toward it. The wind was so strong now that she had to walk at a slant to keep from being knocked backward. "Mother!"

Her mother was standing, facing the storm, screaming.

Grabbing her arm, Mayara tried to pull her away. "Mother, we have to go!"

But Mother wasn't just screaming, Mayara realized—she was screaming words. *Specific words:* "You took my daughter! Now take me!"

"Mother! They didn't take both of us! I'm still here!"

Mother didn't seem to hear her or feel her, however. And as much as that hurt her heart, getting Mother to safety was what mattered. Mayara yanked harder, but Mother resisted, continuing her painful prayer. "Take me, damn you! Take my pain! I don't want to be alone anymore!"

Mayara planted herself in front of Mother and put her hands on her shoulders. "Stop it! Please stop! You're not alone! You still have me! And Papa! And everyone! We all love you! Now please come, before we *both* die!"

At last, Mother seemed to see her. "Mayara . . ."

Her mother wilted, allowing Mayara to guide her away from the cliff's edge. Mayara wondered if she might have taken too long, though. The wind was stronger now and filled with spirits. She had to try anyway. Head down, her arm flung around her mother, she took step after step across the plaza.

She sensed the wild spirits swirling around them, though she couldn't see more than a foot in front of her. She felt their unbridled hatred and rage pour into her until she thought she'd choke on it. She tried to keep her own thoughts small and quiet, so they wouldn't notice her. *Just take another step. One more step . . .*

Rain had soaked her, and her wedding dress clung to her like a second skin, the mother-of-pearl shards feeling like fish scales. Water streamed down her face, and she had no way of knowing if she was crying—and she didn't care.

*Keep moving.*

Her foot hit something soft.

She looked down and saw one of her cousins, Osian, lying on the flagstones. For an instant, she didn't understand why he was lying there. He had to get up! Run! But his eyes were open, and red pooled at his throat.

Biting back a cry, Mayara guided her mother around her cousin's body.

Only to find more dead.

Cousins. Aunts. Neighbors. Her uncle Dolano, who used to swing her into the air in a circle until she was laughing so hard she cried. Porel, the village baker, who made wonderful pastries filled with tart berries. And Helia with her unborn baby.

*Please, please, don't let me find Papa. Or Kelo. Or . . . anyone else. No more!*

With each body, she felt as if a tear split her insides. Her mother became harder to pull. She was bent nearly in half, shaking with sobs. But the spirits were too close—*they'll find us.* Any second, it would be Mayara or Mother on the ground, her throat torn, her body ripped apart, her eyes sightless.

*No.*

And then Mayara saw a black blur ahead: the cave!

She pushed Mother ahead of her into the cave, and she heard a familiar voice cry her name: "Mayara!" Kelo rushed out and grabbed her arm.

As sudden as a scream, she felt a spirit attack—its shriek echoed inside her, scraping her throat as if it were her own cry. It swiped at Kelo with its razor claws. Beside her, he crumpled. "Kelo!" Dragging him into the cave, she turned back toward the plaza.

She saw only wind, rain, and spirits.

"Mayara, get back!" Papa yelled at her.

The spirits were coming for the cave. She could sense their . . . They weren't thoughts, precisely. It was a whirlwind of *need* and *want*. They wanted blood, death, and pain.

They wanted *in*.

The opening of the cave was large enough only for one person.

*I could block it.*

*I could stop them. Stop this.*

She didn't know if that was true. She'd never used her power against so many or faced spirits who were so lost to their bloodlust. It might make it worse if she used her power, by drawing even more spirits toward the villagers.

And in that moment, she had the sudden, terrible thought that she had caused this by using her power during her dive.

But no, the spirits she'd encountered were island spirits, bonded to the queen of Belene. These were wild spirits from the untamed waters far beyond the islands. Spirit storms like this one were freak accidents unconnected to anything anyone did. Yet, if no one did *something* . . .

She called back to Papa. "Is he alive? Kelo, does he live?"

Papa yelled, "Yes! But you need to get inside! Come where it's safe!"

But it *wasn't* safe. The spirits knew where the cave was now—they'd seen Mother and Mayara run into it. They were calling to one another.

*No, that wasn't right. They're calling to one* other.

A sea dragon.

She could feel the shape of the water spirit in her mind—larger than any of the houses in her village, large enough to crush a fishing boat, with a serpent's body and a bat's wings. And then it wasn't just in her mind—it burst through the rain, appearing midair in front of the cave.

Its scales were black as the night sky but flashed like the sea in sunlight. Its eyes were fire red and seemed to flicker. Its wings drove the wind toward Mayara, and she threw her arm in front of her face as water, carried by the wind, slammed into her, within the cave.

She felt the spirit's rage.

*It will kill us all.*

She felt hands pulling on her arms. Papa and Kelo and others were shouting, "Mayara! Get back!" But she shook the hands off and stepped forward, out of the cave. Squinting in the driving rain, Mayara stared up at the dragon.

She thought of the dive within the ancient leviathan's skull. And of her sister, Elorna, who had braved even more frightening dives. And of Kelo, who waited for Mayara, always trusting she'd return to him.

*Trust me one more time, my love. I can do this. I will* do *this.*

Mayara had heard the stories: the heirs kept the islands safe. They sent the wild spirits back into the sea. But Mayara didn't have the training or the strength of the heirs. She had only herself, and she didn't think she could command more than one spirit at a time.

So she chose the dragon, and she crafted a single order: *Protect us!*

The sea dragon resisted. She felt it screech within her head, and it was almost enough to shatter her mind. Gritting her teeth against the onslaught, she held the command steady, focusing all her intent and will: *Protect us! Now!*

The dragon, struggling against itself now, spun in the air. And as the other spirits tried to attack the cave, her dragon fought them.

Sinewy, it slid through the rain-choked air, and it snatched the flying eel-like spirits midflight and flung them back over the cliff. It smashed its tail into a humanlike air spirit who was running across the plaza, teeth bared and claws extended.

*Above you!* Mayara called to it, and she showed it in her mind what she saw: a trio of spirits shaped like massive white birds, with blood spattered on their white feathers, diving at the dragon from above.

The dragon twisted in the air as if it were swimming in water, knocking into them, and bit the neck of the first one, shaking it like a dog shakes its prey, then tossing it aside.

Soon the rain began to slacken. She felt the wind lessen.

Her dragon continued to defend the cave, and Mayara kept her focus on it, but now she could see across half the plaza, where several bodies lay. She forced herself not to look. Keeping her eyes on the dragon spirit, she guided it as it fought its brethren.

She felt the spirits begin to recede, some moving across the island and others returning to the sea, until at last it was only her and the dragon.

The rain faded to a drizzle. The wind fell until it was no more than a breeze. Mayara began to shiver, hard, her dress soaked and heavy, her hair wet and sticking to her skin.

Pivoting in the air, the dragon fixed its fire-red eyes on her.

She felt as if she'd dived too far beneath the water. Black dots danced in her vision. But she held on. And as if she had been given a second breath, she was able to push back.

*Go!* she ordered. *Return to the sea!*

It screamed once more, both out loud and in her head, and Mayara fell to her knees, hard on the stone, and clapped her hands over her ears. But the cry went on and on, receding only as the dragon flew away over the waves.

She looked up and saw the clouds had dissipated, and that during the storm, the sun had finished setting. Stars began to appear overhead, and the moon glowed, heavy and full, through the remaining black wisps of the unnatural typhoon.

Mayara got to her feet, her knees aching. Her mind felt dull and empty. She silently counted the dead: nine, twelve, fifteen. She knew them all. Loved them all. Slowly, she turned to face the cave.

Kelo limped out, supported by Papa. They crossed to her, and Kelo fell into her arms. She held him, and then sank down onto the ground.

"They'll know what you did," Kelo said, his voice a broken whisper.

She knew who he meant: the Silent Ones, the ones who had come for Elorna, the ones who'd taken her beloved sister's future, her hopes, and all her dreams when she revealed her power.

Whenever a woman proved to possess an affinity for spirits, the queen sent the Silent Ones to retrieve her and offer her a choice of two futures: Become a Silent One, one of the queen's enforcers, forsaking your family, your identity, and your voice, and swearing obedience to the queen. Or submit to the Island of Testing, Akena, in hopes of becoming an heir. Only a rare few survived that test, joining the queen's other heirs. Most who tried, like Elorna, died there and were never seen again.

It was a terrible choice.

It was no choice at all.

"They'll come for you," Kelo said, anguish in his voice. "They'll take you."

She couldn't think of what to say. Looking up, she saw her parents were crying, their arms around each other. Others had formed a semicircle, all of them staring at Mayara and Kelo.

There were no words for anyone to say.

She'd saved them. But in doing so, she'd doomed herself.

# CHAPTER FOUR

Mayara wrapped her arm around her mother's shoulders. Her father sat on her opposite side, cradling his wife's hands in his. But Mayara didn't think Mother even knew they were there. Mumbling softly, she rocked back and forth.

Beyond them, the sea was dark but quiet. The waves slapped the shore far below with an even regularity that was almost soothing. The only other sounds were the soft whisper of voices as families consoled one another and the weeping of those who still had the strength to cry.

"She's cold," Papa said. "Mayara—" He cut himself off, as if suddenly realizing there were many things he wanted to say to his daughter beyond the fact that they were drenched.

*If he says anything, I'll cry. Again.* She jumped up. "I'll get her a blanket."

A few of the unhurt villagers were hauling the storm trunks out to the plaza—every family kept a trunk sealed against storms secure in the caves that riddled the islands. She hurried to the nearest trunk and dug through it for the thickest blanket she could find. Musty and old, the blankets stank like cabbage soup, but they were dry. She pulled one out.

A hand clamped onto her wrist. She blinked, realizing that she'd been so focused on her prize that she hadn't noticed Grandmama was sitting cocooned in blankets beside the trunk. Normally, Grandmama was an impossible-to-miss force.

"I'm sorry," Mayara said, not even knowing what she was apologizing for—ignoring her or using her power. *Or not using it soon enough.*

Nearby, the clamdiggers were wrapping the dead in torn sails and then binding them in netting, as was tradition. At dawn, the bodies would be taken to the "death boats," sea-worthy canoes carved with prayers for the dead, and then rowed out to sea.

*If I'd acted faster . . .*

"You should go," Grandmama croaked.

Mayara swallowed, a scratchy lump in her throat. She'd be gone soon enough. It wouldn't take long for the queen to hear of what had happened in the spirit storm. *She probably sensed it the moment I took control of the sea dragon.*

"Before the Silent Ones come," Grandmama clarified. "You should run."

*Impossible,* Mayara thought. "You know I can't. They'll catch me. Besides, my parents need me. My mother—"

"Run and hide. You know this coast. Find caves. Take that pretty new husband of yours and flee!"

Mayara shoved back the wild hope that flared inside her. As tempting as it was, it wasn't possible to run and hide forever, not from the Silent Ones. They were the queen's enforcers, and they used the island's spirits as their eyes and ears. "No one's ever escaped."

"Oh, my little Mayara, pearl of my heart, if no one has done it, then you be the first. Like one of your dives. You've been the first to do the impossible before."

Mayara shook her head, stepping backward. "I . . . I . . . I have to take this to my mother." Clutching the blanket, she fled back to her parents.

Kelo was already with them—he'd brought more blankets,

as well as candles. Lit candles ringed the plaza. Seeing him, she felt her knees buckle, but she didn't let herself collapse, as badly as she wanted to fling herself into his arms. First, she had to take care of her mother. She tucked two blankets around her and felt her forehead. Cold and clammy.

As Mayara straightened, Kelo wrapped a blanket around her shoulders. "You'll catch sick like this," he scolded her. "Can't do that, not now. Let me take care of you." He glanced at her parents, as if asking their permission.

"Go with him," Papa said. He summoned up an almost-smile, and it was tinged with so much sadness that Mayara felt as if her heart were shattered glass.

His arm around her, Kelo led her away.

"I don't need 'taking care of,'" Mayara told him, "but my parents do. Promise me you'll look after them. I need to know they're safe. Mother . . . she isn't going to take this well. Papa will have his hands full watching her."

He didn't seem to be listening, though. "Let's hurry. You're shivering. I've spare clothes in the studio."

His studio wasn't with the rest of the village on the shore, so it wouldn't have been swept away. And protected as it was by all his charmed art, the spirits wouldn't have touched it. Any damage would be from ordinary rain and wind. *I'll change into dry clothes, and then I'll help as much as I can . . . until they take me away.* She was still in her sopping-wet wedding dress. It chilled her skin everywhere it touched.

As they passed through the plaza, Mayara spotted her aunt Beila. She dragged Kelo toward her. "Aunt Beila . . . don't respect her privacy. *Make* my mother be with you. She'll need you, all of you, whether she admits it or not." Last time, with Elorna, her aunts had given her mother space. Mayara had always thought that was a mistake. She wasn't going to let it be repeated. "Promise me you'll annoy her so much that she has to find the will to live, just to tell you to stop."

Aunt Beila clasped Mayara's hand. "Oh, Mayara . . ."

"Please, promise me," Mayara begged. "I have to know she'll be okay."

"We'll be more annoying than fruit flies," Aunt Beila promised. "But you have to promise us you'll try to live too. Make the smart choice."

Gently, Kelo extracted Mayara's hands from her aunt's. "She needs to get into warm clothes, or she won't be fit to make any choice."

Though Kelo was trying to hurry her through the plaza, Mayara paused again and again as she passed more aunts, uncles, and cousins. All of them wanted to wish her well, express condolences for her fate, thank her for what she'd done, or simply say goodbye.

"Why do you have to have so many blasted relations?" Kelo growled.

"I'll change before I freeze, don't worry." Mayara picked up her pace so he'd stop fussing.

They started up the path toward Kelo's studio. It was strewn with debris. Limbs had been torn off trees, and leaves and branches had been flung everywhere. The rope railing that had run along the edge was gone. Mayara wondered how much worse the damage was down in the village.

"I want to be back before the Silent Ones come," she told him. "I want to be surrounded by everyone I love when they"—she swallowed hard, not wanting to complete that phrase—"when I have to go."

He was concentrating on his footing and didn't reply, but she knew he'd heard her. The winding path veered up along one of the ribs of the ancient leviathan's skeleton. His studio wasn't far, but much of the path had been washed away.

"Kelo, you know your art . . ." She wasn't quite sure how to say it. His art was his life, his heart, his soul. He was going to be devastated to see it storm-ravaged. "It might not still be there."

"I have a trunk beneath the floor—that will still be there

even if everything else was washed out to sea. It has the spare clothes. And I can make new art."

She hoped he meant that. Ahead, she saw his studio. Half the roof tiles had been torn away, and the door had been ripped from its hinges. It lay several yards away, broken against a boulder. Around the studio were remnants of his art and his materials: shells, pebbles, driftwood, all tossed together as if one of her toddler cousins had thrown a tantrum. But the structure still stood. His charms had protected it from the worst the spirits could do.

Following him inside, Mayara felt her heart crack at the wreckage inside. Rain had soaked everything. While his studio was built too high up to flood from the tide, plenty of rain had gushed in through the damaged roof. The floor was covered in puddles. *So much beauty, gone in an instant.*

Mayara lifted a driftwood horse out of a puddle. He'd been carving it to be part of a mobile to hang over Helia's unborn baby's crib. *Now it never will.* She choked back a sob and suddenly realized why Kelo had been so insistent on hurrying here. It was hard to say goodbye to the dead; it was going to be a hundred times harder to say goodbye to the living. "I know why you brought me here."

Not looking at her, he knelt in the puddles and yanked at the floorboards. "You do?"

"You didn't want to say goodbye in front of everyone."

*Crack.* One of the floorboards splintered as he pried it up. Over his shoulder, she saw a trunk lying in a pool of water that had seeped through the floorboards.

"Kelo . . . I need you to know . . . you'll always be in my heart." She caressed the bit of carved driftwood, turning it over and over in her hands. "No matter what else they take away. No one can take away that."

Still not looking at her, he opened the trunk and then handed her a stack of clothes.

She peeled off the wedding gown carefully, as if it weren't

already ruined by rain, mud, and blood. Kelo took it from her just as carefully, set a chair upright, and draped it over the back. Drying herself with a blanket, she dressed in the clothes he'd given her: a thigh-high wrap dress plus water-resistant leggings.

These were high-quality clothes, she noticed. Very sturdy. Very practical. And they fit her as perfectly as the wedding dress had. A suspicion began to tug at her mind. "You know my size."

"I just made you a wedding dress," he pointed out. "That shouldn't be a surprise." He was watching her with a wary expression.

The wrap dress had extra fabric that could work as a sling for supplies, and the leggings felt tough enough to withstand the scrape of barnacle-encrusted rocks. She noticed he'd pulled two packs out of the trunk. Most villagers kept only blankets and candles and a few essentials in their storm trunks. This outfit and these supplies . . .

They were made for a journey.

"You know that no one escapes the Silent Ones," Mayara said. "It would be better for my family if—"

"*I'm* your family," Kelo said. "And it would be better for *me* if you were with me. That's what we swore, remember? To share our journeys. So journey with me, Mayara. Away from here, until it's safe to return."

She couldn't ever return. "Everyone knows I—"

"What do you wish Elorna had done?"

Mayara flinched.

He drew her closer. "Your sister did everything she was supposed to, was the dutiful islander, went with the Silent Ones . . . and she died." His voice was gentle, even if his words felt like knife cuts.

"I can't escape this. You know that. I only have two choices: become one of the Silent Ones or go to the Island of Testing." *Why is he torturing me with this? He knows I can't run!*

He pressed his forehead against hers. "I'm asking you to pick a third choice."

"I'm supposed to be the impetuous one. Everyone calls me reckless, chasing after a sister who's gone, as if I could catch her and bring her back." She pulled away and looked at the two waterproof packs. "But I suppose this isn't impetuous of you, is it? You've been planning this for a long time."

"Years," he said.

"You never told me."

"You never wanted to hear."

That was . . . not the right answer. "I thought we didn't have secrets from each other."

He reached for her hands again. "It's not a secret that I want to be with you forever," he said simply. "You know I'm a worrier, Mayara, and a planner. Did you really think I wouldn't prepare for this?"

She wished he'd told her. She would have talked him out of this sooner, so he wouldn't be clinging to this false hope. "Elorna tried to run."

He blinked.

"She sneaked away without a word to any of us. I'd had a nightmare and I woke in the night. I went to go curl up with Elorna—sometimes she let me do that when I was scared. But when I went into her room, her bed was empty."

"What did you do?"

"I climbed into her bed and went to sleep," Mayara said. "I *wanted* her to escape. I didn't want to tell anyone she was gone. I thought if I were in her bed, asleep with the covers over my head, everyone would think she was still there, and I'd buy her enough time."

"What happened?" he asked softly, as if he wasn't sure he wanted to hear the rest of the story.

"She came back, before dawn, before anyone woke, and when the Silent Ones arrived, she was packed and waiting for them. I asked her why she didn't keep running, and she said: 'Because then I lose you no matter what. This way, there's a chance.'"

Mayara had never told anyone about that night. *Maybe we do keep some secrets from each other.* But it was a secret only because it hurt so much to say the words. He had to hear this, though. She continued. "Elorna said if she survived the test and became an heir, we'd see her again. She would have been allowed to visit. But if she ran . . . she couldn't ever return. It would be too dangerous to come back—the Silent Ones would have caught her. She'd have to stay away from everyone she loved and everything she knew. She'd be alone."

It was the law: the Silent Ones had to sever all contact with their families. Supposedly, this was to encourage people to try to become heirs instead of choosing the safer route.

Kelo cupped her cheeks in his hands. "I know how much you worship your sister, but you aren't her. And you won't be alone. I'll be with you, and we'll find a way to see your family again, once it's safe."

She kissed him, her lips sweet and salty from the rain or her tears. "Oh, my Kelo, sweet Kelo, it won't ever be safe again. Everyone *knows.* My family. Yours. Everyone in the village. The spirits themselves."

"So you just want to give up? Because I won't. Not on you. There is nothing I wouldn't do, nowhere I wouldn't go, to be with you." He wasn't arguing—Kelo hated to argue. He was begging, and she loved him for it, even while she wanted to shake him for making this so much harder. "You're my *wife.* We're supposed to have forever."

"No one gets forever," she said gently.

"Well, I'd like longer than a day," Kelo pleaded. "Call me self-ish, but I want as many days as we can get. Now will you stop being so noble and fatalistic and run away with me? Before it's too late, and we lose any chance to choose what happens to us?"

"They'll punish you if they catch us." Maybe even kill him. Death was a common punishment for those who tried to help their loved ones evade their duty. She couldn't let him risk his life.

He was looking at her as if she'd said the most absurd thing ever.

"You don't think they'll catch us," she said, and she couldn't help it—a grin began to tug at her lips. *This is all absurd. I shouldn't even be considering it.* But he'd been thinking about this for years, he'd said, and she knew Kelo. He'd have thought through every aspect meticulously. *Maybe I should trust him. I did marry him, after all.* "You have a plan?"

He knelt again by the hole that had held the packs and pulled out two rolls of sail wrapped in rope. Unfurling one of the rolls, he showed it to her.

Mayara frowned. "I don't understand. That looks like—"

"We can't hide in the village," Kelo explained. "Even if it weren't so badly damaged, that would be the first place the Silent Ones would look. And we can't hide in any of the nearby caves. Every inch of those tunnels has been explored and mapped—they'd know exactly where to send their spirits to search for us. We also can't flee over land—if we tried to cross the island on foot, we'd leave tracks, and the Silent Ones would be close behind."

"So where does that leave us?"

"We hide with the dead. And sail away with the tide."

It was a crazy plan.

Mayara loved it.

He'd constructed two fake shrouds out of old sail and net that mimicked the simple shroud that all islanders used. But these were designed to merely *look* as if the body inside was bound. In truth, they'd fall open at the tug of a rope.

"All we have to do is lie in the boats and wait for dawn. When the b-bodies"—he stumbled over the word, and she saw pain dart across his face; he'd known those who'd died as well as she had—"are carried down to the bay and loaded into the boats, we'll already be there. Just two more dead, indistinguishable from the rest."

Mayara nodded. "They'll row us out to sea and dump us over."

"And then we remove the shrouds underwater." He pointed to the loops of rope on the net that would cradle rocks. "All the shrouds will be weighted to sink the bodies—so they'll sink without us, and we'll swim."

"East," Mayara said decidedly. All the mourners would face the south, toward the open ocean, toward the blue of death, as the boats were rowed out, and then as the bodies disappeared beneath the waves, the villagers would face north, toward land and hope. If she and Kelo swam *east* before turning back toward shore, they'd not only be swimming in a direction that no one would be looking, but they'd also be heading into the sun—the glare would help hide them. "You'll have to stay under, though, until the mourners turn."

"You'll help me," he said, with such unwavering confidence in her that she felt like crying. Except she had no more tears left.

"Always," Mayara said. She took a breath. All right, she was going to do this. *We,* she corrected herself. She thought of Grandmama urging her to flee. *Maybe we should do this.* "It's hours until dawn, and if we don't return, the villagers will send out a search party. So we'll go back to the plaza, be with our families for a while longer, and then slip away near sunrise." She wanted to spend as much time with her family as she could before . . . well, before her life changed. *Or ended.*

Kelo's brow furrowed—it was how she could tell he was unhappy with something she'd said. He didn't like to disagree with anyone. It occurred to her it must have been difficult for him to try to persuade her to run away, knowing how she'd feel about it. She felt a fresh rush of love. "Mayara . . ." he began. He stopped.

"You want to go now?" she guessed.

"We don't know when the Silent Ones will come," he said,

regret in his voice. "It could be tomorrow, but it could be sooner. If it's sooner, it's better that we're gone. And if it's tomorrow . . . everyone will think we have a head start. They'll search farther away. They won't think we're still here. Besides, we can't guarantee we'll have another chance to slip away. And we might need time to find or repair the boats, if they were damaged by the storm."

She studied his face, so earnest and anxious. "You've given this a lot of thought."

"Ever since you first shared your secret," he said.

That was six years ago, three years before Elorna had died. For six years, he'd been thinking about this, planning it, worrying over it. *Six years he's been thinking about the moment he could lose me.* It must have been tearing him up inside. Yet he'd never spoken about it. "You never said a word," she repeated.

This time he simply said, "And ruin your happiness? I wouldn't do that." He then took her hand, as if to lead her out of the studio, but he didn't move. He waited instead for her to lead. *He trusts me to make the right choice, whatever that is.*

Stepping over his ruined art and the shells she'd collected, she reached the threshold. Up would lead back to the plaza. Down to the boats. But she'd made her decision—there was nothing she wouldn't do for Kelo, just as there was nothing he wouldn't do for her. She hurried down the path with Kelo, bringing the false shrouds and the packs of emergency supplies.

On the beach, it was a beautiful night.

The sky was serene, with a pale moon that looked as if it had been drawn onto a backdrop and then smudged slightly around the edges. Stars were sprinkled everywhere. No clouds. No rain. But the shore was a tangle of seaweed and driftwood and boats. Fish had been tossed ashore and lay dead but still wet across the rocks.

Oddly, the death boats were untouched.

Both Mayara and Kelo halted and stared at them. Yes, they'd been tied to trees along the shore, but so had other fishing boats and those had been tossed against one another and onto the rocks. The boats that the villagers used to send their dead into the waves looked as if they hadn't felt a breath of wind. They were perfectly parallel, with no sand or seaweed on their hulls and no water inside them.

"Spirit storm," Kelo breathed. "Maybe this is not a good plan."

"It is," Mayara said firmly. "Don't doubt yourself. Or us."

His lips quirked in an almost-smile. "You know, this isn't how I thought we'd spend our wedding night. You looked just as beautiful as I'd imagined in that dress. Death shrouds . . . aren't quite the same look."

She wanted to laugh but couldn't. Instead, she climbed into one of the boats and lay down. She strapped the waterproof pack with supplies to her stomach, and Kelo did the same. He wrapped the false shroud around her, leaving her head exposed, and then lay down beside her, positioning his shroud around himself.

"Did any spirits see us?" Kelo asked.

Closing her eyes, she felt for whispers with her mind. She heard only the waves lapping gently on the shore. "None." Pulling the shroud up over her face, she closed her eyes. The sail was porous, letting the night breeze in. It was strangely calming. "We should try to sleep." *I can't imagine how we will. But we'll need our strength.* "Tomorrow we swim with the dead."

# CHAPTER FIVE

Mayara woke to voices, low and even, singing the mourners' farewell. She felt the false shroud on her face and had to fight the urge to claw it off. Instead, she lay still.

The sun must have risen, or been close to rising, because she could see a dull glow through the fabric. It was already hot beneath the sail.

She hoped the fabric was thick enough that no one would see her breathing.

*This is the riskiest part.*

She didn't know what the villagers would do when they discovered two additional bodies already in the death boats. Kelo had made the shrouds beautifully. *But no matter his level of craftsmanship, people don't usually miscount their dead.* Someone would notice, and if they spoke . . . if she and Kelo were exposed . . . if the Silent Ones were already there . . .

As the mourners drew closer, she picked out individual voices: Papa's, Aunt Beila's, Grandmama's, mixed with others from their village. *I should be singing with them.* By now, they had to have known she'd run, with Kelo. She wondered if they'd think she was selfish or wise. Her parents would understand, as would Kelo's, and she thought that most of her aunts, uncles, and cousins would too, though she wasn't certain.

*But any of them could betray us. Even a child with an innocent question.* She hoped Kelo had thought through this part in his six years of worrying. Because otherwise, this would be the shortest escape attempt ever.

She wished she'd asked him what his plan was for getting past this moment. It was far too late to ask anything now. As the mourners drew closer, Mayara closed her eyes, as if that would help make her invisible to them. She tried to lie perfectly still.

Her nose began to itch, then her elbow.

She kept her breathing shallow and didn't move.

She heard Kelo's father by the stern of their boat. He was a baritone, like Kelo, with a soft, warm voice. Near him was Grandmama, her off-key belt loud and clear. One of the singers broke off. "Who are—"

*Oh no.* Mayara tensed.

Grandmama's singing stopped abruptly. "Hush, do not speak of the dead. Sing!"

Chastened, whoever it was—one of her cousins, she thought— began singing again, as did Grandmama. She felt her and Kelo's boat lurch forward. It was being pushed over the sand toward the waves. It bumped as it was forced over debris, either rocks or driftwood.

"I will row this boat," Kelo's father said softly but firmly.

*They know,* Mayara thought. And the realization felt like sunshine on her face. She wanted to laugh out loud, but she had better sense than that.

Kelo *had* planned for this. His father must know—he wouldn't have been the usual choice to row a death boat, since he was unrelated to any of the dead. And Grandmama . . . *She must either know or have guessed.* She wished she could hug her grandmother's bony shoulders and tell her how much she loved her.

But she wouldn't be able to tell her that, maybe not ever. She might never see Grandmama again. Or her parents. Or her aunts. Or . . . *Then again, I might. Quit wallowing. You're alive.*

*Stay that way, and you might find a way to see them. Die, and you certainly won't.*

As the boat was pushed into the waves, it rocked, free of the shore. She then felt it tip to the side—Kelo's father must have climbed in.

The drummers began a slow rhythm, and she felt the boat slide through the sea as Kelo's father rowed, matching his strokes to the drumbeats. She felt and heard the crash of the breaking waves against the hull of the boat as it jerked with each wave. Drops of water seeped through the sail shroud, worming down her neck and pooling behind her back.

One lone voice sang now on the shore, a soprano, and for an instant, Mayara couldn't name the singer. She knew the voice was familiar, but whose?

> *The sea calls to me, and I to the sea:*
> *Come to me,*
> *Take my sorrow,*
> *Carry it away in your arms of blue,*
> *Until sweet memory is all that remains,*
> *All that remains of you.*

Mother.

She was singing the final lament.

As they passed the breaking waves, the boat rose and fell gently, propelled forward, and Mother's voice began to fade, swallowed by the wind. Mayara strained to hear.

And then the only sound was the dip of the oars into the water and the light touch of the waves on the hull. At last, she felt hands on her, rolling her toward the side of the boat. Her heart beat faster. Her pack of supplies was pressed against her stomach, tied securely so she wouldn't lose it as she swam. She curled her hand around the rope that would free her from the shroud and hoped the stones had been tied to the net, as

Kelo had said they would be. She didn't have a clear memory of their being tied—shouldn't she have noticed? *Maybe not. And it's too late now.*

She exhaled fully, and then sucked in air, as if for a dive, pulling in fast puffs at the end, hoping she was silent enough. As she was heaved up the side of the boat, she heard a whisper: "Be well."

Kelo's father.

And then she was dropped into the sea.

She sank, pulled by the stone weights, and felt a burst of panic. Instantly, she calmed herself. She'd done dives with more gear than this. Counting to three, Mayara waited, and then she pulled the rope.

The shroud unraveled around her and drifted down, sinking beneath her. Kicking smoothly, she spun in a circle beneath the water, looking for Kelo. His father had, wisely, pushed her off the boat first. He would have known she could stay under for longer than Kelo.

She heard a muffled splash and a spray of water, and she pinpointed the source: a wrapped body falling from the shadow of a boat's hull. Not her and Kelo's boat.

Mayara watched the body sink slowly below the water.

It was both sad and beautiful, as the blue embraced the white sail, pulling it deeper and deeper. She lost track of the seconds for a moment, and then another, closer splash, again muffled through the distortion of water.

Kicking, Mayara swam to the body as it began to move. Kelo!

His shroud fell away, and acting on instinct, he kicked, propelling himself upward. She wrapped her arms around his waist, keeping him from rising to the surface and being seen. He nodded at her, his hair swirling gently around his head, and she released him.

They both swam.

Kelo swam like a dolphin, all smooth movements, and she shot through the water behind him as if she'd been born there. He'd never trained to hold his breath like she had, but short term he was a strong swimmer. *I hope that's enough.*

She didn't know how long they had between the sinking of the bodies and the symbolic turn to the north. She thought she could count on Grandmama to speed the tradition along, and then keep the villagers facing away from the sea. *Just need to swim far enough from the boats.*

Mayara kept her eyes on Kelo, ready in case he faltered. She also kept her senses open for spirits. If one saw them . . . If the Silent Ones were watching through their eyes . . . But the only spirits were by the shore, playing in the shallows and the tide pools, not paying any attention to the two humans swimming through the ocean.

Kelo began to slow.

She knew what he was feeling: the pain, the screaming in every cell for *air, now!* Propelling herself through the water, she caught up to him. He treaded water beneath the surface, apology in his eyes—he couldn't hold on any longer. He had to breathe.

She grabbed his arm and swam upward, bursting up behind a wave.

Both of them gasped, and then Mayara yanked them down again and swam on.

They repeated this as they swam, with her timing it so they would rise behind the swell of a wave, until they were far beyond the shore of the village. Stopping to get her bearings, Mayara treaded water.

The escape plan may have been Kelo's idea, but now they were in her territory. "North," she said, leading the way. She knew the island from the sea, all the coves and caves, all the cliffs, all the reefs. And she knew exactly where they should go.

Leading the way, she set out in strong strokes. Out of sight of the village, they swam on the surface of the sea. In some ways this was easier, because they had oxygen. But in other ways, she missed the smooth unbroken evenness of underwater—the feel of gliding like a fish instead of fighting with the waves.

"Mayara?" Kelo called.

"Don't use my name." She didn't *think* any spirits were listening to them, but it was better to be careful. Quieting her own thoughts, she tried to hear any nearby spirits. It was tricky, given how many worries were swirling through her mind, but she pretended she was preparing for a dive.

She felt the spirits like unnatural ripples in the stillness of her mind.

There was one not far away, a water spirit swimming with a pod of dolphins, and another—this one an air spirit—gliding like an albatross on a current of wind. A half dozen tiny spirits made of seafoam were on the sand.

"Follow me," Mayara said to Kelo.

She aimed for a cave, one that was visible only in low tide. They could rest there. With no trail, the Silent Ones wouldn't be able to track them. The Silent Ones would be forced to rely on chance encounters with spirits, and Mayara didn't intend to encounter any.

*The cave will do,* she thought.

She led Kelo through the water toward a cliff.

"If we climb, we'll be visible," Kelo warned.

"Not up," she said. "Down." And then she led the way, taking his hand and again swimming beneath the surface. She knew the shape of the rocks that marked the entrance, and she spotted them nearly instantly.

She swam unerringly into the cave and then up, bursting out of the water into complete darkness. Kelo gasped in air beside her.

"Where are we?" he asked, his voice echoing.

"Safe. For now."

She picked a direction and swam until her fingers brushed rock, and then she climbed out of the water and collapsed onto the stony shore. "At low tide, the cave will be exposed," Mayara told him. "We'll need to be gone by then. Once the Silent Ones know the cave is here, they'll send spirits to search it. But until then . . ."

Kelo flopped out of the water beside her. She heard him panting in the darkness and the squish of his wet clothes on the rocks. "We can eat and rest—I've food and a canteen of fresh water," he said. "Damn hard to swim with supplies."

"But you did it," she pointed out.

"*We* did it." He squeezed her hand.

"Obviously *I* did. But you swam pretty well . . . for an artist."

He laughed, as she hoped he would.

Reaching out her hand, she entwined her fingers through his. For a moment, they lay there, side by side in the darkness, as their pounding hearts began to settle and their breathing steadied.

"I used to dream about the day we'd finally be husband and wife," Mayara said.

"You were the one who said 'nothing would change because we're already united in our hearts.' Or was that just a ploy to get out of the fancy celebration?"

She smiled, though she knew he couldn't see it. "Living under the same roof. Able to be alone whenever we wanted to be. Of course I dreamed about it. Besides, you know I wanted those shrimp." *I didn't request the spirit storm, though, or all that followed.*

"It was a nice ceremony."

"It was," she agreed. "Until it wasn't."

He lifted her hand, and she felt the brush of his lips on her knuckles. "Whatever else happens, we are married."

"And we're even alone under the same roof," she pointed out.

Rolling onto her side, she moved to kiss him, her body pressed against his. Their noses crashed in the darkness, and they both jerked backward. Mayara began to laugh, and then Kelo was laughing too. Still laughing, they began to kiss once more.

All mirth fled as their hands roved over each other's bodies. They kissed as if it were their first time. Or their last. Slowly, because their muscles still hurt from their escape. Slowly, because the darkness was so complete. Slowly, because they wanted to treasure this night, their true wedding night.

Clinging to her best friend and the love of her life, Mayara knew she'd made the right decision leaving everything and everyone behind but bringing her heart and soul with her.

FOR EIGHT DAYS, THEY EVADED THE SILENT ONES. THANKS TO Mayara's knowledge of the coast and ability to sense spirits, they were able to hide in the nooks and crannies, swimming between them unobserved. With Kelo's supplies, they were able to keep themselves dry and fed, at least sort of—he'd packed a fire starter, and during times they were hidden enough to try a fire and had access to enough bone-dry driftwood, they cooked crabs that Mayara caught. When they didn't dare risk a fire, they ate seaweed and raw oysters. It wasn't copious amounts of food, but it was enough. For water, they collected and drank the freshwater runoff from the cliffs, catching it in shells.

*Such a clever boy,* Mayara thought. *He planned it all.*

She watched him as he chipped the barnacles off a shell he'd selected from the remnants of their breakfast. He was humming softly as he worked. He'd told her he wanted to make her something beautiful and practical—a bowl, carved from an abalone shell, that she could use to drink water or soup.

This was the first morning that they weren't already in the water. Mayara had found a secluded cove with no access from land (unless you wanted to scale a cliff) and with an overhang that kept them from being seen from the sky.

Kelo spoke as he worked. "Once we're certain the Silent Ones have lost our trail, we'll go to the next town and buy passage to one of the other islands. Start a new home in another village, or even a city. We could even go to Yena and live right under the queen's nose if we want. No one will recognize us, and so long as you don't use your power, the Silent Ones won't have any way to find us."

"I won't use my power again," Mayara promised.

He worked quickly and with a steady hand, the knife flicking over the shell. "I can set up shop anywhere—there's always a market for charmwork—and your diving skills are useful anywhere in Belene. And then once Queen Asana and the Silent Ones have forgotten all about us, we'll come home. Might not be able to stay, but we'll be able to see our families."

It was a beautiful plan. She loved how certain he was. He could paint a future in her mind that felt as real as any memory. "How will we know when it's safe to return?"

"I left flags with my father, disguised as charms. He'll fly one whenever the village is free of Silent Ones—that way, we'll know whether we can visit."

"And if we can't ever return?"

Putting down his knife, he glanced at her. "So long as we're together, we can conquer anything." He smiled at her, and she smiled back.

*Maybe he's right. We've come this far.* Leaning back against the cliff wall, she watched him walk to the shore. Still in the shadow of the overhang, he knelt. When a wave kissed the shore, he rinsed the shell.

Without warning, the wave lurched, and a creature launched itself out of the seafoam. It looked like a sea turtle, but its jaws were narrow and studded with teeth. *A water spirit!* "Kelo!" She hadn't opened her mind for spirits. She'd thought they were safe here. "Kelo, get back!"

Lunging for Kelo's knife, she grabbed it as the spirit latched onto Kelo's leg. Screaming, he fell forward, catching himself on his hands. She heard a snap that sounded like bone breaking.

"No!" she cried. Screaming, she stabbed at the turtlelike spirit's neck.

The spirit released him, and Kelo clutched at his leg—it was coated in blood, and she saw his calf had been savaged. She struck at the spirit again, but it evaded her.

The spirit lunged for him again, this time landing hard on his chest.

"Kelo!"

She couldn't let it kill him. She'd promised . . . but there was no choice.

"Mayara, don't!" Kelo shouted.

*Go!* she commanded the spirit. *Leave us alone!*

The spirit scuttled back. It retreated over the sand, snapping its jaws at the air, and then into the water, where it submerged. Then she released her focus and ran to Kelo.

"You shouldn't have—" he began.

"I'm not losing you," she said fiercely. "I told you: I'd do anything for you."

"It will tell the others. A Silent One will read its memories. You shouldn't have— Ow!" He contorted in pain. Blood speckled the rocky shore.

*Please,* she prayed. *Don't die. Please, please . . .* Mayara dug into the nearest pack for a healing kit—he'd packed bandages and salves, plenty of them. *Oh, my clever boy.* Cracking open a jar of salve, she dipped her fingers into it.

He caught her wrist. "Wash the wound first."

"It'll sting," she warned. "We only have saltwater."

"It'll cleanse. Do it."

She scooped seawater into the abalone shell he'd been carving and poured it over his leg. He hissed as it stung. She noticed he was cradling his wrist against his chest. *Broken?* His palms were scraped raw. She poured more water over his hands.

"How bad?" he asked.

She didn't answer.

"Mayara?"

"I'll stitch it up."

"You can't sew worth a damn. Give me the needle—it's a

sterile one, this is what it's for. There's sinew thread in the kit too."

"You aren't going to sew your own leg," Mayara argued. "Do you know how much that will hurt?" But he was the one who always fixed her. He knew how to do this. Her hands were shaking as she handed him the kit.

"Just help me sit up, please."

She braced his back as he leaned forward and saw his leg. *Oh, Great Mother.* It had been torn open. She watched him try to thread the needle, his hands trembling. He dropped his arm down. "Let me," she said, and taking it from him, threaded it.

He then took it back from her, ignoring her protests, and plunged the needle into his skin. He let out a howl that made her heart feel as though it were being squeezed. "Driftwood," he panted. "For me to bite."

She hurried to the shore and returned with a chunk of wood, which she placed in his mouth. He bit into it hard as he sewed his own flesh closed. He spat it out when he finished, gasping, and she eased him backward.

His eyes fluttered closed.

"Kelo?" Her heart pounded so hard that she felt as if she couldn't breathe. She pressed her fingers to his neck. *Still a pulse. He just fainted. Anyone would have fainted.*

She fetched more seawater and began rinsing off more of his wounds. *He'll be okay. He has to be.*

A few moments later, he opened his eyes. "Mayara?"

"I'm here." *I'll always be here.* "Can you move? Swim? Climb?"

She knew the answers:

If he hadn't broken his wrist, he could have climbed. Maybe.

If he hadn't injured his leg, he could have swum. Maybe.

But both?

"You'll have to leave me here," he said. "I'll catch up when I can. Go to Kao, secure a boat—there are enough coins in the blue pouch at the bottom of my pack. Sail with them to Renata. I'll find you."

She looked at him as if he were speaking nonsense. He was the reason she was here. Finding a way to be together was her only purpose. "I'm not leaving you."

"Mayara . . . More spirits will come. You know that. And the Silent Ones will be right behind them. I can't move, and you can't stay."

He was right that more would come. Calming her breathing, she tried to open her mind. She spread her awareness over the ocean beyond them and the cliffs above them.

"Please, Mayara. I don't want our last moments together to be spent arguing."

Mayara pressed a finger against his lips. She shook her head and tried to smile. She failed. "I won't leave you. And I can't leave you. It's too late."

"It's not—"

"It is." She kissed him gently. His lips tasted like blood. Tightening her grip on his knife, she turned to face the sea. "They're already here."

# CHAPTER SIX

Mayara sensed the spirits—the ocean was clogged with them and the air full of them. The nearness of so many made her feel as if ants were crawling on her skin. Scooting closer to Kelo, she watched them approach.

First to appear was a trio of water spirits beyond the breakers, their heads popping out of the waves. From the shoulders up, they looked human, with pale-blue faces and flowing green hair, bobbing in the water, cackling to one another. By the opening to the cove, she saw yet another water spirit, this one orcalike with a smooth iridescent back that rose out of the waves. Above, she saw a spark in the air darting over the rocks—it was a fire spirit that looked like a winged lizard covered in flames. It peeked down at them and then disappeared above the overhang.

*I should have stayed and faced my fate.* If she had, at least Kelo would have been safe and home. Watching the water spirits swim closer, Mayara took Kelo's hand.

"I'm sorry," she said.

"I'm not. Better we're together than for you to die alone."

She snorted. "Better if neither of us dies."

"Well, yes, that would be better," he said mildly. She appreciated how unruffled he sounded. She knew he was faking it, but it was easier for her to stay outwardly calm if he was.

The first of the spirits clawed its way onto the beach: it was shaped like a brilliant blue crab, twice the size of any ordinary crab and with six pincher claws. Then a half dozen tiny water spirits that looked like seafoam tumbled out of a wave as it broke onto the sand. They scurried toward Mayara and Kelo.

She could use these last moments to tell Kelo how much she loved him. Or she could use them fighting like hell to keep him alive. *He knows I love him.*

Beside her, Kelo was breathing heavily. He'd pulled himself up to a sitting position, his back against a boulder. His face was prickled with sweat.

"Take this." She pressed the blood-slick knife into his hands.

He tried to give it back to her. "You need—"

"I have another way to fight." *Or at least I think I do.*

Reaching out with her mind, Mayara felt for the strongest spirit—she planned to seize control of it and force it to defend them, like she'd done with the sea dragon when the wild spirits attacked their wedding. But when she touched the mind of the orcalike water spirit, it felt oddly distant. Even distracted.

*Protect us!* she ordered.

It felt as if she were trying to shout into a heap of burlap—her mental voice felt muffled, and she had no sense that the spirit heard her. She tried communicating with another, the crablike water spirit.

Same result.

She tried the tiny foam spirits. . . . Same.

"Why aren't they attacking? Is it you?" Kelo asked. "Are you holding them back? All of them at once? I didn't know you were that strong."

"It's not me," Mayara said.

She felt the spirits seething with hate, straining as if on leashes, oblivious to her commands. Three birdlike air spirits circled above the cove. She couldn't see them through the overhang, but she could hear them cawing to one another in voices that were both almost human and almost bird. The humanlike water spirits bobbed just beyond the breaking waves, watching Mayara and Kelo with their unnerving inhuman eyes. The orca-like water spirit swam back and forth at the mouth of the cove. The crab spirit watched them without moving, and the tiny foam spirits continued to skitter from side to side each time a wave slapped the sand. Above, the one fire spirit, the winged lizard with flames, darted over the rocks, eyeing them but never coming closer.

A horrible realization came over her. "They're all waiting. Just waiting." Even the wind seemed to be waiting to blow, and the waves seemed hesitant to touch the rocky shore.

He nodded. He didn't ask whom they were waiting for. He didn't need to. "What will you choose?" His voice was even, almost conversational, as if asking what she wanted for breakfast.

She shook her head, unable to answer the question. *Answering would make it real.*

"If you choose to become a Silent One, you'll live." He cradled her cheek in his hand, and she tore her gaze away from the spirits to look into his eyes. He had endless eyes, the kind that swirled with color. She loved his eyes.

"But we won't see each other again. It will be as if I'm dead."

He shook his head. "But I'll know that somewhere on the islands, you still exist. Mayara . . . I need you to exist. If you go to the Island of Testing and you die . . . it would break me."

*But what about me?* Life as a Silent One was no kind of life. He wanted her to live a kind of living death so he wouldn't have to mourn her? At least with the island there was a chance she'd survive, wasn't there?

*Maybe not.*

Her sister had chosen the island. And died. Most of the girls and women sent to Akena Island died. It was supposed to winnow out the weak and unsuitable—every heir had to be ready and able to assume the crown.

*If Elorna couldn't do it, how can I think I'd stand a chance?*

"Mayara, promise me you'll choose to live!"

Looking into his eyes, she couldn't deny him. *If I'm doomed anyway, why not pick the fate that gives Kelo the most peace?* "I'll choose to be a Silent One." Kneeling, she faced him and kissed him. She was crying, but she didn't care. This was their last kiss. Whether she lost herself and became a Silent One or lost her life on Akena Island . . . this was the end.

"We'll find a way to communicate," Kelo promised, when they broke apart. "I'll leave messages for you in my charms, and I'll find a way to get them to you. It may take time, and for that, I need you to *not die.*"

"Kelo . . . it's over—us, our future," Mayara said. "You need to go on with your life." That hurt to say too. She tried to mean it—she didn't want him to be unhappy, and if that meant he had to forget about her and build a new life with someone else . . . then she wanted to give him permission to do so, even if she hated the idea of it.

"My life *is* you."

*Right answer,* she thought. She smiled through her tears. Kelo always seemed to be able to say exactly the right thing, whereas Mayara felt she still had a million more things she wanted to say and would most likely mangle them if she tried.

"Mayara . . ."

"I'll try not to die," she promised. It was the best she could do. She'd make the sensible choice: become a Silent One. It was the only choice that assured her survival.

And she'd have to make that choice soon. She sensed a shift in the spirits—a readiness. The wait was over.

"Stay here and stay hidden," Mayara told him. "I need you to not die too."

She kissed him one more time, as sweetly as the sunrise kissed the morning sky, and then before he could stop her, she climbed up the rocks onto the overhang. The bird spirits screamed louder when they saw her. She stood straight and tall and very, very visible on top of the rocks. And then she turned and ran.

She didn't think she could escape. For one, the overhang stretched only a few yards before it ended in a cliff that towered above her. For another, the spirits had already spotted her. It was only a matter of time before the Silent Ones caught her. *But if I can lead them away from Kelo, it will be worth it. . . .*

She felt the spirits chasing her.

Feeling for handholds in the cliff wall, she climbed fast. Fear fueled her. Fear for Kelo, not for herself. He couldn't defend himself against another attack. And if he survived the spirits, he was still alone and defenseless in a cove. How would he hunt? How would he get back home?

But she couldn't think about that. All she could do was try to ensure he survived today. Tomorrow was beyond her imagination.

She reached the top of the cliff.

The Silent Ones were waiting for her.

Three women in pale-gray robes, their faces covered in white featureless masks with holes for eyes and slits for mouths. Their hair was tied back beneath gray scarves, rendering them featureless. None of them spoke, of course. They stood calmly side by side, with three air spirits circling over their heads.

Mayara ran past them and dived off the cliff on the opposite side.

She knew the shape of the shore, and while she was not certain of the water depth this time of day, she knew how far out to leap to be beyond the rocks. Stretching her arms out by her ears, she tried to think of nothing but the howl of the wind as she sliced through the air and then the shuddering cold of the sea as she plunged in between the waves.

She curved upward as quickly as she could, and she swam. The sea spirits were after her in an instant. Stretching her mind out like fingers, she counted them: the turtlelike spirit, the crablike spirit, the human-shaped ones, the tiny seafoam spirits—all of them followed her away from the cove where Kelo lay injured.

She made it farther than she expected before the orca rose beneath her, lifting her out of the water, where the air spirits seized her shoulders and carried her back to the Silent Ones on the cliff above the cove.

The three women stood side by side, exactly as she'd left them. They faced her with their unreadable masks, their arms motionless by their sides, their robes hiding their bodies.

Lowering her head, Mayara said, "I will come and make the choice." The words tasted bitter in her mouth.

She didn't expect a spoken answer. But she expected some reaction. Peeking up, she saw the woman in the center give a slight nod.

And from far below, in the cove below the overhang, she heard Kelo scream.

"No! Don't hurt him! It was my idea! Mine! Blame me, punish me, but don't kill him!" She launched herself at the Silent Ones, but the fire lizard leaped onto her hand, scalding it. She screamed and clutched her burned hand.

Reaching out with her mind, she tried to stop the spirits—

And then she smelled sweet flowers on a cloth held to her face. The world tilted, and she fell as she lost control of her body—Kelo's screams softened into hazy silence, and then everything was quiet and dark.

MAYARA WOKE IN A DIMLY LIT ROOM TO THE SKRITCH OF A PEN across paper. She heard the tap of the pen against glass, probably the ink jar. *Squid ink,* she thought. And then her thoughts settled into place, memory flooded through her, and she sat upright.

"Where's Kelo? Is he alive?" The words came out jumbled, as if her mouth were full of mud. She swallowed. She repeated, "Kelo—is he alive?"

The sound of the pen stopped, and a male voice said, "Drink water. You'll feel better. The *cartena* flower is effective but does leave one a bit woolly-headed." His voice was warm, as if he were a kindly uncle, but Mayara knew this was a stranger. She tried to see across the room.

"Who are you?" she asked.

"You know, I find it fascinating that none of your questions have been about yourself. Usually, in these situations, the first question is 'Where am I?' followed by 'What's going to happen to me?'"

She blinked—her eyes felt as woolly as her mouth—and she could make out the shape of a large, muscular man at a desk. She couldn't see his features. A lamp was beside him, stuffed with firemoss.

"I know what's going to happen to me," Mayara said. "So it doesn't much matter where I am. Please, tell me if my fiancé— my *husband*—please tell me if my husband is alive."

"If you're resigned to your fate, as you say, does his fate make much difference?" The man sounded genuinely curious. Yet not sympathetic, as if her worry were of scientific interest only.

She could have cried or raged, yelled or pleaded, but she didn't think that would impress this strange man. So she simply said, "Yes."

Trying to sit up more, she winced as her head began to throb. Stubbornly, she didn't lie back down. *I'm not going to face my fate prone.* She spotted a glass of water on a small table beside her and drank it. The water felt cold, stinging her teeth, and it tasted faintly of flowers, but she couldn't be sure if that was the water itself or an aftereffect of the drug the Silent Ones had used on her.

Instead of answering, the man rose and straightened the papers on his desk. She was able to see him more clearly now: dark hair and a pale beard against skin that was striped in swathes of black, white, and bronze. She knew that coloring, at least from reputation.

"You're from the Family Neran," she guessed. "And I'm in your fortress."

That would explain the desk of solid wood—clearly shipped from the mainland. No island tree gave wood like that, with knots the size of her fist. She noticed the room was paneled in similar wood. It must have cost a fortune. *Possibly as much gold as my village makes in a year.* Belatedly, she realized that meant she was most likely addressing someone of importance in the Family Neran.

She added: "My lord."

He chuckled. "Power and intelligence do not always go hand in hand. I'm pleased to see you have both. You may work out fine."

"My lord, can you please tell me if my husband lives?" She kept her voice polite.

"I am here to record your choice and offer you guidance, if you need it." He still sounded kindly, even though she could see no reason for him not to tell her. "Let me present to you your options—"

"I know my choices." She took a deep breath as if she were about to face the sea. "But I will not choose until I know if my husband lived or died. My lord."

He regarded her with even more interest. "I am the head of the Family Neran. Do you know what that means, spirit sister?"

She flinched at the name "spirit sister." It was a title she'd run from for a long time—in some mouths, it was a name of respect. In others, it was a death sentence. And then she realized what he'd said about himself: the *head* of the Family Neran.

This was Lord Maarte himself, head of the ruling Family of her island, Olaku, second only in power and importance to Queen Asana herself and equal to the leaders of all the other islands of Belene.

Her head swam again, and she wished she were still lying down. She'd guessed from the richness of the room that this was someone of import. But she hadn't imagined she'd be waking in the same room as the ruler of their island.

"It means," he continued blandly, "that I am the final say

in all decisions pertaining to this island. I approve the laws. I mete out the punishments. I sign the trade agreements. I determine which villages—"

"Don't threaten my family." The words burst out before she'd considered them.

"Excuse me?"

It was too late to take them back. She plunged on. "You've taken my freedom, my future, my family, my dreams, my everything from me. Fine. It's the law. It's tradition. It may even be necessary. But threatening my family? That's cruel."

"You'll note that I didn't actually threaten anyone."

"You won't tell me whether my husband lives or not, either from sheer spite or because you enjoy feeling powerful. Then you hint at your power over villages. What am I supposed to think?"

He looked stunned. She guessed not many people spoke to him this way. She wondered if she'd misstepped. *Maybe I jumped to conclusions. Maybe he hadn't meant to threaten anyone.* She took another breath to steady herself. She felt embarrassment creeping up her neck, along with fear. For her family's sake, she shouldn't anger him. "If I misunderstood, please accept my apology, my lord."

His lips quirked—was he *smiling*? "Such a pity I did not meet you under better circumstances. Do you always speak first, think later?"

Now she didn't just feel embarrassed. She was mortified. What would Papa say if he knew she was speaking to the head of the Family Neran this way? Secretly, she thought Grandmama would approve. "Nearly always."

"It's charming," Lord Maarte declared. "But as delightful as you are, time is limited. You have been found to have an affinity to the six spirits of Renthia—water, fire, ice, air, earth, and tree—and as such have the potential to someday link yourself to spirits of Belene as queen, a bond that would grant you enough power to protect both our beloved islands and the entirety of Renthia from the deadly wild spirits that slumber in the Deepest Blue. Because of that potential, your fate is our fate. . . ."

He continued reciting the words as if he'd said them a hundred times before. *He probably has.* Every woman of power on Belene had to hear these words. *I just never thought it would be me.* She'd always thought she'd be able to hide her power forever. She'd promised both Elorna and her parents, and for years she'd been able to keep that promise. If the spirit storm hadn't hit their village . . .

For the first time since her wedding day, she asked herself *why* the storm had hit their village. Wasn't the queen supposed to predict the storms? And shouldn't the heirs have been sent to deflect it, or at least to assist them? But no heirs had come.

"Where were the heirs?" she interrupted.

A faint shadow of irritation crossed his face. As if she hadn't asked the question, he said, "In accordance with the laws of our island, laid down by the first queen of Belene, all women with potential are given a choice, to choose a path that is the best match for their temperament. Both choices are noble and necessary."

"The storm that hit my village," Mayara pressed. "It shouldn't have happened. Even if the heirs couldn't stop it from coming, they should have been there to help." She thought of Helia, her pregnant cousin, dead with all her dreams of the future. "My friends, my family, my neighbors—people *died*. And the heirs didn't come. They weren't even there after it was over to help with the dead. Why didn't they come?"

"A queen must make difficult decisions," Lord Maarte said stiffly. "The heirs were needed elsewhere." He then continued. "The Silent Ones enforce our laws by using their power over the islands' tame spirits. They do not face Akena Island and are never asked to risk their lives against the wild spirits, nor are they required to shoulder the burden of becoming queen. In return for their lesser risk, they must swear obedience to our queen and forsake their name, family, and all ties to their prior self."

Mayara saw movement out of the corner of her eye. She turned her head sharply—and paid for it with black spots that filled her vision. When they cleared, she saw that, unlike what she'd assumed, she was not alone with Lord Maarte.

The three Silent Ones stood in the shadows.

As always, they wore their white masks and gray robes. Mayara felt shivers up and down her spine. She'd seen many spirits over her lifetime, both wild and bonded, but none of them were as disturbing as the Silent Ones. It was the way they stood as if they were stone—they reminded her of the bones of the leviathans. There was the same kind of ancient feel to them. She couldn't explain why, but it didn't feel human.

She *knew* they were ordinary women under the masks and robes. In fact, they could have been exactly like her, recent brides from tiny villages who had to leave their families and homes because of a chance accident that revealed their power. But they felt more foreign than the wild spirits themselves. Worse, because she couldn't sense them in the way she could sense spirits.

"Your other choice is to submit to the Island of Testing. Survive for one month, and you will have proven yourself worthy of becoming an heir. Survive, and you will be trained to contend with the wild spirits and taught the secrets of the sea. While the Silent Ones are akin to the queen's police force, the heirs are her army. The heirs are vital to—"

"Is my husband alive?" Mayara asked the Silent Ones. "Did you kill him?"

All their eyes were fixed on her, and she thought she saw slight variation between them: one had narrow brown eyes, one had black eyes, and one had unlucky blue eyes. Death eyes.

"If you killed him . . . then I'd rather die than be one of you. Did you do it?"

"Of course they did," Lord Maarte cut in. "He tried to aid your escape."

Mayara felt as if she'd been hollowed out.

Lord Maarte continued talking, but she didn't hear him. *Kelo . . . dead?* She knew they'd punished him. She'd heard him scream. But a part of her was certain they wouldn't let him die. He'd be back in his studio, making new charms, picking up the scattered shells and bits of driftwood. He'd miss her, but he'd know she was safe. And someday, maybe . . .

She dropped her face into her hands. Her shoulders shook with silent sobs.

"Now you know," Lord Maarte said. "Will you make your choice?"

Mayara lifted her head. "I will."

"Remember: once you make your choice, it cannot be unmade."

*I can never be one of them.*

*They killed Kelo.*

"I choose the island."

# CHAPTER SEVEN

Lord Maarte recorded her choice and stamped the paper with his seal pressed into hot wax. He then nodded to the Silent Ones. Feeling numb, Mayara let herself be ushered out of his office. She'd cried, and now she felt empty.

One of the Silent Ones led, while the other two flanked her. Their white masks facing forward, none of them looked at Mayara. Their robes whispered against the stone floor.

*You killed him,* Mayara thought as she walked between them. But the words felt hollow and unreal. None of this felt real. It was all some terrible nightmare, distorted by the *cartena* flower. Maybe she was still knocked out by the drug and lying on a cliff at the feet of her captors. Maybe she was still asleep in the cove, with Kelo asleep beside her, resting uneasily because she knew they were being chased. Or maybe everything was a dream, and it was still the night before her wedding and the storm hadn't come and none of this had happened.

All that felt more plausible than the truth.

The first Silent One opened an ornately carved door and waited for Mayara to enter. It took her a moment to realize she'd been brought to the fortress's baths.

In the village, everyone bathed in tidal pools, or if you wanted to rinse the salt from your skin, you could venture farther into the island's interior and bathe in one of the freshwater streams that trickled down from the lakes. But in the fortress of the Family Neran, the baths were in a magnificent cavern tiled with blue glass and polished shells. Gilded columns supported an arched ceiling above interlocking pools of steaming turquoise water.

The three Silent Ones positioned themselves within the bathing room, guarding the door. Mayara stood on the edge of one of the pools. It was obvious they wanted her to bathe. Why else bring her here? And as much as she didn't want to cooperate, she also didn't see the point in resisting.

*This could be my last bath.*

She supposed that would be true of many things now. Her last bath, her last meal, her last night in a bed, her last dreams, her last breath. She wondered how many lasts she'd already had: her last kiss, her last day with her family. . . . *Kelo has already had his last everything.*

*No. I don't believe it.*

*My Kelo can't be dead.*

She'd known Kelo forever. They'd been born within a few hours of each other, in the birthing room of the healer's house. Their mothers had nursed side by side while the grandmothers of the village stood outside, welcoming them with the traditional lullabies. When they were a few months old, their fathers had strapped them onto their backs and carried them as they worked on their boats. As toddlers, while their parents fished in the shallows, they would chase hermit crabs on the beach, share pineapple slices, and then fall asleep sticky and sunburned. Older, they studied together—or rather, Kelo studied and Mayara sneaked into the kitchen to steal slices of coconut pie, to help them study. They'd shared their first kiss at age fourteen, and by the time they were sixteen, everyone knew they would wed someday. It had been as inevitable as sunrise.

That summed up Kelo himself: as inevitable as sunrise. She'd never doubted he would be there for her. He loved her with unwavering certainty. To think of that constant as gone . . .

*I can't.*

Very deliberately, she shoved the hollowness, the pain, the grief, and the disbelief into a tight ball deep inside her. Kelo would have told her to feel her full feelings. Emotions, the ability to feel anything beyond hate and rage, were what separated them from the spirits, he said. But she couldn't. *Not now.* They'd swallow her whole, so she swallowed them instead.

Mayara shed her clothes and slid into the water. It was so warm her skin prickled. Steam rose around her. Gliding through the pond, she found the soap, carved into the shape of a conch shell and resting beside a sponge, and she cleaned off all the blood, sweat, salt, and sand that clung to her skin.

She was working her fingers through her knotted blue-streaked hair when she heard voices from across the baths. Ducking down, she debated whether she should stay or go. She didn't want to speak to anyone. *Go where?* Mayara glanced at the Silent Ones—they hadn't moved.

She wondered what they'd do if she jumped out of the pool and ran across the room and out the door on the opposite side that the newcomers had opened. . . . Reaching out with her mind, she brushed against multiple spirits in the corridors of the fortress. A fire spirit writhing in a fireplace. An ice spirit lurking in the kitchen. Numerous water spirits swimming by the dock. She felt their pent-up rage, very different from the unbridled fury of the wild spirits that rode the storm. These were Belene spirits, linked to the queen and to the islands and controlled by the Silent Ones.

In other words, running was a bad idea.

So she stayed in the baths while the women splashed through the pools, drawing closer. There were two of them: a woman who looked to be about Mayara's age or perhaps younger, with bronze skin like hers, anemone-orange hair, and an angular face, and an older woman who looked to be in her fifties or sixties, with weathered wrinkles, black hair with clumps of gray, and a wide mouth.

"It *does* matter what kind of spirit you're controlling," the younger one was saying.

"Not to me," the older one said.

"But say you control both a fire spirit and an ice spirit, and you force them to fight each other. Think about what would happen!" Animated, she was gesturing wildly.

"You'd create steam," the older one said dryly. She gestured to the copious steam that rose off the bathing pools. "Lots of steam for them to hide in and kill you."

"Okay, maybe, yes, but I still think we have to go on the offensive."

"Dying in a blaze of glory is a legitimate choice."

Exasperated, the younger woman threw her arms in the air. "You're so negative! That's what will kill you faster than spirits. Have a little faith!"

"I have faith that the spirits are more deadly than my attitude."

"Heirs are supposed to be heroes, you know."

*Heirs!* Mayara had intended to stay silent, but not if these women were heirs. She had to ask them the question that Lord Maarte had avoided: Why hadn't they come? "Excuse me? Hello?"

Their conversation broke off.

"Who's there?" the older one asked in nearly a growl.

"This is new," the younger one said, surprise in her voice. "I'm not allowed to talk to others. Lord Maarte's orders. Who defies him?"

They didn't sound overly friendly, but Mayara wasn't feeling friendly herself. "There was a storm that hit the south shore. Eight days ago." Maybe nine. She wasn't certain how long the *cartena* flower had knocked her out. She thought of Kelo and then ruthlessly pushed the thought back again. "No heirs came and a village was destroyed. Why didn't you come?"

There was silence for a moment. Mayara wondered if she should have been more polite and if she was about to be in trouble with either Lord Maarte or them. Heirs were even more dangerous than the Silent Ones. The Silent Ones were trained to enforce laws. But the heirs . . . They were, in many ways, above the law. They were trained to fight threats to the islands. *Trained to fight spirits*, Mayara reminded herself. *Not islanders. They're pledged to protect people like me.*

Or people like she used to be. She supposed she couldn't consider herself an ordinary islander anymore. She was officially a spirit sister, her name and her choice recorded by Lord Maarte for all of history.

"She thinks we're heirs," the younger one said.

Through the steam, Mayara saw they were both staring at her. She stared right back. *If they're not heirs, who are they to talk about spirits like that?* Obviously, they weren't Silent Ones, chattering to each other and with their faces bare. Also, Silent Ones didn't fight spirits; they used them—and only the ones they knew they could control.

"I'm sorry to hear of your village," the older woman said gravely. "But we aren't heirs."

"Notice the guards?" The younger one waved her hand at the three Silent Ones. "You don't guard heroes."

Mayara had thought they were here to guard her. *But if they're guarding them too, then that means . . .*

"Take a good look at us," the older woman said, rising out of the water so her entire body was visible. Her wet flesh was soft, as if she'd never lifted a fisher's net or rowed more than a few strokes. She bore scars across her stomach that looked like claw marks. "You'll want to remember us because we'll be dead soon."

The younger one rolled her eyes. "If her village was hit by a wild spirit storm, she's not going to be impressed with your scars." To Mayara, she said, "I'm Roe, and this is Palia. She's having some trouble adjusting to the reality of our situation."

Palia sank back into the water. "On the contrary, I'm well aware of the reality. I'm not the one in denial about our chances."

Politely, Mayara said, "They're very nice scars."

Roe covered a laugh with a snort.

"I take it you're both spirit sisters too, and you also chose the island." Mayara hadn't thought about the fact that she'd meet others like her. Despite everything, she almost felt like smiling. *I'm not facing this alone.*

But the two of them were staring at her as if she'd said the most horrible words they'd ever heard. She wondered if she'd guessed wrong. Surely, though, if they weren't heirs and weren't Silent Ones and were talking about controlling spirits . . .

"You're spirit sisters," Mayara said. "Like I am. Aren't you?" It felt a little strange to admit her power so openly, but it wasn't as if it was a secret anymore.

Palia buried her face in her hands and moaned.

"I'm sorry," Mayara said. "What did I say? I didn't mean . . ."

Roe's voice was subdued. "It's not what you said. It's who you are. You're the twelfth spirit sister to be found. Per tradition, the queen waits until we number twelve before she orders the Silent Ones to start the test."

Palia lifted her face. "Because you've arrived, we all get to die that much sooner. Hurray. So happy to meet you."

Mayara didn't know what to say to that.

"I . . . I thought I'd be more ready," Roe said; then she shook herself, scattering drops of water in every direction. "Had to happen sooner or later. And this must be even harder on you. We've had time to get used to our fate."

"Does anyone get used to the idea of facing death?" Palia asked. She then frowned at Mayara. "You don't look upset at hearing the test is going to start."

Mayara considered that. "Upset" wasn't a word that fit. She felt as if her insides had been ripped out, like a clam pulled from its shell. It was all too much. The storm, the failed escape, Kelo . . .

*Oh, Kelo.*

It suddenly hit her, hard.

Maybe the effects of the *cartena* flower had finally worn off. Maybe it was discussing the test with Palia and Roe. Maybe it was only that enough time had passed that the reality became impossible to ignore.

"Are you all right?" Palia asked.

"Whoa, don't faint," Roe ordered. The two women were on either side of her—Mayara hadn't even noticed they'd moved. "I suppose it's healthy you aren't taking this all in stride. But you'll have to develop a way to cope soon. We'll be taken for three days of intensive training before we're delivered to Akena Island. It will be our last chance to prepare for what's to come. And your first chance."

Mayara didn't care about training or about what would happen on the island. She knew she wasn't going to survive it. *At least Kelo won't have to face a world without me.*

It was a terrible, horrible thought. But he'd said it would break him if she went to the island. *At least he'll never know. He died thinking I'd live.* She felt as if she wanted to burst into sobs, but the sobs were clogged in her throat.

She wished he hadn't asked it of her, to be a Silent One. It wasn't for him to decide whether she should choose death or a life like death. And then she pushed that thought down—he'd only said it because he was afraid.

She wondered if her choice would break her parents. Her mother . . . Would she feel this new pain on top of the old, or would it all mix together in a perfect storm of sorrow? How would her father bear it, losing two daughters? She'd have to trust her aunts and uncles and cousins to watch over them now. Mayara gulped in little breaths, as if she was about to dive. She felt as though there wasn't enough air.

"Three days to train," Roe repeated. "You can do this!"

"Maybe it will be enough," Palia said. "Maybe we won't die."

"Optimism, Palia?" Roe asked. "I'm proud of you."

"I'm lying through my teeth," Palia said. "Obviously we're all going to die. But I didn't think it would be helpful to say that."

Mayara almost smiled, painfully. "You just said it."

"Thattagirl." Palia patted her shoulder. "No more panicking. Gather your courage and all that. Just because it's hopeless doesn't mean we can't act like it's not."

"You're really terrible at comforting people," Mayara told her.

"I blame my upbringing," Palia said. "And Lord Maarte. And the queen. And the archaic traditions that put us in this position. I also blame the spirits, bad luck, and an unripe mango I ate for breakfast. It really didn't agree with me."

This time, Mayara smiled for real—something that she wouldn't have thought possible in the wake of Kelo's death. Her smile died almost as quickly as it came.

*I'll never see his smile again.*

AT DAWN, MAYARA WAS ESCORTED OUT OF THE FORTRESS BY A Silent One. She, along with Roe and Palia, was to be transported to the training site via one of the Family Neran's trading ships—*which would be an honor if we weren't being taken to our deaths,* Mayara thought.

As she stepped through an archway onto a white-and-red dock, she saw the famed triple-masted sailing ship, gorgeous in every detail and worth more than the combined wealth of every villager Mayara knew.

*Kelo would love to see this.*

Just thinking of him made Mayara feel as if a wave had hit her full-on. Halting at the plank that led to the deck, she blinked back tears as she stared at the ship. Kelo would have spent the whole journey gawking at the artistry. Every inch, every plank, every rope, and every sail was as exquisitely crafted as the furnishings in the fortress. The ship itself was made of red-, white-, and yellow-hued planks that had been fitted together to make the hull into a beautiful mosaic. All the ropes were braided with strands of shimmering silver, woven together with water-reed fibers. The sails were a brilliant red to rival the brightest sunset, and the sailors wore clothes as fine as any lord, embroidered with silver threads and studded with bone buttons. Completing the picture, Lord Maarte himself was at the helm. He looked even more intimidating outside in the light than he had in his darkened office. He shone in the sunlight, the gold and silver of his uniform reflecting the sun in almost-painful flashes. His hair and his beard had been tied in multiple braids, and he wore a heavy pendant—his house's symbol, a bird whose wings held the sun. The sails too bore the same symbol, white against the red. Altogether, it was glorious.

And horrible.

"Kelo won't ever see this," Mayara said. "Because of you." She directed the last at the Silent One who guarded her. "He won't see another ship or another sunrise. He won't . . ." She swallowed hard, unable to go on.

The Silent One looked at her, and Mayara imagined she saw a hint of pity in those shadowed eyes—but no, the Silent One was emotionless and unreadable, because the woman behind the mask wasn't human anymore.

Squaring her shoulders, Mayara walked up the plank onto the ship. The Silent One joined her sisters. All three were motionless, except for the fluttering of their robes in the wind. She wondered if they sweat under their masks. Or laughed. Or cried. Or felt guilt over those whose lives they had taken and lives they had destroyed. Maybe they had abandoned all emotion when they'd relinquished their names and identities.

*Murderers,* she thought.

Trying to put space between her and them, Mayara crossed the deck to Roe and Palia.

Roe beamed at her, as if this were an exciting adventure, while Palia humphed, squinted at the sun, and then started to shuffle away.

"Hate ships," Palia said. "Get me when it's over."

The older woman disappeared belowdecks, leaving Mayara and Roe above with the sailors and the Silent Ones. Shouting to one another, the sailors stowed the plank, untied the ropes, and unfurled the sails. Lord Maarte barked orders from the helm. The Silent Ones merely watched. One stood on the prow. One on the stern. And the third not far from her and Roe.

Roe leaned against the railing and looked out at the sea eagerly, as if she couldn't wait to be underway, which they soon were. Mayara faced the opposite direction: looking back at the fortress and her island as they receded.

Wind filled the triple sails.

"This is exciting!" Roe said.

"You're excited to die?"

Roe rolled her eyes. "I don't plan to die."

*How can she be so naive?* Nearly everyone who went to the island died there! The test was designed to weed out those who were unsuited and leave only the best of the best. *And I'm not that.* Mayara had no experience, no training, no strategy for how to survive. *I'm just an oyster diver.* "I'm not planning to either, but it's going to happen. It's the most likely outcome."

"Likely but not certain," Roe said. "Death can't catch me if I chase it."

Mayara stiffened. "What did you say?"

"It's a saying. Haven't you heard it before? It comes from the tale of the first islander." Leaning against the rail of the ship, Roe launched into the story, chattering cheerfully. "He was a fisherman, and in the wake of the first great battle between the queens of Renthia and the wild sea spirits, he couldn't find any fish. All the leviathans had scared them off. So he got into his boat to row out to deeper waters. Everyone told him he was crazy—the deeper waters were where the wild spirits ruled. He'd never survive. And he told them that death was searching for him and everyone else up and down the shore of Renthia, so if he went out to where death lived, he'd be fine. His family let him go, because they thought anyone who was spouting such nonsense was probably going to die soon of some terrible mind disease anyway. Or something like that. Anyway, he went out into the sea, and found that the queens had killed so many of the gigantic spirits that their skeletons had formed the islands. He made his home there and caught thousands of fish. When at last the battle was over, others rowed out to the new islands and found him there, as fat and as happy as could be."

Mayara had never heard that version of the story. She'd been taught the first queen of Belene had founded the island nation, not some stubborn fisherman. But she liked it.

"Sorry—I didn't mean to bore you with the whole tale. I've spent a lot of time listening to my grandparents tell me stories. It's pretty much all I did for most of my childhood."

"It's all right," Mayara said. "It was a good distraction." For a few moments, she wasn't thinking about what she'd left behind or what lay ahead. Of course, now that Roe had finished, it all came back.

As they sailed farther and farther away from the only home she'd ever known, Mayara looked out across the water. Spray spattered her face as the ship sliced through the sea. A pod of dolphins swam parallel with the ship. She watched their smooth bodies leap, glistening, out of the water, one after another. They looked so full of life as they journeyed through the sea.

*And here I am, traveling to my death.*

Death should be sudden. Not this slow march toward inevitability. She wished she felt more like the elderly grandmothers of the village when their time came—she'd seen them leave the world with dignity.

Except Great-Aunt Hollena, she remembered.

On her ninety-ninth birthday, Great-Aunt Hollena had smashed every window in the village and then run off the end of the dock. She might have made it to her hundredth birthday, people said, if she hadn't misjudged the leap, hit her head, and drowned before anyone realized where she'd gone.

*If you can't die with dignity, die dramatically* became a new village saying. As funerals went, it had been a fun one. Great-Aunt Hollena wouldn't have wanted any tears.

*Oh, Kelo, why did this have to happen?*

Mayara didn't want to die, either with or without dignity. She wanted to be home with her new husband, her parents, and her cousins. She wanted to be diving for abalone in the mornings and sipping fish soup with Kelo in the evenings while they watched the fishing boats come into the harbor. She wanted it so badly that it physically hurt in her gut.

They stood by the railing, side by side in silence, each lost in her own thoughts, until Roe pointed at the horizon. "That's where we'll train."

In the distance was a small island, one of the many that dotted the sea around the five major islands of Belene. It looked like a fist rising out of the ocean, covered in green. There, they'd receive their final training before they were deposited on the Island of Testing.

Only in Mayara's case, she hadn't yet had *any* training.

"They'll bring the other nine of us there too. Plus an heir to train us." Of the twelve spirit sisters who chose the island, only the three of them were in the Neran Stronghold. The others had been held on other islands in the homes of other ruling families. "Some of them had nearly a year to prepare. I'd thought I'd have more time."

"At least you've had three months," Mayara pointed out. "I've had none."

"That's true." Roe brightened. "And you know the saying: You don't have to outswim the shark; you only have to outswim the other swimmers." She added quickly, "I'm joking."

Mayara nodded to show she wasn't offended.

"Also, I can't swim," Roe said. "And I'm pretty sure the fastest swimmer might end up dying anyway." She frowned at that thought.

Mayara ignored Roe's musings, because something the girl had said struck her as odd. Mayara had always swum, for as long as she could remember. It felt as natural to her as walking— even more so, because in the water, every movement could be smooth. But she knew, at least intellectually, that there were plenty of people who couldn't. It did seem shortsighted, though, for someone who lived on an island. And a serious problem for someone who expected to survive the Island of Testing. "How do you plan to escape sea spirits if you can't swim?"

"By not going in the water."

*Fair enough,* she thought.

They were both silent for a moment, looking out across the sea at the fist-shaped island; then Roe said, "I heard you tried to run."

"Only made it eight days before they caught us." Mayara sighed. "I suppose it was the height of optimism to think we'd be able to hide from them for a lifetime." She thought of how certain Kelo had been. *I never should have agreed to his plan.* She should have refused to climb into those death boats. At least then he'd have been spared.

Roe boggled at her. "*Eight days?* I've never heard of anyone evading the Silent Ones for more than a single day."

"I know the coast near my village, so I knew where to hide." *And I had Kelo with me.*

"Eight days! Okay, that clinches it. We're teaming up." Roe clapped her hand on Mayara's shoulder.

"I thought you were just going to outswim me."

"Yes, but that was before I knew you escaped the Silent Ones for eight days!" Roe was marveling at her as if Mayara had defeated a leviathan. Mayara didn't feel as if she'd done anything remarkable. After all, she'd failed. "If I could have escaped . . ." Roe trailed off, glancing at Lord Maarte.

"Did you try?"

"Actually, the opposite. I tried for years to get Lord Maarte to admit that I had powers. But every time I tried to rile up the spirits, an heir or a Silent One would shut it down. It was only when I unleashed an ice spirit during one of his feasts, while his magical lackeys were busy elsewhere, that he finally couldn't deny it anymore."

"But . . . why?" Mayara had never heard of anyone who *wanted* to be caught. "You wanted to be sent to the island?"

"I want to be an *heir*," Roe clarified. "It's all right if you don't understand. Palia thinks I'm crazy too." She leaned farther over the railing, holding her hands out to touch the spray from the waves as the ship cut through the sea. "And so does Lord Maarte. He was definitely angry after the feast. Suffice it to say he doesn't like me much."

"What exactly did you do?"

Roe grinned. "Froze his soup. And I don't mean just made it chilly. I had the ice spirit sculpt the soup in everyone's bowls into these frozen waterfalls. And then I made it freeze the doors shut and turn the floor into an ice rink."

"You didn't!" To *the* Lord Maarte, head of his Family, ruler of their island?

"Everyone tried to run and then . . . whoops! Slipped on the ice. I watched it happen through the eyes of the spirit. Looked like a bunch of newborn sheep, everyone wobbling all around."

"You're serious?" She didn't know it was even possible to control the spirits with that degree of precision. And what did Roe mean she watched "through the eyes of the spirit"? *Is that a thing we can do?* Mayara didn't know much about how their power worked. It had been safer to pretend it didn't exist.

Solemnly, Roe nodded. "Lord Maarte's nephew tried to stand up by grabbing on to Lord Maarte and accidentally yanked his pants down."

Mayara surprised herself: she laughed. Roe joined in too. Maybe the story was true, and maybe it wasn't, but it felt good to laugh again. And to feel as if she'd made a friend.

A few of the sailors shot them startled looks. She realized that none of the sailors had made eye contact with them or the Silent Ones. The Silent Ones were considered by all to be . . . disquieting, at best, so that was understandable, and as for her and Roe and Palia . . . *They probably don't want to befriend the doomed.*

Looking out at the sea again, with the sun sparkling on the waves, she thought, *I don't feel doomed*. In fact, she didn't feel any different from how she had yesterday. She felt well fed, well rested, and heart sore. But she didn't feel on the verge of death. *I've stared death in the face before, surrounded by blue. This doesn't feel like that.*

It felt, weirdly, like a beginning.

*A terrible beginning, without Kelo.*

"Do you really think it's possible to survive?" Mayara asked. She had no illusions that she could survive this, but perhaps Roe had a chance.

"Others have. Otherwise there wouldn't be heirs. And if they could do it . . ." Roe gave an elaborate shrug. "Palia says I'm not a realist. She's wrong."

"How have you been training?"

"I've been trying to learn survival skills mostly, at least as much as my grandparents can teach me," Roe said. "I haven't been outside the stronghold in years, so I'm pretty hopeless in the wilderness. But I've learned how to start a fire, boil water, clean a fish . . ." She wrinkled her nose. "After that lesson, I couldn't eat a fish for a week. And when they showed me where roe comes from . . . I nearly changed my name."

Mayara laughed again, then sobered. It wouldn't do her any good to be able to gut a fish if the spirits on the island gutted her first. She looked at the helm, where Lord Maarte stood majestically, his ponytail of braids flowing behind him in the wind, and something finally dawned on her. Roe talked as though she'd grown up in the fortress. "You're Family Neran?" She couldn't imagine him taking his own relative—daughter? niece?—to the island and then leaving her behind. What kind of monster would do that?

"Oh no, I'm not a Neran. My family is under their protection."

She glanced again at Roe and raised both her eyebrows. *Protection from what? Or who?* "Do you know how to protect yourself from spirits? Did your grandparents teach you that?" That was the point of the test: to teach potential heirs how to handle hostile spirits. If they passed, they receive more intensive training, beyond anything a Silent One ever learned.

Roe became serious too. "I've been practicing that as much as possible. But there hasn't been much opportunity. The Silent Ones have been keeping watch over me to ensure I don't cause any more 'incidents,' and Lord Maarte . . . I'd hoped he'd allow an heir to train me or at least give me advice. That's what he's done for the children of his guards and servants who showed an affinity for spirits. But he refused. It causes political problems for him if I survive."

"He *wants* you to die?" That was worse than being expected to die. He could have helped Roe's odds, but he'd chosen not to. *What kind of monster is he?* Mayara clenched her fists as a hot, sudden rage rose inside her—it was so swift and strong that it surprised her, but she didn't try to stop it.

Here was a place to funnel her feelings of anger at the unfairness of it all, toward the law, the queen, the Silent Ones, even toward Kelo who had insisted on his escape plan even though the odds were against them and who had told her to become a Silent One even though that was a fate worse than death. So much anger—she hadn't known it was there; it had been smothered under the sadness.

She had to let it out.

Without waiting to think, Mayara marched across the ship to the helm.

"Mayara, what are you doing?" Roe called after her.

A sailor stepped in front of her.

Clearly he was there to guard Lord Maarte, which was absurd. It was his ship, and he had Silent Ones who could control spirits at his beck and command. "Exactly what do you think I could do to hurt him with three Silent Ones on the ship?"

"Lord Maarte is not to be disturbed."

Mayara judged the soldier was younger than she was, with

barely shaveable scruff on his chin. He probably came from a village just like hers. She fixed him with the kind of look that Grandmama gave youngsters in the village, with one eyebrow raised and her lips pursed. "He's just standing there holding a wheel steady, whereas I'm likely to die in a few days. I think he has more time to spare than I do. Let me by."

The soldier shifted nervously.

"Let her by." Lord Maarte's voice drifted down. He sounded amused. She felt a fresh burst of anger—nothing about any of this was amusing, and how dare he think it was.

The sailor shifted to the side, and Mayara marched up the stairs toward the ship's wheel. "You could have helped Roe prepare, and you didn't because of some political game?"

"Quick to defend a stranger. How noble of you." He flashed her a grin that she supposed was meant to be charming. She wondered if there was anyone on all the islands who could find a man who wielded so much power over people to be "charming."

"And how vile of you," Mayara snapped. A part of her brain shrieked at her to stop—this was Lord Maarte! But another part reveled in letting her rage out. "She was under your protection, and you failed to do anything to protect her."

His grin dissolved into a scowl. "She is the one who insisted on flaunting her power."

"And she should have been praised for it! She *wants* to be an heir! You should have encouraged that, not sabotaged her like some petulant child who wasn't getting what he wants."

He raised his eyebrows. "You should watch your tone."

"Why? I've lost everything and am on my way to die." She remembered Great-Aunt Hollena. "I think that entitles me to say whatever I want in whatever tone I want." But then she thought of her parents and her village. He wouldn't retaliate against them for her words, would he?

"You could have everything again if you survive."

"Except my husband."

Lord Maarte shrugged, then squinted at the horizon. "Perhaps even him, if you still want him. You won't know that unless you survive."

His words hit her so hard that for a moment she couldn't breathe. "He's dead. You told me they killed him."

"How would I know either way? I wasn't there, and the Silent Ones aren't exactly forthcoming about their activities." He flashed her a smile. "Your beloved may yet live."

Mayara felt as if she'd been swallowed by a tsunami. She lost all sense of what was up and what was down. Staggering backward, she clutched at the ship's railing. "You said . . . Why would you . . . ?"

"Because you were about to make the wrong choice," Lord Maarte said. "I was performing my duty, looking out for the interests of Belene. If our strongest women choose to become Silent Ones, their power is wasted. Silent Ones don't receive the same level of training, and they don't perform the same duties—controlling spirits already claimed by the queen is vastly different from fighting wild spirits that aren't bonded to anyone. You stopped the spirit storm—that's strength. And we need our strongest to become heirs, to defend our islands and protect our future!"

*Could it be true?*

Her knees felt weak. She wanted to collapse. *I can't collapse. I have to get off this ship! Back to Kelo!* They'd already sailed several miles from the island, but she was a strong swimmer, and it was a clear day—

A spirit shaped like a pale-blue human rose out of the water and bared its shark teeth. A wave curled around it, in defiance of the current.

She pivoted and met the eyes of a Silent One. "You're doing that?"

The Silent One did not respond, but she didn't have to.

Mayara spun back to face Lord Maarte again. "If he lives, I must change my choice. I made a promise!" She was aware that her voice was spiraling higher. She felt as if her thoughts and feelings were caught in a whirlpool.

"You did make a promise—to your country and its people. Your choice cannot be changed. It was made, witnessed, and recorded." Shaking his head, he clucked his tongue disapprovingly. "Come now, second thoughts don't become a woman on her way to transforming into a hero of the islands. I am disappointed."

"I only chose the test because I believed my husband was dead! Murdered by the Silent Ones. If he wasn't, then I need to do what I meant to do and become a Silent One. Please, my lord, if there's any mercy in you . . ." She dropped to her knees. She'd beg if she had to. Whatever it took to get back to Kelo.

He raised his eyebrows. "As much as you talk, you'd have made a poor Silent One. As for your artist husband . . . all you need to do is survive the test, and then you can find out for yourself whether he lives. If he does, you'll be reunited. Unlike Silent Ones, heirs are allowed private lives, so long as they perform their duty when needed." Lord Maarte flashed his "charming" smile once more. "Of course, if you survive the test, you may decide to do better than a common craftsman. I'd be honored if you would allow me to get to know you better."

She stared at him.

She wasn't often struck wordless, but Lord Maarte had succeeded.

"There's no point in that *now,* of course, because there's no guarantee you won't die." He dismissed his offer with a wave of his jeweled hand. "I try not to form attachments to anyone with a potentially short life span. But I predict I will be seeing you again, spirit sister." He then glanced over her head and nodded.

Mayara felt a hand on her elbow, drawing her away—it was the young sailor. She looked back at Lord Maarte. "You *are* vile."

"I do what I must for the good of Belene. With power comes the responsibility of making difficult choices. You will learn that someday." He flashed her another smile that she wanted to claw off his face before he added, "If you don't die first."

She didn't resist as the sailor pulled her away, and he released her as soon as she was across the deck from the ruler of Olaku Island. Numbly, she stumbled over to where Roe was leaning against the railing.

"He likes you," Roe observed when Mayara had reached her. "Creepy."

She couldn't argue with that. It was worse than "creepy." It was disgusting.

*I don't want him to like me. I want him to let me go home!*

But she knew that was impossible, not without Lord Maarte defying the law, which he was clearly not willing to do. In fact, he seemed to take a weird satisfaction in transporting them to their probable deaths—there was absolutely no reason he needed to be helming this ship himself. But here he was, and in his eyes and the eyes of the law, she'd made her choice, and now she was bound to it, whether she wanted to be or not. *And whether or not I was tricked into that choice.* She would have broken that law, though, if she could, just as she had when they'd run. *I'd swim out of here, if the Silent Ones with their pet sea monsters would let me.*

Mayara squeezed her eyes closed. *If Kelo is alive . . .*

She tried not to think about how hurt he must have been when she found out about her choice. *It would break me,* he'd said.

"What did he say?" Roe asked.

For an instant, Mayara thought she was talking about her beloved. But no, she meant Lord Maarte. "He doesn't know whether or not my husband lives."

"That's good news!" Roe said encouragingly. "Possibly alive is better than definitely dead, right? Um, right? You don't look happy."

"I have to live," Mayara said.

"Again, good news, right?"

"I don't know how to fight spirits."

"That's why we're going to be trained! You'll see. The queen *wants* us to survive. The more heirs Belene has, the safer the islands will be."

Mayara thought of the cove where she'd left Kelo. If she'd been trained, if she'd known more about how to control the spirits . . . If she'd been able to wrest them away from the Silent Ones . . .

She shook herself. *What am I thinking? Overpower the Silent Ones?* There were three of them! All trained to control the island's spirits! And all focused on one task: subduing her.

"Once we're at the training site, we'll have a real heir to teach us," Roe was saying. "Don't worry. It's not like everyone else will be an expert. You'll be fine."

"I'm not so sure about that," Mayara said. In fact, she was sure of the opposite. *Elorna had this special training, and she still died. How am I going to do what she couldn't?*

*I chose this, knowing it meant my death. How can I now expect to live?*

"You'll catch up," Roe said. "If you're willing to try. So are you? You, me, and Palia—we could be a team. Help each other out on the island. Keep each other from dying. What do you think?"

This was her actual choice, she realized: Accept that she was doomed . . . Or fight fate.

And maybe win back the future she'd wanted.

Mayara looked out across the sparkling waves. A flock of pelicans soared low over the water, toward the island that looked like a fist raised to the sky. She filled her lungs, then emptied them, the way she did when she was preparing for a difficult dive, and she imagined Kelo, alive and waiting for her.

"Let's chase death," Mayara said.

# CHAPTER EIGHT

Kelo drifted in and out of consciousness in a haze of pain. Sometimes he woke certain the spirits were still gnawing on his leg and he thrashed, fighting them, until he felt his father's hand on his forehead.

Other times he woke with the taste of soup on his tongue, salty and sweet, and to the sound of his father singing, an off-key crooning sea song, like he used to sing when Kelo was a small child and had trouble sleeping.

He wasn't sure which was the dream: the spirits or his father.

Or maybe both were, and he was somewhere else entirely, wherever souls went after their life ended. At last, though, he clawed his way back to awareness.

He was in his parents' home, in a cot, tucked in with quilts that he remembered from his childhood. His pillow was mostly flat and smelled of seaweed. Turning his head, he saw the walls had been patched with sail fabric that fluttered in the wind. *I should help them fix that,* he thought vaguely. His thoughts felt like they were fluttering too.

And then he tried to sit up.

Pain shot through him, and he clutched his chest, easing himself back down. His torso was wrapped in bandages. Craning his neck, he managed a glance at the rest of him—bandages swaddled his leg as well. And his left wrist was bound. He'd broken it, he remembered.

*I'm alive,* he thought. *How?* The last thing he remembered were the spirits in the cove. . . . He'd been certain they were going to kill him. He didn't know why he'd been spared or how he'd gotten home.

"Mayara?" he croaked.

"She's alive." His father was in a rocking chair by the window. The window looked oddly empty—no charms, no mobiles, no shutters. All of it had blown away in the storm. Kelo noticed other things missing as well: dishes and bowls, everything made of glass. There was a stack of coconut shells, cut in half and dried out, that were stacked beside the sink.

As he cataloged each difference, he tried to wrap his mind around those simple words: *She's alive.* She'd chosen life. And he wouldn't see her again. Or if he did, he wouldn't know it was her. She'd be behind a mask, swathed in robes. She'd have renounced her family, her name, herself. . . . *And it's my fault. I told her to choose that life.*

*That non-life.*

*I shouldn't have done it.*

It had seemed like such a beautiful solution at the time: He'd leave her coded messages in his art, and he'd know that somewhere she still existed. Their love would survive so long as they both did. But now that plan felt empty. And foolish.

"So she is to be a Silent One." He was surprised at how calm his voice sounded, when what he wanted to do was scream and rage against the universe for taking her from him. He'd never felt this rush of anger before. Usually, he went through life as calm as the sea on a windless day. He took pride in being even-keeled.

"Kelo, my boy . . ."

He heard the note in his father's voice and knew he wasn't going to like what came next. He wanted to clap his hands over his ears like a child and not hear whatever it was his father was about to say.

His father's voice was as soft as a lullaby. But the words burrowed into Kelo's heart: "She chose the island."

As soon as he was well enough to move, Kelo booked passage to Yena on a slender ship, a breed of seafaring vessels that were built to cut through the water with speed and stealth—their captains advertised swift passage between the five major and myriad minor islands of Belene with little to no interference from spirits. You paid handsomely for that, but Kelo didn't need to offer gold: he had his skills. Even with one broken wrist and flares of pain from his other wounds, he could still carve.

As the ship sped away from his home island, he unrolled a leather carrying case that held his wood-carving tools, and with his uninjured hand, he set to work on the mast, carving runes that would repel spirits.

Runes weren't effective against all spirits. Neither were charms. *Certainly our village is proof of that.* Kelo had carved charms on many of the houses himself, and he'd supplied the majority of the charms that had hung in the windows and doorways, yet still homes had been destroyed and lives lost. But runes and charms would make most spirits hesitate—and sometimes those precious seconds gave you just enough time to escape. *If the heirs had come, it might have been enough.*

The sea breeze was steady in his face, and as he chipped away at the mast, he kept having to pause to push his hair back behind his ears. If Mayara were here, she would have handed him a hair tie the second she saw him distracted. But she wasn't, and with his injured wrist, he couldn't knot the ribbon. It was only by the tenth time his hair flopped in his eyes, breaking his focus, that it occurred to him he could simply ask someone else.

He missed Mayara so abruptly and deeply that it felt as if a knife had stabbed him in the gut.

She always made sure he tied his hair back, and he always

treated her cuts when she scraped herself on rocks and coral. He cooked her favorite spiced pineapple mash, and she reminded him to eat, even when he was in the midst of an all-absorbing project. . . . *We were a team.*

*We* are *a team.*

That was why it had been such a simple choice for them to marry. It wasn't because of the shrimp buffet, as Mayara had liked to tell people. And it wasn't because he'd wanted to see her in that nacre dress, though he had. *She looked like art. Exactly as I'd imagined.* No, the reason he wanted to marry her was because he wanted his life to be by her side.

It was, he thought, the best reason of all to marry: *Because we want to be together.*

Just that one reason, true and beautiful. Like Mayara herself.

And it was the reason it had been a mistake to tell her to become a Silent One, and why he had to see her again and tell her how sorry he was for asking that of her. They were meant to be together, no compromises.

That's what he planned to tell Queen Asana: she had to stop the test and release Mayara, because if she didn't, then she would destroy something rare and precious. Yes, heirs were needed for protection—but this, the kind of love that he and Mayara had, was what the heirs fought to protect.

He just hoped she didn't think it was all bullshit.

"Hey, charm-maker." The captain of the slender ship poked his shoulder. "Done yet?"

Kelo frowned at the rune he'd carved. It was intricate, with the right patterns to appeal to fire, water, and air spirits— it should work, buying the sailors at least a few seconds. But it should be brighter. He wasn't sure why he felt so certain, but he trusted his instincts. "Do you have any resin?"

"Pitch? Got that."

"Yellow resin."

"Might. Why?"

"It'll make the rune more effective."

The captain grunted. "Never heard of that. Runes are supposed to be bare wood. That's how they've always been done. Yellow resin is not traditional."

"Have you ever heard of the Massacre of Yellowfin?"

The captain scratched his beard. Kelo noted that it seemed to be the captain's favorite pastime. Every conversation he'd had with the man, the captain had had his fingers stuffed into the straggly tangles of his beard. Kelo wondered if the man thought it made him look wise. *It makes him look like he has fleas.* "Can't say I have."

"That's because there was no massacre when there could have been. Spirit storm, but everyone sheltered inside a single house that had been covered in runes highlighted with yellow resin. They came out after the heirs had beaten back the storm, and every building was flattened except for the one they'd taken shelter in."

The captain's eyes bugged. "I'll get you the resin."

"And a cooking can, to melt it."

"Right away."

Kelo turned back to the mast. If he poured melted resin from the top, it should follow the channels of the runes down— he'd carved them so they'd all connect.

A nearby sailor cleared her throat. "You know, I'm from Yellowfin. We didn't have any spirit storm, and we certainly don't have any house with yellow resin."

"Maybe it was a different village?"

"Or maybe you made it up."

Kelo flashed her a grin. "It will look better in yellow."

The sailor laughed.

The captain brought the resin, as well as a cooking cannister. Kelo dropped the yellow resin into the top and waited for it to melt. *I have to trust my instincts,* he thought. *Without Mayara, they're all I have.*

A few seagulls circled the top of the mast, calling to one another. He spent the rest of the journey adding the resin to the runes and imagining what story he was going to tell the queen to convince her to change a far more important tradition.

HE FINISHED THE RUNES A FEW HOURS BEFORE THE SLENDER SHIP reached Yena and had ample time to observe the approach to the glorious capital city of Belene. And it was indeed as glorious as all the songs, stories, and poems claimed:

Built on the back of a turtle shell that was more enormous than could be imagined, the upper levels of the city were carved into the rib cage of a leviathan on top of the shell. Palm trees crested each rib in neat rows, and beautifully delicate homes were suspended beneath the ribs—these marvels were where the wealthy lived. But the rest of the citizenry lived in just as much splendor. Below the ribs, the lower city, on the shell of the turtle itself, was sheathed in mother-of-pearl. And to the west of the dock, at the base of the tallest tower, was a standing circle of vertical ribs, encircling the famed coronation grove.

"I heard the city streets are all nacre," Kelo said to the sailor from Yellowfin.

"Indeed they are," she said with a snort. "Damn impractical too. You aren't allowed any carts or anything with wheels. Hooved animals are right out. Can't risk damaging the mother-of-pearl. I've heard that Yenites spend half their income on repairs."

*Surely the queen of a city that values such beauty will listen to an artist's plea, right?* he thought. "Do you know where I go for an audience with the queen?"

"I doubt they'll let you waltz up to the palace and say hello, but if you want to try"—she pointed toward a tower that looked like a spiral shell—"that's it there."

He thanked the sailor, then the captain as he disembarked with the other passengers, mostly wealthy folk come to visit the city that was the jewel of the islands. He hadn't spoken with any of them, and they, seeing that he was employed with carving the rune, hadn't tried to interrupt him, which was fine with him—he wasn't here to make friends.

Shouldering his pack—and wincing as it bounced against his bandaged wounds—he made his way through the city.

The streets, as promised, were paved with mother-of-pearl. All the buildings too were covered in it. And while he appreciated the effort, now that he was seeing it up close . . . it was overkill. Maybe if the pristine shell could have been maintained—in other words, if no people whatsoever lived in the city, walked through the city, or did anything but gaze from a distance—then it would have been a beautiful sight. But as it was . . . Up close, the city looked sad. Half the shells were broken or missing, giving the buildings the appearance of having been in a fight. *And of having lost,* he decided.

As for the famous streets . . . The sailor was right. Paving city streets with delicate shell mosaics was not practical. Kelo appreciated the vision, though. The original city planners certainly had style.

He weaved between the other pedestrians—everyone was on foot, many carrying loads. Poles were laid across shoulders, with crates or barrels hanging from either end. People also carried pots on their heads, cushioned by a nest of fabric. And everyone, young or old, working or playing, wore thick, stiff sandals. Even the children didn't dare run barefoot through the street. The broken shells would rip their feet to shreds. He wondered why they didn't change the streets. Use the nacre to create some other kind of beautiful art piece, one that didn't need to be walked on.

Musing over this proved a nice distraction from worrying about what to say to the queen, and before he knew it, Kelo was at the palace.

It was only when he stood in front of the palace that he at last acknowledged the massive flaw in his plan: *Who am I to speak to the queen?*

As that question rippled through his mind, he admired the queen's seat of power. The palace was curved like a shell and had a semicircle of spires, each taller than the next, that ringed its heart. Iridescent, its walls looked like a rippling rainbow as the sun played over the mother-of-pearl. As near as Kelo could tell, there was a single entrance: an ornate bridge carved in the shape of a wave. It was the only bit of the palace not covered in the luminous shell. Instead it was carved of a translucent blue stone that was like nothing Kelo had ever seen.

He joined the stream of pedestrians on the blue wave bridge, feeling out of place between the courtiers and palace workers. At the gate—an intricately shaped iron gate that mimicked coral—he was stopped by a guard in a pristine white uniform.

"State your business."

"I must speak with the queen," Kelo said. He was acutely aware of how ridiculous his demand must sound. All the islanders probably wanted to speak to the queen at some point in their lives. What gave him the right to do so?

"Do you have an invitation from Her Majesty?"

"Um, no. But it's a matter of importance. It concerns the spirit sisters being sent to the Island of Testing. I must speak with her before they arrive at Akena Island."

"And the matter of importance?"

"My wife is among them. I wish to speak to the queen—"

The soldier's face softened, and he laid a hand on Kelo's shoulder. "You're not the first to come on such a mission. You won't be the last. Know that if she falls, your wife's sacrifice will be honored, and if she succeeds, all of Belene—indeed all of Renthia—will be the safer for it."

"She can't go! She's my wife, and we—"

"You love her. I know. I've heard it all, believe me. She has elderly parents. Or a baby. Or ten children, all of whom will starve without her. She's sick or injured. Or you are." The soldier nodded at Kelo's bandages. "Perhaps you want to claim she doesn't truly have powers. You aren't the first, and you won't be the last to lose a loved one to our way of life. But it is *because* of the test that we are able to have a way of life at all. I know. I lost a daughter to the island. You think I didn't try to see the queen? You think I didn't plead for her? Even tried to bribe the Silent Ones, and when that didn't work, I tried to rescue her."

Kelo felt hope drain out of him, as if he were a sack of sand that had been pierced. "I'm sorry for your loss. What happened when you tried to rescue her?"

"I failed, of course. One against twelve Silent Ones? She was taken to the island, and she lasted for a full week before the spirits got her." There was pride in his voice—Kelo supposed that was all he had left. *If he didn't feel pride, he'd be swamped with sorrow.*

"Then you must understand why I have to try."

"And you must understand why you cannot see the queen. Every test, she must send twelve women to possible death. She can't listen to the pleas of their families. It would be too much to ask her to bear. You cannot add to her sorrow. Every guard, every courtier, every counselor will tell you the same."

Kelo tried again. "But if she would only consider ending the tests—"

"She cannot, for the sake of all of Belene." The soldier's pity had an edge of steel in it now. "Go home. Rebuild your life. Hope for your loved one to survive but don't count on it."

This couldn't be it! He'd traveled all the way here, and he was so close! The queen was within these walls. She could stop the test before it began. "There's still a chance that this time, the queen calls off the tests. If I could only speak to her for one minute before the test begins—"

"I am deeply sorry, but it's too late. All the spirit sisters have been taken from the strongholds and brought to a secret location for final training. In three days, they will be delivered to Akena Island."

Kelo felt as if the blue stone bridge had shattered beneath him. "No, that can't be." He was supposed to have more time! The tests weren't supposed to begin until there were a total of twelve spirit sisters. Unless Mayara was the twelfth. . . .

Gently but clearly, the guard said, "Your wife's fate is in

her own hands now. You can't help her, and neither can the queen."

QUEEN ASANA OF BELENE WISHED, NOT FOR THE FIRST TIME, SHE could chuck her crown into the ocean. Not literally, of course—the crown itself was a lovely band of black, ivory, and pink pearls that was at least a century old, which, coincidentally, was about how old Asana felt after she'd heard the news that a twelfth spirit sister had been identified and captured. She had received the news from her least favorite nobleman, Lord Maarte, whose oh-so-polite letter had informed her that he and the other Families were delivering the women for their final training.

The twelfth woman had been discovered after a spirit storm had devastated her fishing village—a storm that had hit in the exact location that Queen Asana had predicted, on the southern shore of the island of Olaku. But the Families had decided to dispatch the heirs to protect the Neran Stronghold on the northern shore, near the city of Kao, instead.

It had gotten a bit breezy there.

Innocent islanders *died*, while the Neran Family, snug and safe inside their fortress and guarded by the most powerful women in Belene, lost a few petals off their fancy rosebushes. If this woman hadn't stepped in, it was probable that they all would have died.

*And how do I repay her? By ruining—and endangering—her life.*

Stomping into her private chambers, Asana scooped up a probably priceless heirloom pillow off a couch, squeezed it against her face, and screamed into it. Sadly, it did not make her feel better.

A voice spoke up from one of the other reclining couches. "You could try poisoning someone. That always makes *me* feel better."

With as much dignity as she could manage, Asana restored the pillow to the couch and fluffed it back to its original plumpness. She'd forgotten that she'd requested her new adviser join her after her meeting—her adviser had been, in fact, waiting for Asana already when she'd stormed into her chambers. Keeping her voice mild, Asana said, "I'm never quite sure when you're joking and when you're serious." Her new adviser was from Aratay, where she'd held a position of importance in the Aratayian queen's palace. Her name was Lady Garnah.

"I've been told that's part of my charm." Lady Garnah smiled cheerfully. An older woman with a fondness for many-layered lace ruffled skirts, Garnah did everything cheerfully, from eating pineapple (which she was currently doing, with juice dripping off her chin) to assisting in the major trauma ward in the healer's school (which she'd done this morning). Asana found her relentless joy to be both refreshing and fascinating. *Perhaps because it's so different from my relentless doom and gloom.*

"Come now," the garishly dressed woman said, patting beside her. "Tell old Garnah your problems, and I'll tell you who to kill to fix them. Never met a problem that a little murder couldn't solve."

Asana laughed.

She hadn't expected to ever laugh again, not since she'd been crowned and had her husband, her daughter, and her elderly parents taken from her. She'd had precious little to laugh at.

She'd been introduced to Garnah a month ago, while her capital city, Yena, was recovering from a vicious spirit storm. Asana had collapsed after the attack. Her own physicians blamed exhaustion, but Garnah, a visiting doctor who'd come to the islands to study the medicinal properties of their indigenous plants, had correctly identified a toxin in Asana's bloodstream and cured her.

She'd then helped Asana poison the one who'd fed her that toxin. Not enough to kill them, but enough that they were still vomiting when the Silent Ones arrested them.

Naturally, Asana was fond of her.

"It's the Families," Asana said. "Specifically, the Family Neran. Several days ago, I told them a spirit storm was approaching their island, and they chose to defend their own home rather than help the people actually in danger."

"Can't you overrule them? You're queen."

"A title that comes with surprisingly little power." Queens in other countries in Renthia might have true authority, but not the queen of Belene. The Families made certain of that. Asana flopped on one of the couches and removed her crown. She set it gently on a table, which was inlaid with mother-of-pearl mosaic like nearly everything in the palace. She rubbed her temples, wishing she had at least the authority to send her headache away. "I'm the official scapegoat for all that's wrong on the islands. I've just gotten a report cataloging the extent of the damage, so you can expect a delegation from Olaku to be arriving within a few days to complain in person—rightfully—that the heirs, and therefore I, failed them."

*Ugh, it wasn't fair.*

She felt like a six-year-old thinking that, but it was true. She hadn't asked for this "honor." She'd simply been unlucky. Three years ago, she'd been one of the heirs, a lesser one in fact. It had been her turn in the grove—every heir was required to spend a certain number of days per month in the sacred coronation grove, so that someone qualified and trained was present in case the current queen died. Without a queen, all the "tame" spirits on the island turned wild pretty much instantaneously. But a new queen could be crowned only in the grove. So to minimize the death and destruction between the passing of one queen and the crowning of the next, every heir took their turn there. No one had expected the queen to die on Asana's shift.

*But she did. Lucky me.*

She'd emerged from the grove as Queen Asana, and then she'd found out how much worse being queen was than being an heir. *I wouldn't have thought that possible.*

But it was. The instant she'd emerged, she'd been informed

by the Families that her loved ones had been taken to a safe-hold for their protection. No, she couldn't see them. No, she couldn't know where they were. No, she couldn't know which Family held them. And no, she couldn't tell anyone they'd been taken.

If she wanted to ensure they remained protected, though . . .

She'd tried once to free them, a week after her coronation. In retaliation, the Families had had her husband secretly killed and informed her that her daughter would follow if she did not act "for the good of Belene."

She'd been made a widow, and the Families had seen to it that no one even knew.

Since then, she hadn't dared speak or act against them. Which was why she could do nothing about what happened on Olaku except scream into a pillow and vent to her only adviser who *wasn't* connected to one of the ruling Families of Belene. So long as they held her parents and daughter hostage, the Families were the true power in Belene. *I'm just a puppet . . . and a scapegoat.*

"They'll probably try to kill you at some point," Asana mused out loud. The Families didn't like anyone they couldn't control.

"They can try," Garnah said. "I'm remarkably difficult to kill." She popped another chunk of pineapple into her mouth. "But just so I can be prepared, who precisely do you think will try to kill me?"

"Everyone," Asana said. "Welcome to Belene."

Picking up her crown again, the queen sighed heavily. She had no right to whine like this when her people had suffered. But there was just so blasted little she could do! She had already ordered workers be sent to help with rebuilding, along with supplies of food and fresh water. It wouldn't be enough to replace the lives lost, though. *Unnecessarily lost.*

The thing was, she wouldn't mind the Families ruling the islands if they weren't so damn *bad* at it. *And if they hadn't taken my family and killed my Camuk.* Her beloved Rokalara had been fifteen years old when Asana was crowned. *She's eighteen now, a young woman ready for the world, and I'm not there to guide her.*

*Then again, I can barely guide anyone as queen.*

"You need to find a way to take power," Garnah said, as if hearing that bitter thought. "For your sake and mine. Just because I *can* defend myself against assassins doesn't mean I enjoy the anxiety of being a target."

Asana snorted. "A nice thought, but impossible." She heaved herself off the couch. Her joints ached a little more than they used to—all the constant stress, and the lack of any real exercise. She knew she didn't take good enough care of herself, but it was hard to worry about that when there was always some other disaster that needed her attention, in addition to the primary burden of protecting the land from the sea. She'd been warned about that—the constant strain and the drain of keeping the slumbering giants of the sea safely asleep—but the reality was so much more difficult than she'd imagined. It was the reason she needed the heirs to combat spirit storms; with all her power focused on the Deepest Blue, she didn't have enough strength left over for other battles. And now she needed to find the stamina to handle the administrative duties to see her people through this latest disaster and the emotional fortitude to face the upcoming results of the latest test on Akena Island.

"I must increase the relief efforts in Olaku. And send a 'Congratulations, you must be so proud' letter to the parents of our newest spirit sister. She was all that kept it from being a massacre. An act of heroism that I rewarded by sending her to her probable death, yet another horrible thing in Belene I can't stop or change."

"You know," Garnah said mildly, "sometimes I get the impression that you don't like being queen."

At that, the queen of Belene laughed so hard that she cried.

# CHAPTER NINE

They moored in a vacant harbor at a half-rotted dock. Mayara had the very strong sense that the sailors were happy to see them go, which was proven when she overheard one of them say to another, "Be glad to see the last of those witches."

She made it a point to smile extra sweetly at that superstitious sailor as she walked over the plank to the dock.

Lord Maarte didn't accompany them onto land. He stayed at the helm, watching them disembark. He had, she knew, plans to sail to the Southern Citadel, the southernmost city of the forest kingdom of Aratay, to trade island fruit for mainland wood, but Mayara had expected him to wish them well or at least bid goodbye to his ward. He had to feel *some* responsibility for Roe, since her family was supposedly under his protection. But as far as Mayara could tell, Lord Maarte didn't glance at Roe once.

*Maybe he truly does want her to fail.* She couldn't imagine what "political problems" could be caused by giving a young woman the help she'd need to maybe not die.

He did, though, make eye contact with Mayara and had the gall to look pleasantly amused, as if he were letting the women off the ship for an afternoon picnic. Mayara wished she'd called him more than just "vile." He deserved worse. But she refused to waste any more time thinking about him. Deliberately, she turned her back on him and faced the island.

*We have three days to learn how to not die. Best make the most of it.*

The training island was so tiny that it didn't have any villages, houses, or inhabitants. As far as Mayara could see, it had nothing except a decrepit dock. *Where exactly are we supposed to train? And with whom?*

Mayara, Roe, and Palia clustered at the end of the dock as the Silent Ones swept off the ship behind them. Then the sailors pulled the plank back and untied from the dock.

"Now what?" Roe asked.

Palia plopped herself down onto a crate and stretched her legs. "Ahh, it's nice to be back on land! Shame that means we're closer to our doom." She pointed to another island to the south. It looked innocuous, a smear of beautiful green amid the turquoise blue.

Mayara swallowed hard. "Is that . . . ?"

"Yes, it is," Roe said in a hushed voice. "We're on one of the nearby islands. This used to be a pineapple farm, until spirits destroyed the soil. Now it's abandoned."

"And now we're abandoned too. Yay. And with such great companions." Palia scowled at the Silent Ones.

The three Silent Ones had drifted to the other end of the dock and stood motionless, facing the interior of the island, which looked like a pile of bare rock. Mayara strained to see whatever it was they were looking for. "Any idea what we're supposed to do?"

"Be trained," Roe said, then frowned at the gray, unwelcoming stone around them. "Really thought the other candidates would be here already."

For a while nothing happened, and Mayara started to fidget. Then, in the center of the island, a stream of fire shot up from between the rocks. Mayara felt the heat warm her cheeks. She and the other two women automatically cringed, even though the flames weren't close enough to hurt them. Roe scrambled to her feet, and Palia rose as well. But the Silent Ones seemed unfazed. They merely waited.

Mayara shielded her eyes against the sun as she saw a shape soar toward them. It came from between the rocks, and at first she thought it was an oddly shaped bird. She felt the familiar itch of a spirit, though, as it came closer.

And then she saw someone was *riding* it.

The spirit looked like a bird, but far larger than any bird Mayara had ever seen, with translucent wings that were nearly invisible against the sky. They distorted the clouds. On the bird's back was a woman in a red shirt and leggings.

The bird spirit landed at the end of the dock, and the woman hopped off. She looked to be about thirty, with seaweed-green hair, pale skin, and a thick clump of scar tissue running from her left cheekbone to her chin.

Mayara thought she was the most terrifying woman she'd ever seen.

The woman barked, "Listen up, newbies, you're here to prepare for the island! I am Heir Sorka. It's my job to make sure you don't die before you set foot on Akena. After that, it's all up to you." She marched between them, inspecting them. She sniffed at Palia, raised eyebrows at Roe, and then stopped in front of Mayara. "*You're* our future, the ones who will protect the innocent and preserve our way of life? You're the best the islands have to offer?"

"Not really," Mayara said. "We're just the ones who got caught." As soon as the words were out of her mouth, she regretted them.

Heir Sorka glared at her, and she had mastered the art of the withering glare. Mayara felt as if she'd shrunk to two feet tall and five years old. Behind Sorka, the spirit spread its wings and cawed. It sounded like metal scraping against metal.

"Forgive me," Mayara said quickly, eyeing the spirit's sharp beak.

"It's true, though," Palia said. "Don't regret speaking the truth."

Heir Sorka shared her glare with Palia as well, but the older woman just stared right back. "Maybe in other lands like Aratay and Chell, heirs aren't important. In those other lands, they're spares in case the queen falters," Sorka said. "But here on Belene, our queen must use all her power to keep the worst of the wild ones at bay, which leaves the daily protection of the islands to *us*. That's why the test is so rigorous: because we must each be strong enough to face the task at hand. This test will weed out the weak and unworthy." Sorka positioned herself directly in front of Mayara, her nose only inches away. "Are you weak and unworthy, newbie?"

Mayara wondered what Sorka would do if she said yes.

But she was saved from answering by Roe, who spoke up. "Heir Sorka? Do you think we have a chance, if we train hard enough?"

"There's always a chance, Spirit Snack. Follow me . . . if you can." Sorka strode back to her bird, mounted, and flew over their heads so low that they had to duck. She then swooped up and between the rocky peaks.

All three of them stared after her.

"Um, by follow her, does she mean . . . ?" Mayara began.

"I think she does," Roe said. "It's either fly or walk."

"Exactly how are we supposed to do this?" Mayara asked. So far, every interaction she'd ever had with a spirit had focused on keeping them from killing her. She'd never had any desire to *ride* one. Still didn't.

Three air spirits circled them. Mayara felt the hairs on the back of her neck stand up. Larger than any natural creature, they looked like skeletons carved out of shiny black volcanic rock. Their wings were thin gossamer, like a dragonfly's, and they circled twice before they glided to a landing on the dock.

"I am not flying on a spirit," Mayara said firmly. She'd dive into a leviathan's skull, stay submerged beyond her limits, and brave the dangers of the sea, but she was *not* climbing on the back of Death and allowing it to carry her into the sky.

"It does seem like a terrible idea," Palia agreed.

The three Silent Ones each climbed on, though. Holding on to the spirit's vertebrae necks, they soared upward. They circled above the three spirit sisters, clearly intending to fly above them—or with them, if they chose to summon their own spirits and fly.

*No.* This test might kill her, but it wasn't going to turn her into someone she was not, and she was not someone who played with spirits. *Besides, even if I wanted to, I wouldn't know how.*

"I think it's a nice day for a walk," Mayara said.

Roe nodded. Despite her determined optimism, she was clearly just as unsettled as Mayara and Palia. "We'll stick together. A team, right?"

Palia eased herself off the crate and eyed the rock formation. Mayara wondered how much stamina the older woman had—was it fair to ask her to hike? *On the other hand, what choice do we have?* Fly or walk. That was it. *Lousy choices.* Just like the two terrible choices that had led her here: heir or Silent One.

They began to hike, watching the three circling Silent Ones all the while.

Palia began to pant halfway up the rocks. Noticing, Mayara slowed her pace, trying to make it seem like she was not slowing her pace.

"You don't need to dawdle," Palia said behind her. "I can see what you're doing, and it's not necessary. Do you think the spirits will take pity on me because I spent most of my life sitting at a loom?"

"You're a weaver?" Mayara asked.

"I made sails," Palia said. "Wove the sail that our Lord Maarte used on his ship, not that he knew it. He paid me a pretty penny for it too. It funded half my daughter's education." She panted and groaned less when she talked. *Maybe the distraction is good for her.* Certainly it was helping Mayara avoid thinking about whether or not Kelo lived.

"Tell us about your daughter," Mayara said.

Palia went on to describe a young woman about Mayara's age, who was, by Palia's account, the smartest, most accomplished, most talented, most extraordinary woman ever to grace the islands. She planned to study the tides at the university. As Palia talked, she moved faster, taking the lead. "Shame of it is she won't be able to finish her studies, not without the money I earned us to pay for housing and food. If I'd had another few years to support her . . . But it wasn't meant to be."

"If you become an heir, you'll be able to support her again," Roe pointed out. The families of heirs received a steady stipend, to compensate for any lost wages due to the heir's absence.

"If," Palia echoed. "Face it: I'm fodder."

"You don't know that," Roe said.

Palia heaved herself up onto a peak and stared down the other side. "Yes, I do. Once you show power, you're either a hero or dead. And I'm no hero."

Mayara was about to say something when she caught up to her, but instead she—like the other two—could only gawk.

In the valley, women were riding on spirits, leaving cyclones in their wake that ripped trees from their roots. An earth spirit formed from boulders hefted one woman on his shoulder and then bent down and tore a crevasse open in the earth. Another woman stood in a ring of fire, her arms spread wide and her mouth open in a scream.

In the center of it all was the heir, Sorka, untouched by even a breath of wind.

*Hero or dead,* Mayara thought.

*I wish there were a third choice.*

TWELVE GIRLS AND WOMEN WERE TO BE SENT TO THE ISLAND FOR the test. Mayara made a point to learn who they were, because if they were destined to die together, she wanted to at least know their names.

Tesana was a fisherwoman from northern Kao. She left behind a husband and son.

Amilla worked with stained glass, along with her mother and her sister.

Nissala sold grilled pineapple to early-morning clamdiggers.

Osa hauled crates on and off ships on the docks of Yena.

Quilan didn't like coconuts.

Dayine hadn't cut her hair since she was five years old, when she lopped it off with a machete. She didn't know why her parents let her near a machete, but that was the family story.

Resla didn't talk much, but she wore a necklace made of shells.

Balka had just become a mother.

All of them had people they'd left behind. Work. School. Dreams. Aside from Roe, only one other, a young woman, barely more than a girl, named Kemra, seemed to want to become an heir. She chattered nonstop about how this was their destiny and their duty, and how morally reprehensible it was to hide your power and deny the world your gift. Most of the others ignored her, even Roe, who clammed up about her plans after seeing how unpopular Kemra's views were. The other ten women had all hidden their power, because that was what you did if you wanted to live a long life, and that was what your families begged you to do if they didn't want to say goodbye.

As the twelfth to join them, Mayara expected to meet more resentment—it was her arrival and her failure to hide her power that had triggered the start of the test. But she was treated more with pity. She'd had less time than any of them to accustom herself to her fate, and she knew less of the basics than any of them. She told them she was a deep diver, an oyster gatherer, who'd been married the day she exposed her power. She told them how she'd lost her older sister to the test, and how she'd promised to avoid the spirits and never use her power. As a consequence, she knew very little about how it worked.

The introductions were quickly over, though, and Heir Sorka delivered an opening speech, very little of which made sense to Mayara. As she finished, Mayara leaned over to whisper to Roe and Palia, "What is she talking about? How do we 'expand our consciousness' and 'tap into the essential nature of the spirits'? What 'essential nature'?"

"She means their instincts," Roe whispered.

Sorka pointed to Tesana, Quilan, and Kemra. "You, you, and you! Come with me."

Mayara whispered back, "I thought their instinct was just 'kill humans.'"

Rising to follow Heir Sorka, the fisherwoman Tesana clucked at Mayara. "Such a beautiful bride. Such a shame." She stroked Mayara's hair as if consoling a baby, and then she headed down the hill for her training session.

"Hey, she might live!" Roe called after her.

"She probably won't," Palia said.

Roe glared at her. "Must you?"

Another of the women, Balka, who had been taken from her newborn daughter seven weeks ago, shushed them. "I can't hear the lesson." At the base of the valley, Heir Sorka was beginning to lecture the first three women on how best to subdue an earth spirit.

They were being trained in small groups, at least to start with. Mayara, Roe, and Palia waited near a fire, lit by a lizard-like spirit that writhed over a pile of dried-out driftwood. The others were spread across on the same rocky hill, all focused on Sorka and her first students.

Listening, Mayara tried to follow the lesson.

She felt Roe watching her, and her cheeks heated up as she blushed—*it's obvious how little I know.* "If we're going to be a team, you need to know more than 'spirits are bad,'" Roe said. "Can you handle a condescending lecture from someone nearly your age?"

Relief coursed through her. Yes, that sounded like exactly what she needed! "Pretend I know nothing, since that's close to accurate." Mayara hadn't realized how little time she'd spent thinking about the spirits. She hadn't cared much what they were or how they worked, so long as they weren't chomping on her when she dived.

"She knows they want us dead," Palia said. "That's the important bit."

"She may want a bit more detail than that," Roe said.

The woman who had shushed them, Balka, glared again and moved farther away, but Mayara noticed that a few others—Nissala, Osa, and Dayine—had shifted closer, listening to Roe. That made her feel less like an idiot. *Maybe I'm not the only one who hasn't done this before.*

"Okay," Roe said. "There are six kinds of spirits: water, air, fire, earth, ice, and wood. Sometimes that last one is just called 'life,' but it means plant life exclusively. The spirits vary in intelligence. Some are as smart as us. Others are as dumb as a barnacle. But they all operate on two basic instincts: to create and to destroy. Their creation powers let them shape the natural world. Unchecked, they'll just keep creating and creating until the world is in constant flux and completely unlivable, even for them, which is why they need queens, even though they hate us. In the beginning, the land was—"

Palia cut her off. "Roe, she doesn't need the history of the world."

Across the valley, Sorka was shouting at Kemra, Quilan, and Tesana to fight a fire spirit. Kemra had been burned badly on her arm, and Quilan was running toward a copse of trees. Tesana was cowering behind a rock. *It would be good if I knew more before I have to face* that, Mayara thought.

"Sorry. In addition to their urge to create, the spirits also want to destroy. Specifically, they want to kill us, because they hate how we mess up what they create by living here. But they also need us, as I said . . . or at least they need queens, to keep them in balance."

Every Renthian knew this, but Mayara had never heard it laid out so baldly before. Most islanders didn't talk much about the spirits outside of heroic ballads and stories. *Feels like bad luck to discuss them,* she thought.

*Guess it's too late to worry about bad luck.*

"The queens of Renthia are women of power—like us—who have linked their minds to the spirits of their land. Seriously linked, not just the occasional telepathic moment. This bond can only be forged in a coronation grove. Lots of theories on why, but essentially what happens is the old queen dies, the spirits go wild, and then, after a fun killing spree, they enter this kind of stasis until they link with a new queen while she's in the sacred grove."

One of the other spirit sisters, Dayine, interrupted, "The heirs force them into stasis."

"Right. Anyway, once they bond with the queen, they give her power. Lots of power. Enough to sense and control all the spirits she's linked to at once, and enough to help her fight off the spirits she's *not* linked to, the wild spirits. And . . . I should probably skip to the relevant bits. What this means for us."

Palia snorted. "Oh, I'm sure we can destroy the spirits by boring them to pieces with a history lesson." In the valley, the three spirit sisters, Kemra, Tesana, and Quilan, had failed to defeat the fire spirit—the Silent Ones corralled it as it writhed, blackening the earth beneath its feet.

"You aren't supposed to destroy spirits," Osa, the dock-worker, said. "Not the island spirits, at any rate. They're linked to the land. Destroy them, and you destroy bits of Belene. We're supposed to control them."

"Go on," Mayara urged Roe.

Roe gave Palia a look but continued. "Regardless of how much power they get from the spirits after they bond, all queens start out like us. Spirit sisters. Girls and women with the ability to touch the minds of spirits. We can sense where they are, read their thoughts, and command them—how well we can do this is a mix of how naturally strong we are and how focused we are, which is where the training comes in . . ."

All of them shifted to look into the valley, where Heir Sorka was barking for the next set of spirit sisters to take their turn. Nissala, Resla, and Balka trotted down the slope to face the eager spirits.

One of the women—Amilla, the stained-glass artist—picked up the conversation. "You need to concentrate both on who you are and who they are, to the exclusion of all else. The clearer your thoughts, the clearer the command you give."

"Yeah," Osa chimed in again. "You can't doubt. You just gotta do." All the women drew closer, clustering together around the fire and around Mayara, as if their proximity could give her confidence and courage.

She looked at them and at Roe, earnest and hopeful. *They want me to succeed.* It was a warm feeling, and she felt the same way. She wanted all of them to live.

Turning away, Mayara studied the spirits in the valley. Two of them were attacking Nissala, Resla, and Balka, but most were corralled into a corner, held there by the will of the Silent Ones, waiting until they were needed. As easy as the Silent Ones made it look, she couldn't imagine having enough control over her own thoughts to conquer the will of so many monsters. It was all she could do to keep from screaming in frustration.

*Hero or dead,* she reminded herself.

"So . . . I just concentrate?"

"You're a deep diver, aren't you?" Amilla said. "You have to clear your mind and focus to dive, right? Think of it like that. Except instead of diving into water, you're diving into minds."

That . . . she could do. Maybe.

She met Roe's eyes. *At least I won't be doing it alone.*

MAYARA BREATHED IN DEEPLY, DOING AS AMILLA SUGGESTED AND clearing her mind as if she were about to dive. But instead she focused her thoughts on the spirit that stood in front of her. It was a water spirit, made of sea spray, in the shape of a woman. Her eyes were whirlpools, and her hands were whips of water.

"Your task for the next month is simple, newbies!" Sorka shouted. "Don't die!"

Positioned on the hills that circled the valley, the Silent Ones looked like gray pillars. Heir Sorka was in the base of the valley, on a pedestal of stone that she'd ordered an earth spirit to build for her. Mayara didn't know if the heir and Silent Ones were here to keep the spirits in or to keep the "newbies" in.

*Both,* she guessed.

That was almost the way it would be once they were on Akena Island. There, the Silent Ones would be responsible for making certain they didn't try to escape. Here, though, both the heir and the Silent Ones were also tasked with helping keep them in one piece. Because the queen wanted all twelve potential heirs to arrive on the island alive. They were welcome to start dying within minutes of their arrival, but tradition stated that twelve needed to begin.

But that didn't mean their training had to be easy or pleasant.

"Your task today is to learn how to convince spirits that they haven't seen you," Sorka announced. "Sounds simple, right? Not so simple. You have to trick their minds. Believe it or not, that's easier on intelligent spirits. Dumb spirits don't bother analyzing what they see and hear, but intelligent spirits think like you and me. So how would you convince *me* I don't see you?"

Mayara concentrated on the spirit in front of her, trying to dive into its mind. She pictured herself swimming and . . .

*There!* Her vision split: she was looking both at the spirit and at . . . herself?

Through the eyes of the spirit, she saw an island woman in a practical wrap dress with leggings underneath. She'd chosen to wear the sturdy, water-resistant clothes Kelo had made her rather than the standard outfits the heir had provided them. She was clutching . . . what was she holding? A knife? *But I'm not holding a knife.*

And then the image of herself warped to be a picture of another woman: older, with hair down to her knees, wearing a seal-skin tunic and holding a knife. The spirit hated this woman. This woman had hurt it, and it wanted to hurt her in return.

*I'm seeing a memory,* Mayara realized.

The spirit was merging its memory of some other woman, maybe an heir or another spirit sister, with its vision of Mayara, transferring the old hate onto her. To this spirit, humans were interchangeable.

*That gives me an idea . . .*

She crafted a new image: a monkey, like the kind that lived deep in the island forests of Zanor. She'd seen one once, when a peddler had come through her village. He'd had it in a cage and was hoping to sell it as a curiosity. She'd wanted to free it, but her parents had said no, she couldn't interfere. She shaped a picture in her mind exactly like that monkey, with silvery fur all over its body, and she pushed it into the spirit's mind, in place of its image of her.

She felt the spirit's confusion: it had seen the woman who'd hurt it! Now there was only this animal. But where had the hated spirit sister gone? It could still feel her power, pressing on its mind, but it couldn't reconcile that with the monkey it thought it saw.

Mayara used its moment of confusion to slip away. She scrambled over the rocks and ducked down behind them, wedging herself in between. She felt the spirit drift away.

"Good job, Minnow!" Sorka hadn't bothered to learn any of their names. She'd nicknamed Mayara "Minnow" as soon as she heard she liked to swim. Liking to swim wasn't exactly a unique feature on the island, though. Several of the other women had also acquired fish nicknames.

*At least none of us is Tuna. Or Flounder.*

*Or Chum.*

She tried not to think about the fact that Sorka had picked the same pet name that Elorna had favored for Mayara.

Looking out from her hiding place, she saw Roe was in trouble. She'd gotten herself cornered by two ice spirits. Both of them were shaped like tiny dragons, and they were spitting shards of ice at her. Already she had blossoms of frost on her arms.

"Hey, Spirit Snack"—that was Sorka's name for Roe—"you're going to be an icicle if you don't do something. Distract them! If you can't convince them not to see you, then make them see something they want *more* than you."

"I'm trying!" Roe said. "I c-c-can't concentrate. I'm too c-c-cold!"

Without thinking, Mayara stepped out from her hiding place. "Send them to me!" She pushed her mind toward the two ice spirits. *Come freeze me!*

The two ice spirits pivoted and raced toward their tasty new target, and it occurred to Mayara that she hadn't thought this through. She plunged her mind into theirs, trying to warp what they saw into making them think she was a fire spirit, the same way she made the water spirit see a monkey. She imagined flames and heat—

And they veered at the last minute, revolted by the nonexistent fire.

*Yes, it worked!*

She heaved a sigh of relief—and was encased in liquid. A bubble of water surrounded her, and she hadn't taken in a full breath of air. It distorted the valley around her, making the rocks seem to shimmer. Frantically, she tried to push her way out of it, but it moved with her.

She heard a cackle in her mind.

*Thought you'd escaped,* the water spirit cooed. She heard its voice both in her head and in her ears, burbling through the water. *But oh, no, I found you, you who hurt me, and now I will hurt you.*

The terror was unlike anything she'd ever experienced. It coursed through her, as if it ran through her veins instead of blood. It permeated every thought. *No, no, no!*

Mayara tried to run, but the bubble clung to her. She felt her lungs begin to burn. Familiar black dots danced over her eyes. Roe was there, reaching into the water, and then inside it with her. Mayara saw her own terror mirrored in Roe's eyes as they both fought to break free.

And then the bubble burst.

Mayara collapsed onto her knees, with Roe gasping beside her.

"I can't do this," Mayara said. She still felt the terror thrumming through her. *Can't, can't, can't.* "One I can handle. If I'm lucky. But on the island . . . there will be hundreds. You should find a different team."

"You saved me just now," Roe pointed out.

"And then failed us both." Mayara flopped backward, looking for who had saved them, and saw two of the Silent Ones corralling the water spirit. *They saved us.* She wondered if she was supposed to feel grateful, knowing they'd been saved only because it was too soon for them to die. *We have to wait and die in the right place, at the right time.*

"We have to keep trying," Roe said.

"Or we don't. Maybe it's a mistake to try to 'win' against the spirits. Maybe we should just try to survive them." She thought of Kelo and how they'd hidden in the caves successfully for eight days. "Hide until the month is over."

Heir Sorka loomed over them. "Hide? That's your solution? You want to simply hope you're lucky enough that the spirits don't find you? You won't make it a month on luck. Luck might keep you from the spirits for a day. Even a week. But a month? When they're actively hunting you, and there's no one to jump in and save you if you get in over your heads?" She nudged Mayara's leg with her foot. "Get up and try again, Minnow."

Mayara didn't move. She hoped another spirit didn't decide to attack just yet. She didn't think she could move. Lying on her back, she looked up at the sky. It was blue, the kind of sky that islanders called a dreaming sky, because you could dream up whatever you wanted to fill it. She wondered if Kelo was looking up at the same dreaming sky and thinking of her. *He might be, if he's alive.*

"You aren't going to learn lying there," Sorka said. "Up."

"Is it hard training people you know are going to die?" She'd talked with the other spirit sisters, getting to know them, but she knew so little about this woman they were trusting to train them. Had she volunteered for this? Had she been chosen? Had she trained anyone before? Did she think they had a chance? Would she mourn them if they failed?

"You can't all die this time," Sorka said. "Belene needs heirs too badly." Then she stalked off, shouting to another trainee about how she needed to concentrate or that fire spirit was going to burn her balls off.

Propping herself up on one elbow, Mayara stared after her. "Roe, what did she mean 'this time'?"

"Oh. I . . . Well, there were rumors. . . . All the ruling Families denied it, but I overheard Lord Maarte . . . Last year, a batch of twelve spirit sisters went to the island for the test. None of them survived."

She shifted to gawk at Roe. *"None?"* But . . . She'd never heard that. Surely, if it were true, rumors would have flown from island to island. People would have been outraged. "Really?"

"It was hushed up, but I heard Lord Maarte say it was a shame none of them were worthy. My grandparents, though . . . they think there are too many spirits on Akena. They think the test has gotten out of control. They were furious when I forced Lord Maarte to acknowledge my power and chose the island."

"Why *did* you do it?" Mayara asked. If she'd known that none had survived . . . She supposed that was exactly why it had been hushed up.

"My mother was an heir," Roe said. "If I succeed, I can be with her and reunite our family."

Mayara could understand that—really, it was not so different from the reason that Elorna had chosen the island. If she'd survived, then she'd have been allowed to see her family.

*If I survive . . . Kelo and I can look up at the dreaming sky together.*

"I think we should hide," Mayara said.

"You heard Heir Sorka," Roe said. "Besides, heroes don't hide."

*Dead heroes didn't hide,* Mayara thought. Maybe Palia was wrong and it wasn't "hero or dead." It was just alive or dead. She'd never wanted to be a hero. She'd happily give that up if it meant she'd survive. "You can be a hero if you want. I want to survive."

"Refresh my memory on how you came here again? Facing a sea dragon to save your family? Yeah, sure, you're not hero material. Unless it's to save everybody." Roe flashed Mayara an encouraging smile. "You can do this. Look how you saved me from the ice spirits!"

"My sister was the heroic one, not me." She pictured Elorna, corralling the spirits and making them do her bidding. She probably flew on a spirit the first day of training and was overwhelmed only by the sheer numbers on the island or by bad luck.

"Say what you want. I know you."

"You've known me literally less than a week."

"Under intense circumstances." Another of Roe's infectious smiles. "That makes each day count for about ten years."

"All right then. What's my favorite color?"

She pointed up. "That color."

Correct. "What's my favorite food?"

"Let's see . . ." Propping herself up on an elbow, Roe studied her. Her face was intense and serious. "You look like you like limpets."

"I do not like limpets. No one likes limpets."

"Sautéed in goat butter and seasoned with sea salt."

"Limpets take three weeks to chew." Despite everything going on around them—the spirits howling through the valley, the spirit sisters screaming, the Silent Ones watching—Mayara felt a smile pulling at her lips.

"You especially love them fried and then dipped in sauce. Or raw. It's your secret shame. You have a stash of limpet shells under your bed at home, hidden because you don't want anyone to know how much you love them."

"You realize how badly that would smell?"

"You realize that's the perfect opening for me to tease you about smelling?" Roe was grinning widely. Over her shoulder, Mayara saw a flash of amber flame.

She launched herself forward without thinking, slamming into Roe. Together, they tumbled down the slope as the fire spirit scorched the earth where they had just been lying.

Watching it soar away in a streak of flame, Mayara said, "I continue to think running and hiding is the best plan."

"And I continue to think that when the time comes, you won't."

At the end of three days, Mayara felt like she *should* feel ready. She didn't feel ready, of course. She felt as if she'd been pounded by waves, pummeled by rocks, and flattened by falling trees, which was not so far off from what had actually happened. When Heir Sorka called an end to the training, Mayara collapsed with Roe and Palia by one of the tents.

Palia shared a slice of pineapple with the two of them, as all twelve trainees waited for Heir Sorka to address them for the last time.

"It's not like we don't know the rules," the dockworker Osa complained. "Don't leave, and don't die. Pretty simple. Can't we get on with it?"

"Are you that anxious to die?" the fisherwoman Tesana asked. She had burns that looked like claw marks on her upper arm. One of the other spirit sisters, Dayine, was rubbing a salve onto her wounds. "This is our last night to mourn what we've lost. I intend to treasure it."

Others nodded.

Mayara looked at their faces, all streaked with dirt and sticky with sweat. She did feel as if she'd known them for far longer than three days, as Roe had said. A part of her felt like she'd known them forever, as if they'd always been here, training with Heir Sorka, and they always would be. It was hard to imagine anything or anyone beyond this place and time existed.

"Do you think they know we go tomorrow?" Mayara asked.

"I asked my daughter to light a candle for me on this night, our last night before the island," Palia said. "Told her to blow it out after a few minutes, though, so she wouldn't waste the wax. She'll need to find her own way now. I wish there was more I could do. Always thought I'd be there to help her."

"You might be," Roe said, patting her on the shoulder. "You might survive. We might all survive!"

Palia snorted. "Didn't you hear that everyone died last year?" The rumor had spread through the trainees until everyone believed it. Pooling knowledge, they'd realized no one could name a single new heir from the last test. And more tellingly, Heir Sorka, who had heard the gossip spread, hadn't denied it.

It hadn't done good things for morale.

"But that can't happen every year," Roe said, "or there would be no more heirs. The queen—and Belene itself—needs heirs. If the test stayed that deadly, she'd cancel it. She wouldn't send us to certain death."

*Maybe not certain death,* Mayara thought. *Just very, very likely death.* But she didn't say it out loud.

Roe continued. "We have a chance. If we stick together."

Striding past them, Heir Sorka didn't look as if she cared about any of their conversation, but when she climbed onto the stone in the center of the valley, it became instantly clear she had been listening. "You can't stick together."

She heard Roe suck in air. She felt her own heart plummet.

"Wait—what did she say?" Palia said.

"She can't mean it," Roe said.

Mayara agreed—they must have misheard. If they weren't able to face this together . . .

"Listen up, everyone," Heir Sorka barked. "Here's the part where I give you key advice that will help you survive." She began to pace back and forth on the stone pedestal. It only allowed for three steps in each direction before she had to pivot and pace back. "You will be delivered to the island with nothing but the clothes you wear. No weapons. No supplies. No food. No anything. You may use whatever you find on the island and in its waters to aid in your survival. Your limits are the end of the reef that surrounds the island. Venture farther than that, and you will be turned back."

Sorka glanced beyond them, and Mayara twisted to see that they were ringed by Silent Ones, more than she thought she'd seen before, closer than they'd been. She shivered looking at their white masks.

"Akena Island is home to over one hundred spirits," Sorka continued. "They vary in strength and intelligence, but they all have one thing in common: they have been instructed to hunt you down. Because the aim of this test is to assess your individual worthiness, the spirits have all been ordered to attack those of you in groups first. In other words, you will be safest on your own."

Mayara shot a look at Roe—she looked as if she'd been drained of all her confidence. Her hands were shaking. She met Mayara's eyes with a panicked look that clearly said, *We were supposed to be a team!*

Mayara saw other women around her looking equally troubled—during the three training days, they'd been getting to know one another with the goal of relying on one another. Several groups had already formed, and Mayara knew most of them had counted on sticking together. Certainly she hadn't had any plans to run off by herself. Usually there was safety in numbers against spirits.

"You'll be tempted to clump together anyway—share resources, protect one another. I'm telling you right now, that's a mistake. I've seen it with my own eyes." A shadow crossed Sorka's face, and for an instant, she looked more human than heir. Mayara hadn't thought about the fact that Sorka had been on the island and survived, while others in her year hadn't.

"Well, there goes that plan," Palia muttered. "And every other viable plan."

Roe attempted a wan smile. "I guess we're on our own?"

This was a terrible twist. Mayara wished Sorka had told them earlier. *At least then I could have gotten the additional panic out of the way sooner.*

Sorka continued. "Another tip: as soon as we land, *move*. The spirits are bright enough to know where the new potential heirs come in, and they'll be lying in wait. You want as much distance from this ship as possible. Head inland or up the coast. Either will work. Just get away. Don't be stupid."

Mayara felt her palms growing sweaty. She wiped them on her leggings. *I need some kind of plan. Something without Roe and Palia . . .*

She hadn't realized how much she'd been counting on having Roe and even the fatalistic Palia with her. The thought of facing the island alone . . . *I can't do it!* If she was with Roe and Palia, this all felt possible. *Or at least more possible.*

Roe squeezed her hand and mouthed, *You can do this.* Or possibly, *I can't do this!*

Either way, Mayara squeezed her hand back. She thought of how she'd evaded the Silent Ones. *Keep to the coast, and stay in the water.* She'd have water spirits to contend with, but earth spirits would prefer the land, and fire and ice spirits wouldn't want anything to do with the sea. *As soon as we land on the shore, I'll swim. And then I'll find a place to hide.*

Run and hide. That was her plan. After Heir Sorka's announcement, she was more convinced than ever it was the right choice, heroic or not.

*One month, and then I'll see Kelo again. If he truly lives.* She tried not to think about the fact that she and Kelo had only evaded the Silent Ones and their spirits for eight days, and that was on a familiar island.

*Maybe I'll be lucky.*

She glanced over at Roe again. *Maybe we'll all be.*

# CHAPTER TEN

Akena Island was formed from the skull and neck vertebrae of a colossal leviathan that had attacked Renthia centuries ago. Greenery covered it, as lush as anything Mayara had ever seen, with coconut groves and bamboo forests in overflowing abundance. The cliffs of bone and stone were painted with purple, blue, and red flowers, and dozens of brightly colored birds flew above them. She heard the keening cry of monkeys and the caw of wild parrots. In short, it looked and sounded like a paradise.

But the feel of it . . .

She sensed the spirits even before they sailed into the cove. The island was teeming with them. Like stinging jellyfish beneath the pristine, beautiful surface of the sea. *Except worse.*

"The entire island is barely a mile wide," Heir Sorka called across the ship. "You won't ever see the Silent Ones, though— they'll be stationed on a chain of outer islands beyond the reef. If you try to escape, they *will* catch you, and you *will* be executed. Can't have super-powered traitors in Belene. The Silent Ones will be watching you through the eyes of the spirits that will be hunting you. So if you have that uncomfortable feeling that you're not alone . . . you aren't. You aren't ever alone on Akena, and you aren't ever safe. Get used to it."

Swinging on a rope that dangled from one of the sails,

Sorka crossed the deck and turned a winch to lower an anchor. No sailor would agree to come this close to Akena Island, so Sorka both helmed and manned the ship herself, occasionally barking orders at the Silent Ones and the spirit sisters. Now, though, she plunged the anchor into the reef below without any help.

*When she's finished with us, she'll probably sail off solo and eat a sea monster for lunch.* If Sorka was an example of the kind of woman you had to be to survive the island, then Mayara despaired of lasting a day.

The ship slowed as the anchor snagged on a chunk of rock or coral. Waves broke against its hull as it strained to continue drifting forward. All twelve women crowded on the port side of the ship, looking at Akena Island.

"You expect us to swim to shore?" Osa called.

"I have zero expectations," Sorka said, "except that you will all be off my boat in the next three minutes, even if I have to push you off myself."

They'd anchored inside a cove with a beautiful white-sand beach. Mayara could see coconut trees, heavy with coconuts, and banana trees that were overladen with countless bananas. *I was expecting it to look more ominous. Skulls and decay. Stench of sulfur, not ripe fruit and hibiscus.*

"Remember: the spirits have been without prey for a year," Sorka said. "Do try not to get killed in the first hour." But she wasn't looking at any of the spirit sisters. Her eyes, Mayara saw, were fixed on the island itself. She looked as if she was remembering and the memories weren't nice. *What was her test like?* Mayara wondered. Sorka had strictly, and undoubtedly deliberately, kept herself separate from the spirit sisters. She hadn't chatted with any of them, hadn't shared personal stories, hadn't laughed with them or cried. *Maybe so she won't have to cry for us now.*

"It doesn't look so bad," someone near Mayara said hopefully.

It was true.

A stretch of shallow sea lay between the ship and the lovely sand with its bounty of fruit. The stunningly clear water looked picturesquely perfect: the reef below, with schools of silvery fish. A brilliant green sea turtle glided lazily over delicate fan-like coral that waved in its wake.

"It looks like a trap," Palia muttered beside her.

"Don't swim toward the sand," Mayara advised. "They'll expect that."

Roe was frowning. "I don't sense any spirits anywhere near the cove."

Reaching out with her mind, Mayara raked the waters of the cove. She didn't sense any spirits nearby—all of them were packed tight onto the island itself, like wasps within a nest, ready to spill out. Still . . . the calm beauty of the cove felt deceptive. "I still think we shouldn't swim toward the sand. Go toward the cliffs."

Palia snorted. "Might be fine for you with your young muscles, but that's the easiest place to go ashore. I haven't climbed rocks since I was just married and looking to impress the in-laws."

"Your in-laws were impressed by climbing skills?" Roe asked.

"Not with mine," Palia said.

Roe laughed.

It was, Mayara thought, a slightly hysterical laugh.

All of them were delaying. No one wanted to be the first to leave the ship, the first to officially begin the test. Others were embracing, wishing one another luck, saying goodbye, consoling one another. A few were pleading with Sorka for more time.

"One of us has to go first," Palia said.

"It's shallow enough to walk, right?" Roe said, peering over the edge.

"Swimming will be faster," Tesana advised. "Plus, if the coral cuts your feet, you could get an infection, which will kill you as surely as any spirit."

"I can't swim," Roe confessed.

Palia leveled a look at her. "You're just mentioning this *now?*"

"I can help you," Mayara offered. She'd forgotten about Roe's limitation. "I'll swim with you." She'd done it before in far less idyllic waters, rescuing swimmers who had been caught in currents or swum so far they didn't have the strength to swim back. All she had to do was hook one hand under Roe's armpit. She'd still have her legs and other arm to power her forward.

Roe opened her mouth to answer, but Palia cut her off. "You heard Heir Sorka. Pair up and you'll be the first targeted. All of us have to go our separate ways."

Roe nodded. "She's right. I'll be fine. Tough sandals." Mayara studied her, trying to gauge whether she was serious or not. *I promised we'd be a team.* It felt wrong to split up, even though Mayara knew it was for the best.

*They're my friends,* she thought. *All of them. I don't want to abandon them.* She knew, though, that she didn't have a choice. Heir Sorka had been very clear.

"Still doesn't answer the question of who goes first," Palia said.

"Me," Mayara said.

Roe flashed her a smile, albeit one that quivered around the edges. "See? Hero."

It wasn't that. Not at all. She just couldn't stand it another minute—the worry about herself, about Roe, Palia, Tesana, Osa, Balka, Dayine . . . It was tearing her apart caring about all these other women.

Maybe it had been a mistake to learn their names.

But it was too late now. She *did* care. And if she delayed any longer, she was going to lose her nerve entirely and Heir Sorka would have to force her off the boat and into the gaping maws of whatever spirits awaited them. "Good luck," she told the other women. "Try not to die, okay?"

Roe and Palia called after her—wishing her luck, saying

goodbye, shouting advice—as she strode to the rail, climbed up, and dived into the turquoise water.

All sounds melted away the instant she was underwater, and she swam forward with smooth strokes. She felt the water shift against her as the other women plunged into the bay. She opened her mind as Heir Sorka had taught them, feeling for spirits, as she swam not toward the lovely sandy beach but east toward the rocky cliffs.

She didn't hear the screams. No, this was worse. She *felt* the screams, amplified through the spirits that came streaming into the cove—out of the greenery by the sands and down the cliffs into the waters of the cove. They *had* been waiting, watching the ship arrive, prepared for the moment that the women would jump into the water.

Mayara swam faster. Behind her, the spirits swarmed, spilling out from beyond the cliffs, rising up from below the water, diving down from the clouds above. She felt their greed like claws inside her stomach.

*Must get away!*

She stuffed the thought down fast, trying to keep her panic as quiet and small as possible so they wouldn't hear her. *Keep swimming. Just swim.*

*Feel the water.*

*Only the water.*

*Cool. Quiet. Calm.*

*See the coral below, the fish as they dart. I am one with the water, part of the sea. . . .*

She jerked underwater, her stroke broken, as a ripple of emotion that wasn't hers echoed through her body—it was from the spirits, their terrible glee. She rose up, gasped in air, and looked back toward the ship as she treaded water.

It was a feeding frenzy.

Spirits were swarming around the ship as the spirit sisters tried to swim for shore. The water was churning around them, frothing white with drops spraying high into the air. On the ship, Sorka was raising the anchor. Mayara could see her mouth moving, but the women's screams were too loud for Mayara to hear what the heir was shouting.

The Silent Ones, standing along the railing of the ship, were motionless, watching the water. At least one woman was dead, her body floating in a cloud of red. Mayara tried to rise up in the water to see who.

*Roe! Palia!* Where were they? Were they—

Mayara spotted a few figures climbing out of the water onto the sand. One of them was Roe. Even though she must have walked from the ship, almost certainly slicing her feet, she was helping Palia out of the breaking waves. *Not dead! Oh, thank the Great Mother.*

*I shouldn't have left them.* Never mind what Sorka had said about groups being targets. She shouldn't have abandoned her friends—her new sisters—to their fate. She'd made a mistake, abandoning them. She should have stuck with them, like Roe had . . .

Switching directions, Mayara began to swim toward them—

One of the spirits noticed her. She felt its attention shift to her—it felt as if claws had pinched her brain—and then she saw the spirit across the waves. It was a warped kind of dolphin, with a body covered in iridescent scales and a mouth full of rocklike teeth. Skimming over the surface, it swam for her.

Pivoting in the water, Mayara fled, thinking of nothing but getting away. She didn't try to control or deflect the spirit—and didn't even remember she could. She focused only on the pull of the water against her hands, and she breathed as if she were in a race, sparingly, with efficient gulps that were a part of her rhythm.

Concentrating, she lost herself within the rhythm of her strokes. *One, two, three . . .*

She felt the spirit recede behind her, drawn to easier and more tempting prey.

*I should help them! I shouldn't be running away. Roe can't even swim. . . .*

But Roe had made it to shore. Palia too. And others, though she hadn't gotten a good look at who. *They're safer without me. We're all safer apart.*

Sorka had said the spirits were drawn to groups, specifically targeting anyone who tried to work together, she reminded herself. She'd be safer, and they'd be safer, if everyone went off on their own. She'd seen that Roe and Palia had both made it to shore. She'd have to trust that they'd be able to use the cover of all the chaos to scatter and escape.

She remembered what Roe had said: you don't have to outswim the shark; you just have to outswim the other swimmers. *Which is what I did.*

She felt guilt like a fist in her stomach.

*There was nothing I could do. We were told to split up!*

But she kept seeing in her memory the cloudy red water by the ship and the image of Roe helping Palia out of the water. Roe hadn't abandoned the others to save herself.

The next time Mayara looked back, the ship had sailed out of the cove and was a speck in the distance, its sails bright against the blue sky. The water by the sand was deceptively calm, and Mayara could see a few spirit sisters running and hobbling into the thick green.

Trying to empty her thoughts, she kept swimming. *Don't think about spirits.* But she felt them in the distance, their ugly glee. She was crying as she swam, her salty tears mingling with the salty sea.

Eventually, her arms began to tire. She was used to long swims, but even she couldn't swim forever. Looking back, she saw that she'd swum far enough around the cliffs that she could no longer see the cove or the ship.

*Maybe it's safe to stop.*

She thought of Heir Sorka's final instructions: "You aren't

ever alone, and you aren't ever safe." *Maybe "safe" wasn't the right word, then.* But she had to stop anyway.

Gliding on her side, she eyed the shore. In a way, she told herself, it was not so different from home: there were rocks, cliffs, and even caves. She swam toward a dark slit in between the rocks. Sending her mind probing into it, she felt for spirits. Empty.

*Good.*

Climbing onto the rocks, she wedged herself into the slit.

It wasn't so much a cave as a nook, but it was sheltered enough from view that she could at least rest her limbs and catch her breath. Laying her head back against a rock, she peered out at the sliver of blue: turquoise-blue sea and brilliant blue sky.

It was still morning, she judged. *And at least one of us is already dead. Most likely more.* She hadn't seen whose body floated in the bay, and she was grateful for that. She didn't want to know who had died while she had lived.

*It's begun,* she thought. *It's truly begun.*

# CHAPTER ELEVEN

Shelter, freshwater, and food. Those were her priorities.

*And not dying. That too.*

Mayara fidgeted, trying to find a comfortable position. All the rocks were sharp, with barnacle-coated sides, and slick with seaweed. Not a perfect hiding place, especially not long-term. She'd have to leave soon, before high tide swallowed the rocks.

But for now . . .

Her arms and back ached from swimming so hard, and she was still gulping in air. She'd escaped. *Barely.* She thought of how Sorka and the Silent Ones had watched from the ship while the spirits fell in a frenzy on the potential heirs, and she wondered if they felt any guilt. They must have known that the spirits were waiting and watching, keeping themselves at just the right distance to lull them all into feeling as if it was okay to jump in the water. In fact, Sorka had hinted at as much in her warnings.

*The spirits are hunting us.*

By now, word must have spread that the women were here. Spirits could communicate with one another mind-to-mind. Her best bet was to give them nothing to hunt. Leave as little trace of herself as possible. Hide as much as she could. Avoid the spirits. Avoid the others.

She knew that wasn't what she was supposed to do. She was

supposed to fight. Learn to use her power, and either die in the attempt or succeed and become an heir. That was what the queen wanted them to do, but she didn't believe it was possible. *Not for me.*

*It hadn't been for Elorna.*

The waves lapped at the rocks, as if trying to reach her. Seafoam spirits chattered as they swam by, only a few yards from her hiding place. She sensed their urgency, their thoughts tumbling over one another.

Mayara waited quietly, her heart beating so fast and hard that she was sure they'd hear it. Eventually, they receded. She could still sense them, though, too close for comfort. But they were branching out, searching the island. Cautiously, she emerged, climbing on top of the rocks.

*I have to keep moving. Get as far from the cove as I can.*

Jumping off, she dived into the waves.

Underwater, a rainbow's array of fish sparkled and glittered as they swam among pastel-colored coral. A blue crab scuttled by, and a jellyfish drifted in the current. She swam above the reef, and despite all the terror she felt, she couldn't help but marvel at the wonders around her. The reef was gorgeous—brighter than any she'd ever seen, as if carved and painted by a master artist. The fish were more plentiful too, traveling in shimmering schools and drifting over orange anemones and pink coral. A few sand sharks glided lazily between them.

She swam, keeping the shore beside her, resting on rocks when she needed to, until the frenzied spirits of the cove felt distant, and then she flopped onto the shore.

*I'm still alive!* She felt like laughing out loud—the same kind of high she felt when she'd performed a death-defying dive—but she didn't dare make a peep. It felt wrong to feel such a rush when she didn't even know if anyone else had survived.

Still . . . she lived. And that was worthy of a little joy.

*Kelo, I'm trying!*

Monkeys were calling to one another. Beyond the sand, the

forest of palm trees was dense. She had no interest in losing herself in there where she wouldn't be able to see the ocean or any approaching enemies.

*This will have to do for now.*

The sun was setting. A glorious spread of pinks, oranges, and purples saturated the clouds near the horizon. She calculated that she had a little while to find a place to sleep, and then it would be dark. She'd collected a few oysters on her swim— they'd serve well enough as dinner, plus there were clumps of seaweed that were tasty uncooked.

She picked a set of boulders that were above the high-water line and hunkered down between them. As the stars came out, she ate her oysters and seaweed. Falling asleep, she thought to herself, *I can do this. Shelter, freshwater, and food. Keep away from spirits.*

*Really, it's not so different from home.*

*Right?*

WRONG. VERY WRONG.

This was very, very different from home.

Mayara scrambled up the boulder as it moved beneath her. She didn't know how she'd failed to sense that the boulders she'd picked weren't ordinary rocks but rather part of an earth spirit. Her only excuse was that the spirit had been asleep, its thoughts dulled so that she couldn't sense them beneath the buzz of the other spirits. Because she hadn't tried to command it, it hadn't sensed her either. She clung to its neck as it strode across the dark beach. The rocks in its legs crunched together as it moved.

The moon shed blue light over the sea and the sand. But the sea wasn't behaving as it should, any more than the rocks were. It was writhing as if snakes were dancing vertically on the surface. But these snakes were made of water, whipping fast in thin waterspouts.

*Don't react,* she told herself.

None of them had noticed her. *Yet.*

She tried to keep her mind as small and quiet as possible, which was difficult when everything inside her wanted to scream. Clinging to the earth spirit, she was rocked back and forth as it began to climb up one of the cliffs. It punched the rock to make handholds that it could use to climb.

She tried to clear a small corner of her mind that *wasn't* panicking in order to make a plan. If she brought attention to herself by jumping off, she'd be killed. If this earth spirit went closer to other spirits and they saw her, she'd be killed. So, for now, the best she could come up with was:

*Don't move.*

*Don't think too loud.*

The earth spirit lumbered through the palm forest, crushing trees beneath its massive feet. It continued until it reached another cliff, and she saw it had brought her back to where she'd come from: the cove where they'd first landed, the place she'd tried so hard to get away from.

On the shore were bodies, laid out in a row.

Three of them: Tesana, the fisherwoman who had left behind her husband and son; Dayine, who hadn't cut her hair since she was five; and quiet Resla, whose shell necklace was stained red with her own blood.

She'd known them all. Called them spirit sisters. And they hadn't survived a day.

If their eyes weren't open . . . if there wasn't blood at their throats or spread across their chests . . . if they weren't so very still . . . she could have pretended they were asleep, side by side, looking up at the stars. But she knew that wasn't true.

In the light of the moon, she saw a hint of movement in the trees just beyond the shore. She felt the earth spirit's attention shift. Suddenly, it charged forward, stomping in great strides toward the trees. Clinging to it, she felt as if every bone she had was rattling.

Ahead the trees writhed like a mass of shadowy snakes. She heard a scream—a woman's voice, tearing through the darkness. And then it was drowned out by cries and howls as the spirits converged on the sound.

Mayara held on as the earth spirit strode toward the twisting trees. As it burst through, she saw a half dozen tree spirits. Two looked like knots of wood, with gnarled bodies covered in bark. The others were slender and faceless, with smooth bodies that looked vaguely human. One had wings made of leaves. Another had fingers that were thorns.

Like spiders wrapping their prey, the slender tree spirits were cocooning something in vines. The vines grew fast, as Mayara watched—the spirits seemed to be drawing them out of the trees. The gnarled bark spirits flipped the cocoon over, and in a flash of moonlight, Mayara saw a face.

Kemra, the young spirit sister who'd wanted to be an heir.

Her eyes were open, lifeless, and her mouth was filled with bark. Bark seemed to have burst out of her mouth and encased her cheeks. The spirit with thorns for fingers drove those thorns in between the vines, drew out, and then stabbed her again.

Mayara felt a scream building inside her throat, and she fought to keep it back.

To the east, another cry from another human throat ripped through the night.

The earth spirit pivoted and charged toward it, trampling more vegetation. The trees they pushed through—*I could leap onto one of them*. But what if the spirit saw her? Torn by indecision, Mayara let the moment pass, and soon they had broken free of the trees and were above a cliff. Below, the sea crashed onto rocks.

She sensed the spirit's confusion—it had lost its new target. *Maybe she—whoever it was—escaped?* She hoped that was true. She feared it wasn't. *Four of us already dead. And the rest hunted.* The earth spirit let out an oddly wolflike howl, which was echoed by other spirits across the island. Plunging forward, the spirit headed toward the echoes.

As it stomped through the lush vegetation, the trees creaked and shifted, and the feel of spirits was so intense that the air felt thick with them. Instinctively, she squeezed her eyes shut—as if they couldn't see her if she couldn't see them, which she knew was ridiculous, but she'd never felt so helpless.

*Don't see me.*

It was only meant to be a whisper of a thought. But she felt it spread out from her and sink into the spirits around her. "Oh no," she whispered. She'd meant to hide from them, never using her power, never drawing attention to herself. . . .

"Jump now!" she heard a familiar voice call.

Roe!

Mayara didn't hesitate. She jumped from the earth spirit's neck—arms flung out, she grabbed on to the trunk of a coconut tree. She felt its bark scrape against her as she half climbed and half slid down to the ground.

Searching for her, the earth spirit howled again. She felt the sandy ground buckle, as every rock beneath the sand was called to the surface. The rocks kept growing, piling on top of one another, rising into towers all around her.

Scrambling over and between them, she ran toward Roe's voice.

She tried to run silently, but she was panting in both fear and exhaustion, and she stumbled and tripped over the dark, shadowy ground. "Where are you?" she whisper-called.

"Over here, the nearly dead girl by the tree." Her voice was right beside Mayara, and Mayara spun and jumped—and saw her. Lashed to a tree by vines, Roe was speckled in blood. Her hair was matted to her cheeks. Her leggings were torn, revealing an ugly gash that ran down the side of her calf. The soles of her feet were caked with dirt and blood.

In the darkness, the blood looked black.

Mayara began yanking at the vines, trying to loosen them. She glanced around at the ground, spotted a sharp rock, and began using it like a knife to saw through the vine. "Where are the spirits that did this?"

"Off killing someone else, if I had to guess," Roe said. "Must have figured they could finish me off later. The spirits themselves weren't here—it was a trap, like a snare, and I walked right into it."

"I used power," Mayara confessed. "They'll be after me."

"Everyone's using power. If we can get away fast enough, they won't know which of us did it. Just get me free and run." Roe struggled against the vines—they were wrapped tight around her thighs and arms, pinning her against the trunk.

Listening with her ears and her mind, Mayara kept sawing at the vines. She wished she had her diving knife. That would have sliced through these in no time.

At last, the vines began to fray. She kept going.

One snapped. Arm free, Roe yanked at the others, trying to loosen them, while Mayara attacked the next vine. She felt the hairs on the back of her neck prickle. Spirits were close. It was hard to tell how close or if they were aware that Roe and Mayara were here.

"Get ready to run. You go east, and I'll go west," Roe whispered.

"You're hurt—" Mayara protested.

"I'll be hurt worse if they catch us. How did you escape the water?"

"Guess I outswam everyone." Her disgust in herself permeated her voice. She thought again of the bodies on the sand—Tesana, Dayine, and Resla. *Not "bodies." They had names. Dreams. Lives.* They must have died in the first few hours. She wondered how many more of them were already dead and how many had suffered like Kemra before they'd died.

"You did what you had to do." Roe sucked in air and then winced. She fell forward as the last vine snapped. Mayara caught her and helped her straighten. Roe then sagged, clutching her injured leg.

Mayara made a decision. "Lean on me."

"We can't stay together," Roe said. "You heard Heir Sorka."

"They're already hunting us whether we're together or not," Mayara said. "And you can't run." Supporting Roe, she helped her hobble away from the tree. She noted as they left that Roe was right: it looked like a deliberate trap, a hunter's snare, that would tighten the vines around a body as soon as someone stepped inside. She wondered why a spirit would have to set a trap like that when they could simply control the vines with their minds.

In the distance, they heard another woman scream.

And then they heard the shrill, ecstatic shrieks of spirits.

The scream abruptly cut off.

"How many of us have they gotten?" Mayara asked. She knew of four. She didn't know if any others had been swept out to sea or lay somewhere, silent and still, in the sand between the trees.

"Don't know," Roe said. "Maybe half of us."

"It hasn't even been a full day. How are we going to last a month?"

Roe winced and leaned more heavily on Mayara. "We keep outswimming everyone."

It was terrible but also true. Because the spirits were distracted killing someone else, Mayara and Roe were able to hobble away from the trap. Mayara aimed east, not for any reason but because it fit the requirement "away from here."

In the darkness, every shadow looked like a spirit. She heard them calling to one another in shrieks too high-pitched to be birds'. Sometimes the shrieks held words: *Gotcha, gotcha, gotcha! Gonna get you, gonna tear you, gonna rip you, gonna make you dead!*

Or a sweet, childlike beckoning: *Come, spirit sisters! Come, I'll keep you safe. I'll make you warm. Feel my warmth. Feel it burn. Burn your flesh.*

*Little sisters, where are you? Little almost-heirs, let me embrace you!*

*All we want is you. All you must do is die.*

A giggle, shrill and unhinged, emerged from deep within the coconut forest. Mayara shivered. She couldn't tell which direction that had come from, but it sounded too close. Fear was chasing so fast and loud through her mind that she couldn't focus enough to feel any spirits.

As quietly as she could, Mayara whispered, "We need to hide. If they can't see us or hear us, and if we keep our thoughts small, they won't find us."

"But we're supposed to—"

Mayara cut her off. "We're supposed to live."

The moon cast everything in a blue hue. The shadows were layered in its light, and Mayara scanned the area for any darker patches. Despite the fact that she'd chosen to sleep on top of an earth spirit, she thought her first instinct was a good one: hide between rocks. Leave as little of themselves visible to the world as possible.

She helped Roe over to an outcrop of rocks—it was curved, like an eye socket, and there wasn't much room. But that was good—it meant less space through which the spirits could come at them. With difficulty, they climbed up and over the first boulder. Roe lowered herself between them, and Mayara squeezed in next to her. "Your wound, how is it?"

"Woundlike."

"Deep?"

"Painful. Can't tell if it's deep or not. I think the bleeding sort of stopped?"

"Not to be blunt, but are you going to die right now or can you make it until morning?" She knew how to make the various poultices and salves that Kelo used on her, but she couldn't search for the herbs until she had light. Even then, it wouldn't be safe to forage much.

"Absolutely no idea. If I wake up dead, I'll let you know."

They fell silent after that, listening to the night sounds. Neither of them slept much. And they heard two more screams that abruptly ended before dawn crept over the island.

"STILL ALIVE?" MAYARA WHISPERED. HER THROAT FELT ROUGH AND thick. She had a sour nutty taste in her mouth, so she must have dozed off, though she didn't remember falling asleep.

Beside her, Roe was still, curled in a fetal position. But Mayara could see her chest rising and falling. "Not sure," Roe said back, without opening her eyes. "If I were dead, I don't think it would hurt this much."

"Let me see."

"It's gory," Roe warned. Opening her eyes, she uncurled herself, wincing as she pulled her hand away from where it had been clamped on to her calf. Her palm was painted red with blood, and the gash itself was a clotted mess of deep red, black, and brown. Sand and dirt coated the cut. On the plus side, it wasn't bleeding.

"It doesn't look deep."

That was about the only positive thing Mayara could say, though. Because it did look filthy. If she didn't get that cleaned out, Roe was likely to come down with an infection, and that could kill her as surely as any spirit, as Tesana had warned. Pushing aside the image of the fisherwoman dead on the sand, Mayara ran through the list of herbs that she'd need: Verve leaf. Graymoss. Or sap from a suka tree, if she couldn't find the moss. Also saltwater. And angel seaweed, if there was any. As the list grew longer, she realized how dangerous foraging for all these could be and came to the conclusion that she could make do with just the saltwater and the seaweed. It would ward off infection, and that was the primary goal right now.

If she could find any.

She tried to reach out with her mind to check for spirits. It was difficult to make her thoughts calm enough—she didn't know how the other spirit sisters did it so easily back in the valley with Heir Sorka. She hadn't remembered any of them complaining about difficulty in feeling for spirits. *Maybe I'm just bad at this.*

"They're still here, if you were wondering," Roe said. "I've been monitoring them all night. A few of them are combing the island in a methodical way, but the bulk of them are stupid. They're milling around and hoping they trip over someone to kill. We just need to steer clear of the smart ones."

"How close are they?"

"Entirely too close. In another hour, they'll be here, if they keep the same pace and pattern and aren't distracted by killing someone else."

It was terrible to hope for another's death. But maybe she could hope they just chased someone else without catching them. . . .

*A day in, and I'm already being stripped of my humanity.* She shuddered, then closed her eyes tight. Shaking her head, she opened them and looked at Roe.

"Can you move?"

"Oh, sure. I was thinking a morning stroll might be nice." Roe managed a wry smile. "You know, this hasn't gone the way I pictured it. I thought . . . Guess I was naive." She leaned her head back, looking up at the sky.

It wasn't naive, though. Even as bad as the rumors about Akena were, there was nothing that could have prepared them for this. She couldn't get the image of Kemra out of her head, or the glee in the face of the tree spirit as it stabbed her body with its thorns.

*You weren't naive. You were lied to.*

Roe was still looking up, and Mayara followed her gaze. It was another dreaming sky, blue without even a wisp of cloud to mar the brilliance of its color. In the east, the morning sun tinted it with lemon yellow. The beauty warred with the horror of the last day.

Mayara wondered if Roe was thinking about her mother. Maybe she was regretting forcing Lord Maarte to acknowledge her power. Maybe she was just trying to see something that made her smile before descending into the madness of the island. Either way, it was time to go.

"We need to get by the shore. If I can find angel seaweed—"

"You need to get away from me," Roe said, without looking at her. "I'm a liability. Stay with me, and you're twice as likely to die."

"Yeah, and if I leave you, you're a hundred times more likely to die." She'd already swum away from Roe once, leaving her in obvious danger, and she'd hated how that had made her feel. She wasn't going to do it again.

Roe snorted, and then her snort turned into a cough. "Think highly of yourself, don't you? Actually, that's good. If you believe you can survive—" She coughed harder, the effort stealing the rest of her words.

Mayara didn't like the sound of that cough. It sounded as if it were scraping her throat. She knew another kind of seaweed that would help with that. But again, that all depended on whether or not she'd be able to forage without being caught by a spirit. "Did your tutors in the Neran Stronghold teach you what to do with cuts like that? I've sliced myself plenty of times on dives. I can fix you." *Maybe. Hopefully.*

"Well, I'm obviously not going to say no. Just let it be known that I was planning to be self-sacrificing and noble, and we'll leave it at that." Roe's smile was closer to a grimace, but Mayara accepted it. She already felt better just being with Roe.

"Come on," Mayara said. "Let's get closer to the water." Bracing herself, she let Roe lean on her to push herself up. "I'll help you walk. You watch for spirits."

"And what's our plan if one comes?"

"No idea," Mayara said. "Play dead?"

They hobbled together out of the rock formation. It was just barely morning, with the dawn light bathing everything in a cheerful glow, as if the island wasn't a terrifying death trap. On a morning like this back home, Mayara would be leaping out of bed to race down to the docks to see the fishers off. Or she'd be preparing for a dive, plotting out the prettiest cliffs to leap off before she gathered the abalone below the waves. She liked mornings at home. A fresh day was full of possibility and adventure.

Here, she was less fond of morning.

It was going to be a lot easier for spirits to spot them.

"We need to find a cave," Mayara said. "Judging from what I saw from the ship, there should be a lot of them."

"Probably all occupied by spirits. My plan was to stay on the move. Don't establish any patterns that the spirits can latch onto and use my power to distract them. In some of the books I've read—" She cut herself off. "Above."

Mayara didn't hesitate and didn't look up—she simply reacted. Yanking Roe forward, she flattened them both against the trunk of a suka tree. Its thick leaves were a canopy above them, she hoped shielding them from view.

She felt a trio of spirits fly overhead: one was air, one was water, and one was ice.

She kept her thoughts as quiet as possible by thinking of an abalone shell. In her mind, she traced the swirls of color.

*White* . . .

*Pink* . . .

*Green* . . .

*Purple* . . .

It worked.

When the spirits were gone, Mayara and Roe continued. Mayara heard the rhythmic crash of waves grow louder. She felt calmer as they drew closer, whereas Roe seemed to be more and more anxious.

"My grandfather didn't want anyone to teach me to swim,

but I didn't want to learn either," Roe said, out of the blue. "I hate the idea of all that water beneath me. I mean, not the water itself so much, but all the things in the water that you can't see."

"Then open your eyes."

"But that stings."

"You get used to it," Mayara said. "And a little stinging is better than being blind." She shook her head. "I can't remember not swimming. I think my mother taught me while I was in the womb. She said I could swim before I could walk. Why didn't your grandfather want you to learn?"

"Scared for me, I guess. He thought . . . There are more spirits in the sea, and he thought if I was exposed to them, I'd manifest an affinity for spirits and be taken away like my mother was. He didn't want to lose me too."

"Your mother died on the island?"

"Oh no, she didn't die," Roe said grimly. "Worse."

"What's worse?"

"She became queen."

Mayara stopped walking. She stared at her friend.

Roe gave her a weak smile. "Yes, it's a secret. I'm not supposed to tell anyone, but really who are you going to tell? The spirits? I haven't seen her since she was crowned. Our whole family was taken to the Neran Stronghold. For our protection, they said. And for hers."

"Your mother sent her own daughter *here*?" Mayara thought of her parents and how they'd mourned Elorna and were undoubtedly mourning their younger daughter too. If they'd had the power to stop this and end the tests . . .

"She doesn't know I'm here," Roe said. "How would she? She isn't allowed any contact with us." She said it so matter-of-factly, but it had to have torn her up inside to be without her mother for so many years.

Mayara knew how badly it hurt when her own mother had withdrawn after Elorna's death. Families on the islands were supposed to be close, with everyone staying in everyone else's business even after you were grown up and on your own. You weren't supposed to lose such a vital piece of your family. *When Elorna was ripped away, it nearly destroyed us.* "Did you ever try to contact her?"

Roe laughed, but there was no humor in it. "Only a thousand times. And failed a thousand times. That's why I'm here. If I can become an heir, I'll be with her again."

The words hit Mayara hard, because what Roe was really saying was that she was willing to risk *death* just to be able to talk to her mother again.

Quietly she asked, "Did your mother ever try to contact you?"

"Just once. And the Families had my father taken away in retaliation. So far as I know, she never tried again." At this, a hint of bitterness crept into her voice. Roe wasn't as unruffled as she seemed. And . . . *They took Roe's father? Does she mean "killed"?* No one had ever mentioned Queen Asana having a husband. Or a daughter, for that matter. *Maybe he still lives, somewhere.* "Do you know where they took him?"

Roe shook her head. "When I'm reunited with my mother, we'll find him. And then we can all be together again." She spoke with so much fierceness and sorrow that she sounded far older than she was.

Mayara wished she'd called Lord Maarte worse things than vile for separating Roe from both her parents and forcing her to grow up too fast. She shouldn't have to face Akena Island just to be with her family. *And neither should I.*

But there wasn't any time to discuss it further—they'd reached the shore.

"Uh, Mayara, there are a *lot* of spirits out there."

"Under the water or on the surface?" Mayara sent her own mind probing outward. She had to slow to do it—unlike Roe, she couldn't walk over uneven rocks and pay attention to distant spirits at the same time. Roe had either practiced more or was naturally stronger than she was. Either way, Mayara was glad to have her with her.

"Mostly under . . . Actually mostly under the *islands*. Or . . . within? Can you feel that?"

Mayara sent her mind directly beneath them, through the rocks and into the island itself, and she felt spirits moving *through* the island. "Earth spirits?" But that didn't seem right. She didn't get the sense that they were tunneling. "Odd."

So much about this island was odd.

Ahead was the shore. As they came out from between the rocks and coconut trees, banana trees, and suka trees, they saw the ocean spread before them, turquoise blue, with clear blue sky above and distant purple-blue islands on the horizon.

Mayara made her way quickly to the water's edge. Roe followed more slowly. "You can wait here if you want," Mayara told her. "I'll look for a cave. . . ." There were cliffs on either side of the tiny stretch of shore. Perfect for caves.

"Yeah, not staying behind. That's how I get eaten." Joining Mayara, she eyed the water with obvious dislike. "Maybe we'd be safer in the trees?"

"You were trapped by vines," Mayara pointed out.

As she'd hoped, the cliffs were riddled with holes. *One of them has to work.* It needed to be accessible, ideally with a sheltered route they could take to the shore so the spirits wouldn't see them coming in and out. . . .

She spotted one. *Perfect.*

"That one will do." She began to climb toward it. It wasn't far. Just above the high-water mark, it was a shadow about half her height and twice her width—they'd have to crawl inside. From here, she didn't know how large it was. For all she could tell, it was a divot. *Or it could be just right for two spirit sisters to hide for a month.* She wouldn't know until she looked—

"Mayara!" Roe cried.

She sensed the spirit at the same time as she heard Roe's

warning cry. Midreach, she froze as a spirit shot out of the cave she was aiming for. It was translucent, as if it were made of glass, and shaped like a bird with talons that were as long as its body.

*Don't see me.*

Again, the command slipped out of her before she could stop it. She saw the glass bird wobble in the air, but then it kept flying straight out over the sea. She scrambled up the rest of the rocks into the cave.

It hadn't looked back. But it had to have felt her thoughts. She saw it react. Did that mean it would return? Or that it would tell others?

Crawling into the cave, she strained to see. She sent her mind probing ahead into the darkness, looking for more spirits. She didn't feel any, though she knew she wasn't as good at sensing them as Roe. She inched farther inside. After the entrance, the cave widened enough that she could sit up.

Did the glass spirit live here?

She heard rocks tumble against each other outside and froze again. But it was Roe, hauling herself up the rocks to join her. Enough light sneaked in through the opening of the cave that Mayara could see her expression. She looked halfway between amused and exasperated. "So you see a spirit fly out of a hole and decide that's where you want to be?"

"We'll be out of sight."

"Until the spirit comes back."

"If it does . . . we kill it." It was a lousy plan, light on details, but it was better than no plan. Inside the cave, they couldn't be surprised. *Unless an earth spirit comes through the rock . . . Or collapses the rock on top of us . . . Or . . .*

*Stop it,* she told herself. This was the best she could do right now. Maybe it wasn't going to be their permanent home, but Roe needed a place to hide while Mayara found the angel seaweed and other essential supplies.

Roe crawled farther into the cave and collapsed against

the side. She winced as she positioned her leg in front of her. "Home, sweet home."

"It's above the high-water mark." Mayara defended it. She missed Roe's optimism. She supposed it had drowned in the cove. Or bled out of her leg.

"Until sea spirits create an extra-high wave just for us." Then Roe sighed. "Sorry, Mayara. We're not dead yet, so I guess that means we aren't making terrible decisions. Maybe your idea to hide is a good one. Certainly, I haven't done a great job in fighting them."

She hoped Roe was right. "I'm going to find plants to help with your cuts." She cast around, looking for a chunk of rock. She found one about fist size and handed it to Roe. "If that spirit comes back, bash it. Don't use your power—that won't kill it and using a command risks drawing others. If you hit it fast enough, it won't have time to call for help." She didn't mention that she'd already used her power once. She hoped it was such a minor use that other spirits didn't notice. Besides, she'd touched the mind of the spirit while she was outside the cave. With luck, no spirit would look inside. Roe should be safe enough. "I'll return soon."

"You sure you should go out there again?"

Enough light filtered in through the opening that she could see how ashen Roe's face looked. She was holding her side, and every breath looked like it hurt her. She wore a permanent wince. "No." But she was doing it anyway. Like she'd dived into narrow pools of water. "Keep that rock handy. Just don't bash me when I come back."

"Good advice. And if you don't come back?"

Mayara tried to sound braver than she felt. "Then you'll have outswum me."

# CHAPTER TWELVE

Every second on the shore felt like tempting death. Mayara thought of Elorna's favorite saying: "Death can't catch you if you chase it."

*I still think that doesn't make sense.*

She was grateful for the thought and effort that Kelo had put into the outfit he'd made for her—it was water-resistant for swimming and tear-resistant for climbing. And he'd designed it to double as a makeshift carrier. She felt a breath-stealing pang when she thought of Kelo and firmly pushed the feeling away. *I can't afford to be distracted.* Loosening the wrap, she created a sling from her shoulder to hip using the excess fabric. As she foraged on the rocks, she filled it as quickly as she could with everything useful she could find: angel seaweed (yes!), kelp (edible), winged kelp (also edible), bubble weed (barely edible). She found a sharp rock and used it to pry mussels and sea snails off rocks. She also found a few berries, though she wasn't certain whether they were edible. She harvested them anyway.

When she'd gathered all that she quickly could, she knotted the sling closed and began climbing back over the rocky shore toward the cave where Roe was hiding.

*Shelter, freshwater, and food,* she thought. They had shelter, food, and medicine, in the form of the angel seaweed. On her next trip out, she'd venture off the shore and search for a fresh-water stream. She thought she'd seen some probable areas up near the suka trees—they usually grew near water.

*Of course, I'll need a way to transport the water.* And it would be better if they could boil it, but starting a fire would be too much of a risk, not to mention tricky inside their damp-from-the-sea cave. Maybe it would be safer to harvest ripe coconuts, except that would require climbing a coconut tree, which would leave her exposed.

While she was thinking about all the practical details of preparing to survive, she wasn't worrying as much about the spirits, which was a welcome change. It was the first time on the island when she hadn't felt gripped by terror.

*It's because I'm not alone,* she thought. With someone else to worry over and care about and do things for, she was able to think clearly again. And feel hope.

"Roe? It's me," she whisper-called up to the cave. She'd marked the opening with a smear of suka berry juice—to a spirit, it would look like a bird had shat on the rocks.

Still hidden, Roe cheered, "Hurray! You aren't dead!"

Mayara grinned and began to climb up toward the cave.

"But you need to hurry—the spirit's coming back!"

Twisting to look behind her, Mayara saw the glass bird diving toward her from the cloudless sky. She felt as if her heart ceased to function. Then her brain sped up. "Roe, be ready with the rock, but stay out of sight. Wait for my signal."

Keeping her back to the spirit, she continued to climb toward the cave. *Only a few more feet . . . Almost here . . .* She held her own thoughts tight inside her head, concentrating on the feel of the seaweed-slick rocks.

She reached the cave opening just as the glass bird reached her, and then she flopped to the side, shouting, "Now, Roe!"

Lunging out of the cave, Roe brought the rock down hard on the glass bird. Focused on Mayara, the spirit never saw her. The rock hit its head.

The glass cracked.

Mayara flung herself on top of the spirit.

Using the sharp rock she'd found for prying mussels off rocks, she stabbed hard and fast at its slender neck until it broke. Roe joined her, pounding on the spirit's body with her larger rock until the spirit shattered into pieces.

Panting, they looked at each other. Mayara felt a giddy smile pull at her lips. They'd done it! They'd defeated a spirit! And they'd done it fast—she didn't think the spirit had had time to call for help. At least, she didn't feel any other spirits coming to its aid.

"Yay, us," Roe said weakly.

And then she fainted.

"Roe!" Mayara grabbed her as she tipped forward out of the mouth of the cave. Shoving her, she shifted Roe back inside and then laid her against the wall. "Roe, are you all right?"

She was breathing, right? Yes, she was. Mayara felt for a pulse in her neck.

Roe moaned.

"I've got medicine. Hold on." Untying her sling, Mayara dumped everything she'd gathered on the floor of the cave. She rooted through it until she found the angel seaweed.

Angel seaweed was a leafy plant that held copious amounts of water inside its plump leaves. It also had a kind of healing property to it—Mayara wasn't clear what made it good for warding off infections, but she knew from personal experience that it worked wonders. She squeezed the leaves and the vitamin-rich liquid dribbled out.

Roe's eyes snapped open the instant the first drops hit the gash on her calf. She yelped.

"Just relax. It's me. It's okay. You're safe. Sort of safe. Momentarily safe."

Roe hissed as more medicine hit her wound but didn't flinch away. "What . . . happened?"

"You fainted."

"Impossible. I never faint."

"You briefly lost consciousness because of incredible pain," Mayara clarified. She kept squeezing the angel seaweed over the wound, washing out the grit and soaking the cut in medicine at the same time. She then pressed the hunk of seaweed directly onto the gash. "Hold that there."

"The spirit . . ."

"It's dead," Mayara confirmed.

"We have to hide the . . . body. Is it a body if it's glass? We have to hide the evidence, or other spirits will see it and know someone's here."

She was right. "Keep pressing the seaweed to the wound. I'll be back."

Poking her head out of the cave, Mayara looked in all directions. She took a deep breath, centered herself, and sent her thoughts out, combing the nearby sea and sky. No immediate spirits, though there were plenty not far from them, both in the water and among the trees. The shore was temporarily clear.

Using her wrap-dress carrier again, Mayara quickly gathered up all the shards of the dead spirit. They'd been lucky this one was so easy to defeat. Most weren't. If it had been larger or one of the spirits made of water or rock or fire . . . *We were lucky.*

*We can't count on luck to get us through a month. Or even a week.*

*But I don't want to count on power either.*

*Maybe we can count on being clever and careful.*

*Maybe that will be enough.*

*Maybe . . .*

She retreated into the cave with the shards and deposited them in a corner. She studied them for a moment. Catching a bit of stray light from the opening, one of the shards winked. She picked it up. Its edges were sharper than any of the rocks, though the glass was more fragile. It could be useful. As she retightened her wrap dress, she tucked the glass shard into her belt. She then scooted the rest out of the light so that no one outside would see any suspicious glints.

"We're going to die," Roe said flatly. "Palia was right."

Mayara looked up, surprised. They'd just defeated a spirit! They had the right seaweed to heal Roe's injury! And they even had mussels and snails to eat. Uncooked, the snails weren't the best, but mussels were one of her favorite foods, even without her father's mango sauce. *I wonder if I can find any ripe mangoes on the island. . . .*

"Not today," Mayara said firmly. "We aren't going to die today, and that's all that matters."

Roe smiled. "You sound like me. I was so optimistic—until I hurt myself within the first hour and nearly died within the first day."

"But you *didn't* die, and you're going to heal. All we have to do is keep surviving one day at a time." Mayara put her hand on top of Roe's, gently, over the seaweed pressed to her wound. "Just one day at a time."

THEY CONTINUED TO NOT DIE.

They weren't comfortable. Or clean. Or well fed. But they were still alive.

*Not dying is an excellent start,* Mayara thought, as she prepared to leave the cave for her second trip out. She planned to venture closer to the trees today—they needed a freshwater source if they didn't want to help the spirits out by dying of dehydration.

"You're sure this is a good idea?" Roe asked. "You going alone?"

"It's a terrible idea," Mayara said. "Everything here is a terrible idea. But I don't think there's much choice." She didn't *want* to go out there at all, much less alone. But she also didn't want to wither away from thirst, hunger, and fear.

"I want to come with you."

"You need to heal." She handed her another wad of angel seaweed. *I'll pick up more on my way back.* "Reapply and try to get more of the sand and dirt out of there."

"I hate feeling helpless. You've already done so much. It should be me out there this time, risking myself. Not hiding in here."

"You can help when you've healed."

"And how many of our spirit sisters will die in the meantime? We should be finding them and helping them. I heard another scream last night."

Mayara had heard it too. She'd tried to pretend it was a monkey's howl, but she hadn't been able to stop picturing Kemra's body, strangled in vines and pierced by thorns. "We can't help anyone if we don't help ourselves first. And for that—"

"Fine. But if you don't return . . ." Roe left the threat hanging, presumably because there was nothing to threaten Mayara with.

*If I don't return, I'll be dead,* Mayara thought. *And Roe will need to heal fast or die too.*

"Wish me luck," Mayara said as she crawled out of the mouth of their cave.

She blinked in the sunlight. The turquoise water sparkled. A few water spirits were swimming like dolphins to the west, leaping and splashing in the waves. She judged them too far away to fear, at least for now.

Scampering over the rocks, Mayara hurried up the shore toward the coconut trees. If she could bring back just a few, that would give them enough water to last a little longer without having to venture out for a while. And then if they hollowed out the shells, she could use those to fetch freshwater from one of the streams, or they could set them out to collect rainwater.

She kept her mind open for spirits, watching the sky as well as the trees, as she crept up to a copse of coconut trees. She didn't want to be caught halfway up a trunk. It took a lot not to just freeze. Because even though they weren't that close, her thoughts kept brushing against their minds:

Three water spirits out in the sea.

One water spirit, medium size, in a nearby stream.

Two air spirits, both small, to the east.

One tree spirit . . . No, that was heading in the opposite direction.

Even though she wasn't in their sights, she was still surrounded, and it felt more claustrophobic than the cave. She'd be quick. Up a tree, knock down a few coconuts, down the tree, and then back to Roe. She selected the tree—and then stopped as she saw an odd tangle of vines by the base. Tiptoeing up to it, Mayara knelt and studied the tangle. It was a loop with a knot, laid at the base of the tree, exactly where you'd want to step if you were about to climb the tree.

*It's a trap.*

She backed up.

Odd that there was another snare like the kind that had caught Roe, rather than something more . . . well, *magical,* for lack of a better word. It was more the kind of trap that a human hunter would lay than a spirit that could control the elements. Grabbing a stick, she poked at the vines. She'd never heard of a spirit leaving human-style traps. They were far more likely to force the vines to grow faster than normal and knot themselves around you, like they did with Kemra. *Very,* very *odd,* she thought. She resolved to think about it more when she was safely back with Roe. In the meantime, she scooted the snare to the side with her stick and cleared a space to access the tree.

Checking again for spirits, Mayara unwound her cloth belt and tied it into a one-foot-wide loop. She then stepped into the loop and spread her legs so it was taut between her ankles. That was the trick to climbing a coconut tree: a loop of fabric around your ankles. It would give her feet more stability and thereby give her more leverage. Elorna had taught her years ago. She'd liked to wake early and harvest a few extra coconuts just for herself, before the village harvesters had a chance to claim them. Sometimes she shared with Mayara.

Mayara climbed, wondering if Elorna had tried to scale these same trees. They'd never been told how she died exactly, only that it was on the island. It was a peculiar sensation, that it was here, so far from home, that Mayara again felt close to Elorna. Then she pushed thoughts of her sister out of her mind and focused on her task.

At the top, she twisted the stems and then dropped the coconuts. They thudded to the ground. One, two, three, four . . . *There, that should be enough.* Panting, she began the climb down. Her arms and legs were aching. She hadn't climbed like this in ages.

Concentrating, she almost missed sensing the tree spirit flittering through the grove. She caught the high-pitched giggle of its thoughts when it was only a few trees away. It hadn't seen her yet.

Barely daring to breathe, Mayara flattened against the trunk. She was too visible and too exposed. She looked across the island—and then wished she hadn't.

She knew whose scream they'd heard in the night.

Splayed with her arms and legs wide, Nissala was pinned to one of the closer cliffsides, only a few trees away from Mayara. Her hands and feet were encased in stone, and her head was cocked at an unnatural angle, mostly severed from her body. Her tunic was stained red. She was undoubtedly dead.

*As I'll be, if I'm caught.*

It felt as if Nissala had been left as a warning sign. Or a victory flag.

Mayara looked down. She was halfway up the tree. Not an impossible drop, but not safe either. And if she broke or twisted her ankle or her leg . . .

She felt the spirit draw closer. Felt its bottomless hunger and rage.

*No choice,* she thought.

She pulled one foot out of the sash and then jumped.

Landing on bent legs, she felt the impact shake through her. It knocked her back, but she didn't hear or feel a snap. Getting to her feet, she heard the spirit cry. *It's seen me!* She ran, not down toward the shore but up toward the top of the cliffs. She heard it shriek as it chased her.

Beneath her feet, grasses sprouted higher, growing impossibly fast. They reached for her ankles, as ahead of her vines wove themselves into a net. Thorns burst from the vines as they thickened.

*Faster! Faster!* Mayara ordered herself. But she didn't let the words escape her own mind. She kept a tight lid on her thoughts, focusing on running toward the edge of the cliff.

The thorny vines creeped across the edge of the cliff, growing as she watched. She aimed for a spot higher, bare rocks, not yet touched by the impossible growth.

She felt the spirit's claws snag her hair, but Mayara barreled forward, strands of hair ripping from her scalp. She didn't slow as she reached the edge. She exhaled, still running, then inhaled as fully as she could as she leaped off the cliff into the open air, diving toward the sea.

She plunged into the water.

For an instant, she was cocooned in bubbles. Breaking free, she swam down, deeper, away from the spirit. She felt its anger behind her. *I made it! I—*

And then the spirit claimed control over the seaweed.

The kelp began to grow so fast that it looked as if it were unraveling large skeins of green, leathery fabric. It wrapped around her. Struggling, she pulled out her glass shard and sliced.

Slicing and struggling, she fought her way free. She kicked hard, swimming deeper toward the rocks and away from the reef. Her lungs began to burn. She wasn't thinking—she was only fleeing. *Away, away, must get away!* She saw a gap in the rocks ahead, empty of seaweed, and she aimed for it as she felt another strand of kelp whip her ankle.

She kicked hard and shot into the gap.

She saw a glow above her. Sunlight meant air. *Air!* She swam up.

Bursting out of the surface, Mayara sucked in air. She tried to calm herself, breathing in and out. She caught a trickle of the spirit's thoughts: it was radiating its dismay to as many spirits as it could. It wasn't words, but she guessed the gist. It was calling for others to help it search.

Trying to slow down her panic enough to plan, she took stock of where she was: a hole in the rocks. Open at the top, she could see a patch of blue sky, but the hole was too small for her to squeeze out. Her only exit was back down through the water. But she couldn't go near the kelp again, not with the tree spirit out there waiting for her to do exactly that.

*Can I swim around it?*

It depended on whether the tree spirit had called on any water spirits. Concentrating, she sent her thoughts out again. She brushed against three, aiming for the reef, each filled with glee and hunger so sharp that it made her shake. Fear threatened to choke her, driving away her ability to sense the spirits. Treading water, she tried to force the terror down. She couldn't let them feel her fear.

She could send them away, but she didn't know if she could control so many of them. And whatever spirits she failed to command would come for her. *Right now, they don't know where I am.* That gave her an advantage. *A very slight, very pathetic advantage.*

Calming herself with difficulty, she reached out with her mind again—only to feel a bit of panic once more, as even more spirits were flowing toward where she'd dived into the sea. What kept her from losing her mind completely was the strangeness of it all, since a few seemed to be coming from *beneath* the island rather than from above.

Mayara remembered when she and Roe first found their cave. They'd both felt spirits moving beneath and through the heart of the island. Could there be tunnels that went deeper than the caves that pocked the cliffs?

*Why, though?*

*And . . . can we somehow use that to our advantage?*

She felt an air spirit within the island, in the middle of what should be rock. She tracked it as it swam out of the caves and through the reef toward the kelp forest to join in the search.

It had exited the caves only a few yards away from where she hid. *I could swim there.*

But then what? What if the tunnel never came up to the surface? What if it was completely flooded? Yet the spirit she'd felt had been an air spirit, she reminded herself. As far as she knew, they needed to breathe.

It was a risk. *But staying here isn't—it's certain death. And I can't go out there.*

She made the decision. And committed to it. Exhaling fully, Mayara drew in air, preparing as she would for a deep dive, then propelled herself down.

Mayara swam smoothly, careful not to disturb the water, keeping her senses open and her mind clear. Blue surrounded her. She aimed for the darkest of blues: toward the base of the cliff, where she'd felt the air spirit emerge.

Ahead, there was a break in the rocks, laced with bits of seaweed that waved gently in the current. Mayara swam through it, flinching slightly when she brushed past the seaweed, remembering the last time she'd encountered kelp, but she pushed on, and she left the clear glow of sunlight behind her.

An eerie kind of deep blue wavered around her. Only a little light filtered into the cave. She didn't feel any spirits nearby. A few fish darted around her, streaks of silver. A jellyfish that looked like an iridescent flower drifted by.

The peacefulness of a deep dive settled into her, and she

felt calm as she swam through the tunnel. Ahead, she saw a hint of more light. She swam toward it and then emerged. And breathed.

She was in a cavern. Light streamed through a hole high above her. The cave walls glistened and sparkled blue and green. Swimming to the side, she pulled herself up onto a rock and panted. Near as she could tell, she was alone.

*And not dead. That part's important.*

For several minutes, Mayara thought about nothing else. She just breathed.

And then her brain started to work again. Not only were there caves by the shore, but the entirety of Akena Island seemed to be laced with caves and tunnels. The spirits used them. With a thrill, she thought, *So can we.*

When she had rested enough, she began the climb up toward the light. The cave wall was nearly vertical, but it was rough enough to grip. She focused on not slipping. Reaching the hole, she hesitated, feeling for any spirits.

She felt a clump of them to the north. But none were here.

Climbing out, Mayara flopped onto the grass in the sunlight. Allowing herself only a few seconds to rest, she concentrated on slowing her breathing and her rapidly beating heart. She was exposed now and couldn't afford to stay out in the open. As tired as she was, she had to move. Mayara forced herself to stand. She spared an extra second to smear a handful of suka berries on the entrance of the cavern, marking it so she could find it again, and then she picked her way over the rocks. She was just above where the mess had all started, near the coconut grove not far from her and Roe's cave.

She didn't sense any spirits in the grove now, at least as far as she could tell. They were all out at sea, searching for her. She made her way across the sand between the trees and picked up the fabric loop she'd used to climb. She also stored the fallen coconuts in her sash. She did not look up at the cliffs, tried not to imagine Nissala's body pinned by the stone that the spirits had used to kill her.

Carefully, she crept down to the shore.

She felt prickles on her back and neck as she made her way across the rocks and then into the cave, but nothing attacked. And when she crawled deeper, Roe was waiting for her.

"Lots of spirits out there," Roe whispered.

Mayara unloaded the coconuts and then collapsed against the wall of the cave. Feeling the stone against her back, she again thought of Nissala. "Maybe staying hidden for a while would be a good idea."

MAYARA SHARED WHAT SHE'D LEARNED ABOUT THE CAVES AS SHE hacked a hole in one of the coconuts. Roe, though, didn't seem at all surprised. "I think you're right. While you were going for a refreshing swim—"

"Ha, very funny," Mayara muttered, then shuddered. Nissala's fate could so easily have been hers.

"—I did a little exploring. Our cave goes back. *Far* back."

"How far?" Mayara peered into the darkness. She'd checked several yards in to make sure they weren't sleeping with a nest of spirits, but when the cave had narrowed, she'd assumed it ended.

"I just said 'far back' in a deliberately vague way. No idea. I crawled as far as I could, but the dark was, well, very dark."

"You shouldn't have been crawling around alone and injured to begin with."

"I told you: I hate feeling helpless. I don't want to hide here for a month, waiting until it's our turn to scream until we die. I won't do it. If I can't leave the cave, then I'll go deeper in."

"Fine." She wished Roe didn't have this need to be a hero. Just staying alive was heroic enough for Mayara. But there was no guarantee they'd be safe here—it did make sense to see if they could find an alternate exit to their hidey-hole, in case they needed one. "We'll explore together. *After* you've healed more. I'll try to find some firemoss—"

"You can't go out there again," Roe said. "You nearly got killed."

"For this place, 'you nearly got killed' means we're doing great. It means we're still alive." She finished the hole and tilted the coconut up to her lips. The coconut milk was thin, sweet, and amazing. She took several gulps before passing the coconut to Roe. She'd gathered a total of four, which should last them for a while between the milk and the meat.

"Fair enough," Roe said after she'd taken a long draft. "But promise me you'll be careful. The only thing worse than feeling helpless to protect myself is feeling helpless to protect you."

"I'm careful," Mayara promised—and wanted to laugh. That was one word that no one at home, especially Kelo, would ever call her. She'd always been reckless. But then it was easy to be "reckless" at home, when she was just doing what Elorna had done before her. It was harder here, knowing that she did *not* want to follow in Elorna's footsteps. "We'll explore together, as soon as you've healed enough."

"Good. I've been thinking about it. . . . We both felt the spirits going through the tunnels, right? What if we use *them* to show us the cave system? We can keep track of where we feel them. Draw ourselves a map."

Mayara considered it. The spirits couldn't sense them if they didn't issue any commands. And they had to stay hidden for a while anyway. "It's brilliant."

Roe began riffling through the seaweed and remnants of fruit. She raised up a clump of suka berries triumphantly. "How's this?"

"Perfect." It would work nicely for drawing a map on one of the walls. Taking a berry, she drew the first mark, indicating their cave. Roe added to it, pausing to concentrate on the distant underground spirits.

"Sorka was wrong," Mayara said as they both drew, side by side in the faint light of the cave mouth. "We're better together."

# CHAPTER THIRTEEN

Aside from not dying, the trickiest part about hiding from the spirits was figuring out when and where to pee. *None of the legends or songs mention this part,* Mayara thought. Not a single verse hinted at a spirit sister, heir, Silent One, or queen ever having to worry about where to relieve herself while she fought for her life. No one ever warned about the tedium of constant terror or the amount of time you spent obsessing over simple bodily functions when life itself was no longer simple.

Mayara squatted in the shallows of the sea whenever she needed to, and Roe, while her leg continued to heal, used a hollowed-out coconut that Mayara would dispose of during one of her foraging trips.

It was a risk, of course, every time she left the cave. *Everything* they did was a risk, though. Staying in one place. Venturing out. Even thinking too much or too loudly, if they weren't careful to keep their thoughts from projecting as loudly as a shout. But a few things were unavoidable. For example, they couldn't let odors build up inside their cave or even near it—that would give them away. Better to let the waves wash away any trace of them.

At least there was never a shortage of plants to forage when Mayara did risk a trip out. She even found firemoss growing between the rocks. Firemoss gave off a soft glow that made it perfect to use for exploring caves. It was a lucky find, but given what she'd seen so far on Akena Island, it didn't surprise her. She suspected that if she were able to search for long enough, she'd find just about anything and everything growing there. Already on her short jaunts, she'd seen more kinds of flowers than she ever knew existed, as well as bananas, mangoes, oranges, and all varieties of nuts and berries, even those she knew had no business growing in Belene—some belonged in the cold reaches of Elhim or the mountain lands of Semo. But the spirits who'd grown them hadn't cared—they were free to create unchecked here. Mayara wasn't complaining—each trip, she came back with her sling overloaded.

If it weren't for the constant fear of death—*and*, she thought, *the occasional need to pee into coconuts*—it would have been a wonderful place to live.

After five days of not dying, Mayara and Roe were ready to explore the caves beneath the island. Five days was enough time for Roe's leg to heal, and five days was enough for them to map out at least a few of the myriad tunnels.

It was also enough time to realize that if they didn't start moving, they might go crazy.

Now that there were only a few spirit sisters left—Mayara didn't know exactly how many—the spirits were hunting in packs, combing the island in increasingly frenetic patterns, swarming with greater ferocity when they sensed any hint of their prey. She could feel them every time they neared her and Roe's cave. It wore on both of them.

*We need a secondary cave,* Mayara thought, *for the inevitable day when we're discovered.* Assuming they survived that day.

They wouldn't be able to bring their map with them, of course—it was drawn on the cave wall with suka berry juice—and so they each spent a significant chunk of time memorizing it. It was a bit like memorizing the veins in a leaf. Every cave branched out into a half dozen more, and they would have to be careful not to become lost.

"You know, we're supposed to be learning how to use our power to control spirits so we can become useful heirs," Roe said. "Not hiding out and crawling around in dark, dangerous, unknown cave systems. We should venture *out* instead of *in*."

They'd had this conversation before. Roe felt guilty for not being more heroic and practicing being an heir, like they were supposed to do. Mayara felt no such guilt. "You've sensed how many spirits are out there. Do you want to face them?"

"Well, maybe not right this second, but soon. . . ."

"We need an escape route, in case they find us before we're ready to face them." Mayara didn't think she'd ever be ready to confront them, but she didn't say that to Roe. She'd be fine with avoiding the spirits for the entire month. But there was no guarantee they'd be able to stay undiscovered for so long. "The spirits are still searching. At some point, they'll search here." She didn't like the way their cave made her feel cornered. Every time a spirit flew by, she felt like a mouse pinned against a wall. Any second, the cat was going to see her. Run and hide— that was the plan, but right now, they didn't have anywhere to go. "I don't want to wait for our luck to run out."

"It just doesn't feel right, all this hiding," Roe complained.

"Then think of it as exploring," Mayara said. "You've been cooped up inside a fortress your entire life. But now you have a chance to see something no other humans have seen: the heart of the most feared island in all of Belene."

Roe perked up. "Okay, when you put it that way, it sounds a lot better."

Mayara grinned at her. "Then let's do it."

Bringing the firemoss, as well as other essentials (glass shards and sharp rocks for weapons, a hollow coconut filled with freshwater, seaweed, and enough food for a day), they crawled into the darkness.

The firemoss cast a weak glow a few feet ahead of them, enough that they'd see any bottomless pits or cliff drop-offs, but not enough to shed light on what lay ahead or to alert any spirits. Mayara crawled first and then stood as the tunnel widened. She held the firemoss in one hand and a knifelike rock in the other. Roe followed behind her. It was Mayara's job to watch the terrain, and Roe's job to "watch" for spirits.

"Did you really never leave the fortress?" Mayara asked as they crept through the caves. She kept her voice to a whisper, even though there was no one to hear.

"I've never even been to a market."

"How could your mother let them imprison you like that? She has the power of all the spirits!" Except that she didn't, Mayara realized, because of the Deepest Blue. She opened her mouth to take back her words, but Roe was already talking again.

"I used to blame her," Roe said. "Even hate her. When she became queen, we lost her. My grandparents tried to explain it wasn't her fault, that she didn't want to be queen, that she certainly didn't want to lose us, and that I had to be a good little girl, and maybe someday, when the world wasn't so dangerous, we'd be allowed to see her again. Until then, she needed us to stay safe."

"You *never* saw her? Not once?"

"Once," Roe said. "But only at a distance. And she never knew I was there. She visits each of the Family strongholds once a year. Usually Lord Maarte posts extra guards on us for her visits, but one year, it was a surprise visit. I was down in the kitchen, so the guards didn't get to me as quickly as they were supposed to—and I saw her. . . ." She trailed off as if caught in the memory.

"What happened? Did she see you?"

"I was going to call out to her. And then Lord Maarte himself asked me not to—with a knife to my throat. Never liked him much after that."

Appalled, Mayara halted and looked back at her. She couldn't read Roe's expression in the dim glow of the firemoss. "He threatened you?"

"We lived under constant threat—it just wasn't always so

overt," Roe said. "Why do you think the Families have so much power? The queen knows where the storms will hit and tells the Families. But it's the Families who then tell the heirs where to go, saying they're passing along the words of the queen."

"*That's* why the heirs didn't come to my village? Because Lord Maarte wanted to protect his pretty fortress?" She'd been blaming the heirs themselves, but it was Lord Maarte who let the wild spirits attack her village. *He's responsible for the deaths.* "This isn't right. You have to tell someone. No, not someone. Everyone!"

"Who? The spirits who want us dead?"

"Then you have to survive!" Mayara whispered fiercely. More islanders could die because of Lord Maarte's selfishness. It had to be exposed. His crimes . . . He had to be punished. Or at least made so that he couldn't stand between the queen and saving people!

"That's the plan. Lord Maarte still holds my grandparents. Once I'm an heir, I'll be able to see her and tell her everything, and she'll free them."

"And then what will you do? Once you're all free and together?"

"Eat breakfast," Roe said. "I want to wake up in the morning and have breakfast together, with a view of the sea. And then I want to read a book, with her next to me reading her own book. And take a walk on the beach. Just ordinary things, you know? How about you? What will you do once you're home? If we survive and become heirs, you'll be allowed to visit."

Mayara thought about it. About making love to Kelo. About rejoicing in her survival with her family—they'd want to throw a party, with drummers and dancing and a shrimp buffet. But really, what she wanted was exactly what Roe had said: the ordinary moments. "An ordinary day sounds perfect."

As they crept deeper into the caves, the gray stone began to change. Mica in the rock sparkled as if it were sprayed with diamond dust. It reminded Mayara of dawn light on the sea. And then the gray changed to blue stone, translucent and glowing with a soft blue light of its own. Mayara held the lump of firemoss up to the blue stone. It reflected her face, blurred.

"Still no spirits," Roe whispered. "Let's keep going."

Farther in, the blue tunnel widened into a cavern. White limestone stalactites and stalagmites transformed it into a marvel out of a children's tale. Mayara felt as if they weren't in the world anymore. They walked through it in wonder and silence.

On the other side, the cave narrowed and climbed. Soon, light began to flood the tunnel. Mayara tucked the firemoss into her sling. They peeked out and saw below them the cove where they'd first landed. It was still beautiful, lush, and deadly.

She felt Roe touch her arm—two taps.

Two spirits.

Backing up, they retreated, hurrying through the stalactite cave and back through the blue glasslike stone tunnel until they were safely back in their own tiny nook of a cave. They marked their map: they'd found a route from their cave to the cove.

"I feel like we should celebrate," Roe said. "We explored and didn't die! Yay!"

"More coconut milk?" Mayara offered.

It tasted extra sweet that night.

FLUSH FROM THE SUCCESS OF NOT DYING THE DAY BEFORE, THEY took a new path the next day and were met with a new wonder: huge pink and black crystals that speared the room, crisscrossing at all angles to create a labyrinth of translucent stone. In the light of firemoss that grew in the walls, the crystals seemed to glow with their own light.

"None of this makes sense—both limestones and crystals?" Roe whispered. "I've read geology books; I know how rock formations work. None of this should be here. It's an island built out of a fossilized skeleton. What would make it like this?"

"Spirits," Mayara answered. They must have shaped all this

beneath the surface of the island, making it as whimsically beautiful as they wished, out of sight of the queen, the heirs, and the Silent Ones.

Like every tunnel in this underground labyrinth, it branched in multiple directions. They chose the left fork first, following it up to a part of the island they'd never seen: a beach thick with greenery that seemed to move as they watched.

Roe whispered, "Do you think they're hunting someone?"

*Yes. Us. And anyone else who's left.* She didn't answer out loud. Instead she watched as the greenery converged on the shoreline. A wave rose out of the water, bearing a water spirit who held—

*Oh, Great Mother, not another of us!*

Beside her, Roe leaned forward, squinting.

Hand on her shoulder, Mayara drew her gently back into the tunnel as the spirits within the greenery gave a horrible, gleeful cry. "If it is . . ." She couldn't bring herself to say what they saw was a body. Maybe it wasn't. It could have been driftwood or a dead dolphin. "It might be no one. And if it isn't, she's beyond our help." There were too many spirits, and the shore was too far from their cave. With less prey to hunt, the spirits were swarming each new find in far greater numbers.

"It might not be anyone," Roe agreed. "A trick of the light."

But the spirits shrieked again, and Mayara knew they were lying to themselves.

"If I order them to—" Roe began.

"No." She caught Roe's arm. "You'll draw them to us."

"I'll send them far away, and then you can sneak down and—"

"It's a terrible plan. If just one of them—"

"I can't do nothing!"

Mayara shushed her. "*Shh.* We're not doing nothing. We're staying alive."

"But whoever that is needs—" Roe cut herself off, and Mayara saw her eyes widen. She followed Roe's gaze to the shore.

Four air spirits had lifted the woman—it had to be a woman; she was too far away for Mayara to see her features—into the air. Each held an arm or a leg. "Mayara, they're going to—"

They flew in four different directions, tearing the woman apart in midair.

Silently, Mayara and Roe backed into the tunnels. They didn't speak again until they were in their own cave. Slumping against the wall, Roe said, "I won't hesitate next time."

"And I won't stop you," Mayara promised.

ON THE THIRD DAY OF EXPLORING, THEY FOLLOWED A TUNNEL THAT led to an underground lake, as round as a coin and as black as the night sky. As they skirted the edges of it, Mayara found herself eyeing it, wondering how deep it went and where it led. Did it connect to the sea? But she wasn't looking for a new dive. She stayed out of the water and kept walking.

A tap on her arm.

She ducked behind one of the boulders. So did Roe.

There was a skittering sound up ahead. It snuffled, and she felt a medium-size earth spirit, not overly intelligent. She felt it was frustrated, though its thoughts weren't clear enough to identify why. She listened as it lapped at the water and then retreated.

"Forward or back?" Roe whispered.

"Forward, slowly." They could return the way they came if they had to. It didn't sound as if the spirit was aware of them. It was lumbering away. Creeping, they followed it up and out of the caves.

A squeeze on her arm.

Mayara nodded. She felt them too. Lots of spirits. She didn't even try to see where this path led. They knew enough to know this way was *not* their escape route.

Retreating, they tiptoed back to the lake and then kept going until they reached their cave. So far, they'd explored the three major tunnels. Roe added an X to the writhing green beach, an X to the cliff drop, and an X to the route that led to the mass of spirits.

"We don't know if that's their permanent home," Mayara said.

"We don't know it isn't. Do you want to go back and ask them? Maybe they'll invite us in for tea." Her voice sounded oddly rough. Roe drew a shuddering breath. "I can't stop thinking about her. We don't even know who it was."

"We'd have been killed before we were even sure there was anyone to save," Mayara pointed out. "They brought her out of the sea—she may have already drowned before . . . before *that* happened."

"If we'd been careful—"

"No amount of careful would have been enough. We have to focus on what we *can* do, not what we wish we could." Studying the map, Mayara tapped the path that led through the crystal cave. "This is what we can do. We can set up a second camp here. What do you think? That way, if we have to abandon this place—"

"Home, sweet home," Roe muttered.

"—we'll at least not have to start from scratch. Plus, it will make it easier to explore the other tunnels, since we'll already be deeper in."

Roe agreed.

Mayara liked having a plan. It was easier to avoid thinking about what she'd seen if she kept busy. Sorting through the paltry few items they'd accumulated, they debated what to bring and what had to stay—they'd have to hide their supplies at the second camp, and they wanted duplicates of the essentials, such as the coconut water-carrier and glass knives. Packing didn't take long—*It's not as if we have a lot of belongings,* she thought—but they discussed it at length anyway. It filled the time, and their minds, while their bodies rested.

She checked Roe's injuries. No sign of infection. Then they ate and slept. The next day, they crept back to the crystal cave, bringing their supplies. Mayara felt optimistic—or at least, she did when she could avoid thinking of the woman on the beach.

There were enough nooks between the crystals that they had plenty of places to hide their belongings and themselves. Mayara particularly liked a nook beneath a black crystal—the way it was positioned, she could see out but no one could see her. She tested it with Roe.

"Nice," Roe said, and then frowned. "What's that?" Kneeling, she unearthed a lump wrapped in a palm leaf. She unwrapped it and held up a rusted knife.

Both of them stared at it.

"Guess we weren't the first ones to find this place," Roe said finally.

Mayara reached out and touched the knife handle with her finger, feeling as if she was touching a piece of history. From all the rust, it must have laid there a long time. "I wonder what happened to whoever it was." It couldn't have been good if she'd lost her knife. She felt a shiver up her spine and wondered if this crystal cave wasn't the best place for a camp after all. It was large, with many nooks and crannies. They'd seemed perfect for hiding—but they were also perfect for spirits to hide in. Steadying herself, she reached out with her mind. . . .

They were still alone.

"Maybe she escaped, survived the month, and became an heir," Roe said hopefully. And then her expression twisted. "Or not." She was staring beyond Mayara. Taking the wad of firemoss from Mayara, she walked up to a grayish crystal. She held up the glowing moss.

Blurred from the crystal, a face peered out at them, frozen in a scream. Both of them took a step backward. *Oh no.* The woman, a stranger, had been encased in crystal. Mayara didn't know how. . . .

But she did know.

*Spirits.*

Of course spirits. They must have sped up the growth of the

crystal, trapping the woman inside. She must have died as it solidified around her.

*Everywhere we go on this nightmare island, there's more death.*

"Different second camp?" Roe asked, her voice shaking.

Mayara could only nod.

# CHAPTER FOURTEEN

It was time to forage again. They still hadn't found a second camp that felt safe enough, which made Mayara nervous, and she was developing too much of a pattern with regard to where and when she harvested coconuts and other supplies, which made her even more nervous.

After much discussion, they agreed to try foraging at the cove. Roe argued that none of the other trainees would have stayed by the deadly beach, so the spirits would have abandoned it too.

*It's logical,* Mayara thought. She just wasn't sure that spirits *were* logical. But continuing to forage in the same place was too dangerous. That much she was sure of.

"Do you think any of the others are still alive?" Roe asked.

"I hope so." At least she hadn't heard any screams lately.

*Sad that a good day means not hearing anyone die.*

She couldn't believe she was actually getting used to being here. *Not that I want this to be my new home.* Suddenly, she missed Kelo with an ache so strong that she forgot to breathe.

"Mayara? Pay attention," Roe said.

"Sorry." She yanked her mind back to the present. They were side by side at the lip of the cave, peering down at the cove. It looked just as idyllic as it had from the ship: flush with tropical fruit trees, brilliantly colored birds calling to one another, and flowers of every imaginable hue adorning the rocks. Beautiful white sand in a crescent was kissed by the clear turquoise water. It was so clear that even from here, Mayara could see the shimmer of schools of fish. "Can you tell if any spirits are watching the cove?"

Roe was silent for a moment, her forehead crinkled in concentration. "There are spirits on the ridges, but they aren't watching the cove." She pointed toward the cliffs, and Mayara sent her thoughts in that direction. It was a strange sensation, trying to "see" with her mind. The best way she could think of it was like squinting to see something in the dark or straining to hear a distant sound. Or trying to touch a wispy bit of fluff floating in the breeze. She "felt" them, between the trees and out in the waters of the cove, but she couldn't read their thoughts well enough to know whether they were paying attention to the cove. Roe was better at it.

"Dart in, grab fallen fruit, and come back," Roe ordered. "That's it. Don't waste time climbing any trees. And don't go too far. I swear the spirits get more and more agitated every day."

She'd noticed that. The spirits had taken to traveling in swarms. She felt their agitation like a continuous itch in the back of her mind. "Yeah, I think they miss killing people. They're happiest when they're slaughtering."

"Try not to make them happy."

Mayara targeted a nearby tree with three fallen coconuts. That's what they needed most urgently—more liquid. Getting to the streams was too tricky—they were both watched by water spirits. Yesterday one stream had been frozen by an ice spirit who guarded it zealously.

Ready, Mayara bent her knees. "Bird call, three chirps, if a spirit comes for me."

"And you'll do what exactly?"

"Run. Really fast."

"There's no cliff to dive off."

"Back here then. I'll hide."

"And lead them straight to where we live? And straight to me? You know, you're really bad at making plans. No offense meant."

Mayara tried not to grit her teeth. "Do you have a better idea?"

"No. I'm just pointing out it's a serious risk for a few coconuts."

"You want to starve?"

"Hey, I'm not offering solutions. I'm just pointing out problems. It's my role as lookout." And then her tone shifted. "I just . . . If you die, I'm alone. I . . . can't make it alone."

"Yes, you can. Your leg is better. You have a place to live. You know where to find food and water. But I'm not going to die. I'm going to be quick. Three coconuts. That's it. And if it works, then later we'll try again for more. Okay?"

Roe flashed a smile at her. "When did you become the optimist?"

"My family prefers to say 'reckless.'"

"Your family underestimates you."

"Let's hope the spirits do too," Mayara said. "Ready? Now." She darted out from the hole, scrambled down the hill, and scooped three fallen coconuts into her sling. She then turned to race back before—

A voice croaked, "Mayara?"

Mayara stopped. That didn't sound like a spirit. And no spirit knew her name.

"Who is it?"

Silence.

Then the voice again, cracked and thin. "Help me."

Mayara scanned the trees, and she saw a hint of movement. She pivoted, about to run, but Roe hadn't chirped any warning and Mayara didn't sense any spirits.

Glancing up at the ridges, she crept forward. And saw Palia. She was lashed against one of the trees, in the same kind of snare that Mayara had seen before—the kind that had caught

Roe when they'd first arrived. The older woman looked as if she'd aged decades more. She was caked with dirt, her hair half shorn off her head and matted with blood.

Dropping the coconuts, Mayara ran to Palia's side. Using her glass knife, she began sawing at the vines. "Are you hurt? Can you run? We'll need to run."

"Can't." Her lips were so dry and broken that they'd split and bled.

"What's injured?"

"Weak. Too weak."

Three bird chirps.

*Spirits are coming!*

Mayara sawed faster.

"They come to kill me." Palia closed her eyes. "I'd wondered when . . . they'd . . . come. So long. They didn't see me. Didn't know I was there. Or didn't care. So many days. So thirsty. Do you have water? I would like water. Before I die."

"Getting you out of here. Hang on, Palia. Stay awake."

Another three chirps.

Mayara cast her mind out—the spirits were coming down the ridge. She couldn't tell if they'd seen her, but there were at least a dozen of them, tumbling closer. If they hadn't seen her yet, they would soon.

The vines snapped, and Palia slumped forward.

"You need to try to walk," Mayara said. "I can't carry you." She helped her stand, and they hobbled toward the tunnel. "Don't use your power—that will draw them faster."

Palia stumbled, and Mayara caught her. Arms around her, she helped Palia walk-run. Her breath hissed through her teeth. Mayara didn't look back. She couldn't do anything to stop the spirits if they came. She'd have to hope. . . .

The hole wasn't far, but getting there felt like an eternity. She'd never felt so exposed. Why hadn't they been caught yet? She sent her thoughts back toward the spirits—and felt them spinning away. Their thoughts were distant to the touch.

*Roe,* she thought. *What did you do?*

"Quickly!" Roe whispered. She popped out of the hole to help Palia into it. "We have to get away from here, before they come back."

"You shouldn't have used power!" Mayara said. She thought they'd agreed on that! Run and hide. No power. Nothing to draw the spirits, not until they were ready to face them or until the month was up.

"They'd seen you. What was I supposed to do? Watch you die?" Roe helped Palia down into the hole. "Besides, I wasn't the only one using power."

*Who else is out there?* Mayara wondered. It had to be another of them, but who had survived? And why were they risking themselves by using their power? There wasn't time to discuss it. "We can't use this exit again. And we'll need to hide if they search."

They hurried as best they could through the tunnel. Holding firemoss, Roe led the way, while Mayara helped Palia stumble over the uneven ground. Safe in their cave, they shifted rocks to block the tunnel from any spirit that followed.

The three of them hid motionless and in silence, trying to keep their thoughts as quiet as possible. They heard clicking and scratching from a distance, echoing through the caves. Eventually the sound and feel of the spirits' search receded.

Mayara dug into their supplies for angel seaweed, while Roe gave Palia coconut milk. She drank, and it dribbled down her chin.

"Slowly," Roe said. "You'll make yourself sick. Little sips."

Palia obeyed.

Mayara inspected her wounds. Palia was covered in small cuts, one of which was swollen and red. Mayara applied the angel seaweed, squeezing it liberally on the infected cut. "She looks mostly dehydrated. And probably starved as well." She thought of something. "Roe, what did you mean you weren't the only one using power?"

"It was weird—there was resistance, as if the spirits were listening to someone else. Remember how it felt when we were training and Sorka would command them? It was like that."

"Someone was trying to help us? Who?" Mayara knew it wasn't herself, and Palia hadn't been in any condition to concentrate on anything. Had she? "Did you do it, Palia?"

No answer. Just a moan.

Maybe it was one of the other trainees. Someone else was alive! And close enough to see they were in danger and to help them. *We have to find whoever it is. . . . We can team up.* So far, joining together with Roe had only helped her survive. Sorka had been wrong about that. They were stronger together. If they found this other person . . .

"That was the odd thing," Roe said. "I could hear the command. Well, I couldn't hear the words directly, but I felt it through the thoughts of the spirits—their reaction to it. The other person wasn't helping us.

"She was directing the spirits to *attack*."

Mayara whipped her head around to stare at Roe. Her expression, as shadowed as it was in the cave, was serious. "Why would anyone do that?"

"I don't know. To send them away from herself maybe?"

"But that doesn't make sense. Using power draws attention. You'd be better off just hiding. Unless she'd already been spotted? But we would have felt that, right? Or heard the spirits hunting her?"

Roe had no answer.

THEY SAT SILENTLY THEN, TOO EXHAUSTED AND FRIGHTENED TO DO much else. Still, Mayara mused on what Roe had said, even as she continued to treat Palia, who had passed out. After a few hours, the older woman regained consciousness, asking for water. Holding a coconut for her, Mayara asked, "How long were you trapped?"

"Two days."

"Two days and the spirits didn't kill you?" Roe asked.

That was very unlike them. Spirits weren't known for understanding delayed gratification, especially the less intelligent ones.

"I told you—it was like they didn't know I was there," Palia said. "And I didn't do anything stupid to draw their attention." She then winced, breathing heavily, and leaned back against the cave wall with her eyes squeezed shut.

"Rest," Roe ordered.

Mayara continued to clean Palia's wounds, bandaging them with kelp to hold on wads of angel seaweed. Every time Palia woke, Roe fed her more coconut milk.

When she was well enough, she ate bits of mango that Mayara cut for her. *She looks too thin,* Mayara thought. She wondered how Palia had stayed alive, tied to a tree, for so long. The spirits should have at least come by to check their traps.

*Unless it wasn't their trap.*

But who, or what, else would set traps on Akena?

"What caught you?" Mayara asked, when Palia seemed lucid enough to talk again. "Did a spirit grow the vines, or was the trap already there, waiting for you?"

"It was a snare," Palia said. "A simple hunter's snare. I wasn't watching for anything left by a human. Just for spirits. I was going to gather fallen coconuts. I'd checked for spirits. All clear. The spirits abandoned the cove after the initial attack."

"You're sure it was left by a human?" Roe asked. "That doesn't make sense. Who would do that? And why?"

Mayara thought of the other traps she'd seen and evaded, and the trap that had caught Roe their first day on the island. Those hadn't seemed like something a spirit would do either, but she hadn't spent much time thinking about it. "So someone left traps for people, and then someone guided spirits to chase us when I rescued you. Who would do that?"

"How about someone who wants to be queen? To eliminate the competition?" Roe asked. "Remember there was another woman, other than me, who wanted to be an heir? Do you know if she survived?"

Palia frowned. "No one would want to kill heirs. Without heirs, all of Belene is vulnerable."

Mayara shook her head. "She's dead. Killed shortly after we arrived—I saw her. Besides, the first snare I found was too far from the cove. It had to have been set before we'd arrived. There's no way that anyone could have gotten ahead of me and laid it."

"The Silent Ones?" Palia suggested.

"They're bound by tradition not to interfere with the test," Roe said. "And why would they want to kill us?"

Mayara thought of the Silent Ones on the cliff as Kelo screamed. *He's not dead,* she reminded herself. *At least, I choose to believe he isn't.* "We don't know what they want." She had another thought. "What if . . . the Silent Ones might not be acting on their own," Mayara said slowly, thinking it through. She knew that Roe's family was kept as hostages so that the Families could control the queen. And she knew if Roe survived the island and became a fully trained heir, Lord Maarte couldn't touch her. She'd be too powerful. And she'd be protected by the other heirs and all the spirits they could muster. She'd be free to tell the truth. In fact, that was her plan: tell her mother everything, free her grandparents, and expose the Families. "What if it's you? What if Lord Maarte told the Silent Ones to fix the test so *you* wouldn't survive?"

He wouldn't care about other collateral. So what if more heirs died? He hadn't cared if a village's worth of people died, so long as his power and his fortress were untouched. She could easily see him sacrificing all of them to ensure Roe died.

Except that seemed like a rather complicated plan. If he wanted Roe dead, why not just kill her while she was in his fortress? And then Mayara understood.

*Because then he couldn't blame the spirits.*

If Roe died on Akena Island, he was blameless. No one was surprised when an heir died during the test.

The more she thought about it, the more plausible it seemed. He'd already refused to train her. This was just the next step.

It was the Silent Ones, guided by Lord Maarte, with the goal of killing Roe.

"Why would a lord want to kill Roe?" Palia asked.

Roe was shaking her head. "He had easier ways to kill me. Poison. An 'accident.' Plus, remember the last test? All those spirit sisters died too. The test could have been rigged long before my power was discovered."

Mayara liked her own theory better. But she wanted to explore Roe's—it passed the time, if nothing else. And it was helping distract Palia from her injuries. She was looking and sounding more alert than when they'd brought her inside. "You think the Silent Ones . . ."

"Or just one of them," Roe said. "They can't all be involved. That would mean the queen wants us dead, and that doesn't make sense. The queen, more than anyone, knows how vital heirs are."

"A rogue?" Mayara couldn't imagine any Silent One disobeying the queen. They chose their fate because it was safer than the island—why would they risk her wrath now? "But why? Lord Maarte at least has motivation."

"I don't know," Roe said. "Revenge for all they're forced to give up? Jealousy over all the heirs are allowed to keep? If they survive. It's not a fair or kind system for anyone."

The three of them fell silent, sunk into their own thoughts. Bad enough to face the spirits, but to have someone directing them? Someone with knowledge of who they were? Someone who thought like a human, who wasn't just acting on instinct like the spirits? The island suddenly felt a whole lot more dangerous. *And unfair,* Mayara thought.

*We have more enemies than we knew.*

# CHAPTER FIFTEEN

The guard had been clear: Kelo wasn't permitted to see the queen because it would add to her sorrow. So Kelo reasoned, *Perhaps I'll be allowed to see her if I ease it.*

Shutting himself in a dilapidated rented room, Kelo devoted his days to creating an art piece that would ease the queen's sorrow. It had to be beautiful, the most beautiful piece he'd ever made, fit to capture the queen's eyes, mind, and heart.

He started with one of the abalone shells he'd brought, one that Mayara had harvested on her last dive. It was shaped like a bowl and larger than both his fists. Inside were swirls of shimmering green, blue, and purple, which he smoothed and cut into geometric stylized wave-patterns to catch the light, which came together to create a perfect map of the islands of Belene. For the outside, on the mottled, bumpy shell that most considered ugly, he shaved away the imperfections and carefully carved an image of Queen Asana with her arms spread wide— the effect, he hoped, was of the queen cradling all of Belene safely in her arms.

It was the most detailed work he'd ever done, the most precise and the most unforgiving of mistakes. Once you chipped a bit of shell away, it was gone forever. He didn't want a single error. *It has to be perfect,* he thought.

He barely ate, and what he did eat, he didn't taste. He got used to a constant ache in his not-yet-healed wrist. He slept at the table he'd set up as his workstation, by a window with a view of the castle—or a view if you leaned out and looked left between two other buildings.

Then you could see a sliver of the tallest spire.

He wasn't looking up that much anyway.

When he finished, it was two o'clock in the morning, three days later. He leaned back in the rickety chair, rubbed his neck, and looked outside at the quiet street. Firemoss lamps bathed the broken mother-of-pearl walls and street in an amber glow.

He'd never made anything more beautiful.

It wasn't the kind of statement he would have said out loud. He knew it would sound like boasting. But he knew his work, and he'd never done better.

He wished he could show it to Mayara.

He had no way of knowing if she was even still alive. *I have to believe she is.* Crossing to the window, he leaned out to glimpse the sliver of a spire, a shadow against the night sky. He wanted to rush there with his creation . . . but he knew that would make him look unprofessional and unmannered. Or, more likely, crazed. Certainly no one who should be allowed near the queen.

*I'll present it at dawn.*

*Please, Mayara, stay alive a little longer.*

He tried to sleep, laying himself down on the lumpy cot. Staring up at the cracked ceiling, he listened to the sounds of the city: the murmur of voices carried on a breeze, the atonal chime of bells, the bark of a dog, other clangs and thumps and squeaks that he couldn't name. . . .

He woke when the scent of cinnamon curled into his room from the bakery downstairs. Getting up, he felt stiff, worse than when he'd slept at the table. But the art piece was finished, perched on the desk where he'd left it the night before, and just as ready. It was barely dawn, but he'd waited long enough.

Wrapping the carved shell in soft linen, Kelo scanned the room to see if there was anything else he needed to bring. There wasn't. Just himself and his masterpiece.

He'd worked feverishly for this moment, but now that it was here, he was more nervous than he'd ever been in his life. But he thought again of Mayara—when she committed to a dive, she didn't back down and she didn't hesitate. *Take the dive,* he told himself.

Leaving the inn, he nodded at the sleepy innkeeper, who ignored him. Shrugging, he then strode to the palace as if he felt full of confidence. *I am an accomplished artist, bringing my magnum opus as a gift for my queen. My work is worthy of the woman who keeps a whole nation safe. I have no space in my heart for doubt or fear.*

He crossed the blue stone bridge and joined the line of those seeking to enter the palace. At this hour, most were workers: cooks and cleaners, as well as a few courtiers carrying scrolls and books. He waited his turn, outwardly polite and patient, even though his insides churned like a whirlpool.

"State your business," the guard said.

It wasn't the same guard. This was a woman with no-nonsense eyes, a scar that obliterated her left eyebrow, and a prosthetic left leg. She had three knives strapped to her waist, and their scabbards had seen use. Kelo had the feeling that if he'd come to her with the same request as the prior guard, she wouldn't have been as kind. She would have dismissed him without a word of explanation or comfort.

"I am Kelo, master artisan and charm-maker, visiting from the island of Olaku, and I bring a gift for the queen." He held up the package with the shell. It wasn't heavy, but he kept a firm grip on it with his uninjured hand. "May I be permitted to present it to her?"

"It will be inspected for poison and given to the queen." The guard took the package and passed it to a courtier who looked too small for his uniform.

Kelo pressed again. "I would prefer to present it myself."

"If the queen wishes to buy more of your wares, you'll be contacted. Leave your name and where you can be located." Sounding bored, the guard nodded toward a moustached man who sat on a bench with an open book.

He'd guessed it had been too much to think that he'd be allowed to present his gift in person. He had to hope his work spoke for itself and that she'd want more—and want to speak to him.

Nodding his thanks to the guard, he moved to the moustached man and gave his name. All the while, he watched the young courtier carry the package with Mayara's life into the palace.

THE SUMMONS FROM THE PALACE CAME THE NEXT MORNING.

Kelo woke to a knock on his door. When he opened it, the sleepy innkeeper, now looking very awake, was bouncing from foot to foot. "You're wanted at the palace! The queen wants to see you! Why didn't you tell me you were a master artist? I'm moving your room. You'll have our best view. Our best bed!"

Kelo interrupted. "Thank you. But I should dress. I don't want to keep the queen waiting."

"Oh yes, of course, can't delay a summons, and when you return, I will have a meal prepared. Perhaps you should have breakfast on your way, so you aren't meeting the queen on an empty stomach. . . ."

He closed the door while the innkeeper was still babbling.

Kelo dressed quickly, ignoring the twinge in his wrist, and then hurried out, nodding a quick thanks to the innkeeper, who hadn't moved from the hall outside his room. He guessed it wasn't often that a guest at a cheap inn was summoned to the palace. "I'd be delighted to accept your hospitality when I return," he said as he ran down the stairs, two at a time.

"Of course!"

He strode quickly through the street, nearly at a run, and reached the palace in half the time it had taken yesterday. His heart was beating hard in his chest.

*This is it. My chance. Mayara, you'll be home soon.*

Presenting himself to the guard—yet a third soldier—he stated his name and his business. "Kelo of Olaku Island. The queen requested to see me." He pitched his voice to sound confident, as if this sort of royal summons happened to him every day. He wasn't sure he succeeded.

The same moustached man as yesterday consulted his book, then gave a nod, and the guard stepped aside. Kelo continued across the blue stone bridge into the palace, slowing as he stepped inside the grand entry chamber.

Whereas the outside of Yena was scarred by weather and wear, the inside of the palace looked exactly the way it was supposed to: sheathed in polished shell, lit by chandeliers of firemoss, and draped in sumptuous ivory-colored buntings. A broad staircase led up, and four gilded doors led away. It was absolutely gorgeous . . . and he had no idea which way he was supposed to go.

"Artist Kelo of the island of Olaku?" a voice asked briskly. He turned to see a woman in a gold tunic that mimicked the doors. Her face was smooth, as if she never laughed nor cried. "You will follow me, please. Her Majesty has a full schedule, but she insisted I make time for you." The woman sounded as if she didn't approve.

Kelo wondered if she was one of those people who believed art was frivolous, an extra to life rather than central to it. He'd never understood those kind of people. But he trailed after her obediently. *Obviously, Queen Asana can't be like that, or I wouldn't be here.* That thought gave him hope.

He was led to another chamber, just as stunning as the entryway, but much smaller in scope, with murals of glass on the walls and two chairs carved of a red-colored wood he'd never seen. The woman left him there, with instructions to wait until he was summoned.

He didn't sit. Instead he studied the artistry of the mosaic and tried to stay calm.

He heard a door open. Another, older woman entered. Unlike his smooth-faced escort, this woman had laugh lines in her cheeks and around her eyes that looked like the tracks of a sandpiper. She also wore clothes utterly unlike anything he'd ever seen an islander wear: a yellow concoction with ruffles on top of ruffles. It made her look as if she were drowning in fabric. She also wore a hat of feathers that was so garish it made his eyes hurt. She studied him openly, as if assessing an outfit she wanted to buy. "So you're the one who carved the shiny shell. You made the queen cry."

Kelo felt a flutter of worry. He'd meant to touch her heart, but he'd explicitly set out *not* to add to her sadness. Had he mis-carved? "That wasn't my intent."

The court lady snorted. "Of course it was. All art is about manipulation. Tricking someone into seeing things your way."

Offended, Kelo couldn't let that comment slide. "That's not how I'd describe it." Yes, he'd had certain goals with his carving, but it wasn't about manipulation. Art was about reaching out, connecting with another person, and giving them what you knew they needed, even if they didn't know . . .

Wait—was she right?

"Luckily for you, Queen Asana was impressed with your tricks. She'll see you now." She gestured to the door she'd come through. "Just as a reminder, you should bow, be polite, and don't say anything you'll regret later. Regret is for those who lack conviction."

Unsure if that was a warning or advice, his heart pounding harder than he'd ever felt, Kelo walked through the door to face his queen. The courtier followed behind him, closing the door. She then plopped herself onto a chair next to Queen Asana. Her ridiculously voluminous ruffles poofed up around her.

Queen Asana sat straight-backed on a thronelike chair. His carving was displayed in front of her on a table made of suka wood. It lay in a nest of black velvet.

In some ways, Queen Asana looked like a work of art too: the skirt of her dress was paneled with painted scenes of the sea, and the bodice was embroidered with countless pearls. Her hair was wrapped in intricate braids and woven with strands of both white and black pearls.

In other ways, though, she looked like she could be any woman from his village. Her cheeks were soft and lined with wrinkles. Her eyes looked weary, and her smile was as kind as Kelo's own mother's.

Kelo bowed. "Your Majesty, you honor me."

"It is I who am honored. You are the artist who made the shell portrait? Am I correct to think it is a portrait of me?"

"It is you, my queen, embracing Belene, as you do every day." He added, "And it was made with the hope of speaking with you."

Her lips pressed together, and he could sense her withdrawing. "I see."

He glanced at the court lady, who looked smug. *It's not manipulation.* "And the hope of bringing you joy. I think"—he took a risk and plunged on, thinking of Mayara diving into the cool blue sea—"you don't have enough of it in your life."

Her expression didn't change. "And you see that, without ever having met me?"

"You're our queen," he said. "You bear the burden of the world. One of the guards, when I first asked to see you, said he couldn't allow me to add to your sorrow."

"This is a curious conversation," the queen said. "I expected you to ask for my patronage. I am prepared to offer it, you know. Yet I don't think that's why you're here. Why did my guard think you would add to my sorrow?" She'd brought him here to praise his work, he knew, perhaps commission more, which should be what any artist would dream of. *But that's not my dream, not now,* he thought.

All he wanted was a return to the life he should have had, with Mayara.

"Because I have come to plead for my wife's life," Kelo said. "And he believed you wouldn't grant me that. Your Majesty, I am an artist. A charm-maker. A craftsman. I spend my days making mobiles for newborns, to keep them safe and keep them calm and make them smile. I sew bits of shell onto dresses to make brides feel beautiful and loved. I carve runes onto ships and into houses to keep the spirits at bay and give people the hope that they'll survive to see another dawn. I craft joy and hope, and I cannot do that if my joy and hope is gone."

The queen's face was unreadable.

The ruffle-wearing courtier looked oddly entertained.

Ignoring the courtier, Kelo dropped down to his knees before his queen. "Bring my wife home from the Island of Testing. Let others become heirs. Her destiny is with me. We've known it since we were children. We make each other better. We make each other whole."

For a moment there was silence, and Kelo worried his audience was over. Then the queen spoke.

"You wish me to do this because your wife is your *muse*? That is one I haven't heard." She looked even more weary than she had before, and Kelo realized he'd done exactly what the guard had feared: he'd added to her sorrow. *She's going to say no.*

He'd had so many words prepared. Fine, poetic words. He'd planned to convince her to save Mayara on behalf of true love. Before he'd hit on the idea of the shell carving, he'd planned to bring Mayara's storm-ravaged wedding dress to sway her. He stood up, feeling his face burn. *I was trying to manipulate her,* he admitted to himself. *But it was for Mayara.* And it hadn't worked. Yet. "Your city's a mess," he said bluntly.

"Excuse me?" The queen raised both eyebrows.

Perking up, the courtier said, "Ooh, that's new. I like him."

"Mother-of-pearl makes a terrible paving stone, and you can't cover a city that's exposed to wind and rain in it. It's a tradition that may have made sense at the time it began, but it can't withstand the test of time." When the queen didn't stop him, he continued. "The Island of Testing is the same way. It may have worked once, but now it's just destroying all that is good and beautiful about your people. Everyone with power lives in fear, and so do their families. But it doesn't have to be this way. You're the queen! You can change it!"

The queen looked sorrowful. "It is the way it must be."

"Why?" he asked.

"Liking him less now," the courtier said. She looked at Kelo. "You do not tell the queen how to do her job. She's the queen! She knows the extent and the limits of her power. You make pretty stuff and believe that grants you emotional and intellectual depth. Trust me—it doesn't."

The insults hit home. *I'm failing. One chance, and I'm messing it up.*

"Lady Garnah, be gentle with him," the queen admonished. "He's worried about his wife." She favored him with a sympathetic smile.

"Bah. Everyone's worried about someone," the ruffled courtier, Lady Garnah, said. "Your pain is no more important than anyone else's, young man. The queen cannot change the world to appease you. And you should know better than to ask her to."

He bowed his head. "Forgive me, Your Majesty. But if you know your people are suffering, then why don't you fix it?"

"Because the world is more complicated than that," Queen Asana said, her voice tired.

"End this audience, Your Majesty," Lady Garnah said, rising.

She patted down the ruffles of her skirt. "You don't owe him any explanation. You're queen. He's not. End of story." She turned to Kelo. "Many condolences. Much sympathy. And so forth. Please leave."

Crushed, Kelo began to retreat. "I'm sorry, Your Majesty. It truly was not my intent to add to your sorrow." *The guard was right. I failed. And I caused my queen pain.* He knew little about being queen or about the decisions she had to make every day. He didn't understand her burdens, other than to know they were there. Still, he looked to Queen Asana, hoping against hope that she'd change her mind in the last minute . . . and knowing that he had no right to believe in that hope.

"I mourn every death," Queen Asana said as he neared the door. "And if it were within my power, every spirit sister would live long, beautiful lives, with their families around them. No one should ever have to be separated from a loved one." She nodded at the carving he'd done. "I will treasure what you have made me, and hope that someday you will think better of me."

Lady Garnah sighed dramatically. "Just throw him out already."

"You are dismissed," Queen Asana said.

Kelo backed out of the room and shut the door. He then stood outside, in the beautiful chamber, and stared at the closed door as if it had answers. How had that gone so very wrong? He'd won an audience with the queen. He'd prepared what to say.

He didn't know what he had expected—a list of reasons, maybe. Facts that he could argue with. A defense of tradition. He thought the queen would say she wouldn't end the test.

He never expected her to say she *couldn't*.

QUEEN ASANA PICKED UP THE CARVED SHELL. *SUCH A BEAUTIFUL thing.* She hadn't expected it to come with a heap of guilt and a shovelful of sorrow. "That was a mistake."

"Just to clarify: do you mean inviting him or saying no?" Garnah sounded conversational, even bored, as she examined her chipped nails. Unlike most of the court, both the women and men, Lady Garnah did not have lovely, manicured nails. Hers were blackened and broken. When Asana had asked why once, Garnah had cryptically answered, *My work.*

"You don't approve?" Asana allowed an edge to creep into her voice. While she enjoyed Garnah's honesty, occasionally she also forgot who was queen here. Asana wondered if she spoke to the queen of Aratay in the same way, and if the other queen had tolerated it.

*Or did she let her come here just to be rid of her?*

"Of inviting him or saying no?" Garnah flashed her a smile. "I thought he was a delight. So much earnest need! Really, I could listen to him orate for hours. Or at least a quarter of an hour, before it grew old and I had to silence him. I do know some species of lichen that will cause temporary damage to vocal cords. Tastes terrible, though, so it's tricky to get your target to ingest it."

"Garnah." She pinned her with her gaze. Asana had mastered her no-more-nonsense look not when she became queen but before, when she became a mother. Her daughter had had strong opinions from a very young age. *I wonder if she still does.* "Enough."

"You invited me to be your adviser. Don't you want my advice?"

"You seemed to agree with me when I spoke with him," Asana said.

Garnah rolled her eyes. "I'm not going to contradict you in front of the peasantry."

"We don't call them the 'peasantry.'"

"You should. Nice ring to it. Establishes the hierarchy with no room for confusion. That was his problem—he seemed to think he could talk to you person to person, when he wasn't, in fact, talking to you at all." Garnah grew more serious. "Was he?"

"Of course he spoke to me."

"Your Majesty, let me ask you a question: If it were up to you, and if there were no other factors to consider, would you have agreed to save his wife? Would you save all of them? You know the Belenian method of training heirs is not the only one possible. As queen, you could—"

Asana cut her off. "It's tradition, and it's not within my power to change."

Leaning back, Garnah propped her feet up on the suka table that held the artist's masterpiece. "And that, my dear, is the heart of it, isn't it? You don't have the power. Not to grant that overly sincere boy his request. Not even to fix the disaster of your city streets, which, by the way, he was right about. They're a mess."

Asana ground her teeth together. Today Garnah's unrelenting bluntness grated.

Garnah continued. "And you should. You control all the spirits on Belene—there's no reason for you to bend your will to others."

*Oh, there's reason. And that reason has names: Rokalara, Mother, and Father.* "You don't understand." She glared at Garnah's feet, too close to the beautifully carved shell. That piece was everything she wished she could be: the protector of Belene. *Except I can't protect everyone.* She knew she was misdirecting her anger—she wasn't truly angry at Garnah. Or the young artist. She was angry at the Families, who kept her hands tied.

Garnah removed her feet from the table. "But I *do* understand. You aren't free." She studied the queen until Asana wanted to squirm under her gaze. Squirm and fume. At last, Garnah asked, "What do they have on you?"

All the anger drained out of her. "How . . . how did you know?" she whispered.

"Because I'm not an idiot. And I understand power. You don't have it, which means someone else does—and you don't seem happy about it, which means it's not voluntary. Tell me. We'll fix it."

"You can't 'fix' it. Not without . . ." She shook her head.

"Is it a 'what' or a 'who'?" Garnah pushed. "I can't help you unless you tell me."

There was truth in her words. *She really means it. She wants to help me. But . . . why?* "What is it *you* want?" *In other words, why should I trust you?*

The thing was, that's what Asana desperately wanted. To unburden all her pent-up truths. To have someone she could be fully honest with, to share her pain, to understand. . . . She'd never had anyone she could trust in that way. Everyone around her had ties elsewhere, families and people who depended on them, other pulls on them that had the potential to conflict with what the queen needed. But Garnah . . .

"I want to be needed." Garnah let out a little laugh. "Isn't that amusing? Me, who doesn't value anyone else, likes being essential. I learned that about myself with Queen Daleina of Aratay. I don't particularly care who lives or dies, so long as I play a vital role."

There was truth in her words. *Maybe she isn't trustworthy, not in the traditional sense. But I'm sick of "tradition."*

Taking a deep breath, Asana said, "They took my family. On the day I was crowned, the Families kidnapped my parents, my husband, and my daughter and took them 'under their protection.' If I try to free them or even try to see them . . . They had my husband murdered to prove their power and ensure my obedience, and they hold my other loved ones hostage."

Garnah sat up straight, her eyes bright. "Where are they being held?"

"I don't know." Asana spread her hands. "I'm not even allowed to know which Family holds them or which island they're on."

"Then you need to find out."

Asana shook her head. "Exactly what are you proposing?"

"We need to change the balance of power in Belene, and

to do that, we need to free your family. To do *that*, we need to determine where they are."

"If I try to find—"

"Not you. Me."

"But everyone knows you're my adviser. Any investigation you conduct will be traced back to me. I cannot take that risk." As tempting as it was.

She'd tried before, though. And had paid the price. Since then, she had been docile, obeying the Families, chafing under their rule, hating them.

"Then we employ someone who isn't known in the palace. Someone so earnest that no one will suspect him. Someone who will swear absolute obedience to you, if he knew his actions would lead to saving his beloved's life."

Asana felt a fluttering inside her as she realized what Garnah was saying. It felt an awful lot like hope. She picked up the artist's masterpiece. "I can offer him a position as royal artist," she mused. "He'd have permission then to roam through the palace. Perhaps I commission portraits of influential members of the ruling Families. They wouldn't say no to that, not with their egos. The palace could use a portrait gallery, don't you think?"

Smiling placidly, Garnah nodded. "It would greatly enhance the place."

"Summon him back," Asana said. "You will meet with him alone, so that his connection to me is minimized. Tell him what he needs to know. Realize, though, once he knows the truth about what the Families have done to my loved ones . . . if he doesn't swear to cooperate, you will need to kill him."

"Obviously." Garnah was unperturbed by the idea of killing an innocent man. "I told you the truth. I don't care who lives or dies, so long as I am useful."

"Then go and be useful," Asana ordered. She then leaned back in her thronelike chair, cradled the shell carving against her breasts, and thought of her daughter.

# CHAPTER SIXTEEN

Mayara thought dismantling the snares all over the island was a terrible idea.

"But we can't leave them out there," Roe protested. "They could catch someone else, like they caught Palia. And like they caught me, remember?" The three of them were holed up in the cave, which was now quite cramped. Ever since returning with Palia, they'd been careful to leave only for absolute essentials—quick strikes for food and water and to relieve themselves.

*She's stir-crazy,* Mayara thought. *That's why she's making reckless suggestions.*

"We know now to watch out for traps around trees," Mayara said as she shifted, trying to find a better position between the coconut shells. "That's good enough. We can simply avoid them."

"But we shouldn't have to," Roe said. "They shouldn't be there at all. It's unfair, and it's wrong. All we're supposed to be worrying about is the spirits, not . . . sabotage!"

"I *am* worried about the spirits," Mayara said. "It's why I'm not interested in the traps. It's unnecessary time out in the open."

"It's necessary if it saves a life." Roe addressed Palia: "You wouldn't have suffered if we'd destroyed the snares when we first found them. Tell Mayara you wish we'd removed the snares."

Palia still looked terrible, her cheeks sunken and her lips cracked. They'd used up the majority of the angel seaweed on her many cuts, most of which she'd gotten before the snare. She'd been on the run ever since they'd landed on the island, and she hadn't been as lucky as Mayara and Roe. "It would have been nice not to be caught."

"See? I'll do it," Roe said. "We know where they are—it'll be quick."

"Roe, think for a minute, please! We've only stayed alive so far because we've been smart and careful." She kept her voice low even though she wanted to shout. "This is reckless! We don't even know that anyone else is still alive!"

"I said if I got another chance to help someone, I wouldn't hesitate," Roe reminded her. "And you promised you wouldn't stop me. Mayara, I couldn't do anything when the Families took us away from my mother, and I couldn't help my father when they took him away from me. I *can* do something to save someone here—someone who might have a family they want to see again."

She was so earnest that Mayara knew she wasn't going to talk her out of it. Mayara glared at Roe, then threw her hands up in surrender. "Fine. But if we're going to do this, we're going to do it as safely as possible. So that means you can't be the one to go out there. Your leg isn't perfect yet. I can run faster. Besides, you're better at sensing spirits anyway. You watch for them. Give three bird chirps if the spirits notice me, and I'll bolt for the nearest cave."

Thanks to their explorations, they knew the island was like a beehive of stone and bone beneath the surface. The coconut grove was near at least three openings. If Mayara was quick enough, she should be able to outrun the spirits, hide in the tunnels, and return via underground routes. Provided there weren't any spirits in the caves, of course.

"I'll be your lookout," Roe promised. "I won't let the spirits catch you."

"Just because I'm agreeing to this doesn't mean it's not a terrible idea."

"I need this," Roe said. "I can't just hide here any longer. It's the same reason why I forced Lord Maarte to send me here— yes, I may have been 'safer' as his hostage, but at some point choosing to be safe can destroy your soul."

*Maybe that's true,* Mayara thought. *But this better not get us all killed.*

As the sun dipped below the horizon, Mayara crawled out of their cave and scrambled over the rocky shore. The sky was an array of colors: clouds stained rose and deep orange; the sea was black with blue, amber, and rose glints. It crashed against the rocks in rhythm. Out above the reef, water spirits were dancing. Three of them, vaguely human-shaped with bodies made of water, pirouetted on the waves. Their watery arms stretched and waved like grass in the wind. Every once in a while, they'd seem to merge, swirling together, and then they'd break apart.

*Ugh, this is a terrible idea.*

But Roe hadn't given her much choice. *She has too much of a selfless streak in her. I just want to go home; she still thinks she can save the world.*

Mayara kept low and to the shadows. They were far enough out and so absorbed in their dance that they shouldn't spot her, but she wasn't going to take that chance.

Creeping up to the coconut grove, she unearthed the first snare, half buried in the sand. Using her glass-shard knife, she sliced through the vines, dismantling the trap, and then she moved on to the next one. *How did anyone have time to set so many?* she wondered. *And why would they do it?* There were traps on nearly every other tree. She worked as quickly as she could, relying on Roe to be her lookout.

She was halfway through when she heard three bird chirps.

She did a quick calculation: the closest bolt hole was on the other side of the coconut trees, behind a clump of suka berry bushes. Dropping the vine she was cutting, Mayara ran. She cast her mind out—it was the three spirits who'd been dancing on the waves. Drawing a stream of seawater behind them, they were speeding toward the land. As Mayara ran, they slashed through the sand.

And then, up ahead, near the mouth of the cave, she saw movement.

*Another spirit!*

She tried to feel with her thoughts and met only emptiness. *Nothing's there.*

It wasn't a spirit, she realized. A spirit sister? Or a Silent One? Mayara didn't see the telltale gray robes or white mask. Instead she saw a wave of bright hair as the woman jumped back into the hole. She didn't remember any of the other spirit sisters having red-streaked hair.

*Who is she? How did she get here?*

*And why is she fleeing from me?*

*Did she set the snares?*

Maybe the stranger had alerted the three spirits as well.

Mayara chased after her. She reached the hole as the spirits' wave crashed behind her. She didn't slow—she jumped in and kept running. Pulling out a clump of firemoss, she squeezed it until it shed enough light to see the rocks directly in front of her.

Ahead of her, in the darkness, she heard the footfalls of the other woman. Behind her, she heard the spirits—they'd followed her into the cave. They shrieked to one another in wordless screams. She hoped they couldn't see in the dark. She held the firemoss close to her chest, ready to snuff out its light if they drew too close.

Moving as quickly as she dared, she kept trailing the stranger, hoping that the other woman had a plan for escape.

At the same time, she needed to make sure the spirits weren't led back to Roe and Palia.

Ahead she saw the glow of firemoss light—*I know this place!* It was the cavern with the underground lake. She saw the silhouette of the woman just before she dived into the water.

*Brilliant!* she thought.

Without hesitating, Mayara dived in after her, plunging herself into liquid darkness. She felt the cool water close around her as she propelled herself deeper.

It was dark, and though her eyes were open, she saw only murky grayness. She hoped she'd been fast enough and the spirits hadn't seen them dive.

As the swimmer went deeper, Mayara followed, trusting the other woman knew where she was going. Mayara didn't know if this pool was endlessly deep or if it led anywhere. But she knew she couldn't return to the surface, not if she wanted to live. She figured the woman wasn't suicidal, so she pressed on.

The water had a greenish glow to it, as if there was another light source ahead. With it, she could see the faint outline of the other swimmer, as well as feel the movement of the water. She kept her own movements as smooth as possible so that the other woman wouldn't sense her.

The woman began swimming up—there must be another cave, deeper but with air. Mayara doubted the stranger could hold her breath for as long as an oyster diver could. She waited just a bit until the woman surfaced and started moving away again. Mayara then followed, and her head soon popped out of the water.

She was in another cave with a ceiling covered in firemoss. It glowed as if the stars had been stuck between the stalactites. Gathering herself, she saw that the other woman was swimming for the cave's shore. Mayara swam faster, reaching the shore first, scrambling onto the rocks, and drawing her glass knife.

The woman pulled herself out of the water and lay on the shore panting. She was mostly in shadows, and it was difficult to see her face. Her ribs were visible, pressing against her skin as she panted. "If you're going to kill me with that, please wait until I've regained my breath."

"I'm not going to kill you—not yet anyway," Mayara said, hoping her voice belied her revulsion at the idea of killing another. With more conviction, she asked, "Why are you trying to kill us?" She expected the other woman to deny it.

But the woman didn't. Instead, she said, "It was nothing personal."

"My death is extremely personal." Mayara gripped her knife, but the other woman didn't make any move to go for a weapon. Mayara wasn't sure what she'd do if the woman did. She'd never even punched anyone, much less used a knife against another person.

Glancing around, she saw that the other woman had set up a camp here. Or more accurately, a home. There were driftwood shelves that held rows of coconuts, an array of palm fronds in one corner, a pile of shells in another. She had a bed—a bed!—of leaves and even a stack of clothes. How long had she been here? And how had she survived the spirits? Mayara had thought she and Roe had done well with their little hole in the sea cliff, but this seemed . . . permanent. "Who are you? What do you want? Why did you set those traps?"

The other woman hadn't moved. "My name is Lanei."

"Why are you here? What do you want?"

Lanei didn't answer her. Instead she said, "You're lucky those spirits didn't follow us here. If they'd found this cave, we'd both be dead."

"Then I'd say you're just as lucky. But I'm not sure you're actually all that worried about the spirits."

Lanei just lay there.

Mayara pressed harder. "Your traps nearly killed my friends.

We're supposed to be surviving the spirits, not each other. Why would you do this?"

"For the greater good," Lanei said simply.

"No."

"No? Just 'no'?"

"You don't murder innocent people for 'good.' Try again."

"Then I did it for all the women and girls who wake up one morning and feel the spirits dancing on the waves and hear their thoughts and know if they tell anyone, horrors will befall them. I set the traps to end the test for all those future spirit sisters."

"Still not a good excuse for murder," Mayara said. "You'd better start making sense, or I will call those spirits and tell them where you are."

"Then they'll find you too," Lanei said, shrugging, and propped herself up to sitting, and for the first time, Mayara got a good look at her. She had bronze, sun-beaten skin and black hair with fire-red streaks. She was wearing a tunic made of a black leathery hide that didn't look like any animal Mayara had ever seen. Could it be a spirit hide? She was barefoot, and her feet were cracked and calloused. Her hair had been chopped just above her shoulders and was matted. She was thin, only muscles and bones, with the look of someone who never had enough food.

"How long have you been here?"

Lanei shrugged again. "I lost count of days. A week, a year, forever? Sometimes I think I have always been here."

Mayara thought of the snares near her and Roe's cave. Her first reaction had been to think they'd been laid a while ago, before their group of spirit sisters came to the island. She hadn't imagined that the person who set them was still on Akena. "How did you get here?"

Lanei pried herself off the ground and stood.

Crouching, Mayara gripped her knife tighter, but Lanei made no move toward her. Instead she crossed the cave and plucked a mango off a pile. Sitting on a rock loosely shaped like a chair, she began peeling its skin with a sharpened sliver of stone. "Want a slice?" Lanei offered.

Mayara didn't lower her knife. "Are you a Silent One?"

Lanei let out a humorless laugh. "Do I look or sound like one of those monsters? No, I'm just like you. Or I was."

"You can't be," Mayara said. "The last group came a full year ago! How could you have survived here for that long? And why? The Silent Ones should have taken you home."

"Like they took the others home? Oh, wait, they didn't, because the others died."

Mayara eyed the water. She knew the way back, if she had to flee. She couldn't be sure the spirits weren't still there, searching for them. "Did you kill them?"

"I haven't killed anyone."

"Your snares . . ."

"Failed. I spent months laying them, but you set free the only two people they caught. So you can stop waving that . . . is that supposed to be a knife? You can stop waving it around because I've never successfully murdered anyone," she said with a tinge of bitterness.

"Most people would consider that a good thing."

"When the Silent Ones came with an heir at the end of the month, I was ready to leave. I was the only one who had survived, and I was about to present myself. But then I heard her talking: the heir, saying to the Silent Ones that the queen would have to end the tests if there were no new heirs. She'd have to find a different way. A less cruel way. And I knew I couldn't show myself. If I did, the tests would never end. And others would have to go through what we went through. But then your group arrived. And I knew one failed test hadn't been enough. Everyone needed to die again. *Then* the queen would have to end this! If Belene has no more new heirs, she has to find another way to train spirit sisters. I thought if no one survived for a second time, it would be considered too costly to continue the tests. These deaths, *your* deaths, could put an end to all future deaths on this forsaken island."

"So you decided to help the spirits murder us? *That* was your solution?"

"Sacrifice! Not murder! Your deaths would have served the greater good. It's what we've always been told anyway, right? Believe me, this was not something I did lightly."

"And I thought *I* had bad ideas." Mayara tried to keep her tone light, but she didn't release her grip on the glass knife. Lanei had not only set snares, but she'd set an overwhelming number of them, nearly every other tree. That wasn't the sign of someone who was thinking rationally. "Here's a better idea: How about we work together to survive the month, and *then* find a way to end the tests?"

Lanei shook her head sadly. "It will never work. If any of you last the month, the queen will think the test is fine. It will continue."

A thought hit Mayara then. "Maybe there's another way to convince the queen." *Other than our gory deaths.* "I'd like to introduce you to one of my friends. Her name's Roe, and she's the queen's daughter."

"What? That makes no sense. She sent her own daughter to be tested? Our queen is more depraved than I could have imagined—"

Mayara interrupted. "She doesn't know her daughter is here. This island isn't the only place our traditions aren't what they seem. And once Roe survives the month, she'll have the queen's ear. She can talk with her mother—heir to queen—and convince her to end the tests."

Lanei shook her head. "I wish I could have faith it would work. . . ."

"Can you be certain your idea will work? It didn't last time. So come meet her," Mayara said. *Meet the people you're trying to murder.* If she saw them face-to-face, talked with them, then maybe it wouldn't be so easy to think of them as disposable.

And if Roe could convince Lanei there was another way, they could all work together to survive this place.

Lanei looked as if she wanted to refuse.

"At least talk with her," Mayara pleaded. "If we can't convince you our way is possible, then you can go back to trying to kill us."

She added silently, *And we'll stop you.*

THEY MET IN THE CAVE WITH THE LAKE, FIRST ENSURING THERE WERE no spirits nearby. Mayara drew the line at bringing Lanei to their home cave. It would have made it far too easy for Lanei to summon spirits to attack them while they slept. Perched on a rock, Mayara listened while Lanei explained her vision to Roe and Palia.

"It has to end!" Lanei declared.

*She's passionate,* Mayara thought. *You have to give her that.*

"Far too many women have died," Lanei said. "And too many others live in fear of exposing their power, when they could be using it to keep the islands safe!"

"You're not the first person to have thought that," Palia said. She was looking a little better, Mayara thought. Not *well,* exactly, but out of immediate danger. "Every family with a girl who shows power feels that way."

"Exactly why extreme measures are necessary! Everyone has accepted this 'tradition' for far too long, despite knowing it's wrong. We need to remove all benefit from it and expose it for the horror it is. Force the queen to admit that a change must be made."

"So you've planned a dramatic murder-suicide?" Roe's tone was cheerful, as if they were discussing the weather, and Mayara admired how completely she rejected Lanei's speech with a single perky question. She was obviously not persuaded by Lanei's passion.

"I'll kill as many as it takes, until no one is sent to die anymore."

"How noble of you." Roe turned to Mayara and said conversationally, "Just so we're clear, if she calls to the spirits to end it all now, we'll push her into the lake, right?"

"Or hit her with a large rock," Mayara agreed. She wasn't able to match Roe's cheerful tone. Truthfully, this entire conversation unnerved her. She'd never met anyone who talked so eagerly about murder. It made her skin crawl.

Palia held up her hand. "No threats. She came to us to talk, didn't she? Lanei is right—too many of us have had to live in fear, both for ourselves and our loved ones."

"But her methods!" Roe burst out. "You can't seriously be listening to this?"

"Don't you want the tests to end?" Palia countered.

"Of course!" Roe said. "But this isn't the way! If you wanted the heirs to think the test failed, you could have just brought all of us down to the caves and hidden us. Make them think we all died. Instead of trying to kill us!"

"I couldn't have hidden all of you," Lanei said. "That never would have worked."

"So your solution was to let people die slowly and horrifically from starvation or dehydration if they weren't found, tortured, and killed by spirits? That's cruel!"

"How do you propose to change the world?" Lanei challenged. "You want to ask your mommy nicely to alter hundreds of years of tradition? She's been so badly suckered in by the myth of the Deepest Blue—believing the worst problems of Belene lie out in the ocean, when they're all here on our shores."

But that was the thing: Mayara had never wanted to change the world. She just wanted to survive long enough to return to Kelo. As she saw it, there were only two outcomes to this test: win (and leave this nightmare) or lose (and die). Mayara didn't like the idea of losing. In fact, she was adamantly opposed to it. And Lanei was just as adamantly opposed to any of them winning.

Roe and Lanei began arguing, with Roe saying killing the

innocent was never a solution to anything, and Lanei saying she was merely hastening the inevitable.

"Our deaths are not inevitable," Roe said. "*You* didn't die yet. Why do you think we're doomed? We survived this long. Admittedly, it hasn't been pleasant, and I would trade my right arm for a bath with soap, but day by day, we're surviving. And maybe others are too."

Palia chimed in. "How many others are left?"

"Besides you three?" Lanei said. "I don't know."

"Then there could be others surviving too!" Roe said.

"So what if there are? What happens next? You all go out and fight for the queen? How long will you survive that?" Lanei asked. "Do you know how few heirs ever make it past thirty? Surviving here isn't a guarantee to a long life. Heirs are lost in every wild spirit storm. They're lost in storms we don't even know about that never make it to shore. The queen uses those losses as an excuse for the atrocities of the test—because the battle after is so tough, it can only be fought by the best. But why not just train *all* of us to fight? Select a few to be actual successors, but leave the rest of us alive to defend our homes. No more dying on Akena. No more Silent Ones. All of us trained to fight side by side."

Palia looked impressed. "You have plans."

"Yeah, murderous plans!" Roe said.

Lanei smiled. "Think how effective it will be when Queen Asana learns that her adherence to tradition has resulted in the death of her daughter. She *will* cancel the test. Hundreds will be saved, and the world will change!"

*And this conversation just took a turn for the worse,* Mayara thought.

Gripping her glass knife, Roe jumped to her feet.

"Wait," Palia said. "We all want the same thing here!"

"I really don't think we do," Roe said, eyeing Lanei.

"Palia's right," Mayara said. "Sort of. We want the test to

end, don't we? But we also don't want to die if it can possibly be avoided. Can we all agree on that much?"

Roe didn't lower her knife as she nodded. Lanei was still smiling creepily, but she also nodded. She seemed unnaturally calm, as if she thought she had control of the situation. On a hunch, Mayara reached out with her mind, scanning the nearby tunnels for spirits, but she felt nothing. So far, they were safe. *Just a nice, safe, calm conversation about our own murders.*

"Future generations should not have to live like this," Palia said. "Our daughters . . . shouldn't have to fear their future. Lanei's goals are worthy."

Lanei beamed at her as if the older woman were a child who had remembered her manners. "You have to ask yourself: What would you give to end the tests? How far would you go to save those you love? Those are the questions you need to ask. I'd give my life. And yours."

"The thing is: my life isn't yours to give," Mayara said.

"Right. And besides that, how do you know for certain our deaths will end the tests?" Roe asked. "They didn't stop after all the spirit sisters died last time. Why should it be any different now? I have a much better chance of convincing my mother alive than dead! Everything she does, she does to keep me safe! If I survive the month and become an heir, I can talk to her. Persuade her."

The three of them continued to argue, but those words echoed inside Mayara. Mayara thought of Kelo and how he'd persuaded her to try to escape from the Silent Ones. *I'm asking you to pick a third choice,* he'd said. "A third choice," she said out loud.

The others stopped.

"What was that?" Roe asked.

"We need a third choice. We're talking as if the choice is survive the test or die. Win or lose. What if there's a third choice?" Her heart began to beat faster. This felt right. "What if we just don't play?"

"Cryptic," Lanei said. "Go on."

"You say your mother would never do anything to endanger you, right?" Mayara asked Roe. "That's the whole reason your family was taken. As collateral against her good behavior. A way to control her. So if she found out you were on the island . . ."

"She'd stop the test," Roe said. "Yes, but there's no way to get word to her from here. Believe me, I tried for years to reach her from Neran Stronghold—you know, *before* we were imprisoned on a remote island guarded by Silent Ones and plagued by bloodthirsty spirits—and it was impossible then from there. It's more impossible now from here."

"Then we escape," Mayara pushed. She was aware that wasn't an easy thing to do, but neither was surviving here, right? "We leave the island, we find the queen, and we tell her that she either stops the test right now and saves whoever is left, or her daughter will risk death fulfilling a tradition that should have been abolished years ago."

"No one has ever escaped the island," Palia said.

"No one has ever survived the island for more than a year," Mayara pointed out. "No one has ever stayed here voluntarily, gotten to know its caves and tunnels, and stayed hidden from not just the spirits, but also the Silent Ones. No one . . . until her."

All of them looked at Lanei.

"But the spirits—" Palia began.

"The spirits aren't our real enemy," Mayara said. "It's the Silent Ones who are keeping us here. Lanei, you know the secrets to staying out of their sight. And if we can stay out of their sight, we can escape."

"They're watching all the time," Roe objected.

Lanei looked thoughtful. "They aren't watching as much as you think. The Silent Ones are, almost by definition, afraid to risk themselves. That's why they opted to renounce their former lives instead of choosing the test in the first place. So they don't set foot on Akena. They watch from afar, on islands just beyond the reef, through the eyes of the spirits. To survive, I left evidence that I'd died, and then I made sure no spirit ever saw me."

Mayara didn't want to ask what that "evidence" was.

"So we just have to make sure spirits don't see us," Roe said, beginning to smile. "And then what? Swim to my mother's palace and knock on the door?"

"Beyond the reef, the spirits aren't under the command to kill us," Mayara said, warming to her idea. "We use them to travel to the capital, and then yes, we knock on the door of the palace, say who you are, and ask to see the queen. She won't refuse to see you."

Roe blinked at her. "She won't. You're right. That . . . actually sounds like a plan."

"And no one else dies, either now or in the future." Mayara looked at Lanei. "Well?"

Lanei was quiet for a moment. "A third choice, huh?"

They all fell silent, considering it, sensing all the spirits swarming over the island and outside of the caves, and trying to figure out how to get past them.

Because if they could, there was a chance to end this once and for all.

# CHAPTER SEVENTEEN

"A third choice," Kelo said. "That's what Her Majesty is looking for. The Families offered her either obey or her loved ones suffer. But she needs a third choice."

He was still trying to wrap his mind around the fact that he was back in the palace, with the queen's personal adviser, Lady Garnah, in a room inlaid with more turquoise than he'd ever seen, listening to secrets that he wished he didn't know. Kelo had received the summons while he was politely informing the innkeeper that he'd be leaving. The innkeeper had been crushed to hear his customer wasn't about to be showered with riches and then elated when a slightly harried courtier had arrived to insist Kelo's business at the palace wasn't finished.

"Exactly, a third choice." Lady Garnah looked as if she wished to pat him on the head like a well-behaved dog. "Smart boy. She needs her power back."

"You mean, she needs her family back."

Lady Garnah waved her hand airily. "Same thing."

"And once she has them back, she'll end the tests?" Kelo asked.

"Yes—permanently. There are other ways to train heirs." She said it so easily, as if she weren't proposing upending generations of tradition, as if everything she'd told Kelo wasn't shocking.

Kelo felt as though his view of the world had been dropped into a mixing bowl and stirred. He, like all islanders, had regarded the queen as the source of both ultimate protection and ultimate power. To learn she'd been hamstrung by the Families . . . "It's not right, what they've done and what they're doing."

"Agreed." Lady Garnah was watching him closely, as if he were a fascinating new species of bug that she'd been proud to find.

"But I don't understand why you're telling *me* this," Kelo said. "I'm a simple charm-maker. How can I possibly help you with Families and heirs?" He'd never expected to encounter any of this. Certainly never intended to become wrapped up in politics. He just wanted to make his art in his studio and see his new wife when she came home from a day of oyster diving.

Lady Garnah rolled her eyes. "Really, master artisan? You're claiming you're too lowly to do what needs to be done to save your wife? After coming all this way? Admit that you're a coward and go home alone, then."

"I'm not a coward! Tell me what I need to do, and I'll do it."

"The queen can't investigate the whereabouts of her family," Lady Garnah said. "If they think she's involved, her family will suffer. You, however, are an unknown. You can access the Families. You are hereby commissioned by Her Majesty, blah blah blah, whatever official language you need to hear, to create portraits of the most influential people on the islands. You'll start with the members of the Families who work in the palace, and once we know which stronghold to visit, you'll continue your work there until you've found the queen's parents and daughter."

He considered that. It was clever. And doable. Portraits were within his skill set, even with a broken wrist. It would be easier than carving. "I'll have hours alone with them if they pose for me. But how can I possibly convince them to tell me where the queen's family is?" It wasn't as if it would come up in casual conversation. Often portrait conversations became deep, as the person unfolded more of their personal and emotional life than they intended. But still, he doubted they'd include a confession of kidnapping the queen's family. That seemed beyond the normal range of even the most intimate conversation.

"They'll be parched after posing for you for so long," Garnah said. "You'll give them a drink. It will . . . include an extra flavor that will relax them. You'll be able to ask them whatever you want after they drink it."

"There's such a 'flavor'?" Kelo had heard about people who could create potions and powders that could confuse the mind and warp the body. He hadn't expected to find one so close to the queen. "Are you a poison-maker?"

"I know a few herbs," Garnah said with a smile. "You just do your art, ease their thirst, and ask the question. A simple task."

"Won't they remember what they told me?" Kelo said.

"You let me worry about that. Will you help your queen? And by doing so, help your wife?"

The choice was clear. He didn't even have to consider what would happen if he refused. He didn't want to refuse. "Of course, Lady Garnah. When can I begin?"

Garnah kept smiling, all her many laugh lines crinkling, yet it wasn't a joyful expression. It was, he thought, the kind of smile you'd find on a skeleton, as if the laughter was at something you couldn't comprehend. It made the hairs on the back of his neck stand up. He wondered what he had gotten himself into, but like Mayara when she dived, he didn't second-guess his decision. "Today."

KELO CHOSE CHARCOALS TO SKETCH WITH. HE LAID THEM OUT IN front of him and tested each pencil until he found one that smeared nicely across the parchment. *Lucky the spirits broke my left wrist, not my right,* he thought. And then felt absurd for thinking that any of this was "lucky." He was merely trying to make the best of a bad situation—and trying not to feel so terribly out of his depth.

"You know, it doesn't matter what the portraits look like," Lady Garnah said. She'd come with him to prepare her "flavored" drink. Once it was ready, she'd remove herself from the room, and it would be up to Kelo to placate the lord or lady, create a portrait, and coax information out of them. While Kelo prepared, Garnah was laying out an array of salt-laden snacks that she'd said would encourage the models to sample the beverages.

"It matters to me," Kelo said.

"It shouldn't. You should reexamine your priorities."

"If the portraits are bad, then no one will want them done. And then this will fail. Unless you think we'll be lucky and the very first model will be the one with the information we need?"

Garnah added to a pitcher a pinch of powder from a vial she'd kept in one of the many pockets of her dress. It sparkled as it dissolved. Kelo was trying not think about what else was in the other pockets. He'd heard stories about poison-makers—none of them turned out well. "Have it your way. I'm happy to hear it's not just about your 'artistic integrity.'"

"That's important too," Kelo said. "If I betray my art, I betray my soul."

"You really spew a lot of bullshit for one so handsome."

He bristled, but he pushed down the feeling and said, "Someone like you wouldn't understand about integrity." He tried not to wince visibly at his own words. He'd never thought of himself as someone who would say anything that pretentious, but Garnah was exquisitely unsettling. It made him want to prove he was different.

"There is *no* one like me," Garnah said with a tinkling laugh. "But there are plenty like you. Earnest young men and women who think they'll never compromise their ideals because they've never been in a situation where they've had to.

The queen was like that. My son was like you too. So above everyone. Until it was time to make the difficult choices. And then . . . he made me proud."

"Just because you're jaded and bitter—"

"There isn't a shred of jaded bitterness in me. I am sunshine and delight. Especially now that we have a purpose. Are you ready?"

He'd positioned his stool and the model's stool so that the angle of light from the window would be perfect. He had his easel and all his supplies. He had his own water to drink from, so he wouldn't be expected to share with the model. And he was nervous.

*Terrified,* he admitted. So much rode on this.

A knock sounded on the door.

"I will be on the other side of that door," Garnah said, pointing to a smaller door that led to a closet full of various instruments. He'd been positioned in one of the palace's music rooms. "If anything goes wrong, simply shout for me."

That was *not* reassuring. "What do you expect to go wrong?"

"Occasionally people have an adverse effect to the 'flavor.'"

That was alarming and sounded like something that should have been mentioned sooner. "What kind of 'adverse effect'?" But Lady Garnah had already swept through the door and closed it behind her with a click.

He told himself not to worry, smoothed his tunic, and then crossed to open the main door to the room. Flanked by two servants, a woman in silver-fish-scale pants marched in. "Are you the artist?" the woman demanded. "I was told there would be no charge."

Kelo bowed, unsure of the exact protocol with ladies of the court. "Welcome. You were told correctly. Her Majesty has issued a request to create a portrait gallery in the palace with images of the most important people in Belene. It will be paid for by the royal treasury."

"The most important people in Belene, you say? Do you know who I am?"

His throat felt as if it were stuck. He hadn't thought to ask who he'd be interrogating. He felt like the worst intelligence gatherer in history. *Please don't let me fail so soon.* "I'm sorry, my lady, but I was only told where to go, not whom I would have the honor of depicting." He tried adding a bit of flattery. "Truth be told, I am relieved to see my first subject is someone of elegance and beauty. It will make my task simpler."

She snorted, but seemed pleased. "You will have more of a challenge with some of my peers. Very well. Let's begin. I am Lady Biliarn of the Family Culo. You will do to concentrate efforts on my nose. I'm told it's my finest feature."

"It's the pairing of your nose with your cheekbones," Kelo said promptly. And honestly. Lady Biliarn *was* a striking woman. *Striking not unlike a venomous snake, but still striking.* "The way your face catches the light. The angles are perfect."

To his surprise, Lady Biliarn laughed. "I have been complimented on many things in my years, but never on my angles. I am not displeased." She positioned herself on the stool he'd provided and tilted her face up to catch the light.

"This may take a while," he cautioned. "I want to be sure I do you justice."

"I will clear my schedule." She gave a nod toward one of her servants and barked, "Clear my schedule. Give polite rejections to the people I like and aloof ones to those I don't." To Kelo, she asked, "One hour?"

"That should do," Kelo said, then hesitated. "You can dismiss both your servants, if you have things you'd prefer they accomplish while you are occupied. I have refreshments already here, as you can see, and can tend to your needs."

To his relief, she dismissed both servants with a litany of instructions, and then resumed her position on the stool. He began to sketch.

She really did have nice cheekbones, he thought. He worked on them first, catching the angle. Soon, he lost himself in the work.

"I have not had my portrait done since I was a girl," Lady Biliarn mused, breaking the silence.

He opened his mouth to ask her not to speak—it made it difficult to capture the line of her neck—but then remembered she was supposed to be talking. He'd gotten so caught up in his task that he'd forgotten his purpose. "I'm sorry. I am making you sit for too long. Would you like a break?" Standing, he felt stiffness in his own legs. How long had he made her hold still? How much time was left in the hour? He scurried to the refreshments table and reached for the pitcher to pour her a glass of Garnah's beverage.

"I'm not thirsty, but is that goat cheese?"

"Infused with . . ." He had no idea what was in the cheese. "Herbs?" He composed a plate for her, adding salted nuts, salted crackers, and salted dried figs, and then carried it to her. "You mentioned having your portrait done before. Was it for a special occasion?"

"A coronation. Not of Queen Asana. This was before her." She nibbled on the nuts and figs as Kelo returned to his stool. He wondered what he'd do if she wasn't thirsty before the hour was up. "The prior queen was originally from our island, and so I was given the honor of crowning her, after she emerged from the grove. She had to be cleaned up quite a bit before her portrait. Bloody work, being crowned. The artist was only too happy to paint me while we waited for her to be dressed."

He wondered if he could get her to talk without the drink. She seemed to want to chat.

She ran her tongue over her teeth. "A bit too salty, isn't that?" She looked with distaste at the cheese, then sniffed her fingertips. "And perhaps a bit off."

He sprang up. "Let me get you something to drink—"

But before he could reach the table, Lady Biliarn slipped

off her stool. She landed in a heap on the floor and began to twitch.

He ran to her. "Someone, help! Help!" he cried.

The closet door burst open. "Shush, you ridiculous man." Lady Garnah hurried across the room. "Stand back and no more noise."

"But she—"

"Appears to be having an allergic reaction to the cheese, poor dear."

"How do you know—"

"Because she just *appears* to be. I laced the food with terracet powder, in case our targets didn't get thirsty. Incidentally, what took you so long? I was bored in there. I detest being bored."

"I'm sorry," he said automatically. "Are you sure we shouldn't call for a healer?"

Garnah had pinned Lady Biliarn down with a knee to her chest. She pried open Lady Biliarn's eyelids and peered at them. Lady Biliarn continued to twitch. "I *am* a healer. Of sorts. Hold her legs steady."

"Do you know how to help her?"

"She's supposed to be helping *us*, remember?"

"Well, she's not doing that right now."

Lady Garnah gave him a quelling look and then pulled out a vial and let a drop fall into Lady Biliarn's mouth. The twitching slowed. Lady Biliarn's breathing became more steady. In a broken whisper, she said, "What have you done to me?"

"Poisoned you," Lady Garnah said matter-of-factly. "You've had one drop of antidote." She wiggled the vial in the air. "If you tell me what I need to know, you may have the rest. If not, the one drop will wear off, you'll be in excruciating pain, and then you'll die in your own excrement. It will look like an allergic reaction to—oh dear, is that anemone-laced cheese? You have an anemone allergy, don't you, my dear?"

Kelo backed away. "What have you done? You said it would make her talk . . ."

"This *will* make her talk," Lady Garnah said. "I had no idea you were squeamish."

"But she knows who we are and what we've done!"

"She won't remember. I've added a helpful herb to the antidote that will ensure that," Lady Garnah said. "If she survives. The survival bit is up to her. Antidote or no antidote, Lady Biliarn?" She held up the vial again.

Lady Biliarn sucked in air. It sounded as if she were breathing through a tiny hole. Everything in Kelo made him want to yell out for help. Lady Garnah was clearly insane, and she was killing Lady Biliarn.

But if he were found here like this . . .

If they didn't learn who held Queen Asana's family . . .

He didn't move.

"What do you want to know?" Lady Biliarn asked, her voice so strained it was hard to hear. He leaned closer.

"Very simple. One question. One answer. Who holds Queen Asana's family?"

"No one," Lady Biliarn whispered. Her legs began to twitch again. "They live happy, prosperous lives." She gasped like every breath cut her throat.

"Ooh, the drop of antidote is wearing off. How much pain are you willing to withstand? Tell me: Where is her family?"

Lady Biliarn began to cry. Fat drops slid down her perfect cheekbones. "I do not know. I swear to you, I don't."

"You know they were taken."

"It's how it's always done. But who holds them is secret."

"Then tell us who would know."

"Only a member of the Family who has them. And that's not mine. Or if it is, I am not important enough to know it. Please, the antidote. This is the truth!"

Lady Garnah didn't move. She studied Lady Biliarn's face as the woman began to twitch again and gasp for air. "Give it to her!" Kelo cried.

Shooting him an amused look, Garnah poured the vial

down Lady Biliarn's throat. Her head flopped to the side. "Now you may call for help. She had an allergic reaction, remember." Standing, Garnah swept across the room and closed herself in the music closet.

Kelo ran to the door. "Help! Someone, help!"

In the distance, he heard footsteps. When the courtier reached him, he said, "Please, help, Lady Biliarn has had an allergic reaction. She ate a wedge of anemone cheese and collapsed."

*IF I HAD INTEGRITY, KELO THOUGHT, I'D STOP THIS.*

But he didn't. He set aside the nearly complete portrait of Lady Biliarn, displaying it by leaning it against one of the harps. The new arrivals would be able to see his work and anticipate how he'd capture their best side. He'd done a nice job on her portrait, before she'd eaten the cheese. He'd captured her dignity and majesty in the moments before she lost both.

Lady Garnah emerged from the closet and, using tongs, she plucked the cheese off the plate and dropped it into a bag that she slid into another of her many pockets.

"Don't we need that?" Kelo asked.

"Two allergic reactions in a row would be suspicious, don't you think? No, for the next one, encourage them to drink the beverage. You'll be able to question them freely."

"Wait—it really does work as you said?"

"Of course. I don't lie. Unless it suits me."

"Then why didn't you put the same stuff on the food?"

"Because that wasn't for them," Garnah said. "It was for you."

He recoiled. She'd planned to poison him? Why? It didn't even make sense. "But I wasn't going to eat any of the food."

"Not for you to ingest. For *you*. I needed to see how far you're willing to go and how much you're willing to compromise your ideals to achieve your goal." She gave him a motherly smile. "I think you'll do nicely."

He pointed to the spot in the carpet where Lady Biliarn had fallen. "You did that . . . put her through pain . . . to prove a point to *me?*" This . . . it was wrong. It was appalling.

"Yes," she said, nodding eagerly. "Also, it was fun."

A knock on the door. Kelo tried to compose himself as Lady Garnah hid again in the closet. This time his model was a dignitary from the Family Toral, and he came without servants. Near as Kelo could glean, he was a lower-ranking official. But Kelo obediently offered him the beverage, and he drank before even sitting down to be painted.

Tense, Kelo waited for him to collapse to the ground or start foaming at the mouth, but he didn't. He just started to talk. And talk. Before long, Kelo had learned the official's every dirty secret—and the man had a disgusting array of them—but not who held Queen Asana's loved ones.

Kelo finished the portrait, working as quickly as he could so he'd be done with this odious man sooner. It was a challenge to keep his contempt for the man out of the lines of his work. If he hadn't been handsome, it would have been much trickier, but luckily or unluckily, his ugliness was within, hidden behind a strong and symmetrical face. "Would you like to see it?" Kelo asked politely.

The man blinked. "You're remarkably fast."

*Lady Garnah's potion must be wearing off,* he thought. At least he'd timed it well.

Kelo managed a weak smile. "Thank you for coming." With his uninjured hand, he turned around the portrait, and the man gushed his praise. Kelo was happy to see him go.

Lady Garnah emerged as soon as he left. "Pity we didn't poison him."

Secretly, Kelo was inclined to agree. Then he banished that thought in horror when he realized Garnah might be right that he was suited for this kind of work. He quickly set up for the next portrait, while Lady Garnah stirred a new beverage. He had the unnerving sense that the poison-maker guessed his thoughts and was amused.

The next model came in, and Kelo repeated everything: the praise, the offer of a beverage, the questioning while he sketched the portrait. This courtier was less vile than the last, but Kelo still learned more than he wanted to about affairs within the woman's family.

By the end of the day, Kelo was thoroughly disgusted by humanity and no closer to learning who held Queen Asana's family. He glared at the row of portraits as if it were their fault.

"Don't despair," Lady Garnah said, as she bottled her special beverage. "We hunt the long hunt, as they say in my home forests. Actually, I don't know if anyone says that, but it sounds like something a gruff, burly hunter would say."

"Every hour we waste is another hour Mayara is in danger."

"I'm sure she's having a delightful time. All your islands are tropical paradises."

He snorted. "With death lurking around every corner."

"Death always lurks around *every* corner," Lady Garnah said, steel in her voice. "You can die for arbitrary, stupid reasons just as easily as you can die in a grand gesture. The key is how you live before that moment."

"This—drugging people, listening to their torrid secrets—is not how I planned to live," Kelo said. He'd created such beautiful portraits of people with such ugly souls.

"Maybe not. But you have to admit, it's terribly entertaining. So many secrets! So much drama! Imagine the blackmailing potential of all that you've learned today. You could be a wealthy man, if you played it right."

"I have no interest in wealth. I just want Mayara back."

She rolled her eyes. "Eh, more for me, then."

He fixed her with a glare that he hoped looked imposing, even though he found Lady Garnah, beneath all her ruffles and ridiculous hat, to be the most terrifying person he'd ever met. "We have one purpose and one purpose only. Don't jeopardize it for personal gain." He was certain she'd laugh at him.

And she did, a full belly laugh that shook her shoulders. When she caught her breath again, she said, "Silly boy. I don't care about wealth. If I did, I'd sell my potions for a fortune. Or just use them on someone with a ridiculous amount of gold and take it for myself."

He couldn't tell if she was serious or not, so he elected not to respond.

"Cheer up," she told him, patting him on the cheek. "Today was just the first wave. We saw the lower-ranking people. Once word spreads of the quality of your work, then we'll begin seeing people with actual information. They'll come. And we'll learn." She rubbed her hands together in gleeful anticipation.

Kelo hoped she was right. He wanted this over as quickly as possible.

QUEEN ASANA DIDN'T EXPECT THE ARTIST TO SUCCEED. SHE DELIBerately kept her hopes in check, careful to dismiss it from her thoughts while she went about her daily routine.

On the third morning after the covert interrogation began, she shut herself in her chambers and sat in the center of the floor. Her joints creaked as she lowered herself down and folded her legs. Placing her hands on her knees, she steadied her breathing.

She thought of her daughter.

She held the image of her as she'd last seen her, years ago, in her mind, and then gently packed it away. She sometimes let herself wonder what little Roe looked like now, grown into a woman, but today wasn't a day for wondering.

Wondering felt too close to hope, and she didn't dare feel that.

Freeing her mind, Asana swept her thoughts out of the palace, south through the sea. She let her awareness flow through the wild spirits, the ones not bound to her, sensing their unrest. When that unrest built into uncontrollable anger, they'd pick a target: one of her islands, and she'd spread word of a coming storm. Often, the heirs were able to dispel it before it even reached landfall. *Not always, though.*

She stopped that thought too.

She needed her mind fully relaxed to reach into the Deepest Blue, and that was where she had to go. It was the queen of Belene's responsibility to keep the largest of the wild spirits safely asleep. It was the reason she couldn't use her own power to subdue the storms, or to bend the wills of those who opposed her. She needed all her power for this task, which had to be repeated every few days.

It hurt to reach so far. She felt as if she were fraying.

The leviathans slept fitfully, in dreams that were drenched in ancient memories of the birth of the world. They'd been there when the Great Mother had called for the creation of the land and the sea. They'd reveled in her boundless love, and their rage when she'd died had been immense and unquenchable. It was that old rage that drove them still, churning the waters while they slept.

All heirs, after they completed their testing, were taught how to subdue the sleeping monsters. You had to guide their dreams: keep them remembering the days when the Great Mother ruled all, before humans arrived, when spirits created beauty and didn't know death.

It was remembering death that woke them.

If you could pull their dreams back far enough away from that cliff, they'd continue to slumber. Guiding the dreams of spirits was a trick that any heir could do, but only a queen had the power, drawn from all the spirits who were bound to her, to reach so far and influence such old, powerful minds.

When she finished, she drew herself back, feeling as if she were pulling in a mile-long strand of seaweed that snagged on rocks and coral. She had to pull carefully so that it didn't tear.

It was so tempting to let her mind flow free, mixing with the water, losing herself in the chaotic swirl of the countless numbers of wild spirits who lived beyond the borders of the known world. But if she did, she might truly lose herself.

She couldn't risk that.

She thought of Rokalara once more, who was waiting for her to someday return. She'd promised they'd be together again, knowing it was a promise she might never fulfill. Queens stayed queens until they died.

*Unless Garnah and Kelo succeed.*

That thought jerked her back to her body so hard that it felt as if she'd fallen. She felt aching and bruised. *It's getting harder and harder.*

What was she going to do if it got too hard to withstand?

"I'll die then, I suppose," she said out loud.

A voice behind her said, "I'd prefer you didn't, my queen."

She turned, wincing, to see Lady Garnah had entered the room. She wondered how long she'd been there.

Asana thumped the heels of her palms on her thighs, trying to remind her blood to circulate. As she understood it, her whole body slowed when her mind wandered that far. She kept breathing, and her heart kept beating, but it was sluggish. She'd had a healer watch over her once, at the beginning, and he'd remarked that her mind-travel was not so different from what he'd seen in dying patients. Her body was empty, and so it began to shut down.

It was all rather horrible.

But necessary.

"I'm surprised the guards let you in," Asana said. She didn't try to stand. She knew her legs wouldn't be functioning properly yet. Her guards were under orders to keep everyone out while she communed with the spirits of the Deepest Blue.

"They didn't want to, but I convinced them," Garnah said, then flashed her usual delighted-with-the-world smile. Asana wondered what it would be like to go through life like her, without concerns weighing her down. "They'll wake up in a few hours, feel guilty for napping on the job, and be none the worse for wear. It's a delightful powder. Also useful if you're having trouble sleeping at night. You wake up so refreshed!"

Looking at Garnah's oh-so-pleased-with-herself expression, Asana allowed a hint of hope to creep in. "Either your attempt was a success or a failure. You wouldn't be here unsummoned otherwise."

"It was educational," Garnah said.

Asana stretched her fingers and shook them as feeling began to return to her extremities. Her heart was already beating faster. *Don't get your hopes up. Don't start believing. Wait to hear what she says.* "Oh? It was?"

"And entertaining."

"Out with it."

Garnah pouted. "I was going to lead up to the dramatic reveal. You're ruining my timing." But then she took one look at the expression on Asana's face and said quickly, "The Family Neran. Your parents and daughter are in the Neran Stronghold on the island of Olaku."

Asana felt as if she'd been shoved underwater. It was hard to breathe, and her lungs felt as if they were being crushed from the pressure. *Lord Maarte.* "Are you certain?"

Garnah turned serious. "Absolutely. Our informant was . . . informative."

She wasn't going to let herself rejoice until she was certain all was well. "Did you endanger my family? Does the Family Neran know that I know? Can you be certain your informant won't tell anyone that he told you?"

Garnah smiled again, and this time it was a predator's smile, all teeth and no humor. "He won't tell anyone anything."

"Please tell me you didn't kill him," Asana said. Her heart sank. She knew it was too good to be true that this would go smoothly. "If there's a death, there will be suspicion. The Family Neran may react. They could move my family. Or retaliate—"

"I didn't kill him," Garnah said. "Great Mother, I wish one day someone would just understand that I know what I'm doing," she complained, mostly to herself. Louder: "To be honest, it *was* my first choice. Death is so much neater than other options, but your good little artist boy wouldn't have it."

"Then what did you do?" Asana demanded.

"Oh, just took a few precautions," Garnah said. "Nothing you need to concern yourself with. What you should begin focusing on is what we're going to do with this information."

"Garnah—"

"I destroyed his mind," Garnah said cheerfully. "A very clever potion that mimics an illness, a brain parasite. But he won't recover."

"Then he's worse than dead."

"Your pet artist begged me to spare his life. He wasn't more specific than that. I do believe he's learned his lesson: be careful what you wish for. Or perhaps the lesson was: don't stand between a queen and her family."

Asana did not ask who the man was they'd destroyed. She didn't want to know. *Kelo learned the right lesson: don't stand in my way.* "I believe it's time for a formal visit to the Neran Stronghold."

# CHAPTER EIGHTEEN

There was a reason that no one ever escaped from Akena Island. *And that reason is that it's impossible,* Mayara thought. But she wasn't going to say that out loud, and besides, "impossible" had never stopped her before.

*If you chase death, it can't catch you.*

Their plan was simple: first, they would reveal themselves near the cove. Draw as many spirits there, to the north side of the island, as possible. And then Lanei would lead Mayara, Roe, and Palia through the underground passages, some of which were submerged and some of which weren't, until they all reached the south side of the island.

While the spirits searched for them in the north, they'd swim across the reef to the south, toward the deeper ocean. It was an illogical escape route, one that led *toward* the wild spirits and *away* from the islands of Belene, but that would be to their advantage, because the Silent Ones wouldn't expect it. They'd be busy watching all the spirits flood into the cove on the opposite side of the island. From the other side of the reef, Mayara, Roe, Palia, and Lanei would compel a stray spirit to bring them to Yena.

Mayara thought it must have been tried before. But the piece that was new was Lanei: she knew the island's caves better than anyone. She'd been using them for more than a year and knew the fastest routes and the best hiding places. She could lead them across the island, beneath the island, faster than any spirits or Silent One could anticipate.

*Idea is we'll be gone before they even think to look.*

It *could* work.

Certainly it was better than Lanei's original plan.

As they prepared, Mayara found herself daydreaming about Kelo. She wondered what he was doing right now, if he'd repaired his studio, if he was carving anything new, if he was thinking of her. Her heart was still holding out hope that he was home and well and waiting for her. He must know she wanted to survive and would do anything she could to get back to him. *Including doing what's never been done before . . . what not even Elorna had done.*

Mayara peeked out at the cove. Today it was a riot of colors, every flower in full bloom so that it looked as if a painter had chucked pot after pot of bright paint over all the greenery. A few spirits were already there, playing with a breeze by the shore. "Roe, I think you should stay hidden. You're the key to this working. You can't take risks."

Roe snorted. "Like I'm going to let you go out there without me. You've taken far too many risks on my behalf. From here on in, we do it together."

Reaching over, Mayara squeezed her hand.

"Aw, how sweet," Lanei said.

Both of them ignored her.

"Besides," Roe said, still holding Mayara's hand, "the more of us the spirits see, the more spirits will come. And it won't work unless they come."

"We can do this," Mayara told her. "Look at what we've done so far: survived when it shouldn't have been possible, with me untrained and you injured. And Palia . . . she shouldn't have survived being trapped, but she did, and now we have the chance to do what no other spirit sister has ever done."

"Nice pep talk," Lanei said. "Just to be clear, though, if you get yourselves caught, I won't help you. Succeed or fail, I win. Remember that."

"Remember that we can't trust you? Yes, I think we'll remember that," Mayara said.

"I'll watch her," Palia offered. "As much as I like her goals, she did set the trap that nearly killed me." She patted Lanei's shoulder with false friendliness and added, "You know, you really shouldn't try to murder someone who has nothing left to lose. You've made me desperate. I'll be watching your every move."

"Your daughter still lives," Roe reminded Palia. "And you're going to see her again. Don't lose faith now. We have a plan, and it's going to work!"

"Are we going to keep giving speeches, or are we going to do this?" Lanei asked.

"Do we have a plan for attracting the spirits' attention?" Palia asked. "Or should we just jump around, wave our arms, and shout, 'Come eat me!'"

Roe crawled out of the hole above the cove. "Something like that. Follow my lead. I have an idea." Mayara and Palia, with Lanei, followed after her.

Before them, the cove was its usual gorgeous paradise self: white sand beach, trees heavy with tropical fruit, brilliantly colored birds calling to one another, and a few monkeys screeching in the distance. Roe closed her eyes.

Mayara didn't reach out yet. She waited to see what Roe would do.

And then she heard it, echoed through the minds of the spirits:

*Attack the Silent Ones.*

"Clever," Lanei said with approval.

Mayara smiled. She knew she shouldn't hate the Silent Ones, especially since they didn't kill Kelo. Or might not have killed Kelo. But she couldn't help it. They were the ones who had torn her away from her family and her life. Besides, they could defend themselves. She added her mental voice to Roe's: *Go north, to the islands beyond the reef. Attack the Silent Ones.*

She felt the spirits respond. This was a command that they all liked. She was certain it had been tried before, but perhaps not as a distraction.

The earth spirits moved. The air spirits flew. The water spirits boiled up from the cove. All of them flowed north. And the four spirit sisters ducked back into the cave.

Without a word, Lanei led them.

They hurried through the passageway toward the underground lake, and then, into the lake. Roe hesitated at the edge. Mayara repeated what she'd said, "Remember, we're doing this together. Take my hand."

Roe took her hand, and together they jumped in. Mayara pulled Roe through the water, swimming strong enough for both of them, following Lanei and Palia.

They surfaced, breathed, and then swam on, with Mayara continuing to pull Roe, who flopped through the water as awkwardly as a baby sea turtle. She wished there had been time to teach her to swim. *I'm strong enough. We can do this.*

Climbing out of the water, they followed a dark path, lit only by firemoss.

It rose up.

Ahead, Lanei was whispering furiously to Palia. *Warnings or threats?* Mayara wondered, but there wasn't time to ask.

In the distance, they could feel the churning of the spirits. The Silent Ones were equipped to defend themselves, and the spirits were under orders not to leave the reef. But they could make life unpleasant, beginning wind storms, tossing waves at the shore, hurling boulders out of the sea. For now at least, there was chaos. *If we can just be fast enough . . .*

They emerged on the southern side of the island. Palia was breathing heavily, with a wheezing hiss at the end of each breath. Hands on her knees, she bent over. "Are you all right?" Mayara asked. "Can you make it?"

"For my daughter," Palia said. "Yes."

"Roe?"

Roe nodded. "Ready."

Mayara was awed by how strong they both were. Roe, unable to swim, yet going underwater inside caves. Agreeing to plunge into the ocean. And Palia, who was clearly hurting and pushed beyond her limits. *Roe wants to see her mother, and Palia her daughter. Just as much as I want to be with Kelo. We all want the lives we were supposed to have.*

She wondered if there was anyone out there whom Lanei loved.

Palia dived into the water first, then Lanei. Roe was next, followed by Mayara, who immediately swam to Roe, supporting her in the waves. "You watch for spirits," Mayara told her. "I'll take care of swimming." Any sighting could spell disaster—one spirit could alert the others. They'd have to silence it fast.

The reef was teeming with fish: silver, purple, yellow, orange. Eels slipped between the fans of the coral. The coral itself was overlapping layers of lace. She didn't fear any of them—they were animals. But a spirit could hide between them. *That* she feared. All it took was one.

And there was one.

"Mayara . . ."

"I feel it. Palia, Lanei, keep Roe afloat!" She pushed the younger woman toward them.

Lanei and Palia each caught her under an armpit. "Push the water down," Palia advised her. "Don't just flail around. *Push.* That's it. You call for a wild spirit, and we'll help keep you afloat until it gets here."

Kicking, Mayara swam down toward the spirit with a powerful thrust. It hadn't noticed them yet. She drew her glass knife. The spirit was a translucent wisp, drifting between the coral.

As Roe, Palia, and Lanei crossed the line of coral and began summoning a spirit not from Akena that would be strong enough to carry them to Yena, the little island spirit noticed them—and as it did, Mayara sank her knife into it. She cut off its cry.

She hoped she'd been fast enough.

Silvery blood spread through the water, and Mayara rose to the surface at a distance from her friends. She opened her mouth to call to them to wait for her, then felt a hand close around her wrist and yank her down. She had half a second to suck in air.

Ready with her knife, she spun under water—but it wasn't a spirit.

It was a woman with a white mask. Her gray robe clung to her limbs, and she was seal-slick gray. Underwater, they both stared at each other.

Dimly, beneath the panic and fear, Mayara had the space to think: *She's a deep diver.* Neither of them were fighting for air. *She's like me.*

Then another part of her thought: *I have to keep her from calling the spirits.* She had to give her friends a chance to escape. Instead of trying to pull away from the Silent One, Mayara launched into her, kicking hard against the water to propel herself into her.

She knocked her down, into the reef, holding her against the coral.

Fish scattered.

The Silent One struggled to break free.

*Let's see who's the deep diver now,* Mayara thought. She held the Silent One down, silently urging her friends to hurry. She hoped they had the sense to go without her.

She felt the Silent One begin to slow. *I won't kill her. Just let her lose consciousness and then . . .* She could deposit her on one of the outer islands and escape before she woke.

But the Silent One didn't black out.

Instead, spirits came: three of them, from the island.

She felt them inside her head, as if they were clawing the

inside of her skull. Mayara released the Silent One and swam to the surface. She popped up and sucked in air and saw three dolphin-shaped spirits aimed toward her.

Pivoting, Mayara looked for her friends.

Just beyond the reef, where she knew they were, a storm had sprung up. The sky was blue on either side of it, so she knew it wasn't a natural storm, even without feeling the swirl of wild spirits within it. She glanced back.

The Silent One had risen out of the water, on top of a tortoise-shaped spirit.

Mayara wondered if she could pit her strength against a trained Silent One. *There's only one of her. So far.* She reached out to spirits of her own. She'd avoided trying to control them, but now she didn't have a choice. . . .

"Mayara."

The Silent One had said her name. *Out loud.*

Mayara stopped. She pulled her thoughts back, treading water. The three dolphin spirits didn't attack. Instead, they circled around her as if corralling her. "You spoke."

The Silent One glanced right and left. And then she removed her mask.

# CHAPTER NINETEEN

*I held my breath too long.*

*I'm dead.*

Because there was no way she could be seeing what she was seeing.

Mayara stared at her sister's face, a little older, a little paler. Her eyes were sunken, as if she hadn't slept in days. She wasn't sure if she whispered or shouted when she said, "Elorna?"

It couldn't be.

She felt a lurch beneath her, and suddenly, she was sprawled on a rock. Not a rock. A spirit, with a shell like a turtle, buoyed her in the water. It was a match for the spirit that held her sister.

If it was her sister.

"Don't be afraid, little minnow," Elorna said.

Her voice cracked and wavered, as if her throat had been sanded raw. *Or,* Mayara thought, *as if she hasn't spoken in years.* Beneath the crackling, though, it sounded like Elorna. Or Mayara thought it did. She'd had so many imaginary conversations with her lost sister in her head that this wasn't proof of anything. "You're *dead.* Am I dead?"

Elorna grinned, and it felt like a wave hitting Mayara. Her grin was the same. Mayara's memory had conjured up that grin a thousand times, but she'd never imagined it creasing the face of this older Elorna, dressed like a Silent One.

"We don't have much t-time," Elorna said. Her voice broke. She swallowed, then continued on, stronger. "My silent sisters will notice I'm not fighting beside them. They'll wonder why I'm on this side of the island. C-clever to send the spirits against us. It's been done, of course, so we knew to expect it, but how did you reach the other side of the island so quickly?"

"You died on the island," Mayara said, still not able to process what was happening. "We mourned you." For years. And she wasn't . . . And she didn't . . . "Elorna."

"I chose to become a Silent One. I knew . . ." Her voice seemed to fail, and she continued in a rough whisper. "I knew you'd be disappointed in me. I asked them to lie for me, so you wouldn't be ashamed. I knew you'd lose me either way. And I'd lose you. I'm deeply, truly sorry."

Mayara felt as if a whirlpool had formed inside her. Joy. Anger. They swirled around each other so fast that she had no idea what she felt or what to say.

"Go back to the island," Elorna said. "I'll help you survive, as best I can. If you're careful, you'll be able to make it the full month. And then you'll be safe." With every word she spoke, her voice was stronger.

"I can't abandon my friends."

"If you leave, you'll be on the run forever, until they catch you and they execute you. It's treason to abandon the test."

"And it's treason for a Silent One to speak," Mayara replied.

"That's why we have to talk fast. Go back, Mayara. Don't do this. It's not your destiny. You're supposed to survive the island, become an heir, and keep our family, your Kelo, and all of Belene safe."

*Kelo!* "He's alive? Truly?" She had hoped, even believed, it was true, but Lord Maarte had proven himself a liar and even he didn't know for certain. She'd been relying on pure faith.

"Yes. I stopped the spirits. That much I could do for you."

*Kelo lives!*

*And my sister . . .*

"That was you, on the cliff? You were there?" She'd never imagined, when she looked at those masks, that she'd been looking at her sister. Elorna hadn't given any sign, any hint, any hope—

"I was there with you," her sister said. "And I've been here watching. Mayara, you can do this! You've always been the strong one, the brave one."

*I'm not the brave one, though.* That had always been Elorna, chasing after death. Mayara had merely tried—and failed—to live up to her, to fill the void she'd left. "I'm not a hero."

"You are," Elorna said. "I could see it in you, even when we were little. You were afraid and you'd do it anyway. I wanted to be more like you, my fearless little sister. I wanted you to be proud of me. But in the end, I failed you. You, though . . . you have a chance to do what I couldn't do!"

"I don't want to live the life you should have lived," Mayara said. As she said it, she realized it was true. She'd tried that, for far too long. Now she just wanted this to end. She wanted to be back with Kelo, home in her village. That was a big enough world for her. She was making a third choice—not heir or Silent One, and not hero or dead.

"Mayara . . ."

"We won't be running forever," Mayara said. "We're taking Roe to the queen in Yena. She's Queen Asana's daughter. Once they're reunited, Roe will convince her mother to end the test. Women with power will be safe."

That startled Elorna. "Her daughter! But how . . ."

"She was taken from her mother when Queen Asana was crowned. She's been held against her will by the Families to ensure Queen Asana obeys them. That's why the Families have so much power. That's why they're the ones who say where the heirs are sent and how the Silent Ones are used. If we can reunite Roe and her mother . . . it will reveal the truth. The queen will be able to take power away from the Families, end the test, and pardon us all. Maybe you could even come home."

Mayara didn't dare blink out of fear that Elorna would vanish. This had to be a dream, a hallucination before she died from lack of oxygen. She'd imagined Elorna before. "Please, come home."

"Mayara . . ." Her voice was full of wonder, and then she abruptly straightened. "They're coming."

Mayara saw Elorna's face harden—it was a familiar expression, the look she got when she'd made a decision. Kelo had once told Mayara that her face looked the same, just before she was about to do something reckless.

"Listen to me, Mayara. The queen isn't in Yena. She's on a formal visit to the Neran Stronghold. If your friends go to Yena, they'll be caught, and they'll fail."

"Then even more reason you have to let me go! Let me warn my friends."

"You really think Queen Asana will change the world for her daughter?"

"I do. There's a lot we'd do for the ones we love." *For Kelo,* Mayara thought. *For you.* She'd changed herself for Elorna's memory, risking herself in dives to feel the kind of wild joy that Elorna had shown her. And she was risking herself now for Kelo, for the chance of returning to him and reclaiming the life she'd planned.

"Then go," Elorna said. She placed the mask back on her face. "I will delay my sisters."

"*I'm* your sister."

"Always," Elorna said, and then she turned and rode the spirit back toward the shore. Mayara dived off the back of her spirit and swam beyond the reef into the storm.

THE SPIRIT STORM WAS CENTERED AROUND ROE.

Mayara felt it whirl and twist. Water rose in giant hands and then slapped down, creating twelve-foot swells that slammed into each other and erupted like geysers. And her friends were at the heart of it.

Rain was falling so hard that she felt as if she were underwater. The waves churned the sea so that it was all white foam. Dozens of wild spirits were both beneath and above her. Focusing on swimming, she kept her thoughts close to herself. *Don't notice me.* Not that she had much to fear at the moment—all their attention was focused on the heart of the storm.

At the center was Roe, standing on the back of a whalelike spirit. Her arms were spread wide and her eyes were closed. Palia was huddled at her feet on the whale's back. She was snarling at the waves and flinging spirits away with her mind.

Reaching them, Mayara climbed onto the slick back of the wild whale spirit. Its skin was shimmering black, as if it had absorbed the night sky, and its eyes were blue flame. "Roe! Palia!"

"Thank the Great Mother, you made it!" Palia cried. "We thought you were dead!"

"Can you stop the storm?" Mayara shouted to Roe over the howls of the wind and the crash of the waves. Beneath her, she felt the whale's thoughts, sluggish and dark. They were an itch it wanted to be rid of, but Roe held its desires tight, as if in a net.

Face clenched in concentration, Roe didn't answer.

"The queen is at the Neran Stronghold!" Mayara yelled. "We have to go to Olaku! And we have to go now, before the Silent Ones come to investigate this storm!"

Roe nodded, so Mayara knew that she was getting through. Roe held out her hands. Mayara grasped one, and Palia the other. They clung to one another.

"Where's Lanei?" Mayara asked.

"Lost!" Palia shouted back.

Mayara felt a pang—she hadn't liked Lanei, but she'd admired how she'd survived a year on the island. And then to die in something that was Mayara's idea . . .

But this was neither the time nor the place for guilt.

"Hold on!" Roe called.

She dropped to her knees and so did Mayara and Palia, all of them flattening against the spirit's back as it hurtled forward. They plowed through the other wild spirits.

"Send them away!" Roe called.

While Roe directed the whale spirit, Mayara and Palia concentrated on sending the wild spirits toward Akena Island. They didn't target the Silent Ones this time; they aimed them at the island itself.

*Destroy the island!*

That would help end the test, wouldn't it?

She didn't think they'd succeed—the island's spirits would defend against the wild spirits. But while the spirits were fighting one another, Mayara, Roe, and Palia could slip away.

*Maybe.*

But it was looking better and better. With luck, the Silent Ones would have their hands full reining in the spirits on the island and quelling the storm that Roe had raised.

Soon, Mayara, Roe, and Palia left the storm behind them and shot through the water. Glancing back, Mayara wished they could have searched for Lanei. She didn't deserve to die like that. "Did she drown, or was it spirits?"

"Neither! She swam off of her own volition," Roe replied. "Said she'd draw them away and that I was the one who had to get to the queen. Told Palia to make sure I made it."

"And I will," Palia said. "Keep going!"

Lanei could have left the island, but she chose to stay behind. That was brave. "I know she tried to kill us," Mayara said, "but she wanted to do what's right. I don't think she was a murderer. I think she wanted to be a hero."

"We won't waste her sacrifice," Palia said. "We'll make it."

"Wow, Palia," Roe said. "That almost sounded like optimism."

Mayara glanced back again. South of Akena, the Silent Ones were arriving at the storm. They rode on the backs of spirits, both in the air and through the water. Mayara saw their silhouettes for only the briefest of moments before wind whipped sea spray around them, obscuring them from view.

Mayara hoped they found Lanei in the storm and were able to save her, though she didn't know what they'd make of a potential heir who had stayed beyond the end of her test. Would they treat her as a hero or a traitor?

*Which was she? Hero or traitor?*

The same question could be asked about Elorna.

As they sped across the water, Mayara kept looking back at the spirit storm. Elorna was somewhere in there, distracting her silent sisters from following her birth sister.

She remembered so clearly the moment she'd been told that Elorna had died. It was a rainy day, and she'd resented being trapped inside. She'd been sorting shells that she'd collected on the beach the day before. Three piles: good, broken, and smelly. Kelo had already started making wind chimes and mobiles, and she wanted to give him a present. Mayara didn't know who had delivered the news to her parents, but she remembered that it was her father who had told her. He'd held her while he said the words: "Elorna isn't coming back."

She remembered the way the rain seemed to slow when she heard those words. She'd felt the thump of her blood through her body, so loud it drowned out whatever her father said next. But it was the next day that was the worst, when she woke up in the morning and the sun was shining and she remembered all over again. She ate her breakfast without tasting it and listened to her mother crying in the other room. Their mother cried for days, heavier than the rain, and she didn't come out of her room, even though Mayara desperately wanted her to. Mayara didn't want to be alone with her sorrow—it was too big and too scary. She spent the days instead with Kelo. Mostly, they sat quietly side by side. He seemed to instinctively know that words would make it worse, that there were no words that would fix the way her heart felt empty or the world felt dimmed.

But gradually, she'd resumed the business of living again, because you had to, unless you were their mother, who seemed to retreat more and more into herself. *Leave her alone,* everyone said. *She needs her space.* But she never seemed to have enough space. Instead she just created more and more space around herself—a buffer against having to feel anything.

Mayara attempted to push her way in anyway, mostly with things Elorna had loved. She taught herself to dive deep. She'd always been a strong swimmer and a good diver, but in Elorna's absence, she tried to fill the world with Elorna's bravery, as if that would make up for the emptiness.

It didn't. Especially for Mother. Losing Elorna had shredded their mother, and no matter how fully Mayara had tried to live her life, it hadn't been enough. In a way, Mayara had lost both her sister and her mother on that day.

*But Elorna was never gone.*

*She chose to leave us.*

She knew as she had the thought that it wasn't fair. Elorna hadn't wanted to leave them. She'd chosen to live, which was the choice that Mayara had planned to make until she thought Kelo was dead. How could Mayara blame her for doing as Mayara had planned?

*Because I blame her for lying—for letting them tell her family she'd died.*

If they'd known that Elorna still lived, maybe their mother wouldn't have withdrawn so much. Maybe their father wouldn't have nearly fallen apart trying to hold their family together. Maybe Mayara . . .

Actually, she didn't know how it would have changed her.

She wished she could have talked with Elorna longer. There was so much she wanted to ask her and tell her. *And now I may never have another chance.*

A Silent One was sworn to not only hide her identity but reject it. Elorna shouldn't have spoken—it was treason to tell Mayara who she was. Then again, sitting atop this spirit, Mayara was committing treason too. She just hoped she would have a chance to tell her parents that Elorna lived. She ached for that.

She wished she'd thought to tell Elorna that she understood why she'd lied. Elorna had been afraid. *Of course I understand that.* She'd chosen to live, even if it meant a life without her loved ones. She'd asked the question: How far would you go to be with the ones you love? And she'd found an answer, a limit to how far she'd go and how much she'd risk. Fear had stopped her.

It was a revelation in and of itself. Mayara had never thought her sister felt fear. But she had, and it had shaped the rest of her life. *And mine.*

As Mayara struggled with the excitement that Elorna lived and her desire to forgive her sister, they sped toward the island of Olaku.

*So close to home. To Kelo.*

*And yet it could just as easily be a lifetime away.*

# CHAPTER TWENTY

Queen Asana's ship docked at Neran Stronghold on the island of Olaku. She stood at the prow, her hands lightly clasped in front of her, her face as placid as she could make it. She couldn't stop her heart from thumping as wildly as a bird's wings beat, but she could give every outward appearance of calm. She had practice at that.

As the sailors tied the ship to the dock, she studied the fortress. It was built into the rocky face of the island's bones, and it radiated both elegance and power, like the Family who owned it. Curved like a conch shell, the stronghold spiraled in on itself, with the heart of the fortress protected by thick walls that looked as though they would weather a thousand storms.

Asana wished she could unleash a thousand and one storms on them. But only after her family was safe. *And not even then,* she admonished herself. She didn't want an internal war—she couldn't afford one. She wanted only to seize her power back. To make sure the ones she loved were no longer under threat.

Generations ago, when some member of some Family hit on the bright idea to control the queens with hostages, the power had shifted. *Today I shift it back.*

She plastered a pleasant smile on her face as Lord Maarte and his entourage approached the dock. Lady Garnah fell in beside the queen as Asana swept forward to greet him.

"Not a word," Asana murmured to Garnah.

Lord Maarte was not the type to be amused by Lady Garnah's outspokenness. It was best if he didn't notice Garnah at all, and she wished the woman from Aratay would have worn something a bit subtler. Asana wouldn't have any freedom of movement once they were in the fortress. It would have to be Kelo and Garnah who worked to find her family while Asana provided the distraction. Still, Garnah knew what she was doing—she always seemed to winnow out the necessary secrets.

*And I'll do what I must.*

Even if it meant being patient when all she wanted to do was rip the fortress apart stone by stone.

Asana summoned up a warm smile. "Lord Maarte, we have missed you in Yena."

He greeted her with a bow and then a kiss bestowed on each cheek. Asana bore them without flinching, much as she wanted to claw off every trace of him from her skin. She held out her hands, and he clasped them.

"You honor us, Your Majesty," Lord Maarte said. His voice was sonorous, and his gaze was intense. It was the kind of gaze given by someone firmly convinced of his own handsomeness. She bet he'd never had a moment of self-doubt in his life. Odious man. "We had not expected your visit until next spring."

"Blame my new discovery." Asana gestured toward Kelo, who bowed on cue. She had decided to stick to the truth as much as possible, to hide the lies. "He's an artist whose wife recently undertook the test. He came to me on her behalf, but it wasn't sympathy that moved me. It was admiration for the beauty of his work. I am sponsoring him in a grand project: to create portraits of all the most important people on Belene. Since he's from your island, I thought here was an appropriate place to start."

"Wise and kind," Lord Maarte said with approval. She plastered a smile on her face, as if flattered by his condescension.

Surveying Kelo, he said, "He may have lost his wife, but he will gain fame and fortune thanks to your benevolence."

"It was within my power to grant him this," Asana said. She kept her voice light so no hint of her bitterness would seep into her words, and she was gratified when Lord Maarte smiled at her benevolently like he was a proud father. Like he hadn't imprisoned her own father. She smiled back with surprising genuine happiness.

It was actually delightful to have a reason to hate him.

He hadn't lowered his voice when he talked about fame and fortune, and Kelo had visibly flinched, but she doubted Lord Maarte noticed. Kelo had been labeled and explained, and so Lord Maarte had dismissed him.

*Good,* she thought. It helped that Kelo looked so little like a threat with his pretty face and with his wide eyes admiring the structure of the fortress. She knew that until he'd come to the capital, he'd never left his village. Maybe he'd visited a few other towns to sell his charm art, but he wasn't accustomed to wealth and the kind of beauty that wealth could buy. She hoped that seeing all this wouldn't change him too much. His innocence was rare and charming. *He is exactly the kind of soul that a queen and her heirs should protect.*

In a way, she was doing this for him and others like him, as much as for herself and her family. *But my family first. And then I can save whoever else needs to be saved.*

"He'll need a room with good light, preferably away from other distractions." Asana had been in the fortress enough times to know which room would fit the description she gave—it was isolated enough that any screams wouldn't be heard.

As she hoped, Lord Maarte took the bait. "The east tower. He will not be disturbed there, and the views are lovely."

"Thank you."

"And while he works, I will show you the wonders of our little slice of paradise. You'll be pleased to hear we've acquired a new chef. . . ." As he continued to extol the luxuries of the

Neran Stronghold, Queen Asana allowed him to escort her off the ship. She didn't look back at either Lady Garnah or Kelo. They knew what to do.

KELO DIDN'T KNOW HOW HE HAD ENDED UP HERE. HOME BUT NOT home. As he set up his easel in the east tower of the Neran Stronghold, he looked out over the turquoise water and tried not to feel as if he'd fallen off a cliff and was still falling.

*I can do this. For Mayara.*

"It will be the same as in the palace," Lady Garnah murmured. "Calm yourself."

This time, Lady Garnah would be present for the interrogations. There was no point in hiding Kelo's connection with the queen anymore—he'd come with her. If they failed, it would reflect on the queen.

*We can't fail.*

His first portrait was a young girl who squirmed as he tried to sketch her, one of Lord Maarte's nieces. She greedily drank the beverage with Garnah's potion, but she knew little about who else lived in the stronghold. Her world centered around her tutors and her games. She didn't venture far beyond her wing.

Next was an elderly man. And then a steward of the fortress, who should have known every detail of what happened within the walls but didn't. Kelo began to wonder if they were asking the right questions.

If a girl and her grandparents had lived here for years, shouldn't someone be aware of it? He began to wonder if their information was wrong, if the queen's family wasn't here at all.

But then they had luck.

It came in the form of another child, younger than the niece. Kelo missed how this one was connected to Lord Maarte's family, but the boy hadn't missed much. He was a little explorer and told them that proudly, even before he drank the beverage. He claimed he'd seen every inch of the fortress.

Kelo's hand shook as he laid a streak of charcoal across the easel. He knew he should feel guilt over drugging a child, but he didn't. He felt hope.

"In all your exploring, have you seen a family of three: a girl who would now be eighteen and her two grandparents?" He described them carefully, exactly as Queen Asana had described them to him: the girl had anemone-orange-colored hair, the grandfather had eyebrows that looked like sea cucumbers, and the grandmother walked with a limp and sounded like a dolphin when she laughed hard enough.

"Oh yes," the boy said happily. And he proceeded to tell Kelo about a caretaker's house within the gardens. Most people ignored it, but he noticed that it always had guards around it. It wasn't obvious—no soldier standing at attention the way they did outside the treasure room—but there was always one walking by, resting on a bench, chatting "casually" with another guard. It made the boy think there was something special inside, but that Lord Maarte didn't want anyone to know there was something special inside.

Which is exactly why he *had* to see what was inside. He was very good at finding special things, he said.

And so, one day, he pretended to play in the garden and tossed his ball up too high so that it flew over the wall into the caretaker's yard. He scrambled up the wall after it—and that's when he found her. A young woman with anemone-orange hair was weeding in the garden. She handed the ball back to him, asked his name, and talked to him until a guard found him and dragged him out by the ear. She'd told him her name was Rokalara.

They let the boy scamper away when they were finished, and Lady Garnah burst out in a cackle. "I love children! A dozen adults, and they don't see a thing. They only see what they expect to see. But a child . . . Beautiful! That was delightfully easy. Bodes well, doesn't it?"

Kelo was smiling too. If all continued to go as planned,

they'd save Queen Asana's family tonight, and then he'd be home with Mayara tomorrow.

"I will tell the queen." She then frowned at Kelo's easel. "You realize you made that child look like a rabbit, don't you?"

Startled, he looked at the canvas. He'd been so distracted that he hadn't captured the child's features at all.

"If this works, that will become a part of history—the moment the rabbit boy changed the world. You might want to burn it before history gets ahold of it."

He carried the canvas over to the fireplace and set it into the flames. But he wasn't burning it because he was ashamed of his mistake—he was burning it for the rabbit boy, to protect him, so that later, whether this succeeded or failed, no one would guess that boy had been the key and no one would punish him for it. *No more innocents will suffer,* Kelo thought.

Tonight, they were going to set the world right.

It was a risk to pull her mind away from the leviathans in the Deepest Blue and concentrate on the spirits of Belene, but Queen Asana had recently reinforced their dreams. She thought she could spare some power for tonight's task, so long as she returned to impose her will on the monsters within a few hours.

*It will be over soon.*

The years of separation. Of loss. Of fear. Of failing to be both a mother and a daughter. She hadn't been able to save her husband, but she hoped he'd be proud of her after today.

Smiling at Lord Maarte, she patted his hand. Lord Maarte had had his new chef prepare a luscious feast. Asana made her move after the soup course.

"Tell me about trade with Aratay," she said to Lord Maarte. Reaching out with her mind, she touched the spirits in the garden. Lady Garnah was already there, moving through the shadows. She saw her through the spirits' eyes as Garnah blew her purple sleep powder into the eyes of the guards. They collapsed, and Asana used the spirits to bind the guards in vines. She then called on an ice spirit to freeze the locks.

Garnah tapped the frozen locks with a rock, and they shattered.

Inside the garden, Asana felt the spirits ordered by the heirs to watch her family. She overrode their minds, tapping into her anger at Lord Maarte for using heirs for such a purpose to fuel her. She doubted the heirs knew who the prisoners were, only that Lord Maarte had ordered the heirs to guard them, probably claiming it was the queen's wishes.

She commanded an earth spirit to burrow a tunnel from the garden to the shore. Garnah would lead her family through the tunnel to freedom. Kelo had been instructed to meet them on the beach, to keep watch over their escape route. Her family would be frightened, unsure if they could trust either spirits or strangers, and she hoped Kelo would reassure them until she could arrive.

She felt the earth spirit burst through the soil. Everything inside her itched to be there. Soon she'd see her family. Soon her daughter would be in her arms again. Politely, she dabbed her lips with a napkin. "The soup is divine," she told Lord Maarte. "Please give my compliments to your chef."

She continued the meal, listening as Lord Maarte extolled the virtues of a proper diet. Fruits were the key, but it had to be the right kind of fruits. Mangoes, for example, were excellent, but you needed the proper ripeness for the full nutrients. "You must inform the palace chefs that they need to serve you at least one mango a day," he told her.

"The palace chefs look after my health admirably."

"You are Belene's most valuable asset," Lord Maarte said. "Are you feeling well? You seem distracted."

"Only by the glorious flavors of the meal," she replied with a smile. "Tell me how you came to learn so much about the quality of food. I know you have many responsibilities."

"Observation, of course. I am keenly aware of my surroundings at all times. It's important to be present in the moment, don't you think?"

"Mm-hmm."

Her family was in the tunnel . . . but why did she see only two figures? She couldn't tell, her vision distorted through the spirits' eyes, who was missing. Her heart clenched, and she ruthlessly shoved every shred of fear deep inside her. Bearing down with her mind, she sent wind spirits into the house, searching through every crevice.

*Find the missing one! Now!*

She felt like screaming when they found no one else. If they'd separated her family . . .

Or if they'd done worse . . .

She thought of her husband and then ruthlessly shoved the memory away. She was committed to this course of action, and this time she wasn't going to fail.

"Speaking of moments," Queen Asana said, smiling brightly at Lord Maarte, "I wish to see the sunset."

He frowned. "Are you unwell?" he asked again.

She rose, which forced the rest of the diners to quit eating as well. "Continue, please. Your meal shouldn't be allowed to cool to satisfy my whim. In the palace, I view the sunset every evening. I did not realize I would miss the moment this much. And in truth, I could use some fresh air. Perhaps the sea travel has left me unsettled."

"Allow me to escort you," Lord Maarte said, popping out of his seat.

She'd rather have dropped the soup bowl on his head than take his arm, but she did, and they glided out of the dining hall. She saw the other courtiers looking at each other, unsure of whether to continue or not. Protocol said they shouldn't eat if the lord and queen were not eating, but with both of them leaving the room . . . She hoped they ate. It wasn't the chef's fault that this was happening, and the soup *had* been delicious.

Especially once she'd added Garnah's antidote for poison.

It was strong stuff, Garnah's special blend to combat several different kinds of poisons, so it would eventually make Asana queasy, but Garnah had insisted she dose every dish before eating, as a precaution. *Lord Maarte won't be happy with you,* she'd said, *for visiting off schedule.* While Asana didn't believe he'd go so far as to poison her, she saw the sense in not taking risks, especially when she was so close to having what she dreamed.

She wondered if it meant anything that Lord Maarte had asked twice if she felt well. She wished she dared ask if he had tried to poison her—and if so, why? Did he know she was close to being reunited with her family? Did he suspect he was close to losing every shred of power she could rip away from him?

They walked out of the spiral shell to see that the sun was already beginning to melt into the horizon. The clouds were stained rose red and orange.

"I often thought that the sun resembles a ball of liquid gold, pierced so that it appears to drain out," Lord Maarte said, halting to admire the view. Asana had to halt as well, though what she wanted to do was run down to the shore and see who was missing.

"I didn't know you were a poet," Asana said. "That's a lovely image."

"I'm told I have a way with words. Your Majesty . . ." He paused. "I hesitate to bring up something delicate, especially while you are feeling indelicate, but your visit here . . . it's unusual."

"It's not unusual for me to visit the strongholds," Queen Asana said. "I merely changed the order." She flashed him her brightest, friendliest smile. *He suspects. How can he?* If he tried to interfere, she wondered how far she would go to stop him.

*As far as it takes.*

She hoped, though, that she wouldn't have to prove it.

And she hoped, too, that his new chef hadn't used an uncommon poison in the soup. *Finish this,* she told herself. *Get to Garnah and your family, and all will be well.*

"I know," Lord Maarte said smoothly. "But I'm also curious. My Family strives to serve you in every way possible. Are you displeased with us?"

"Of course not," Asana said. "You have been loyal to Belene." He probably believed he was loyal. *He probably sees himself as a hero. Pompous ass.*

"Your artist . . . I deeply regret what happened to his village. It is my concern that this is what your visit is truly about. We deployed the heirs as we thought best, for the good of the island of Olaku. The damage to his village meant that this fortress was protected."

She almost smiled. He'd given her another reason to be here—perhaps he hadn't guessed her true purpose after all. "You are correct. I wished to hear how that affair had been managed so poorly. I gave you advance warning of the storm. It should have been prevented."

"The heirs misjudged its trajectory. They disagreed with your assessment on where and when it would make landfall. Forgive me, but I thought their information was more accurate, since they were closer to the storm."

"An understandable decision." Or more accurately, bullshit. "Have you sent workers to help with rebuilding the village?"

"Of course."

Queen Asana knew he'd sent only minimal workers. Most had come at her expense from the capital, but she said nothing of it. "Do you have thoughts on how we can prevent a repeat of this?"

"You must trust our judgment," he said immediately. "We want what is best for Belene."

*Really? His answer to "you messed up" is "trust me more"?* But Queen Asana knew the routine. She bowed her head. "Do you know if my parents and daughter are well?" It was common for her to ask about them, with whatever ruling Family she spoke with. This time, though, she desperately wanted an answer. There was someone missing, and she wanted to know who and why.

Both her parents were elderly. If one of them had faded and they hadn't allowed her to say goodbye . . .

Or if Roe had sickened and they hadn't been able to cure her . . .

The Families wouldn't want to lose their leverage by telling Queen Asana one of their hostages had died.

*Don't leap to conclusions,* she cautioned herself.

"I have heard reports that they are," Lord Maarte said kindly.

"And are they happy?"

"Of course," Lord Maarte said. "Their needs and wants are all of utmost importance. As I have said before, you do not need to worry about them. That's why they are being looked after so carefully, to relieve you of the burden of worry."

"I appreciate that," Queen Asana said. "Those in the Deepest Blue are restless. They sense a coming shift in seasons. It touches their dreams."

"Are they giving you difficulty?" he asked, concerned.

She was pleased he accepted the change in topic. It was good to remind him why he needed her. No one but a queen could keep the worst of the wild spirits asleep. The heirs lacked the reach. It required the extra boost of power provided by bonding with the island spirits. "This time of year is always tricky. Requires an experienced queen." The implication was: they were lucky to have her.

He understood her subtext. "We are grateful for your efforts." He studied her closely. "Would you care to sit down? Your cheeks look flushed."

"No, thank you. Indeed, I wish to see the sunset from the shore. Will you show me the best route to the sand?" She didn't think he would allow her to wander alone, especially since her family was on the property. Plus if she kept him with her, she could ensure he didn't learn of their escape before she was ready.

"It would be my honor and delight."

He looked neither delighted nor honored, but he acquiesced and escorted her down a path. Guards marched behind them, and she called on the tree spirits to pull them away and subdue them, wrapping them in branches in the growing shadows, silencing them with leaves.

By the time they reached the shore, it was only her and Lord Maarte. They were out of sight of the battlements, hidden by the shadow of the cliffs. Out of the corner of her eye, she saw Kelo a few yards down the beach, waiting for her family to emerge from the earth spirit's tunnel. She reached into the pocket of her dress and withdrew some of Garnah's purple powder.

"One question, Lord Maarte, now that we're alone."

"Yes, Your Majesty?"

"Did you poison me?"

He stared at her for a moment, and she could see the calculations behind his eyes—he thought she looked unwell, and the guards were too far to hear either of their words . . .

"Yes, Your Majesty. Your visit here, unannounced and off schedule, was alarming, yet another indication that your obedience is not as complete as the Families would like. A final straw, if you will. For the good of Belene, I did what I had to do."

She blew the powder into Maarte's face with a smile. "For the good of Belene, so did I."

He collapsed on the sand.

Hiking her skirts up to her knees, Asana ran across the shore toward where her family should appear any moment now. *I'm coming, my dear ones!*

# CHAPTER TWENTY-ONE

Kelo saw the queen running across the sand as he helped the queen's father out of the tunnel. Her father was followed by her mother, then Garnah, with a pleased cat-who-spilled-the-milk-but-will-deny-it expression.

The older man let out a half-cry, half-moan as he stumbled across the beach toward Queen Asana. His wife followed, and soon they were all in one another's arms. Kelo felt tears well up in his own eyes. This was how it should be. This was right!

"Very touching," Lady Garnah muttered. "But let's move it along."

"They haven't seen each other in years," Kelo objected. "Give them a moment, for pity's sake." You could almost taste the emotion flowing from them—the love and relief and joy radiated from the three of them. The first star of the evening shone in the deepening blue sky, as if it were blessing them with its approval. His fingers itched to capture the moment in a sketch. It would make a gorgeous work of stained glass, with the sea and the sky just past sunset.

"The queen's family isn't free yet," Garnah snapped. "Not until they're back in the palace and the truth is known. If the queen and her parents are killed here, in the shadows of the fortress where no one can see, then this will have all been for nothing."

"No one will kill the queen. Everyone in Belene needs her alive." Even the most self-interested would balk at removing the one who kept the worst of the monsters asleep.

"You're adorably naive. It's going to get you killed, you know. We need *a* queen. And I've been told that by tradition, there's always an heir in the Belene grove, ready to take control should the current queen unexpectedly fall, which is a beautifully practical solution that has the flaw of making the queen expendable."

*She could be right.* He felt chilled, as if he'd been dunked into the ocean.

"If you're right, we need to leave." Kelo started toward the queen and her parents. They were hugging, laughing, crying, and talking over one another all at the same time. "Wait, where's the queen's daughter?"

"She wasn't there," Garnah said, watching Queen Asana and her parents. Her voice was expressionless, but her eyes were a mix of hungry and sad, as if this moment were conjuring up memories. Kelo would have asked what she was thinking of, if the words she were saying weren't so horrifying. "The queen's parents said she's beyond the Families' reach and not to wait."

"If she's not there, where is she? Is 'beyond their reach' a euphemism for dead?"

At the same time, he heard the queen ask, "But where is my Rokalara?"

Silence.

"Not . . . ?"

Her father spoke. "I'm sorry, Asana. We hid her power for as long as we could, but she insisted on displaying it in front of the lord. There was nothing to be done."

The queen looked fragile, as if a hard wind would blow her into pieces and she'd scatter like a pile of fallen leaves. "Lord Maarte looked me in the face and lied. . . . After he tried to poison me, of course. Perhaps I shouldn't have expected any different."

*Poison!* Kelo thought.

But Lady Garnah didn't look concerned or surprised at this revelation. He tried to feel reassured. If anyone knew how to counteract poison, it would be her. *Lady Garnah won't let anything happen to her.* Other people might suffer—Lady Garnah was remarkably unconcerned about protecting innocent bystanders—but Kelo was certain of the poison-maker's loyalty.

Queen Asana drew herself straighter, looking like a queen again, not a long-lost daughter. "Tell me: What did my little Roe choose?"

"She's on the island," her mother said.

"Not for much longer," Asana said firmly. "I have promised an end to the test, for the sake of one who has aided me and for the good of all Belene. And I will end them *now*."

Kelo was about to step forward, to suggest that they leave before they attracted trouble, but the appeal of stopping the test now, of saving Mayara, was too great. He stayed silent.

Queen Asana closed her eyes in concentration—and then her eyes popped open. Kelo tried to decipher the look of wonder and amazement on her face. Had she done it already? Was the test over? What did it mean for the test to be over? Was Mayara coming home? Before he could ask any of the questions that wanted to spill from his mouth, Asana said, "I don't know how or why, but Roe is coming! She's nearly here!"

Her parents both began talking at once.

"How did you do that?"

"How do you know?"

"Why is she coming?"

"How did she leave the island?"

"Is she all right?"

"Is she coming by ship?"

Their voices tumbled over one another. And Asana: "She's being chased by Silent Ones. I'm going to help her outrun them."

Kelo noticed that Lady Garnah was frowning up at the fortress. He stared too.

"Do you think the Silent Ones will interfere?" Kelo asked.

"That's not my worry," Garnah said.

"Then what is?"

She pointed to the battlements where archers paced along the perimeter. So far, they hadn't noticed the small reunion on the sands in the shadow of the cliffs, but how long would that last? "The queen has to do whatever she's going to do *quietly*."

And then the sea seemed to explode.

Water shot into the air, and a spirit breeched the surface. It looked like a whale but with shimmering scales. It began to swim away from the shore. Wave after wave hit the sand, and each was filled with dozens of seafoam spirits.

"Yeah, she's not being quiet," Kelo said, his heart thumping faster.

From the fortress, he heard shouting. He looked up to see the archers congregating by the walls. But none seemed to be aiming their arrows at the people down on the beach. Their attention was fixed on the chaotic sea.

"I take it back," Garnah said with a wolfish grin. "She can be loud. So long as she's also spectacular."

It was spectacular, to be sure. The waves parted before they hit the shore and chased unnaturally along the side of the island without breaking. He saw the shadows of sea creatures within the water—turtles, dolphins, fish—and then the water swept past them.

In its wake, he saw a spirit shaped like a whale coming toward them, with three people clinging to its back. It was pushed along by a swell of water.

As they reached the shore, Kelo saw their faces.

Three women. But he cared about only one of them.

*Mayara.*

She was here!

MAYARA FELT THE SURGE IN THE WATER, AND THE WHALE SPIRIT lurched forward. "What's happening?" she cried. Looking back, she saw the sea was churning. "Is it the Silent Ones? Are they following us?"

"I don't know!" Roe called back. "I can't touch its mind!"

It was being controlled by another. *They must have found us!* The spirit storm had delayed them, but not forever—Mayara saw, in the midst of the froth behind them, the shapes of women in gray robes. They stood side by side on the peak of a wave.

"Focus on the spirit!" Palia cried. "Break this hold!"

The three spirit sisters battered at it with their minds, trying to break through, but still it didn't respond. Instead, the whale spirit brought a swell of water that propelled them forward so fast that the wind screamed in their ears.

"Stop! Mayara, Palia, stop fighting it!" Roe shouted. "It's not taking us back!"

She was right—they hadn't reversed direction. *But where's it going?* Mayara wondered. It had to be controlled by the Silent Ones who chased them, but then why weren't the three of them returning to Akena Island? Why were they still speeding toward their destination?

"We could jump and swim," Mayara suggested. The waves were high on either side, hemming them in, and the force and speed of the current made her uncomfortable. But she had experience with riptides—you swam with the current until you could break out of it.

"I can't swim in water that strong," Palia said. "I know my limits. I'd drown in minutes."

Roe nodded. "I'd last seconds."

"We could use other spirits—" Mayara began.

"No." Roe was focused on something far away. Mayara tried to reach out as well, to see what Roe saw, but all she sensed was the implacable resolve of the whale spirit. Whoever had imprinted their will on it had overpowered all other thought—and that was almost more terrifying than anything else. Who was this strong? How many heirs and Silent Ones awaited them? And how could they escape?

The wind spat in their faces as they rushed through the sea between two walls of water. Ahead, Mayara saw the familiar shape of the Neran Stronghold. "Who's doing this?"

"I think . . . it's my mother!"

The fortress, lit by torches and framed against the evening sky, was in front of them. Propelled by waves, the whale spirit carried them so fast that Mayara felt as if they were flying.

She saw figures on the beach: five. From their outlines, she guessed two were men and three were women, but she couldn't see faces. Were they heirs? Guards? Silent Ones? Or was Roe right—had they found Queen Asana?

The wave lifted and then deposited them on the sand like seaweed, in a pile. Mayara scrambled to her feet, feeling for her glass knife.

But she didn't need it.

Roe launched herself off the sand. "Mother!"

Mayara dusted off her knees as she watched the reunion. Roe was embracing an exquisitely dressed woman drenched in pearls. An older man and woman clustered around her. Roe's grandparents, she guessed. They were all talking at the same time, laughing and crying and asking why and how. . . . And then Mayara heard the best sound in the world: Kelo's voice.

"Mayara? You're alive?"

"Kelo?" How could . . . But it was! He was here! With a cry, she threw herself at him. His arms closed around her. "You're here! How are you here? Why—"

He kissed her, and she kissed him back. He tasted exactly as she'd been daydreaming ever since they were torn apart.

"You're alive!" she said when they finally had a chance to breathe.

"*You're* alive!" he countered. "I thought—"

"I thought too! I was so afraid—"

"I was too. When they told me—"

"They told me too! You were dead. And then you weren't. Or maybe you were, but I didn't know. I believed you lived, but I didn't know. And now you're here." He hadn't died that day in the cove! He was alive and real! Elorna truly had saved him. He kissed her again. She kissed him back, feeling as if the rest of the world had faded into mist around them. She heard nothing, saw nothing, felt nothing, and tasted nothing but Kelo.

Then he drew back to look at her, only a few inches, and she studied him as if she wanted to memorize every curve and angle and crease. Tears were running down both their faces. She touched his cheek, half expecting him to vanish. How could this be real? It felt as if she were living inside a dream. "It's a miracle," she said.

"*You're* a miracle. Mayara, I'm sorry I told you to be a Silent One. It was selfish. I thought if you lived, there was hope. But I should have trusted you, trusted in your strength."

She cupped his face in her hands and started kissing him again. In between kisses, she asked, "But how is this possible?" She'd dreamed she'd find him after it was over, not so quickly and easily, as if fate had delivered him like a present wrapped with a bow. "Why are you here?"

"To find the queen's family and stop the test." He pulled back again. "Why are *you* here?"

She laughed. "Same. To find the queen and stop the test." A secret part of her had been so afraid that Elorna was wrong or lying. She hadn't let that part speak up, but it was there. She'd heard his screams. But he was here, and he'd been trying to save her all along. . . .

"All these reunions are lovely," a woman in a ruffled skirt

said, "but it would be even more delightful if they could be happening somewhere else." She nodded significantly down the beach, where the prone body of a man lay.

Mayara couldn't see who it was. She wondered if they'd killed someone. She wasn't sure she wanted to know. But the guards at the fortress—they'd noticed the body too, and they clearly *did* want to know. Dozens were pouring onto the stairs to the beach.

Then an arrow struck the sand.

Mayara and Kelo both tried to step in front of the other, to protect each other from the guards. Together, they backed away. *I won't let them hurt him,* she thought. She'd use her power if she had to. The ocean was still thick with spirits.

"It's time to leave," the queen said. "We must return to Yena and announce—"

Her eyes went wide, her mouth slack. Blood blossomed on her ivory bodice and spread between the pearls. The woman in the ruffles spun to scan the fortress battlements, as did Kelo. Roe reached for the queen. "Mother?"

And then Mayara saw Palia.

She stood behind the queen and held a glass-shard knife that was stained with blood.

"Mother?" Roe cried.

Queen Asana slumped forward into her daughter's arms.

"No, no, what's happening?" Roe asked. "Mayara, the angel seaweed . . ."

Angel seaweed couldn't help this. Blood was darkening the sand as it leeched through the queen's pearl dress. "Palia, what did you do?" Mayara breathed.

The woman in ruffles was uttering curse after curse. She knelt beside the queen and pulled powders and vials from her pockets. "Put pressure on the wound." She ripped ruffles from her skirt and balled them up, handing them to Roe to press onto the spreading scarlet.

Blood soaked through the ruffles.

"She's pierced a damn lung," the woman said. "No potion in the world can fix that. Dammit. This was *not* the plan. Your Majesty . . ."

In two strides, Mayara reached Palia and grabbed her shoulders. She shook the older woman. "What did you *do*?"

Palia didn't meet her eyes. Staring numbly at the queen, Palia let the knife fall from her fingers. It landed in the sand.

"Why?" Mayara asked.

"Because my daughter has dreams," Palia said, her eyes fixed on Queen Asana slumped in the sand with Roe sobbing against her.

"Your daughter?" That made no sense. She thought back to what Palia had told them about her daughter, how she'd studied the tides, until Palia was taken and there was no more money to support her dreams. "This won't help her! You were supposed to go home, go back to weaving sails, and send her to her last years at university. You were going to help her live her dreams. Remember?"

"She has dreams, but she also has powers," Palia said. "She'll lose everything if she's discovered and forced to choose. It has to end. No more test. No more Silent Ones."

Mayara wanted to shake her. "Roe was going to ask her mother to end the test!" This was the entire reason they'd come here! Everything they'd done to escape the island was for this very purpose, so why would—

"And it would work . . . until her family was in danger again," Palia said. "Queen Asana has proven time and again that she can be controlled. The second her family is recaptured by them"—she pointed toward the guards who were running down from the fortress toward the sand—"the test will resume. My daughter won't be safe with her as queen. We need a queen with no ties. Lanei will be the queen that Belene needs."

"Lanei! How could you listen to her? She tried to kill you! Plus, she's not even an heir! She can't be queen." Mayara wanted to scream in Palia's face. It was utterly illogical and idiotic—a queen could be crowned only in a grove, and Lanei was back on Akena Island fending off the Silent Ones and the spirits. She hadn't even escaped, had she?

"She's trying to save the future spirit sisters of Belene, which includes my daughter," Palia said. "She's willing to sacrifice for the greater good. How can I do less?"

"Easily!" Mayara shouted. "It's very easy *not* to stab the queen!" How could Palia do such a thing? *I know her! She's not . . .* But what did she really know about Palia? All she really knew was Palia loved her daughter and would do anything for her. Anything. "How could you put your trust in Lanei? Over the queen? Over us?"

"Everything Lanei has done has been to end the test. What about Queen Asana? What has she ever done to save any of us? She's sat by while spirit sisters died. Everyone in the last group of spirit sisters died, and she did nothing. Just sent more of us to die. I can't risk that happening to my child."

"Why blame Queen Asana? You heard Roe! It's the Families who are to blame. Lord Maarte and those like him! They took Queen Asana's family, threatened their safety."

"And Queen Asana wasn't willing to sacrifice them for the good of Belene," Palia said stubbornly and sadly. Mayara remembered how she'd seen Lanei whispering to Palia—she hadn't imagined *this* is what she'd been saying or that Palia would be so weak and fearful as to listen. "Lanei will sacrifice anyone and everything. She'll end the test permanently. Queen Asana couldn't do that. Look at her and Roe. Queen Asana would sacrifice us all for her."

From across the sand, by the prone body, there was shouting. She felt Kelo's arms close protectively around her, pulling her back from Palia. The soldiers had reached the sand. *And we're with a dying queen.*

ASANA KNEW WHAT IT FELT LIKE TO BE SUBMERGED IN WATER, HELD down until your lungs burned and your thoughts fractured.

This felt like that. She tried to focus on her daughter's face, but it blurred in front of her. Roe's voice sounded distant, wobbly.

She heard others talking about a woman who wasn't an heir who was to become queen, if she understood correctly. *That's not possible. There's always a trained heir in the grove, ready in case the queen falls.* She tried to sift through their words, to think like a queen and handle her responsibilities. But Roe was weeping. . . .

"Mother, I just found you," Roe was saying. "Don't leave me again."

"Oh, my sweet girl," Asana whispered. "I never left. My heart was with you, always." She tried to think of what she could say, wise and true, that Roe would be able to treasure. Something to fix this. There had to be words she could find.

She'd never been a great orator. Every speech she'd ever given was written by one of her chancellors or a representative of the Families. Her audiences had cheered because of the crown she wore, not because of what she said or who she was.

Lady Garnah was beside her, swearing colorfully, which made Asana smile. And then she coughed, which hurt. "You're going to die," Garnah said bluntly. "My potions can clean a thousand poisons from your blood, but this . . . I can't heal you, Your Majesty. You'd better say what you want to say."

*What do I want to say?*

*I want to be sure Roe lives. And if the leviathans wake . . .*

She could suffer through the pain a little longer to tell them what they'd need to know to live.

"I wasn't a very good queen," Asana said. "But I kept the leviathans asleep. The next queen *must* be a trained heir, or the leviathans will wake. They're restless already, and they'll feel my death. When the spirits on Belene are released with my death . . . the leviathans will wake with them. The new queen must send her thoughts to the Deepest Blue. This woman, the non-heir—she won't know how to do that. The Deepest Blue . . . She must send her mind to the Deepest Blue."

"We'll tell her," another woman promised—Asana didn't know who she was, but this must be Kelo's wife. He was clinging to her like a barnacle. *At least I brought someone joy.* That was nice. He was a nice boy.

"Where is the Deepest Blue?" Roe asked.

"To find it . . . follow the dreams."

"Mother, that doesn't make sense. Please . . . don't . . ." She choked on her last word.

*"Die." That's the word my Roe won't say.* Asana wanted to tell her that it would be all right. She'd gotten to see Roe, and that was a wonderful gift. Her Roe, all grown and beautiful and strong and clever and kind. She'd escaped the island and come here—Asana wanted to tell her how proud she was and how sorry.

She felt a prick in her side. Energy rushed through her, and her muscles tensed and twitched, her legs spasming.

"What did you do to her?" Roe cried.

Ignoring Roe, Garnah said to Asana, "This won't fix you, but you should feel more awake. Talk fast."

Pain came with being awake. She wanted to sink into it, make it stop. "The monsters dream of the beginning of the world. They must be convinced those dreams are real. Only then will they sleep and not destroy everyone and everything. You must tell the new queen that. She must trick them into believing that time hasn't moved on, the Great Mother never died, and humans were never born. Or everything . . . everyone . . ."

She heard shouting. *Guards?*

With a piece of her mind, Asana summoned air spirits—they whipped across the sand, creating a wall of wind that kept Lord Maarte's soldiers at bay. She also summoned water spirits to keep the Silent Ones from reaching the shore. "Promise me you'll tell her. I need to know I'll leave you okay. You must be okay. Promise me!"

Roe whispered, "I promise, Mother."

Good. That was good. She felt a little of the tension leave her limbs. It didn't hurt quite so much. Each stab of pain felt more like a bubble bursting inside her. Asana touched Roe's cheek, and left a smear of red on her daughter's skin. "I've missed you. I am sorry I was too afraid to save you. But after they had your father killed, I lost heart. And hope."

"Father is . . . dead?" Roe's voice broke, and Asana's heart broke with it.

"I am so very sorry, my sweet." She wished there were time for more words of comfort. She wanted to tell her so many things and to listen to everything Roe wanted to say and to learn what she was like now that she was nearly grown. But there wasn't any time left. "You must go now."

"Now? But . . ."

"Go now. Go, or Lord Maarte and his men will take you again. I couldn't bear that. Did you know he tried to have me poisoned? Garnah's foresight saved me from that. You can trust Garnah. Do not trust Maarte. He is not a good man. Promise me you will never let him have power over you."

"I promise," Roe choked out.

"Good girl. Now leave me. I will distract them. Kelo . . ."

"Yes, Your Majesty?"

"Take my mother and father to your lovely little village. Give them new lives."

"I will, Your Majesty," he promised.

That was very good.

"Garnah?"

"Yes?"

"I want it to hurt less."

"I can do that," Garnah said.

"Roe, I love you," Asana said.

Roe was crying. "I love you too, Mother."

As Garnah lifted a vial to her lips, Asana swallowed. She felt warmth spread down her throat and then through her body. Her skin tingled, but the pain began to fade. So did any feeling in her legs and arms. She didn't think she could move. But that was all right. She smiled up at her parents, who were clutching each other and crying. She wanted to tell them that she didn't hurt and that they'd be okay. Kelo would take them to his village, where they'd live out their lives in safety and obscurity. She thought she had enough strength to summon a spirit to take them. As for Roe, she had too long a journey to trust a spirit—Asana couldn't guarantee that she could hold on to life for the length of her trip. She'd have to travel by ship. Conveniently, Lord Maarte had plenty of those. Asana could generate enough confusion on the dock with her spirits to cover her escape. "Take a ship," Asana told Roe. The words felt like marbles in her mouth. She rolled them around her tongue, tasting each of them. "Sail as fast as you can to Yena. Find this non-heir and warn her. Save yourself and the islands."

There. She'd done all she could.

Asana's eyes landed on the woman who had stabbed her.

"Would you like me to kill her?" Garnah offered.

"No. Let her take the blame," Asana said. "She deserves that." The Silent Ones from Akena Island would be here as soon as Asana's power failed, and they'd find a dead queen and a woman with a bloody knife. They'd know what had occurred. They would arrest her murderer, try her, and then give her to the spirits.

Her fate was sealed. *And so is mine.*

*But it's up to me to make sure Roe is free to claim hers.*

Her murderer had fallen to her knees and was weeping, but Asana couldn't feel pity for her. Through the eyes of her spirits, she saw Lord Maarte's soldiers trying to force their way through the wall of wind her spirits had created. They wouldn't cross until she let them. Or until she died.

"Let me be queen one last time." *Or perhaps for the first time.*

# CHAPTER TWENTY-TWO

Kelo clasped Mayara's hands. He had his instructions from Queen Asana. Take her mother and father to safety. Take them home. He knew the other villagers would hide them. They'd be safe, in case the Families wanted any kind of retaliation.

They'd be able to build new lives.

"Mayara . . ."

"I know. You have to go."

"Come with me! The queen's daughter will deliver the message. You and I can go home, with the queen's parents. Keep them safe." But he knew as he said the words that she was going to say no. And this time, he was going to respect her choice and let her go.

She shook her head. "Roe needs me. She can't face the woman responsible for her mother's . . . for what happened . . . on her own. And I . . . Kelo, I'm the one who introduced Lanei to Roe and Palia. If it weren't for me . . . I have to help fix this."

But when she was done doing what she had to do, and when he was done fulfilling the queen's request, they'd be together again. He believed that. He knew now the lengths he would go to for her. "I understand. But when it's over, come back to me, if you can. Or I'll come find you. I'll always come find you."

"We'll be together again," Mayara told him, and kissed him.

Then there was no more time. He had a thousand things he wanted to say, but he thought she knew them all. She knew that he would come after her and wanted to save her and that he didn't want to be parted from her. He'd go with her, if he could. But Queen Asana had asked him to save her parents, and he couldn't defy a dying queen.

He shepherded the queen's father and mother toward the whale spirit. They splashed through the eerily calm water. Boosting the queen's mother onto the whale's back, he looked back at the beach. Only a few yards away, a wall of wind tore through the sand, obscuring everything beyond it, buying them all time. He had to hope that Queen Asana lived until they reached the village. They'd all die if she lost control of the spirits too soon.

So they had to be quick.

He climbed onto the back of the whale, trying not to think, trying not to doubt, trying not to mourn, trying not to fear. He braced Asana's parents. "Ready?"

"I don't want to leave her," her mother said. "I need to be with her!"

"She wants to know you're safe," Kelo said. "That's what she needs."

"But she—"

Kelo cut her off. "You can give her this gift. Ease her sorrow." His words sank in, and he saw the queen's mother deflate. Her father cradled his wife's shoulders. A moment later, it didn't matter what they felt or thought or wanted, because the whale was shooting through the water.

Kelo felt spray in his face, tasted the sea. It tasted like tears.

He never dreamed he would leave Mayara so soon after he found her. But he'd also never imagined he'd be complicit in torture or that he'd be willing to drug children. If he didn't help save the queen's family after all he'd done, then he wasn't worthy of being with Mayara.

*This, then, is the line I won't cross.*

Clinging to the back of the whale spirit, he rode with the queen's parents along the shore of Olaku toward his village, while the night darkened and the wind howled as if it knew what was coming. *Maybe it does.* The spirits must be able to sense the queen's impending death—they were linked in a way he couldn't begin to comprehend. Once she died, they'd be free of all commands, free to kill the hated humans, free to behave like wild spirits with no one to stop their destruction, until the new queen took control.

*Almost there,* he thought.

He saw his village up ahead. The beach with the boats, the white houses nestled into the cove. . . . He felt the whale spirit buck beneath them. The queen was losing control.

"Swim," he ordered.

He helped Asana's parents slide off the whale spirit. Pacing them, he shouted encouragement as they swam through the churning sea. When Asana's father slowed, Kelo doubled back and hooked a hand under his armpit. He kicked sideways, pulling her father through the water.

Waves broke over them, and he sucked in air. He kept his eyes focused on the shore ahead. Around him, he heard shrieking cries, spirits calling to spirits. Something smooth brushed past his leg.

And then his knee scraped against the pebbly shore. He pulled Asana's father to his feet. Her mother was already crawling out of the surf.

Bells were ringing in the village, and he saw his friends and neighbors running for the caves. Drawing Asana's parents with him, he urged them onward. "Quickly!"

They clung to him as they stumbled away from the shore. Behind them, Kelo heard the waves crash like thunder, and cold water slapped his back. He didn't turn around.

*Crack.*

A tree crashed across the path that led up to the caves. Asana's mother screamed as debris struck them.

He risked a look back at the sea.

The spirits looked as if they were fighting themselves, writhing and churning in the water. *She's fighting them for control,* he thought.

They had, at most, minutes.

There wasn't time to find a way around the tree.

Instead he led them up another path, one he knew so well he could have done it blindfolded. They climbed the path up above the village to his studio. It was still draped in charms, exactly as he'd left it when he'd begun his journey.

He pushed through the door and shepherded Asana's parents inside. He secured the door behind them with a stone that he rolled in front of it. Running to the windows, he slammed the shutters closed. They were still damaged from the last spirit storm, but he thought maybe they'd hold one more time.

Gathering up charms that still lay scattered around the floor, he began draping them around the interior perimeter of his studio. Without speaking, Asana's parents joined him, stuffing charms into cracks and hanging them over the shuttered windows.

Outside, the spirits of Belene went wild as the queen died.

MAYARA WATCHED KELO DISAPPEAR ACROSS THE WAVES AND HAD the terrible feeling that she wasn't going to see him again. *He came to save me. With the queen, somehow.* That felt as wondrous as a sunrise after a storm. She wished she could have asked him how he'd left home, how her parents were, how he felt about her choice. She wanted to tell him about Elorna and the Island of Testing and everything she'd felt and done and seen. . . .

But he was lost in the frothing blueness of the churning sea.

*I should have gone with him.*

But the choice was made.

Kelo would be safe, but Roe needed her.

*We need to be apart now, so we can have a chance to someday be together.*

Spirits were dancing within waterspouts, swooping over the cliffs, and tearing up the sand all around them. Their shrieks mingled with the crash of the waves and the roar of the wind to encase them in a steady cyclone of noise.

Queen Asana was instructing the lady in ruffles. "Garnah, swear to me you will keep my daughter safe." Her words came out as a harsh whisper, and her breath had a whistle to it, as if she'd swallowed the wind and it was now tearing her up from within. It was a terrible sound that Mayara wished she'd never had to hear.

*This must be a thousand times worse for Roe.*

Roe was crying in heaving gulps. "I don't want to be 'safe'! I want to be with you! I never chose to be safe. I never wanted you to sacrifice anything for me."

The woman in ruffles, Garnah, said, as if she were trying to be helpful, "No one will be safe when the queen dies."

Roe let out a sound like a wounded gull.

"Promise me!" the queen rasped to Garnah. "See that Roe reaches the new queen and delivers my message unharmed. Protect her by any means necessary! She will need you, before this is through."

Garnah's eyes shifted to Palia. "'Any means' is my specialty. You have my word."

Mayara felt a shift in the spirits—they knew the queen was weakening. She felt their eagerness and their hunger. It made her feel as if claws were tearing at her skin from the inside out. She stretched her own mind out, trying to soothe them, but it was like shouting when everyone else was already screaming.

"Mother!" Roe cried.

*She must feel it too.*

*The queen won't last much longer.*

"You must go, my little Roe," the queen said. "Go now, while I can still help you."

With a gentle hand on her shoulder, Mayara tried to draw Roe away, but Roe pushed her off and collapsed across her mother. "You can't die!" she cried. "You can't! I just found you, and I can't lose you!"

Mayara felt the spirits' hunger soar—if the queen died before they left this beach, they'd all be torn apart. Lowering her voice, she asked Garnah, "How much time does she have?"

"Not enough," Garnah said grimly. "Can you do something about the girl, or do I need to? We can't stay here. Also, do you know how to sail one of those ships?"

"A small sailboat, yes. A big sailing ship, no." She'd been out on the village fishing boats, and she could maneuver a small craft around the harbor like any islander could, but the trading ships . . . They were as different from the village boats as a whale to a minnow.

"Then we'll need a sailor."

Mayara pointed to the prone body of Lord Maarte, lying untouched in a ring of sand, surrounded by spirits. "He can sail. If we can make him."

Garnah smiled humorlessly. "I can make him—I can make a man do *anything.* Bring the queen's daughter." Raising her voice, she said to the queen, "Asana, we need a path to Lord Maarte, then a path to the ship. Can you do that?"

Mayara wrapped her arm around Roe's waist. "Roe, we have to go!"

Roe fought her, elbowing Mayara in the stomach and trying to yank herself out of Mayara's grip. "I'm not leaving my mother to die alone! My father died without my even knowing! I can't leave my mother!"

Wincing at the stomach jab, Mayara thought of her own parents but didn't let Roe go. "The leviathans will wake. Assuming she had a plan for how to reach the grove, Lanei has to be warned. If we go now, we'll have a chance of catching her before it's too late."

Reaching up, Asana laid one hand on Roe's cheek. "I am not alone. I can feel you and see you through the spirits. Knowing you are gone from here . . ." She then broke into a violent cough. Red spots stained the sand. A drop of blood hit Roe's forehead. It dripped in a streak down her temple and then mixed with her tears. "Go."

"I love you, Mother!"

"My little Roe, I love you."

"I will avenge you and Father!"

"Avenge us by living," the queen ordered.

Mayara kept an arm wrapped around Roe as she shuttled her across the sand. In front of them, the wind wall split, opening a path. Sand flurried on either side of them as they hurried through.

Reaching Lord Maarte, Garnah blew a handful of powder in his face. He spasmed, then coughed, waking. "I demand—" he began.

"I am Death," Garnah said flatly. "You will demand nothing of me."

Mayara felt the coldness of the words slide into her.

Garnah continued. "You will sail us to Yena, per order of the queen, or I will visit every member of your family, down to the most distant cousin, and end their existence. Your line will be wiped from the world."

She'd expected that Garnah wouldn't be subtle, based on how she'd acted already. Still, she wasn't prepared for *that*. It wasn't merely the words that were chilling; it was the *way* she spoke. Hollow, as if she truly could murder a family and feel no remorse. Mayara did not doubt that she meant it, nor that she could do it. *We're trusting our lives to her?*

"You wouldn't!" he blustered. "You'd be murdering innocents—"

"I am not capable of pity," Garnah said to Lord Maarte, and Mayara believed it. *What kind of person has the queen sent us with?* She tightened her arm around Roe's shoulders as Garnah bore down on the island's ruler. "Or guilt. No regret.

No mercy. Your family will die if you do not obey, and I will feel nothing but the satisfaction of honoring my promise to one who valued me. In fact, it will be my pleasure."

Lord Maarte struggled to his feet without another word and then followed them through the narrow path between the spirits to the dock. The trading ship was tied to the dock, though it strained against its ropes as the wind threatened to topple it. The dock itself swayed and creaked so loudly that Mayara thought it was going to splinter into a thousand pieces beneath their feet.

She saw water spirits around the posts, shoving against the dock. Their faces were split with mouths filled with shark teeth, and their bodies writhed in the waves. The water was so churned it looked as if it were boiling. She didn't know how anyone could sail in this.

But then, with shrieks as if they were in pain, the spirits retreated. They swarmed the shore, forming a barrier of sand between them and Lord Maarte's guards and a barrier of water between them and the Silent Ones from Akena.

The sea around the ship became calm.

Unnaturally calm. It looked like a mirror, with only the faintest wave to mar its surface. Farther out, the sea bubbled as if it were boiling, but not here.

Garnah herded Lord Maarte onto the ship. "To Yena."

He didn't protest, which Mayara thought was wise. He had a sense of self-preservation, at least, and his shore, swarming as it was with barely contained spirits, was no place to stay. He ran back and forth across the deck, preparing the sails and untying the ship from the dock. Mayara joined him, helping where she knew how, as did Roe.

Garnah merely watched them all with arms folded, and Mayara was reminded of the Silent Ones and the way they stood guard, faceless and voiceless. Except that Garnah's face was her mask, and Mayara didn't know if there was anything more human beneath it.

Still . . . it was working.

In mere minutes, they had the ship ready. Mayara helped unfurl the sails, while Lord Maarte took the helm. She felt an air spirit shift its attention from the shore to their sail, and a blast of wind filled the sail. It puffed out, and they sped away from the dock.

The air spirit separated from the others, following them. It was lithe and translucent and unnervingly elongated—it looked like a man who had been stretched so much that he'd become thin enough for light to pass through. It had arms and legs that wavered at its sides, thin as seaweed, and its face was distorted in a wordless cry as it blew into the sail.

"When she dies, you will need to fight it," Garnah said softly. "Wise that the queen only chose to send one."

Mayara jumped. She hadn't realized how close the other woman had come. Sweat prickled her arms and back—she had been running around the ship, readying it to sail. "I don't know if—"

"Kill it if you can. Or drive it toward me, and I'll take care of it."

Mayara swallowed. And then nodded. *She's right. When the queen dies . . .* An heir was always present in the grove so that the transfer would happen as smoothly and quickly as possible, but there would be a few minutes where no one controlled the spirits.

They'd have to survive those minutes, out on the open sea, with a spirit filling their sails.

"This is unnatural!" Lord Maarte called from the helm. "The ship isn't built to withstand these speeds!" He hurried away from the wheel to secure a line that had loosened. The sails were straining against the mast, and the ship was keeling in the water as it sliced through the waves.

"If it breaks, we'll swim," Mayara said.

"Do you have any concept of how far—"

She stole a little of the cold darkness she'd heard in Garnah's voice as she interrupted him. "Then you should make sure the ship doesn't break." She crossed to Roe, who was leaning against the port railing. Behind them, in the distance, the island of Olaku looked as if it had been swallowed in mist and foam. It was the spirits, she knew, churning up the sea, but it felt as if her island had been erased, smudged out of existence like a smear of paint on a canvas.

She hoped Kelo had made it home.

"I thought it was possible I'd die on the island," Roe said. "I was all right with that. Not that I *wanted* to die, but I'd accepted it as a possible result of my choice. And I was willing to take that risk, because I didn't think I could live with myself if I didn't at least try. But this . . . was not in any of my plans."

"I know." Mayara tried to think of more she could say. She thought of how she'd felt when Elorna had died . . . or when she'd believed her sister had died. But she didn't want Roe to feel like she was comparing their pain. "I'm sorry."

Roe leaned farther out, letting the spray hit her face and dampen her arms. "Lanei will pay for this."

"If she's queen—"

"Queens can die," Roe said. "As we've seen."

"You aren't a murderer," Mayara said. She knew the rage that Roe was feeling—after Elorna's death, she'd had the intense need for someone to blame. She'd railed against the queen, the world, even Elorna herself for not hiding her power better. But with time, the pain had softened, though it had never gone away. "Killing her won't bring your mother back."

"She's a murderer who doesn't deserve to be queen," Roe said.

Mayara opened her mouth. Closed it. "Yes." She knew she should say more, try to talk Roe out of this unhealthy line of thought. She didn't know if talk of mercy or moral high ground would have any impact. "But your mother wouldn't want you imprisoned for the rest of your life. She'd want you free, alive, living your life. After my sister died . . ." She stopped. It was impossible to talk about Elorna now that she knew the truth.

Beside her, Roe gasped and stepped back.

Mayara felt it a second later—like a rip inside her. She heard the air spirit scream both in her mind and in her ears, the kind of sound that made her bones feel as if they would shatter.

"She's dead," Roe gasped. "I've lost both my mother and my father."

If it had been Mayara, she knew how she might have felt: gutted, empty, broken. It was how she'd felt when she'd heard the news about Elorna's death. She remembered the world seemed to fade around her, the way it did when she dived deep, and she wouldn't have cared if a volcano had erupted and claimed the island in its embrace. She expected Roe to do the same, especially because of the way she'd shattered on the beach after her mother was stabbed.

But instead Roe howled.

She fixed every bit of her rage at the air spirit that was hurtling toward them, with death and blood in its heart—

And Mayara heard the command echo through the spirit.

*Destroy yourself!*

The force of the command was so powerful that Mayara reeled backward, stumbling against the side of the ship. In the air, the spirit tore at its own flesh, ripping holes in the translucent thinness as if it were tearing paper.

It didn't bleed. Instead it rained. Silver drops fell on the ship's deck.

And then all was silent.

The sea barely lapped. The wind barely blew. The ship's sails fluttered, slapping against the mast. It happened so quickly that Mayara had barely had time to be afraid, much less to react. "Roe . . ." She stopped. She didn't know what to say.

Roe was panting, her hands on her knees, her head hanging down.

"That was amazing!" Garnah crowed. She then turned to Lord Maarte. "Get us to Yena. As quickly as you can. There's wind still, stirred by the wild spirits. Use it."

As they sailed, Mayara worked to coax the sails into holding as much of the wind as they could catch. Lord Maarte barked orders, and she scurried over the deck, adjusting lines, tightening pulleys, and ducking under the boom. She would have resented the orders, except he was running back and forth between the lines and the wheel just as much as she was.

He'd shed his embroidered coat, leaving it in an ignoble heap on the deck, where it soaked in spray from the sea. His sleeves were rolled up beyond his elbows, and sweat mixed with saltwater. Maybe it was self-preservation, but he was at least trying to keep them moving forward.

In the absence of the queen, the heirs and Silent Ones had performed their duty: banding their thoughts together to "freeze" the spirits of Belene. The spirits would exist in a kind of suspended state until the next queen seized control over them. *Which should happen any moment now,* Mayara thought. Until then, the ship was sailing on whatever stray breeze came off the wild, untamed ocean.

At least they'd survived the moments of queenless wildness. Mayara thought again of Kelo and hoped he and Asana's parents had made it to shelter in time. Now all that was needed was for a new queen to take control before the wild spirits noticed that Belene was unprotected—and before the leviathans woke.

She hoped it wouldn't be Lanei.

A trained heir was supposed to be in the grove, ready for this moment. She should be the one to take charge, and if she did, she'd know how to quiet the leviathans and this whole journey would be unnecessary. *And I can return to Kelo and resume my life.*

Or at least she hoped she would.

She wondered suddenly how a new queen would feel about how she and Roe had abandoned the test. It was considered treason. Elorna's warning whispered in her ear.

What if they arrived in Yena and were arrested for treason?

"Roe . . . what if Lanei is *not* queen?"

"Then no one will call it regicide," Roe said.

Across the deck, Garnah burst out laughing. "I *like* her."

Mayara didn't believe Roe would truly kill anyone. It was one thing to feel that rage when it was merely a faraway concept, but faced with looking straight into another's eyes . . . *She won't do it. She's not like that.* But that wasn't what she wanted to talk about. "We quit the test. How do you think a new queen will react to that?" Mayara lowered her voice, but it didn't matter—with the low wind, her words traveled across the ship.

"You'll be jailed," Lord Maarte said cheerfully. He was at the helm, sailing with all the confidence of a man who believes he's destined to win. "Unless someone with influence intervenes for you."

"And are *you* volunteering for that?" Roe asked. "You, who separated me from my mother? You, who kept us imprisoned, even though we were innocent, for years?"

"It's a heavy responsibility the Families bear, to sacrifice the happiness of a few for the safety and well-being of all Belene," Lord Maarte said.

Mayara thought of her village and the spirit storm that had claimed so many while the heirs guarded the Neran Family stronghold, miles away from danger. "You never had to sacrifice your *own* happiness, though. You only ever cared about yourself and your own family."

"Not true! Rokalara, were you and your grandparents ever treated unkindly? Were you not given everything you needed? Indeed, you had the best of everything."

"Except my parents. Did you know my father was dead? You must have. He's been gone for years, and you never told me."

"We thought it was a kindness to keep it from you."

"And my mother? You kept me from her, and now I've lost her too." Roe advanced across the ship. Her hands curled into fists.

Mayara saw Lord Maarte glance at the sky, as if looking for spirits, and then he relaxed when he didn't see them—there were no nearby spirits to draw. "As it appeared to me," he said, a mild tone to his voice, "you were the one who brought her murderer close to her."

Roe lunged at him.

Mayara caught her by the waist. "We need him to sail us to Yena. And maybe sail us away, depending on what we find there." She tasted the guilt, sour in the back of her throat. *He's right, though. I brought Lanei to Roe and Palia.* If she hadn't chased after her . . . If she hadn't tried to work with her, instead of labeling her an enemy . . .

"Just to interject one wee little detail you should be aware of," Garnah said. "Lord Maarte did attempt to have Queen Asana poisoned, well before your friend with the knife joined us."

"That's nonsense," Lord Maarte said, though his eyes were wild. "You have no proof."

"I have the queen's word."

Roe again launched herself at Lord Maarte, and Mayara held her back once more. Then Roe steadied herself and drew herself upright, looking very much like her mother. "You will face judgment for what you've done to my family. I promise you that. You'll live while we have use for you, and then, for the good of Belene, you'll die."

Lord Maarte smirked. "That's what I told your mother."

"Gag him," Roe ordered.

"With pleasure." Garnah tore a ruffle from her skirt, stuffed it in his mouth, and then knotted it hard at the back of his head. "Remove it, and I'll remove your tongue," she said sweetly.

The wind began to blow again, stronger, and Mayara felt a

kind of tickling sensation in the back of her mind. She wasn't certain what it meant, but she thought—

"There's a new queen," Roe said.

Yes, that was exactly what it meant.

"But who?" Mayara asked.

The ship began to pick up speed as the sails filled with wind.

Not long after, when they saw the glimmer of the mother-of-pearl-coated city of Yena, the jewel of Belene, they tied the gagged Lord Maarte belowdecks. The three women then guided the ship into the city's dock alone.

# CHAPTER TWENTY-THREE

The first thing Mayara heard was the city bells. It was as if every tower and spire were singing, all the melodies crashing together, bubbling like seafoam. She saw the city before her, rising up from the harbor as if it were crowning the sea. It looked luminescent in the sunlight. Every surface was covered in mother-of-pearl.

*I wonder what Kelo thought of this.*

She wished they were seeing it together.

"Wish they'd stop that," Garnah muttered. "Damn bells giving me a headache."

"It's tradition," Mayara said. "The bells both to mourn and rejoice." Even in their little village, the bells had rung when an old queen passed and a new one ascended. It was a mix of sadness at the loss of life and a celebration of not being all dead.

"You have irritating traditions." Garnah lifted her skirts as she stepped off the ship.

An official scurried toward them down the dock. He wore a crisp white uniform and carried a ledger. Mayara felt a rush of fear—if anyone guessed who they were . . .

"You need permission to dock," the man barked. "No ships from the Neran Stronghold are scheduled—"

"I am Rokalara, daughter of Queen Asana," Roe said, cutting him off, "and this is Lady Garnah, companion of the queen." *So much for anonymity,* Mayara thought. It was too late to shush or interrupt her. She hoped Roe knew what she was doing. "We've come to fulfill Her Majesty's final wishes and pay our respects to the new queen."

The official blinked at them.

He looked at his ledger. Peeked at them. Looked at his book.

Apparently, this wasn't a situation he was used to dealing with.

"Can you tell us the name of the new queen?" Mayara asked.

"I'm sorry, but it hasn't been announced yet."

"How about the old queen?" Garnah asked. "Any news on how she died?" She was beaming at him, as if they hadn't just witnessed Queen Asana's murder on the sands of Olaku Island.

He didn't know.

"Do you know where we can find the new queen?" Roe demanded. "Is she in the palace? Or is she still in the grove?"

Again, he didn't know.

"Can you point us in the direction of the grove?" Mayara jumped in.

He seemed relieved, perhaps because she'd asked a question he knew how to answer. "Yes, of course. Left at the end of the docks, then keep to the shore. It's at the base of the palace's tallest tower. Can't miss it."

"Thank you," Mayara said.

"You'll want robes. You can't walk through the city today like that. Not on Coronation Day. There are extras at the end of the dock."

Both Mayara and Roe thanked him as Garnah began to complain that she didn't want robes, her dress was delightful, he was rude, and couldn't he do something about those damn endless bells? Coming up beside her, Mayara shepherded Garnah past the official.

"Mark down that it's the queen's ship," Roe suggested to him.

Looking relieved, he made notes in his ledger. "It's a difficult day," the man said. "It's important to heed the rules on difficult days."

Garnah made a snorting sound, and Mayara heard her grumbling about "small people with small minds clinging to their minutiae" as they hurried down the dock.

"Please don't cause trouble," Mayara whispered to her. "We can't draw attention to ourselves."

It was important that no one stopped them before they reached the queen. The quicker they did this, the better. Especially if the queen was Lanei.

Stepping off the dock, Mayara saw a heap of white fabric on a cart. She drew three robes out of the pile. They were more like cloaks, designed to wrap around whatever you wore, with a simple ribbon at the neck to tie them on. As they dressed, Mayara noticed that unless they were in uniform like the harbor official, everyone wore similar white robes.

Mourning robes.

Her village didn't keep with that tradition, but the city did.

"It's to symbolize that we're all the same," Roe explained. "We've felt a loss, yet we still live. We're sharing our pain. It's meant to be comforting. Like the bells."

"I am not comforted," Garnah said. "And my pain is no one else's business."

"Think of it as wearing a disguise," Mayara offered. In the robes, they'd blend in. She thought the Silent Ones who knew them from Akena were all on Olaku Island, but it was best not to take unnecessary risks. "Come on. If Lanei is still at the grove, we might be able to talk to her alone. If it is Lanei."

They followed the official's directions, turning left down a shell-encrusted path along the shore. It was only a few minutes before they saw it.

The grove lay cradled in the bones of a leviathan. A rib cage, polished by the wind, protected it from the sea. Just beyond the bones, waves slammed against the shore, and just behind it was the soaring spire of the tallest tower of the palace. The tower was doorless, and the windows were so high that Mayara saw them only as smudges on the iridescent shell wall.

"No guards," Garnah noted.

"Is that a bad sign?" Roe asked.

"The grove is sacred," Mayara said. "It shouldn't need to be guarded." She'd heard stories about the coronation grove since she was a kid. Every country had one: a special place where a woman of power could bond with all the spirits linked to their land. Entering it when one wasn't an heir ready to take the reins of power was . . . tacky, at best.

Most likely, they'd enter the grove, find an heir at her post, and have to answer a slew of potentially embarrassing or incriminating why-are-you-here questions. *That's the best case.* In the best case, a trained heir was the new queen, and Lanei had never made it to Yena.

"That's stupid," Garnah said. "Of course sacred spaces should be guarded. You have an unwarranted faith in people's ability to respect what's important." She lifted her ruffled skirts to climb over a chunk of rock.

"Without a queen, we all die," Roe said. "It's fear, not respect."

"So that's why no guards," Mayara said, hoping she was right. There was something eerie about the emptiness of the path to the grove. Behind them the city was filled with white-robed men, women, and children, mourning the death of the old queen and rejoicing the ascension of the new. Every bell had been ringing nonstop, an endless proclamation of the fact that the world had changed again and they'd survived. *Or at least survived so far,* she thought.

"Still think it's short-sighted," Garnah said. "You can't post a few guards for a place this important?"

"It always has an heir stationed here," Roe argued. "She can call on spirits to defend the grove against whoever wants to disrespect it."

"You people trust in tradition too much," Garnah said.

"You realize if Belene cared less about tradition and more about—"

Roe cut her off. "Stop."

She rushed forward, down the final curve of the path and in between two vertical ribs. Mayara wondered what she'd seen and felt her stomach lurch. It couldn't be good. She felt as if she was beginning to forget what a good surprise felt like. Yes, she'd seen Kelo and had confirmation that he wasn't dead, but she'd also been parted from him again ridiculously quickly.

Mayara and Garnah followed after, coming into the grove behind Roe.

Inside the bones, there was a circle of blue stones with cracks that ran like veins through them, with smooth obsidian in the middle.

A body lay facedown in the center.

"It's an heir," Roe said flatly.

Mayara saw the uniform. *She's right.*

Blood pooled, rich red against the black stone. No one else was in the stone circle. "Did spirits kill her?" Mayara asked. *I can't believe I'm hoping for that.*

Garnah knelt beside her. "Not unless Belenian spirits kill with knives." Nudging the body over, she revealed the hilt of a blade buried in the heir's heart.

Mayara stared at the blade, seeing again the queen on the beach, dying. It was hard to breathe. Placing her hands on her knees, she tried to suck in enough air so that her head stopped spinning. It was like being underwater for too long, with dark bubbles popping in her vision.

This must have been Lanei's plan. All of it. Murder a queen. Murder an heir. And all the while, see herself as the hero righting the wrongs of the world.

"We need to tell someone," Mayara said.

Garnah snorted. "And be accused of her murder?"

"Lanei is queen now," Roe said, her voice hollow.

*She's right.* That's what this meant. And if it were true, then an untrained woman was now the only one who could keep Belene safe . . . a woman who didn't know what she needed to know to protect the islands. Mayara thought of Kelo and their village. "We have to find her before it's too late."

"Exactly what do you call 'too late'? My mother is dead! This heir is dead!"

Gathering herself, Mayara straightened. "'Too late' is everyone dead. Come on. We have to deliver your mother's message." She made herself look at the heir's body. "It's my fault. If I'd left Lanei on the island . . ."

"She would have killed us," Roe said.

"The spirits hadn't killed us," Mayara said. "We could have hidden from them and from her. All we needed to do was survive a few more weeks."

"I'm the one who told you to remove the traps."

"You wanted to save people."

"Mayara—stop it. If anyone is to blame, it's Lanei," Roe said firmly. "And she'll pay for it."

"But you can't touch her," Mayara said. "She's the queen. She'll be defended by both soldiers and spirits. She's a hundred times more powerful now that she's linked to the spirits of Belene. Plus, we *can't* kill her. Belene needs a queen. You felt it when all the spirits were wild."

"Another heir will take her place," Roe said. "She shouldn't be queen. She's a murderer. I don't know that I believe her that she hadn't killed before. She said she didn't kill anyone in the first group. What if she was lying?"

"You still plan to murder her?" Mayara said. "Roe, that's not you. You're the one who thinks of others, not herself. You're the one who believes in what's right. You're the one who always wanted to be a hero. I only wanted an ordinary life." She was grateful that Garnah had stayed silent, watching them with a vaguely amused expression. Mayara focused just on Lanei. "She needs the information we have, about how to reach the Deepest Blue before the leviathans wake. We find her. We *don't* kill her. And she makes sure the monsters stay asleep. Exactly as you promised your mother."

MAYARA WRAPPED HER ROBE CLOSE AS THEY HURRIED THROUGH THE streets. She felt as if the blood she'd seen had stained her somehow, even though her eyes told her that the cloth was still crisp white and that she looked no different from any of the other Belenians on the streets of the city.

The bells still rang, but she barely heard them anymore.

*I don't belong here.*

It hit her hard. On the beach, saying goodbye to Kelo, she'd been so certain that accompanying Roe was the right thing to do. But maybe this wasn't a dive she should make.

This should never have been her responsibility. Except that she had been the fool who trusted Lanei, who believed she'd convinced her to go along with their plan . . . and instead, Lanei had been the one convincing Palia. . . . *How could I have misjudged them both so badly?*

Around them, the city was flooded with people. Shops were closed, and every islander was in the streets. Sugary candies were being given out from carts that would usually have held fruits, flowers, and fish—it was part of the Coronation Day tradition, to remind everyone that life can be sweet even while it can vanish as quickly as sugar melts on the tongue.

She remembered tasting the sugar drops years ago, when Queen Asana had been crowned. It hadn't meant much to her then—the transition had been quick, and no one had died before the new queen asserted her dominance over the spirits. So it was just a nice treat. No lessons. Just sugar. That afternoon, she and Kelo had played on the rocks, poking at starfish in the tidal pools and watching the crabs scuttle back and forth. They'd been allowed to stay up late, and Grandmama had pointed out the constellations, naming them and telling stories about the leviathans whose bones comprised much of the islands.

She wondered if Kelo was remembering that day too. Had he

eaten any sugar drops? Was he all right? Had he made it to the village in time? What had he told the others about the queen's parents? She wondered if they were able to mourn while still hiding who they were.

She wondered who would be mourning the heir who still lay in her own blood in the grove. *Another heir would be coming to replace her. She'll be found soon.*

The heirs wouldn't allow the grove to be unguarded for long.

She wondered what they made of Lanei, an untrained heir as queen. *Maybe one of them has already told her about the Deepest Blue. Maybe we're worrying for nothing.*

She imagined they'd tell Lanei, and Lanei would inform Mayara and Roe that it was all taken care of. Maybe she'd even have an explanation for what happened with the queen—that Palia had misunderstood and had acted rashly and independently. But Mayara knew even as the thought blossomed that it was ridiculous. Lanei had maneuvered herself into position to become queen. She'd murdered an heir. Of course the queen's murder hadn't been a "misunderstanding."

*What will she do to us if we go to her?* Lanei would know they knew the truth. *But we promised the queen. And if Lanei isn't told . . .*

"Maybe another heir has already told her," Mayara said. "Maybe it would be better if we left. Got as far away from here as possible." Back home. To hide in the village she came from. She'd never told Lanei where her home was. She could live out her life in anonymity. . . .

Unless Lord Maarte came for her.

Unless the Silent Ones returned.

Surely Elorna would help protect her. And Kelo would hide her and Roe. *And Garnah, I guess.* Except that Lanei didn't know who Garnah was.

"Are you willing to risk your islands on a 'maybe'?" Garnah asked.

"Lanei won't be happy to see us," Mayara said. "Maybe you

could tell her, Lady Garnah. She doesn't know you know what she's done."

"She doesn't know me at all," Garnah said. "She may not listen."

"Are you afraid of her?" Roe asked Mayara.

*Of course.* She was more afraid than she'd ever felt on Akena Island. At least then she'd been certain she was doing the right thing by hiding. Here, she was doing the opposite of hiding. She was diving through a monster's skull, but there was no clear pool of water at the bottom. "Yes. She's a murderer, and now she has the power of a queen."

But neither Roe nor Garnah slowed. And so Mayara kept pace with them. She saw the palace rising up before them. It was curved like a shell, and a bridge made of translucent blue stone broke like a frozen wave through the gilded doorway.

A crowd of white-robed islanders had gathered by the blue bridge. Many were laying flowers and sugar drops at the foot of the bridge. A few were singing the mourner's lullaby. Others were embracing and laughing, grateful to be alive.

It was an odd day, Coronation Day.

Usually most islanders felt relief.

*They won't feel relief if the leviathans come,* Mayara thought grimly. She didn't turn aside. Instead she followed Roe and Mayara to the blue stone bridge. She waited for a moment, wondering if they would be allowed across, while Lady Garnah spoke with the guard.

Then they were waved through.

She tried to remember the Mayara she used to be, before the island and before Lanei. She'd been fearless, reckless even, trying to live large enough for two. She didn't feel like that Mayara anymore. She'd seen death and fear and loss. But she was diving in anyway.

# CHAPTER TWENTY-FOUR

Beyond the known world, beyond the horizon, beyond where any ship had ever sailed, deep within the sea, where the currents were thick and powerful and the sun was a weak shadow of nearly forgotten daylight, slept the wild spirits.

They were all water spirits and all ancient. They could remember a time before humans when they were supreme, when they were the only ones who created and destroyed.

They felt when the queen who told them such soothing lullabies died. Her absence was like the removal of a blanket. They felt the water on their skin, the coolness of the depths, and their minds churned sluggishly.

Another would come. Sing them back to sleep. Give them the dreams they so desperately craved. They *wanted* to sleep, to dream, to exist again in that long-ago age and forget that the world had moved on. Being awoken was like feeling the Great Mother die once more. Once more, they remembered they were alone.

They woke and they waited.

But no one came.

And slowly, they remembered everything.

Three of them woke, giant monsters that dwarfed imagination. One was shaped like a dragon with a scaly serpent's body, blackened wings, and eyes that were white-hot embers. Another was a kraken, with tentacles the thickness of a ship's hull. And the third was a many-headed snake, with a body that could wrap around the city of Yena.

They swam unerringly toward Belene.

INSIDE THE PALACE, MAYARA FELT AS SMALL AND DRAB AS ONE OF the swallows that nested in the eaves. Everything was encased in nacre. *Like my wedding dress.* She thought again of Kelo. She wondered if he'd come here to meet the queen—there hadn't been a chance for him to tell her his story. She felt as if she'd plunged into a world in which she didn't belong.

If she stayed in it long enough, she wondered if she'd lose herself, the way she did when she dived deep, becoming one with the blue until she forgot she still had to breathe.

They'd all given their names to an official who'd told them to wait. Mayara could tell that the others wanted to storm in and demand to see the queen, but it was more sensible to be invited. They'd have a better chance of convincing Lanei to listen if they didn't barge in.

They waited for several minutes, with both Roe and Garnah growing more impatient by the second. Roe paced back and forth over the iridescent tiles, while Garnah sat, drummed her fingers on the armrest, then stood, then sat again.

Mayara wished she were home.

*I don't belong here.*

A courtier wearing a white uniform edged with gold approached them. His hands were tucked into his sleeves across his body, and he inclined his head as he approached them. "Lady Garnah, welcome back to the palace."

"Am I welcome?" Garnah asked. "That's nice to hear. I know there's a new queen. Will she hear my council?"

"I am most sorry, Lady Garnah, but she will not," the courtier said. "You, of course, are still welcome to the comforts of your room. The new queen, however, does not wish to consult with those who were closest to the old queen at this time. She wishes you to use this time to mourn and to decide the shape of your future."

Garnah snorted. "She's afraid of me."

Roe stepped forward. "Will she see me? I only want to speak with her. She owes me at least this much."

The courtier shook his head. "I am sorry, Lady Rokalara, but the only one of you that the queen has agreed to see is the one called Mayara." He turned to Mayara. "Am I correct in thinking that's you?"

Mayara stared at him for a moment. "Me? Yes. Yes, that's me."

"Very well," the courtier said. "Follow me."

The courtier proceeded out of the room, expecting Mayara to follow.

Mayara didn't want to talk to Lanei alone. She didn't want to talk to her at all. But she'd come this far, and Kelo was counting on her to do this, to make sure that the islands were safe. She started forward.

Roe caught her arm. "You can't let her get away with this."

"She's the queen," Mayara said. "The important thing now is to keep her from killing everyone else." Revenge would have to wait. She didn't say that out loud, but she hoped Roe understood it was true. Their first responsibility was to fulfill the promise to Queen Asana and make sure the new queen knew how to keep the monsters in the Deepest Blue asleep.

Garnah dropped a pouch into one of Mayara's pockets. "In case you change your mind."

"There's no heir in the grove," Mayara said. "Even more would die."

Garnah glanced at Roe with a significant look. "I'll make sure someone worthy is in the grove." She then flashed Mayara a smile. "It'll be fine. We'll be queen-makers."

Mayara didn't have the heart to tell them she didn't want that. This wasn't *her* plan. She wasn't a murderer. All she wanted was to ensure her village survived.

She didn't have to say it. Roe could read it in her eyes. "You aren't going to do it, are you, Mayara? Even after . . ."

"I'm sorry, Roe."

"She killed my *mother*. Your queen. She used Palia. She murdered that heir in the grove. You can't think that such a person would be good for Belene. She has no morals."

"That's less of a problem than the fact that she's stupid," Garnah said.

"She outsmarted us," Mayara countered. "Maybe she is what Belene needs. A ruthless leader to overthrow the Families and keep us all safe, not just the wealthy and their relations."

"You don't believe that!" Roe said.

Maybe she did. Or maybe she'd just had enough of death. And if Lanei could put a stop to it . . . "It's not that I forgive her . . ."

The courtier poked his head back into the waiting room. "Lady Mayara?"

"Just Mayara." She was an oyster diver and a spirit sister and a wife and a daughter and a niece and a cousin, and she'd never wanted to be anything more.

"Follow me, please."

Mayara hesitated for one fraction of a second more. She glanced at Roe, whose face was flushed red, with unshed tears making her eyes look glossy, and she wanted to say she was sorry again. She didn't know how to fix this. There was nothing she could say to Lanei, or even do to her, that would bring Queen Asana back.

She had one responsibility now: fulfill her and Roe's promise to the dead queen.

And then go home.

*If I can.*

*If she lets me.*

Roe and Garnah might think she could kill Lanei, but Mayara knew better. Lanei would now have the power of all the spirits of Belene at her disposal. She'd be twice as strong as any heir, and Mayara was never the best of them. Three days of training and then days and nights of hiding on Akena wasn't enough. *I don't have a chance against her.*

She only hoped that Lanei would listen to her.

As she left the room, she heard a new voice behind her, addressing Roe: "Spirit Snack, this is a surprise. You're supposed to be on Akena." Heir Sorka! For an instant, Mayara hesitated, wanting to go back and explain everything—but Sorka might keep her from talking to Lanei. Might try to send her back. Roe and Garnah would have to handle Heir Sorka on their own.

"The queen awaits this one," the courtier informed Heir Sorka.

Mayara followed the courtier up a spiral hallway. On either side were portraits of queens. So many queens. She studied them as she passed. Their eyes looked out, always painted with the sea behind them. Some were dressed in elaborate robes. Others were in simple tunics. Others, wrap dresses. Some were beautiful. Some plain. *All dead,* she thought. That was the one thing they had in common.

They continued to spiral up and up. Mayara was puffing, her sides sore. She couldn't remember when she'd last slept. Or had a proper meal. Or had enough clean water to drink. She wondered if she was being brought up this far to be tossed out a window. It wouldn't have surprised her.

She wondered if she was strong enough to summon an air spirit to catch herself. She'd never tried such a thing. Maybe she wouldn't feel so intimidated if she'd used her time on the island to learn how to use her power like she was supposed to have.

*But I'm not here to fight Lanei.*

The courtier halted and gestured to a doorway. It was blocked by a gossamer fabric. Pushing it aside, Mayara entered. She was in a round room with arched windows all around. This had to be the top of the palace.

The sea was visible in all directions.

Lanei stood by one of the windows.

*Queen Lanei,* Mayara corrected herself.

She was dressed in white silk, and she wore a crown of shells. Mayara tried to think of what to say, but all she could do was suck in air and try to shake the dizzy feeling of climbing too many steps on too little sleep.

"I think I hate the water," Lanei said. "Unfortunate for the queen of an island nation."

"Lanei . . ." Mayara began.

"Queen Lanei." Lanei then turned to her and smiled. "But you can, of course, call me Lanei. Without you, I wouldn't be here. You gave me the way to make this happen. Because of you, I can fix everything that's wrong on our islands. So I owe you a debt of gratitude."

"You aren't going to kill me?"

Lanei laughed. "What you must think of me! No. Of course not. Why would I?"

"Because I know what you did." She was talking without thinking again, she knew. It might have been smarter to dissemble or plead or flat-out lie, but it was too late now.

"I became queen, that's what I did," Lanei said. "And everyone will forgive the rest, because they want to live. Renthians need queens. You don't replace them lightly."

There was so much wrong in everything she said. She had replaced a queen, and it sounded as if she were threatening the country. "Lanei, there's something you don't know about the Deepest Blue. Queen Asana told us before she died—the way to keep the leviathans asleep. Have you spoken to any of the heirs? It's something they're taught after they survive the island."

"I know all about the Deepest Blue," Lanei said, with a dismissive wave. "It's a lie. Used to limit the queen's power and to control people, by keeping them afraid."

"What? No—you're wrong." She'd heard the fear in Queen Asana's voice. The dying queen had used her last moments to warn them and to send her daughter with her warning. She wouldn't have done that if it weren't true. "Everyone knows—"

"Do they? Have you ever met anyone who has seen a leviathan?"

"The bones of our islands—"

"—are just that. Bones. The leviathans are gone, long ago."

She'd heard the tales and the songs. She'd grown up knowing what every Renthian knew: that the queens of Belene protected everyone from the monsters of the deep. This was why the heirs were needed, because the queen had a greater duty. It was dangerous lunacy to believe that a danger wasn't real just because you hadn't seen it for yourself. "But the queens—"

"Oh, innocent Mayara, there are no monstrous spirits to threaten our people. All the monsters are within. The Families. They are the ones whose power needs to be subdued and contained. I am going to create a new way forward by dismantling the ways things have always been done. It's the dawn of a new age."

"The Deepest Blue is real," Mayara said. "Queen Asana—"

"Lived in fear. Afraid of the Families. Afraid of her power. Afraid of myths. Bound by tradition."

"She was very specific about how to get them to sleep," Mayara said. "You have to convince them that the world hasn't changed, that humans don't exist. Lull them into dreams of the world before the Great Mother died, when there were only spirits. And they'll be content. And you can find them by following the trail of their dreams. Can you at least try? Please? Just to be sure."

"I'm not putting myself in a trance and making myself vulnerable to you," Lanei said with a light laugh. "I assume you have poison in your pocket that's meant for me? I was told you came with Queen Asana's daughter and her favorite poison-maker."

Mayara's hand went to her pocket. Should she deny it? Say she didn't plan to use it? Tell Lanei that she despised what she did but knew Belene needed a queen, even one as broken as she was. "Check for the monsters. I'll leave the room. You'll be safe."

"There are no monsters. You can either trust me or not."

"I can't trust you. Your brilliant plan was to kill us all!"

"But I'm letting you live now. I'm giving you what you want. Freedom. You don't need to be a spirit sister anymore. You never wanted to be. I know you never wanted to use your power, never bothered to learn how. You can go home. So can Roe. And that poison-maker, whoever she is, is free as well. You'll be happy to know that your surviving spirit sisters—a grateful two survived—as well as any Silent Ones left on Akena have been evacuated from the island already. The test will be canceled, and future heirs will be drawn from spirit sisters who are willing—with the understanding that the only danger of death will come from the spirits themselves. No more Akena Island. In fact, I'm thinking of destroying it. It's only made of bone, you know, and riddled with holes. Get enough spirits into those holes, and the whole island could be torn apart. Don't you like that idea?"

She didn't want to like anything Lanei said. The two others that survived—how many more would have lived if Lanei hadn't been working against them? Did she even know Lanei had told the truth when she said she hadn't killed anyone?

Still . . . it was hard not to like what she was saying. No more tests. *I could go home. With Kelo. And maybe even Elorna.*

But Queen Asana had seemed so worried about the Deepest Blue.

How could it be a lie?

It didn't make sense. If it was a lie, then Queen Asana should have had the power to rescue Roe. She shouldn't have been under the thumb of the Families. Roe should never have been without her mother or sent to the island. . . .

"Stand with me," Lanei said. "And watch as I destroy Akena Island. Then you'll understand. I only want to make the world a better place. Come and see." She held out her hand, and Mayara walked to the window.

It was open, with no glass in between them and the world. She could still hear the bells, mixed with the wind. It smelled like the sea, even so far above the water. Below them was the coronation grove. Around them, the city. Beyond . . . This high up, she could see a distant smudge of purple on the horizon to the north—the mainland. And if she turned and looked across the island to the south . . . Akena Island.

*Two others survived,* she thought. She wondered which two. At least there was no one left on Akena, living in fear. . . .

Out on the waves, she saw spirits spiral up out of the water. Water spouts began to form. "Are you doing that?" she asked Lanei.

The new queen grinned. "Oh yes. Keep watching." She then laughed out loud as the spirits began to swirl faster, the spout rising higher. Ice spirits flew around them, and the seawater froze, breaking into a million shards of ice as the water below continued to churn. "Finally, I have power. Queen Asana was a fool not to use it. To allow others to use her. No one will ever hurt me, or anyone like me, ever again. And, my dear Mayara, so long as I have this power, no one will ever hurt you or your family ever again either. How does that sound?"

It sounded . . . like everything she wanted.

# CHAPTER TWENTY-FIVE

Mayara watched as Lanei, laughing, forced the spirits of Belene to destroy Akena Island. They swarmed over it like ants over a ripened fruit. Waterspouts tore into its shore. Fire tore across its forests. She saw the flames grow, coalescing into the shape of humans with long fiery limbs that tore at the distant green. She was so far away, she heard nothing, but even from this distance, the level of destruction was so clear, it blackened the sky.

"Tear it!" Lanei urged. "Rip it, rend it, drive it into the sea. . . ." Every spirit in Belene was there in a froth of rage and destruction.

Backing away from the window, Mayara tried to keep her mind closed to it, but the fierce rage seeped in. It felt like boiling water being forced down her throat. "Lanei, you need to stop."

"Not until it's done!" Hands on either side of the arch, Lanei screamed, "Destroy it!"

Mayara fell to her knees. The rage—it was too much, filling her veins, making her feel as if she were going to fly apart. She felt it rushing through the sea.

The tower door slammed open. "Your Majesty!"

Though her head was pounding, Mayara lifted it and tried

to force her eyes to focus. She recognized the person in the doorway—no, not person. Three people: Heir Sorka with Roe and Lady Garnah.

"Your Majesty!" Heir Sorka called again. "Stop!"

"You can't stop me," Lanei said. "This is what it means to be queen! Take power. Use power. Make the world better. You don't understand that a true hero cannot be bound by the rules and limitations of an ordinary person. The few must die so the many—"

Garnah cut her off. "No one cares. Murder whoever you want. Just do your duty—"

"I care," Roe said. "She killed my mother!"

"Priorities, Roe," Garnah said. "Focus."

"You've woken the Deepest Blue," Sorka said. "Can't you feel them coming?"

"You can't frighten me with your myths!" Lanei cried. Her arms were spread wide, and they were shaking. Her face looked euphoric.

"Idiot," Garnah snapped. "A rock would make a better queen. But you're what we've got right now, so quit playing and do your job! Put them back!" She pointed south across the island, toward the ocean beyond.

And Mayara realized *that* was the rage she'd felt. It was rolling in with the surging tide. She pushed herself to her feet and stumbled to one of the windows. Out where the horizon should be were three smudged shapes, rushing through the water. One of them reared, and she saw the silhouette of many, many heads. "How far?"

"Not far enough," Sorka said grimly. To the queen, she ordered, "You must focus on the leviathans. You're the only one with the power to do it. We'll hold the Belenian spirits." To Roe and Mayara, she said, "Keep them away from the inhabited islands. With them riled up this much, that's the best we'll be able to do. Especially with *them* on the way."

"This is impossible," Queen Lanei said. "The monsters of the Deepest Blue . . . they're a myth created by the Families to control the queens. They're fairy tales! They don't exist!"

"Tell that to them," Sorka snapped.

"Try to get them back to sleep," Roe urged. "You need to convince them their dreams are real—that they're still living in a time before humans. That's what my mother said."

"She's right," Sorka said. "You would have been taught this, if you'd bothered to obey the law and become a proper heir. They must be kept in a state of perpetual sleep. Otherwise, they'll destroy the islands. And when they're done with Belene, they will move on to the rest of Renthia. *This* is the purpose of our queen! This is what you agreed to when you bonded with the spirits of Belene. You must use the power the island spirits gave you in order to keep the monsters at bay. Like every queen who came before you."

"I was supposed to be different from every queen that came before!" Lanei cried. In the distance, her spirits were still gleefully dismantling the Island of Testing. It had been swallowed in a swirl of smoke, steam, and water.

"If you are, we all die," Sorka said. "Do your job, Your Majesty, and put them back to sleep! Now!"

Staring north, Mayara saw what looked like a surge of sea coming toward the city. The leviathans had circled the island and were rapidly approaching Yena. "They look *very* awake." She wanted to run and dive into the ocean and swim as far away from all of this as possible, all the way home to Kelo.

Closing her eyes, Lanei focused her attention.

Mayara felt the Belenian spirits shift their attention from Akena Island toward the other islands. The spirits were still hungry. They wanted to destroy more. *Stop,* she thought at them. *Calm! Rest!*

There was no sign that any of them heard her.

"Keep them at Akena," Sorka ordered.

*Stay,* Mayara thought. *Tear it to nothingness.*

They liked that.

She didn't know what would happen when every shred of the island was gone. *Stay. Destroy where you are.* She glanced back toward the leviathans.

A wall of water was moving toward the island. "Is that . . . ?"

"Tsunami!" Roe cried.

"You have to stop them!" Sorka begged. "They'll drown the city!"

Lanei was on her knees. Sweat poured down her face. "They aren't listening to me!"

"Lullaby," Mayara said. "It has to be like a lullaby. Soothe them back to sleep." They did *not* look soothed or like any creature who could ever be soothed. There were three: a dragon as black as char, a kraken with tentacles that looked as if they could pull down the moon, and a snake with more heads than she could count. They rode the waves, so high above the sea that they looked as if they would swallow the whole ocean and all the islands.

"Your Majesty, they're coming closer!" Sorka called.

"She can't do it," Garnah said.

"If she can't, no one can," Sorka said. "She's the queen."

"She's a bad queen," Garnah insisted. "Her own ambitions cloud her focus. She's too much like them. Too much rage and ambition."

Mayara wondered if Garnah was right. But there was no other choice. Lanei was the queen now, for better or worse, and she had to be the one to face down these monsters. Mayara knelt by Lanei's side. "You can do this. I know you can. You're strong! You lived on that island alone for an entire year. You evaded all the Silent Ones. Stayed alive despite all the spirits. And you did all that before you had the power of a queen! Use your power."

"I am! They won't listen!" Lanei spat out the words. There was blood on the corners of her lips, as if she'd bitten her cheek or tongue. Her hands were curled into fists, and Mayara saw blood weeping from her palms where her nails had dug into her flesh.

Still the tsunami came closer.

"The bells should be ringing," Sorka said. "I'll alert the guards and rally the heirs. They'll need to be ready to fight." She strode toward the door of the tower.

"The Silent Ones too," Mayara called after her. "They can help!"

"That's not their function," Sorka said.

"They'll do it if the choice is this or death." Mayara was certain of that. They'd chosen to become Silent Ones out of fear of death. "Tell them Mayara says they have to choose between death and life. It's time to fight for their families."

"They know who you are?" Roe asked.

*One does,* Mayara thought. And if they could reach one, she didn't doubt that Elorna could persuade at least some of her "silent sisters" to fight too. At the very least she'd know the message came from a trusted source. "It might help."

"Heir Sorka, can you pass along Mayara's message through the spirits to the Silent Ones?" Roe asked.

"Yes, but—"

"Do it," Roe commanded. "Send the message to the Silent Ones, rally the other heirs to control the Belenian spirits, and order the guards to sound the alarm to evacuate the city."

Sorka ran out of the tower room, shouting for guards. Out the window, the leviathans were approaching. Mayara didn't know what more she could do. She wasn't powerful enough to even think of stopping them.

"They won't sleep!" Lanei cried. "We're going to have to fight them." She then turned her attention to the spirits on the island. "We'll use the spirits."

"That's a terrible idea!" Roe cried. "If we start a spirit battle, it will destroy everyone."

"The tsunami is coming!" Lanei said. "We're out of options!"

"Not quite," Garnah said. She then grabbed for Mayara's

pocket, stepped forward, and flung powder into Queen Lanei's face. Lanei collapsed, and Garnah pried her mouth open and dumped a vial of purple liquid that sloshed out around her lips.

"What did you do? She's the queen!" Mayara cried.

"She was."

The two young women stared at her.

"You have ten minutes to reach the grove and fix this," she told Roe and Mayara.

Pivoting, Mayara grabbed Roe's hand. Together, they ran for the stairwell and flung open the door. If they could reach the grove in time . . .

But then the tsunami reached the shore. And there was no time at all.

# CHAPTER TWENTY-SIX

The sea wanted to swallow the world. It swept toward the island. At first, it sounded like a continuously breaking wave. And then, as it reached the boats and the docks, it sounded like crunching gravel. And then louder, as it broke buildings.

Water rushed through the streets in great torrents, peeling shells from the walls. From high above, Mayara watched as the city flooded. She couldn't hear the screams, but she could see the people, running from the water, fleeing into the palace, and climbing as high as they could on the islands.

"We have to help them!" Roe cried.

Mayara heard her commands echoed through the spirits. Roe was calling to any she could reach, ordering them to carry people up out of the floodwaters. But the spirits, so caught up in their glee in destroying Akena Island, didn't respond.

Garnah grabbed her arm. "Forget the people. Get to the grove and stop the monsters."

"It's too late! It's flooded!" Roe pointed out the window, and Mayara realized she was right. Directly below them, at the base of the palace, the grove was buried beneath water that already reached half the height of the tower. "All we can do is save as many islanders as we can. Without a grove, there can't be a new queen. You've left us queenless, Garnah. And as soon as the spirits realize that . . ."

Mayara saw the queen's adviser, for the first time, look afraid. And that frightened Mayara more than anything. She hadn't realized how much she'd been relying on the strange poison-maker's unflappability.

She looked down at Lanei. The queen was still breathing, but shallowly. She didn't doubt that in a few minutes, those breaths would stop completely. And then, without a queen, against the monsters of the Deepest Blue—the people of Belene wouldn't stand a chance. *We will be wiped from the face of the world, like Akena Island.*

"Do you have an antidote?" Roe asked.

"You want me to *save* her?" Garnah asked. "The woman who killed your mother? You want her to be queen, to have the power of life and death over you and everyone you care about? Think carefully on what you ask of me."

"My revenge isn't worth the life of everyone on the islands," Roe said. "Save her. Let her be queen. Let her save us all."

"And if she can't? I didn't go through the trouble of poisoning her because I thought she had a chance of success. I did it because our only chance is without her. We need a new queen."

"You don't understand," Roe said. "We can't reach the grove! Look how much water is between us and the grove! We can't reach it! Please, I'm begging you. Use the antidote. Bring her back. I will accept her as my queen. I will forgive her. If that's what it takes to save Belene."

"You're asking for something that may not—"

Mayara quietly said, "I know how you can reach it."

Garnah stopped. "What did you say?"

She thought of her dive on her wedding day. "Summon an air spirit to give you air on the way down to the grove."

"You know I can't swim," Roe said. "Much less dive."

"I know," Mayara said. "But I can. You bring the air, and I'll get us down to the grove. Then you become queen and save all of us."

Roe licked her lips. Looked at Queen Lanei. Looked out at

the waters that were filling the city. The leviathans had nearly reached the shore. Once they came, the devastation would be beyond imagining. "You want me to be queen."

"You can do this," Mayara said firmly. "And I swear I can get you there."

She held out her hand.

Out the window, the waters rose. The three leviathans were close enough to hear: their screams sounded like cracks of thunder.

Roe took her hand.

Together, they walked to the edge of the tower.

"Just jump," Mayara told her and released her hand. "I'll follow."

"Are you sure . . . ?"

"Yes," Mayara lied. She wasn't sure about any of it. Except that Roe could do this. *And I can help.*

She emptied her lungs. Emptied her mind. Drew in air. She filled her lungs until they were ready to burst. The world narrowed to just her and the water below. She thought of Elorna and let that thought give her strength. Somewhere, her sister was out there, maybe fighting too.

Looking at Roe, she nodded.

And Roe jumped.

Leaping off the tower, Mayara arched through the air after Roe. She heard the wind scream in her ears. The bells had stopped, she realized dimly. And then they hit the water, slicing into it. Cold squeezed her.

She heard Roe hit the water beside her. Pivoting, she scanned the sea around her. It churned with dirt and debris—*there! Roe!*

She swam toward her, grabbed her hand, and then she propelled herself down, pulling Roe with her.

Kicking her way down, Mayara focused only on what she had to do: go as deep as they needed to go. Dimly, she sensed Roe calling for a spirit.

She felt her lungs burn, and then she passed the moment

and became one with the water. She sensed the spirits all around them, but oddly they didn't scare her. She felt as if she were one of them.

Ahead, below, she saw the rib cage of the grove.

She swam toward it, pulling Roe with her.

And then the water wrinkled as a bubble of air expanded around her. She glanced sideways to see a spirit attached to Roe. It was an air spirit, shaped like a bird but with scales in place of feathers. Its wings were wrapped around Roe's chest, and it was exhaling a steady stream of air.

Mayara tried sucking in just a swallow.

It tasted pure. Like the air you breathed on an empty beach, far from the smoky fires of the village houses, far from the mingled scents of a dozen cooked dinners, far from the stench of bodies and life. She breathed in more as she swam between the rib bones.

Pulling Roe down, she aimed for the obsidian floor. The air pocket around them grew, widening to encompass their whole bodies, and they fell to their knees on wet stone.

Sea swirled all around them. Mayara saw the palace wall through the slits between the ribs. It was distorted from the murky water and looked as if it were wavering, dreamlike.

It was silent within their air bubble.

The air spirit made a chittering sound, looking at them.

"When the queen dies, I'll lose control of it," Roe said softly.

Mayara nodded. "The water will rush in, and the spirit will try to kill us." She looked around, hoping for a bit of rope. There was nothing here. Even the heir's body had either been found and taken or had swept away in the water. Quickly, Mayara untied the piece of her wrap dress that had served her so well as a sling on the island. She tied it around her waist and Roe's, and then tied it to one of the ribs.

The spirit watched them.

They breathed.

And waited.

Mayara felt the leviathans nearing the city. They'd come from impossibly far away, but had traveled fast, their vast bodies propelling them through the water at incredible speeds. She felt the vastness of their hunger. It was an ancient hunger that reminded Mayara of the space between the stars. An empty void that felt as if it would obliterate any speck of light that dared break through its darkness.

"You'll need to make the spirits fight them," Mayara said, "as soon as you have control. Drive them away from the islands, back into the deep, before you can make them sleep."

"I don't know if I can do it," Roe said. "I didn't mean to try to become queen. My mother . . . She's supposed to be queen. All I wanted was to be near her, to get a chance to know her. And now I don't get that."

"You'll have a chance to get to know who she was," Mayara said. "By being like her. By bonding with the same spirits she bonded with."

Roe was staring up at the debris-choked water. Bits of the broken city swept by. A wheel from a cart. A chair. A body. "But I won't get to know *her*."

"The spirits knew her," Mayara said. "You could get to know her through their memories, once you're bonded with them. I know it's not the same. But it's something."

Roe considered it.

It was almost peaceful in the pocket of air within the grove. None of the debris came through the rib cage. It brushed along the outside. If it weren't for the roiling of the water and the pressure in her head, Mayara could have believed there wasn't a disaster in the city, that there weren't people dying right now.

"It is something," Roe said at last. "If I live long enough for it."

"Not dying," Mayara said. "That's what we do, right?"

Roe squeezed her hand. "Right."

The moment came both fast and slow. Slow because they

had been waiting for it. Fast because they could have waited forever and Mayara still wouldn't have felt ready.

The air spirit screamed.

Water collapsed the bubble, and Mayara had only time to half fill her lungs with air before the spirit shot through the water toward them, hate and rage and death in its eyes.

Roe screamed silently. Mayara heard her through the minds of the nearby spirits. *Choose me! Make me your queen! Choose!*

Mayara echoed her: *Choose her. Choose Roe.* She didn't know if it would help, but she pushed the thought out as hard as she could.

Water bashed against her. She clung to Roe's hand.

The spirit that had given them air latched onto her arm. Twisting, Mayara fought it off. She pulled the glass knife from her belt and plunged it into the spirit's throat. It reared back as silvery blood spurted into a cloud around it, obscuring it from view.

She felt her lungs begin to burn.

Roe didn't have experience holding her breath. She wouldn't know how to resist it. She'd begin to lose focus and then consciousness.

Mayara shifted her concentration to the wounded spirit. It was weak, but not dead. *Air,* she told it. *Make air.*

It resisted.

It was free of the queen. It didn't want to obey. And Mayara wasn't strong enough. . . . *I am strong enough.* She was the one who had dived the impossible dives. Not Elorna. She was the one who had survived the island. Not Elorna. She'd come here, despite all her fear, and spoken to a murderous queen and dived to the sunken grove. *You will obey me. Make air!*

The spirit breathed out. A bubble drifted through the water to Roe's face.

*Can't. More.* The spirit felt weak. It wasn't going to be able to make more air. Not enough for Mayara too.

*Just her. Make air for her,* Mayara told it.

That was what mattered. She could hold her breath. It was Roe who needed the time. She needed to become queen. She had to save them all.

Mayara thought of Kelo.

Once Roe was queen, he'd be safe.

She thought of Lanei, asking what she'd do for her loved ones. *I'd give my air. That's what I'd to.* Roe would banish the leviathans back to the dark depths of the sea, and she'd tame the island spirits once more. And Kelo would be unharmed.

He'd live for both of them, make art and think of her, take care of their parents. He'd . . .

She lost consciousness as blackness claimed her, the last of the air inside her gone.

# CHAPTER TWENTY-SEVEN

"Wake up, Mayara! You need to wake up!"

She was floating. And it was loud. So very loud. As if all the drummers in the village were hitting their drums as hard as they could but off-rhythm. She felt as if waves were crashing inside her head.

"Please, wake up!"

Who was yelling so loudly? She tried to open her eyes to tell them to be quiet. She only wanted to rest. But the voice was so loud. And so angry. No, the voice wasn't angry. It was scared. She felt the anger inside her, squeezing her stomach, making her insides feel as if they were being wrung out like a wet towel.

"Mayara, they're here! And I can't stop them!"

She opened her eyes. Breathed in to say . . .

Breathed in.

*I'm breathing.*

*There's air.*

She blinked hard, but it was near darkness around them. "Roe?"

"Yes! Oh, thank the Great Mother! Mayara, I'm queen. All the Belene spirits are here in the city, fighting the leviathans. But, Mayara . . . we're losing."

Mayara tried to make the words fit together in a way that made sense. "Did I die?"

"Yeah. A little bit. Maybe. But you're better now, so please . . . I don't know what to do. I ordered them to fight, and they're fighting. But they're dying. Oh, Mayara, I can feel them dying! It feels like pieces of me are dying with them!"

"You have to put the leviathans to sleep."

"It's too late for that. You were right—they won't sleep when they're here inside the city. I can't trick them into thinking humans don't exist when the evidence is all around them."

Mayara felt the monsters' hate coiled inside of her.

*Not hate,* she thought. *Pain.*

They hurt.

She looked up, and the sky was a wavering gray. A cloak drifted by, undulating above her. She and Roe were in a sphere of air, within the grove and beneath the sea. Untying herself from the rib cage, Mayara stood shakily.

Above them, the battle raged. She saw the dragon, its blackened wings extended, distorted through the murky water. It was expelling torrents of water at the palace tower. The tower's nacre walls were torn, as if shredded by claws. It looked scarred.

Hundreds of tiny spirits clung to the dragon's wings. Howling, it thrashed in midair, and the spirits flew backward and slammed against the tower, knocking away even more mother-of-pearl.

Roe was crying. "I can feel my spirits die. And when they die, bits of Belene die—they're tied to the land, Mayara. I didn't know! I'm destroying the islands by trying to save them."

"Can you concentrate on just the leviathans? Order them away!"

"They won't listen!" Roe said. "Mayara . . . I think . . . you need to do it."

*What? Impossible!* Only a queen had that kind of power. That was the whole point of diving to the grove and crowning Roe! "I can barely command a little tame spirit! The leviathans won't listen to me."

"They would," Roe said, "if you were *their* queen."

That was a crazy idea. No one was queen of the leviathans! *Especially not me!* She wasn't even supposed to be here. She should have died on Akena Island like her sister . . . except that Elorna hadn't died. She was out there, somewhere, maybe fighting the spirits too. "You're the queen of the island spirits. Can't you be their queen too?"

"I'm at my limit—I can't take any more inside my mind. It would swallow me. But you . . . you have the power. You're here in the grove. Reach out to them! Claim the spirits who have never had a queen! Make them choose you!"

"But I can't tame them! No one has ever tamed *them!*" Mayara insisted.

Mayara couldn't do it! She was just a village girl. That was all she'd ever wanted to be. An oyster diver. A wife, a daughter, a niece, a cousin, a granddaughter. Kelo's muse.

She'd *liked* her life. She'd been happy! She'd hidden her power, only using it when she had no choice but to save her family, or as much of her family as she could. . . . *Like now.*

This battle was destroying the islands.

She didn't know how many had died already, between the flood and the spirits and the leviathans, but if the devastation wasn't stopped here, it would spread to all the islands, including her home. The leviathans wouldn't be sated by swallowing one city.

Roe was on her knees with her hands pressed to the side of her head. Her lips were moving, and she was rocking back and forth—guiding the spirits, fighting the battle.

Tentatively, Mayara reached out with her mind.

There were three leviathans.

One felt cold, sluggish, as if its hate had frozen long ago.

Another was like fire, ready to burn everything until it all disintegrated into ash.

And the third was hollow, as empty as the eye of a tornado, with a stillness that could crush you and a void inside that could swallow you.

She did not want to link her mind with theirs.

If it was even possible.

There had to be someone else who could do this. Heir Sorka. Any of the other heirs. Or other spirit sisters. But she and Roe were in the grove. And Roe was unreachable now, drawn into the minds of the spirits, waging a war in the sea above the grove.

*There's no one else.*

She took a breath. And committed to the dive.

Reaching out, she touched the first of the leviathans, the dragon. *Let me be your queen. Choose me. Bond with me.*

She heard the dragon howl with rage. Or was it pain? She remembered what she'd felt when she first woke: pain, from the leviathans.

*You don't have to feel this anymore,* she told him. *You don't need to be alone.*

His voice was a whisper in her head: *Die.* It echoed through her body, making her bones shake within her and her heart thump unevenly. She wanted to curl back and withdraw her mind. But she thought of Queen Asana, lying wounded on the beach, telling them about the dreams of the Deepest Blue.

*I can help you dream again.*

*I will remake the world,* the dragon said. *It will burn, and I will have my dream. You, little worm, have no place in this.*

*You're angry because you woke, and the world wasn't what you wanted it to be.*

*The world is not how it should be!*

She felt his cry, and she shuddered as the dragon hurled his body against the palace tower. She could see the city, partially through his eyes. Flames and water were everywhere. The tops of the towers were above the waves, but the streets were rivers. She saw humans clinging to whatever they could, and she saw the spirits of Belene fighting, lost in bloodlust, against the many-headed snake and the kraken.

She touched all three of their minds.

*Go away*, the kraken's voice oozed, thick as lava. She sounded even older than the dragon, and Mayara could feel the coiled power within her.

*Interesting*, the snake thought. *We can hear her. Why can we hear her?*

*Let me be your queen*, Mayara thought at them. She pushed down every hint of doubt and fear, exactly as she did before a dangerous dive. She concentrated only on the three voices.

*You are not the queen*, the snake said. *There's another. We felt her. We shunned her. She tried to order us away. We will not go. It's our time to stay.*

*It's our time to kill*, the kraken said.

*She's in the grove*, the snake said. *That is why we hear her.*

*Then we destroy the grove*, the dragon said. He felt close, as if his breath was on her neck. She wanted to scream. But she didn't.

Instead she pushed again. *Bond with me. You know it's what you need.* She thought back to what Roe had said long ago, about how the spirits needed queens at the same time as they hated them. Without queens, they would destroy and destroy until there was nothing left. *It hurts you, doesn't it? Destroying so much.*

*We must destroy!* the dragon said. His voice was a claw inside her mind. She flinched, her hands over her ears. But the voice was unblockable inside her.

*Why?* she asked.

*Why?* the kraken repeated.

*A rich question from the spawn of those who wrecked the world*, the snake said. *Eons ago, we made the world. Us and our brethren. We made it beautiful. And then your kind came—it was not your time. We were not finished. And so we want to begin again. It is only right.*

*You can't begin again*, Mayara said. *There's no going back. We're here. You can't erase that.*

*We can erase you*, the kraken said. *Remove you and your kind from the face of the world. And then . . . it will be as it was, as She intended it to be.*

*You can't bring her back,* Mayara said. *She died. Time moved on.*

The rage at those words . . . and the pain.

*You miss her,* Mayara said. *You're lonely. You think if you do what she wanted you to do . . . You think if you live enough for her . . . it will hurt less. It will be like she didn't die. You think you can go back to being who you were, but you can't. There's a hole in you now, and you're trying to fill it by destroying us. But it won't work.*

She felt them listening.

*It might help,* the snake whispered.

*It won't,* she told him. *I know.* And she opened her mind to them, showing them her memories: her and Elorna. She remembered when she was little, watching her sister run around the house, ribbons flapping after her, laughing as she ran from Mother's hairbrush. She remembered waking from a nightmare and going to Elorna, who would sit with her until dawn telling her stories. Elorna, whom she worshipped. Brave and beautiful and smart and funny, everything she aspired to be. She remembered how Elorna would scream and stomp sometimes when she didn't get her way. How she'd climb out the window when she was forbidden to leave. She remembered how Elorna would laugh when the wind stole socks from the laundry line, and how she'd run full tilt along the edge of the cliff, as if it were impossible she'd ever fall. She remembered how Elorna had taught her to swim, how she would duck her head under the water. She remembered how they'd pretend to be spirits, wild and free in the waves, and how they'd both be scolded. She remembered the first time Elorna used her power and how afraid her parents had been—she'd called in a little spirit, and they'd giggled as they'd played with it in a tidal pool. It was the first time she'd seen Elorna scared, not of the spirits but of their parents. And it had only made Elorna worse. She would climb to the rooftops and be gone from lessons. She'd dive off anything. She'd hold her breath underwater so long while making Mayara count that Mayara would be crying in fear before Elorna popped up through the surface of the water.

But she'd always pop up, laughing at Mayara for her fear.

Until the day they took her, when all the running and laughing wasn't enough.

Mayara relived that day, seeing her mother collapse on the ground, seeing her father take his ax and hack the hull of his boat—the boat that Elorna had taken out when she had drawn the spirits. She'd been seen in the harbor with them, calling them to her.

Elorna had made her promise not to use her power. Not to let anyone see. To do everything that she hadn't done and everything she couldn't do. To run on the cliffs. To dive off the rocks. To swim in the sea. But never to make her mistakes. To do it all alone.

*I didn't want to be alone.*

She saw Elorna taken away by the Silent Ones.

*And I wasn't.*

She showed them Kelo. He was by her side every day. Whenever Elorna ran off, he was there. He'd been her companion ever since she was a child. And after Elorna was gone, he filled that void.

*Except not fully.*

There was always an Elorna-shaped hole inside her.

*And there always will be. But I can still feel happiness and love.*

That had been her mother's mistake. She had let the hole consume her and didn't allow herself to feel happiness or love. Instead she cut herself off and never stopped feeling alone.

The leviathans didn't need to make that mistake. *You can feel that again too. Even if you never lose the pain of loss. You can find joy. Like I did.*

The dragon clawed through her memories and found the one of Elorna taking off her Silent One mask. He held it as if it were a pearl, displaying it for her to see. *But she lives! The Great Mother died. She can't return. We are alone forever.*

*Elorna has changed,* Mayara thought. *And maybe she wasn't ever what I thought she was. Maybe she was scared too. Maybe that's why she ran so fast and dived so deep, because she was trying not to be. The Elorna from my childhood, the one I idolized, is gone. I have a new sister now, one that I barely know.*

She didn't add how badly she wanted to know her.

*I do not understand,* the kraken said. *Your little lives have nothing to do with us.*

*It has everything to do with you!* Mayara said. *Don't you see? You're me! Running along the cliff. Diving into the sea. Trying to flee what you're afraid of. Trying to fill the hole inside of you!*

*We do not fear,* the kraken said. *We are fear. We are Death.*

Mayara thought of the woman in ruffles, Lady Garnah, who had murdered Lanei without hesitation or remorse. And she thought of how she'd let her. She'd stopped Roe from pleading for an antidote and had stopped Garnah from reversing what she'd done. *You're not. You're just like me.*

The ancient horrors hesitated.

*You need me,* she told them. *You are in pain. Like I was when I lost Elorna. You are alone. Like I am when I'm not with Kelo. Join with me, and I'll soothe your pain. Join with me, and you won't be alone anymore.*

She felt them—they were listening.

"Roe, pull your spirits back," Mayara said.

"But they're winning!"

"Do you trust me?" Mayara asked.

"Of course," Roe said. Holding out her hand, she squeezed Mayara's. She took a deep breath and closed her eyes.

Mayara felt the spirits withdraw, pulling back from their attack. The three leviathans breathed, thinking, feeling, hating—but not attacking.

*You don't want to be here, do you?* Mayara whispered to the leviathans. *You were happy in the Deepest Blue, asleep with your dreams.*

*We know they're dreams now,* the snake said.

*So? You've fought, and you've destroyed. Are you happy now?*

*We are not,* the dragon said.

*Then dream again. But dream with me. So when you wake, whenever you want to wake, you won't be alone. You'll still have the hole and the pain from what you've lost and what has changed. But you'll have new joy too.*

She fed them other memories: playing on the sands with Kelo, dancing with the villagers on the cliff, diving into the sea. Little moments. Little joys. She gave them images of the children of her village playing with one another and of the grandmothers clamming on the beach. She gave them singing and dancing and drumming. She gave them listening to stories.

*It's not the same, I know,* Mayara said. *But maybe it can get better.*

*Choose better.*

She felt them, thinking, feeling.

And hoping.

*Yes,* the dragon said.

*Yes.* The kraken.

*Yes.* The snake.

And she felt their power rush into her, with their thoughts and memories, fears and pains, hopes and dreams. Without her issuing any command, the three leviathans withdrew from the city and swam deep out to sea.

# CHAPTER TWENTY-EIGHT

Kelo stepped out of his studio into the sunlight. He blocked the glare with one hand and squinted out at the sea. Silhouetted against the bluer-than-blue sky, he saw impossible myths: a dragon with wings that looked like a slice of night across the daytime blue, a kraken whose tentacles writhed against the horizon, and a many-headed snake. Torn between wonder and fear, he watched them shrink as they swam away from Belene and then vanish, leaving behind only the turquoise blue of the sea.

"It's over," he said.

He didn't know how he felt saying those words. Over? What did that mean? He didn't know what had happened in the capital, who was queen, if Mayara was still alive. . . . He knew "over" didn't address all the rebuilding still to come, the loss of boats and nets and homes and lives, or the mourning that had just begun.

Behind him, he heard shuffling. Queen Asana's mother and father joined him by the cliff, looking out at the sparkling sea.

"We shouldn't be here," the queen's mother said. Her voice had an emptiness that hurt to hear. "No parent should outlive their child."

Kelo stood for another moment, watching the sun sparkle on the gentle waves. He wondered if the abalone shell he'd carved for the queen had survived. *Probably not.* Perhaps he could make another, to help ease that emptiness. If anything could. "I'd like you to meet my wife's parents."

He picked his way down the path. Much of it was covered in rocks and branches. Chunks of houses had been tossed up as well—a bit of a roof, a door. Slowing, he helped the queen's parents climb around a boat that had impaled the cliff. It stuck half out of the rocky sand, its mast broken and sails tattered.

At last, they reached the storm-shelter caves. Villagers were beginning, slowly, to come outside, blink at the sun, and marvel at the fact that they were still alive.

The village itself, at the base of the cliff, looked to have sustained less damage than it had experienced in the spirit storm—their village had been the target of that storm. In this disaster, Olaku had experienced only peripheral damage. Most of the spirits' rage had been focused elsewhere.

*Not on Mayara. Please, let her have survived.*

It might be days, even weeks, before he heard word. She'd come home when she could, *if* she could, but given the damage in the harbor . . . It would be difficult to find a ship to sail her.

*And I don't know if they'll let her sail anywhere.*

She'd deserted the test. That was treason.

*Maybe she'll be forgiven.* She must have delivered the queen's message—the leviathans had departed, and the storm had ended. All was well, wasn't it?

As the villagers poured out of the cave, Kelo located Mayara's parents and then let Queen Asana's parents introduce themselves as Horam and Pesana. He didn't think those were their real names. "Horam and Pesana recently lost their daughter," he told Mayara's parents. "And their home. I was hoping they could stay with you until we're able to fix up a house for them."

"We don't know the condition of our home—" Mayara's father began.

"Yes," Mayara's mother said. "Of course you will stay with us, as long as you need."

Mayara's father stared at her for a moment, then an almost-smile touched his lips. He caught Kelo's eye. *I was right to bring them,* Kelo thought. Mayara's father said, "As my wife said: yes, of course." And he clasped their hands, welcoming them.

Kelo moved away, searching the crowd for his own parents. He found them quickly—his mother with a bruise on her cheek, his father with a faint limp he hadn't had before, both dirty, in clothes that were wrinkled and torn, like everyone else's. But they were alive. He embraced them both at once.

"Mayara?" his father asked.

"I don't know," Kelo said. He looked out again to the sea. "But I have hope. And faith in her."

MAYARA LIFTED THE CROWN ONTO HER HEAD AND FELT LIKE A KID playing dress-up with their parents' ceremonial clothes. Except this was worse, because the crown was worth more than every fish ever caught and sold by her village.

"Do I have to wear this?" she asked Roe.

"You're Queen of the Deepest Blue."

"Yes, but it's not like there's ever been one before. Maybe the queen of the Deepest Blue doesn't wear a crown."

Roe rolled her eyes. Her crown was made of delicate pearls of different shades. It had been her mother's crown and had most likely been worn by generations of queens before her. It was lovely, Mayara thought, and without many pointy bits. Mayara's crown was newly fashioned of too much gold, and its filigree twists poked at her scalp. "You just don't want to be a queen," Roe said. "No matter what the headgear."

"You know what it's like to have three monsters crawling around in your mind?" Immediately, she added, "Sorry. Of course you do." Roe, in fact, had hundreds of them in her mind. Just smaller and not quite as ancient.

*Death,* the kraken whispered in her mind. *Blood.*

Their dreams were filled with glorious destruction, tearing the world apart so that fire spewed from the sea floor and the ocean spilled over the land, and then rebuilding it from the ashes—she didn't know if they were dreaming of a time before humans or a hoped-for time after. But at least they were sleeping again.

For now.

Every few hours, one of the three would rise to the surface of her mind, and she'd have to persuade them again that today was not the day for them to destroy humanity.

*At least, though, they're listening to me.*

Sometimes she had the suspicion that they were only waking to make sure she was still there. They'd lost the Great Mother, their creator. While she knew she was a poor substitute for a god, she was at least something. They'd been alone for a long time.

*You're not alone anymore.*

She sent the thought, not knowing if they'd hear it, but their dreams shifted to swimming through great oceans of kelp, shafts of sunlight filtering through the green. Grateful for that, she pulled her mind back into her own body. It was an effort, even though she was bound to them—she couldn't imagine how much it must have cost the queen of Belene to send her mind out so far without that bond.

"All right. I'm ready. Let's do this," she said to Roe.

"Lady Garnah, if you would be so kind . . ." Roe said, gesturing to the door.

Garnah flashed them a smile. "I'm never kind. It's one of my best features. But yes, I will tell the poor lambs it's time for their slaughter." Humming to herself, she crossed the throne room . . . or what was left of the throne room.

There was very little that remained of the once-shimmering palace. Nearly all the towers had been reduced to rubble, and only the most sturdy of the interior still stood. A few rooms had been cleared out to serve as the queen's chambers, and they'd converted one of them into the ad hoc throne room.

The queens had called for representatives from each of the

ruling Families, and indeed it was tradition for them to meet with the new queen after a coronation—a tradition that Lanei had eschewed. They'd also attend the funeral for the prior queen and lead memorials for the dead from their islands.

This time, though, there had been rumors that the queen would *not* be friendly to the Families, based on a "misunderstanding" over . . . And here the rumors were garbled. Neither Roe nor Mayara had dispelled or clarified those rumors. Yet.

This had been based on Garnah's advice. Let them worry. And ask the Silent Ones to ensure they all attended the traditional meet-the-new-queen ceremony.

As the Families shuffled into the throne room, Mayara concentrated on looking regal. She watched the Silent Ones file in behind them, creating a semicircle that blocked the exit, and she wondered if one of them was Elorna.

Lord Maarte entered third, his formal jacket more tattered than it had been, though his hair was still in neat braids. She tried not to betray her shock that he'd survived. *I might have known. Rats always find a way to flee disasters.* He smiled back at her surprise, and she marveled at his self-confidence to smile at her, when he'd been responsible for the imprisonment of the new queen standing beside her.

All of them were responsible.

Jointly the Families had terrorized the queens of Belene for years. *Tradition,* they'd called it. Some traditions needed to change.

She wondered if Roe would be able to do it. *I don't know if I could.* Luckily, she didn't have to. She only had to stand there and support her friend.

Stepping forward, Lord Maarte bowed. "Your Majesties, on behalf of the ruling Families—"

Roe cut him off. "On behalf of the country, you stand accused of treason."

"Excuse me? I have but served Belene—"

"You oversaw the kidnapping and imprisonment of myself

and my grandparents for the purposes of blackmailing the late Queen Asana into doing your bidding. You knew of and did not prevent the murder of my father, to ensure my mother's compliance. And you are responsible for the attempted murder of my mother, as witnessed before her death."

Lord Maarte had beads of sweat on his forehead. "Your Majesty, as you well know, the late queen was stabbed by a rogue spirit sister, who has already stood trial and been punished."

Mayara had heard the news—Palia had been judged and given to the spirits. She and Roe had mourned her in private, and then Roe had sent a letter to Palia's daughter, with funds from the royal treasury to pay for her to complete her studies.

*Someone else is going to have to mourn Lord Maarte,* she thought.

"Palia was punished," Roe agreed. "And now it is your turn."

"But you need the Families—"

"I don't," Roe said. "Or more accurately, I don't need *you.* I do need governors for the islands, but I don't need puppet masters who seek to control the queen through threats." She addressed the other lords and ladies, who were cowering together. "Let Lord Maarte's fate serve as an example. From here on, things are going to change."

Lord Maarte drew himself upright. "And what is to be my fate? If you wish to begin your reign with the murder of the man who has watched over you as if he were your father—"

"It is not murder," Roe interrupted. "It is justice."

She nodded once to Lady Garnah.

Retrieving a bowl from a tray, Garnah carried it to Lord Maarte.

"I had our chefs prepare you soup," Roe said. "It is the same recipe you fed my mother. If you are innocent, eat the soup and live. If you are not . . . then all will bear witness to your admission of guilt."

He studied the soup.

He looked at Queen Roe.

He did not eat.

"I have done what I have done for the good of Belene, and I regret none of it."

"So be it," Roe said.

Mayara wanted to squeeze her eyes shut. But she forced herself to sit straight, like a queen, like Roe, with her hands clasped on her lap.

Lord Maarte drew himself up, as if he were posing for a portrait. "I merely acted on behalf of the Families, taking on the difficult tasks that had to be done. Yes, it was I who imprisoned you. Yes, it was I who had your father executed. But it was for the good of all islanders and for the future of Belene, as determined by all the ruling Families. You cannot punish all the ruling Families—the islands need us. And you cannot punish me when we are all to blame!" The other Families gasped at his words, but he ignored them. Wrapped in his confidence and arrogance, he waited, clearly expecting Roe to make a speech in which she recognized his nobility and pardoned him.

But Roe didn't. She merely said, "Yes, I can."

Garnah dropped the soup bowl, drew a knife, and jammed it into Lord Maarte's throat. Blood spurted around the blade. His eyes bulged. He landed hard, with a thud, on his knees, and then he sprawled onto the floor.

"Messier than poison," Garnah complained.

Mayara had schooled herself not to react. They'd planned this. Lord Maarte *had* to die, or the others wouldn't understand there were consequences to their actions. He had to die in order for Queen Rokalara to allow the others to live.

Yet it was brutal to watch.

She reminded herself of the others on Akena. Kemra choked by vines. Nissala crucified on the cliffside. The other to-be-heirs they weren't even able to identify, torn apart in the air or trapped in the crystal.

*That had been brutal too.*

"Our people need your help to rebuild their homes—you

have the resources and experience to aid them," Roe said to the other Families. Her voice was steady, as if there weren't a dead man lying on the throne-room floor. "But in return for allowing you to keep your positions and lives despite the crimes you have committed against my family, I require a pledge of allegiance."

Lady Garnah stepped over Lord Maarte's body. "Let me clarify: Her Majesty may find you useful as a whole, but as individuals, you are expendable. You don't harm her, you don't harm her family, and you protect your people. Keep to this, and I won't slip poison into your drinks that will make your blood turn to acid, your brain turn to mush, and your heart liquify in your chest. Does that about cover it, Your Majesty?"

Mayara suppressed a smile despite the tension in the room. She could see why the late queen had relied on Garnah. She was direct, and she had the skills to back up her threats. She was glad the ruffle-clad poison-maker was on their side. "Or I could have a kraken eat them," Mayara offered helpfully.

Queen Rokalara blessed them all with a sunny smile. "I think that about covers it, at least for now. I will be meeting with each of you individually to discuss how this will work going forward. But the essence is this: Don't threaten my family. Don't threaten me. And we'll rebuild our islands together."

She paused, and the two queens and the royal poison-maker allowed the Family representatives to whisper among themselves. When the whispers began to grow louder, Queen Roe spoke again. "Now who will offer me their allegiance and be pardoned for their crimes?"

All of them stepped forward and knelt beside Lord Maarte's body.

AFTER THE FAMILY REPRESENTATIVES WERE DISMISSED AND THE BODY was removed, Mayara wanted to sink into her throne, which was merely one of the few unbroken chairs in the palace, but they weren't finished.

"Silent Ones, please remain," Queen Roe said.

The Silent Ones waited while the Families filed out of the throne room. When only the Silent Ones remained, Roe raised her voice, "Heir Sorka, would you please enter? This matter concerns both heirs and Silent Ones."

Heir Sorka, who had been waiting beyond the throne room, entered and bowed to both queens. Whatever she felt toward the two spirit sisters who'd escaped the test, she didn't let it show on her face. She folded her hands in front of her and waited, more patiently than any of the Family representatives had.

"Here's the situation," Roe said, when the throne-room doors were closed. "I'm queen of Belene, bonded to the spirits of the islands, but unlike prior queens, I do not have to use my power to control the leviathans of the Deepest Blue." She nodded to Mayara.

Mayara stepped forward. "I'm the queen of the Deepest Blue. I'll use my power to keep them in check, leaving Queen Roe free to fight alongside the heirs."

She saw Heir Sorka's eyes widen as the implications sank in. She wasn't surprised that their trainer understood before they'd even put it into words.

"This means that being an heir won't be as deadly, and it won't require such sacrifice," Roe said. "Going forward, there will be no more test. Just as there is no more Akena Island itself." She paused, as if expecting Heir Sorka, or even one of the Silent Ones, to object.

They didn't.

Mayara chimed in. "*All* spirit sisters will be trained. The most powerful will be encouraged to become heirs, and the others will serve as new Silent Ones."

"We still need both heirs and Silent Ones," Roe said. "Heirs to serve as our army—fighting against the external threats of the wild spirits. Silent Ones to serve as our police—ensuring our people remain safe from internal threats. Our islands aren't safe places, and we need women of power to do their duty. But we think, without the test and Akena Island, more will choose to be heirs willingly, and therefore changes can be made that will improve the lives of both heirs and Silent Ones."

Heir Sorka's forehead knit into a frown. "Without the test . . ."

"A school," Lady Garnah piped up. "Like on the mainland. Train your heirs in a more civilized way. You'll still lose some of them, obviously, but you should be able to lower the death rate by not chucking them in the water and hoping they learn to swim, so to speak. Teach them."

"Exactly. And we want you to lead the school, Heir Sorka," Mayara said.

Her mouth formed an O.

It was kind of nice to render their old trainer speechless.

"You trained us well enough in three days to survive the island," Roe said. "Imagine what you could do if you had a year to train spirit sisters. Or longer. With me fighting alongside the heirs, you can take the time to train new spirit sisters properly. All we ask is that when your students graduate, they are as ready and capable as you and the other heirs."

"And that they're alive," Mayara put in.

"Do you accept?" Roe asked.

Heir Sorka looked as if they'd handed her the moon. "Yes, I accept."

*Good,* Mayara thought. That was the first step. She hadn't thought Sorka would refuse, but there was always a risk. Stepping forward, Mayara said the next part of their planned speech. "If choosing to become an heir becomes less dangerous and therefore more appealing, then that also means that becoming a Silent One doesn't need to be such a terrible option."

"You must still be Belene's enforcers," Roe said, jumping in. "We need you. There's no question about that. In fact, I need you to watch the ruling Families especially carefully. Despite their pledges, I don't trust them. We need to ensure they make decisions for the good of the people."

"To clarify, we want to ensure that they don't decide life would be better if they murdered the new queens and went back to the old ways," Garnah said. She twirled a pouch on one finger—Mayara wondered if it held poison. *Probably*, she thought.

Roe continued. "I need you to wear your masks and keep your silence while you serve—the islands aren't ready for so much change in our ways. But during the times when you are *not* on duty . . . Being a Silent One shouldn't be a punishment for those who didn't want to die on Akena Island. To that end, I am changing the law for the Silent Ones. I want your loyalty. And I do not want it out of fear. I want it out of gratitude. I know you have served out of threat to your families' lives and well-being. That ends now. From now on, you will reclaim your names, your voices, and your families. You will have the opportunity to join Heir Sorka's school and even reconsider your choice, if you wish—and in exchange, you will serve the queen of Belene. I ask you to pledge your loyalty to me."

One after another, the Silent Ones lifted their masks and pledged loyalty to the queen.

The first to raise her mask was Elorna.

ANNOUNCEMENTS WERE ISSUED AND SENT TO ALL THE ISLANDS.

Akena Island was no more.

The test was over.

Spirit sisters still had to come forward or risk being charged with treason, but instead of facing death, they would be trained to live. All of them. Those who wished to and those who showed the aptitude for it would serve as heirs, fighting alongside the queen of Belene. Those who preferred not to fight the wild spirits would don the masks of the Silent Ones but keep their names and their families in exchange for their willing service.

Tradition would not be destroyed. But it would change. Not because there was a new queen of Belene, though she was instrumental in implementing the altered laws. But because there was now a queen of the Deepest Blue.

It was the combination of Mayara and Roe that made change possible.

And the two queens made sure everyone knew it.

# CHAPTER TWENTY-NINE

The funeral for Queen Asana was simple. With so many of the islands still in ruins, Queen Rokalara ruled that an elaborate spectacle was not appropriate. And as she'd told Mayara, she didn't believe her mother would have wanted that anyway.

Mayara wore her uncomfortable crown, though, and told no one that a leviathan was awake and watching the ceremony through her eyes. She couldn't have explained why she was allowing the dragon to inhabit her mind instead of forcing him to sleep.

They wouldn't have understood if she'd said he was lonely.

*I do not understand such sadness for a life that was destined to be short anyway,* the dragon said.

*You know what it means to lose and to mourn. Don't pretend you're so superior that you're beyond grief. I have a city in ruins that says otherwise.*

She felt the dragon flinch. *If you expect me to apologize . . . I do not apologize to humans. I destroy them.*

Across the street, the Silent Ones carried a casket. There were no bells, no voices, no sound from the watching people. They stood along the sides of the wrecked buildings, in the muck that still remained from the flooding, and watched the procession. Many held hands. A few were crying quietly, into the shoulder of their neighbor, or openly, with tears streaming down their cheeks unhindered.

*You dream a lot about destroying then rebuilding. . . . What if you skip the destroying part and just build?* Mayara suggested. *Not right here. This part of the sea is already occupied. But there's a lot of ocean out there. What if you made some new lands?*

This time, she felt the dragon's surprise. And she thought a bit of his curiosity. They'd been so focused on what they lost that the leviathans had never considered they could build anew.

*Think about it, okay? If you're tired of sleeping, there are other options besides raining death and destruction down on your neighbors.*

The dragon felt like a swirl of confusion.

*Build,* she ordered him. Then added: *When you're ready.*

He withdrew, but she could still feel him watching and thinking. It was a start, at least.

Standing beside her friend, Mayara watched as the procession led to the steps of the palace. Then she began to softly sing the mourner's lament. Around her, other voices joined in. Roe sang loudest, her voice breaking over the words.

It spread until the whole city was singing, and perhaps the whole island:

> *The sea calls to me, and I to the sea:*
> *Come to me,*
> *Take my sorrow,*
> *Carry it away in your arms of blue,*
> *Until sweet memory is all that remains,*
> *All that remains of you.*

AT DAWN, MAYARA LEFT THE CITY.

She said goodbye to Queen Rokalara and Lady Garnah in the privacy of Roe's chambers. A ship was waiting for her at the docks. Roe clasped her hands. "I wish you'd stay," she said.

"I'll visit. Often," Mayara promised. "But you don't need me to be queen by your side. You just need me to keep the monsters from eating everyone alive. And I can do that from my village as easily as a palace."

"Plus she'll be harder to find and murder in an obscure village," Garnah put in. "You'll have to watch out for any treachery from the Families, of course, but you'll have the Silent Ones to protect you and keep them in line." She nodded to a Silent One who waited by the door.

Mayara shot a smile at the Silent One. "I'll be fine." *I'll be home.* "You need to promise me you'll keep Queen Roe safe," she said to Garnah. "She needs you." Garnah was one of the few people in Belene without conflicting interests. She had no family here, no ties, no other allegiances. She only had a dying queen's wish to fulfill. Despite the fact that she was as bloodthirsty as a spirit, Mayara trusted her.

"It'll be fun," Garnah said with a wolfish grin. "You say hello to that artist of yours. Get him to make you a less uncomfortable crown."

That was an idea she liked. She could leave her gold crown with Queen Rokalara. It belonged in the palace anyway, not in a fishing village, and it wasn't like the leviathans were impressed by a shiny circlet.

*Not impressed,* the kraken murmured.

She reached her thoughts out, but he was still asleep, albeit an uneasy sleep.

"Everything all right?" Roe asked.

Mayara clasped Roe's hands. "More than all right. Don't look so nervous. You're going to be a great queen. Your mother would be proud of you. Look what you've done already!"

"So far, Heir Sorka has five students," Roe said. "She expects many more will come, after word spreads that they're alive after a month or two. Change will be slow, but it's already starting to happen."

"Kind of helps that everything is a mess," Mayara said. And that caused Roe to smile, a small one, but it still counted.

"Everyone's too distracted with how Lanei's disaster changed their own lives that they aren't noticing how you're changing their world. And when they look up and do notice . . . they'll see you made it better."

"I hope so," Roe said, then hugged Mayara. "But it wouldn't be possible without you."

Mayara hugged her back. "That's why no one is going to stop me going home, right? And coming back, whenever I want?"

Roe laughed. "No one is going to make the woman with the leviathans do anything she doesn't want to do."

"Good," Mayara said.

They separated, still holding hands.

There were other things she wanted to say to Roe, about how they were still in this together, even if they were on different islands, and about how she thought of her like another sister. *She knows,* Mayara thought. *She feels the same way.*

"I'll see you again soon," Mayara promised.

Escorted by the Silent One, Mayara walked through the still-ruined city streets down to the docks. She wore the same kind of wrap dress she'd worn when she left home—a new one, since her original dress had been through too much to be wearable anymore, but an ordinary one so she wouldn't be recognized as anyone connected with royalty or power.

She and the Silent One boarded a small ship. An air spirit was lingering by the sails, ready to blow them home on her command. Unwrapping the lines from the dock, Mayara pushed away. The air spirit—a glass bird—filled the sails with air.

They slid through the harbor.

Mayara stood at the prow of the boat and looked at the ruined city, slowly being rebuilt by humans and spirits under Queen Rokalara's direction. The palace towers were broken, as if sheared by a massive knife, but the grove still stood, above water once more, its rib cage gleaming. She knew Roe had stationed two heirs in the grove at all times, in case of double tragedy and to guard against another Lanei. In the city itself, people scurried between the wreckage of the houses, carrying tools and supplies.

*It will heal,* she thought. *We all will.*

"Ready to go home?" she asked the Silent One.

The Silent One removed her mask. She kept her back to the city, out of either habit or caution, so no one would see her, but Mayara saw. And she saw her sister was smiling. "Yes," Elorna said. "Take me home."

SHE BROUGHT THE MONSTERS HOME, INSIDE HER HEAD, BUT SHE also brought her long-dead sister. *Reasonable price to pay,* Mayara thought. Standing at the front of the boat, she leaped onto the village dock—it was mostly mended, she noticed. She wrapped a line around one of the posts, securing the boat, and watched the air spirit as it flitted away across the harbor.

It bothered her a little that the spirit knew where she lived. But then she felt the power coiled inside her, drawn from the three leviathans who napped fitfully in the Deepest Blue, and she stopped worrying about a little bird.

Elorna hesitated. "What do I tell people?"

"Tell them it's a miracle. Or tell them you were unjustly imprisoned. Or tell them the truth. Or tell them a different truth every day they ask. The ones who love you won't care. They'll just care you're alive and home." Mayara held out her hand.

Elorna took her hand and climbed out of the boat. It rocked gently behind her in the waves of the harbor.

In front of them was their village. It looked better than the city. Granted, it hadn't started out as grand, so perhaps it looked good to Mayara only because it hadn't had that far to fall. *Or maybe it's beautiful because it's home.*

She pulled Elorna along the dock, stepping gingerly over broken boards and hopping over holes, and then they were on the sand. The clamdiggers were out, bent over the shore, baskets on their backs, trowels in their hands. On the rock jetties, the grandmothers were perched like waiting cormorants, except with fishing poles.

One of them was Grandmama. She saw them first—her sharp eyes missed nothing. "Could it be true? Have our lost girls come home?"

"Yes, Grandmama," Mayara said, running across the sand to hug her. "We're here."

Elorna lagged behind, as if suddenly shy, but after embracing Mayara, Grandmama reached past her to squeeze Elorna's hand. "Makes me feel twenty years younger to see you girls. Or else question whether I'm still alive. Nah, back hurts too much to be dead. Give me a hug." She pulled Elorna in for a hug too.

Mayara saw tears brightening her sister's eyes.

All the clamdiggers and fisherwomen clustered around them, touching Elorna's gray robes, clucking over Mayara as if she were a chick that had wandered off from the henhouse. She didn't tell them about the monsters in her head, and they didn't ask how Elorna was still alive. Seeing the gray robes, they'd probably guessed. Or maybe it was enough for them that the sisters were home.

After they'd greeted all the elders, they walked hand in hand toward their parents' house. It was in the heart of the village, and all around them people came out of their houses to stare, hug them, cry, tell them the latest news, offer them food, and welcome them home. By the time they reached their parents' door—which was battered but still standing and, Mayara noticed, decorated with Kelo's charms—they had a small train of people following them.

"I'm scared," Elorna said softly.

"Think of it like a dive," Mayara said. "Deep breath. You'll feel strange at first, and then you'll belong."

*And then you'll drown,* the snake said in her head.

*Shut up.*

Mayara opened the door. "Mother? Papa?"

From within, she heard, "Mayara? It's Mayara!" Papa's voice.

She guided Elorna inside and saw her parents had guests: Queen Asana's parents. She recognized them from the rescue at Neran Stronghold. *Kelo made it safely!* If they were here, he must be too! She wanted to see him so badly that for an instant she couldn't think. But then she remembered where she was and pushed Elorna forward.

"Papa?" Elorna said. "Mother? I'm home."

Mother gave a cry like a wounded gull. Papa staggered, steadying himself on the back of a chair, but Mother flew to her without hesitation. She touched Elorna's cheeks, her hair, shook her shoulders, squeezed her tight, pushed her back, and then began to cry.

*This is what joy looks like,* Mayara thought.

*Humans,* the snake said. *So excitable.*

*You woke up grumpy and decided to destroy a city, remember?*

She thought she felt the snake laughing but then thought that must be impossible.

A hand squeezed hers—the queen's father, sitting in one of her parents' chairs. "Our granddaughter, Roe. Is she . . . ?" He couldn't complete the sentence.

"She's fine," Mayara said. "She's the queen, and she's fine." *Or should that be "she's the queen,* but *she's fine"?* There was a difficult road ahead for her, shouldering as much responsibility as she was. "When she's certain it's safe, I think she'll send for you."

"We'd heard rumors, but . . . thank you."

She stayed longer, letting her parents fuss over them. And then she excused herself. Waving to people as she passed, Mayara ran the rest of the way up to Kelo's studio.

The path along the cliff was in the process of being cleared. Mayara could see the indents where boulders had fallen and then been pushed aside, and there were recent saw marks on fallen trees, cut away so that it was easier to walk. She had to climb over a boat that was impaled in the cliffside.

The shells on the last bit of the walkway had been washed

away by the rain, and the studio itself looked like a patchwork quilt: fresh wood hammered over the damaged logs. But there was something beautiful about it: new patching the old, pale green against the knotted, weathered gray.

She stopped at the doorway, listening to Kelo puttering around inside. He was whistling a sailor's song, and she heard the sound of wood being sanded. *He's making art.* She wondered what kind of charm it was and whom it was for. And then she wondered why she was delaying.

She just wanted to drink this moment in and make it last.

*It won't last,* the dragon told her. *Your lives are so fleeting.*

*I know. And that makes every dive special.*

Mayara opened the door to the studio. "Kelo? I'm home."

He dropped the block of wood he was sanding, and it clattered onto the floor. A bird, she saw. Maybe for a child's mobile or an over-the-window charm. He looked tired but perfect. A smudge of soot on one cheek. Scraped knuckles. Hair askew. All perfect.

He didn't say anything. He just crossed the space between them, wrapped his arms around her, and kissed her.

As she tasted his lips, she thought her heart had been deep in the blue for a long time. But now it was rising, could see the sunlight, could see the surface. It broke through. The cold was replaced with the warmth of the sun, and the darkness in her vision was replaced by the brightness all around. She was once again back where she belonged.

Once again, she could breathe.

# ACKNOWLEDGMENTS

When I first created Renthia, I drew a map. I could see it all so clearly: a world with out-of-control nature spirits would be a world of extreme natural beauty, as well as danger. Lothlórien-like forests with cities nestled in the branches. Mountains so high they pierced the clouds. Endless glaciers. And an ocean filled with sea monsters. In the Queens of Renthia trilogy (which starts with *The Queen of Blood,* continues with *The Reluctant Queen,* and concludes with *The Queen of Sorrow*), I got the chance to explore the forests of Aratay and the mountains of Semo.

But I wanted more.

I wanted to know what was happening on those islands I'd doodled to the south. How did the people there live? How did they survive the spirits and the sea?

I'd like to thank my incredible editor, David Pomerico, for exploring the islands and braving the seas with me. And I'd like to thank my wonderful agent, Andrea Somberg, for believing in me from the start, and my amazing publicist, Caro Perny, for always being awesome. I am so grateful to them and to Jennifer Brehl, Priyanka Krishnan, Pam Jaffee, Angela Craft, Shawn Nicolls, Kayleigh Webb, Virginia Stanley, Chris Connolly, Lainey Mays, Ronnie Kutys, Debbie Mercer, Kara Coughlin, and all the other phenomenal people at HarperCollins for bringing this book to life!

I'd also like to thank my family and friends.

A lot of characters in fantasy books are broken. Don't get me wrong—I love stories about broken characters who heal, whose scar tissue over their wounds makes them stronger than they ever could have been before. But I also think that strength isn't born only in pain. Strength can be born in love.

I met my husband when we were both freshmen in college. We were next-door neighbors, and we often say that us getting together was either fate or we're both just really lazy. We meant to send flowers to the university housing department on our wedding day, but never got around to it—which I suppose is a point in the "really lazy" column.

From the very beginning, he embraced my dream of becoming a fantasy writer and made my writing a part of his dream too. Since day one, we have shared every step of this journey. We face life, with all its ups and downs and twists and quirks, together. And that has made me stronger.

So I wrote this book because I wanted to write about a woman who is made stronger by love—her husband's love, her family's love, and her friends' love.

Of course, I am not Mayara. I could never dive off an ancient skull or face a sea monster. Truthfully, I don't even like dunking my head underwater, even in the shower. But I am stronger, braver, and happier because of the people in my life.

Thank you, from the bottom of my heart and the depths of the deepest blue, to my husband, my children, my family, and my friends for being my light and my joy.

# ABOUT THE AUTHOR

Sarah Beth Durst is the author of seventeen fantasy books for adults, teens, and kids, including the Queens of Renthia series, *Fire and Heist,* and *The Stone Girl's Story.* She won an ALA Alex Award and a Mythopoeic Fantasy Award and has been a finalist for SFWA's Andre Norton Award three times. She is a graduate of Princeton University, where she spent four years studying English, writing about dragons, and wondering what the campus gargoyles would say if they could talk. She lives in Stony Brook, New York, with her husband, her children, and her ill-mannered cat.

sarahbethdurst.com
Facebook: sarahbethdurst
Twitter: @sarahbethdurst

# More titles from Sarah Beth Durst

### The Queen of Blood
#### Book One of The Queens of Renthia
The spirits that reside within this land want to rid it of all humans. One woman stands between these malevolent spirits and the end of humankind: the queen. She alone has the magical power to prevent the spirits from destroying every man, woman, and child. But queens are still only human, and no matter how strong or good they are, the threat of danger always looms.

### The Reluctant Queen
#### Book Two of The Queens of Renthia
In T*he Queen of Blood*, Daleina used her strength and skill to survive the malevolent nature spirits of Renthia and claim the crown. But now she is hiding a terrible secret: she is dying. If she leaves the world before a new heir is ready, the spirits that inhabit her realm will once again run wild, destroying her cities and slaughtering her people.

### The Queen of Sorrow
#### Book Three of the Queens of Renthia
The battle between vicious spirits and strong-willed queens that started in the award-winning *The Queen of Blood* and continued in the stunning *The Reluctant Queen* comes to a gripping conclusion in the final volume of Sarah Beth Durst's Queens of Renthia trilogy . . .

### The Deepest Blue
#### Tales of Renthia
The natural magic of the classic *The Island of the Blue Dolphins* meets the danger and courage of *The Hunger Games* in this dazzling, intricate stand-alone fantasy novel set in award-winning author Sarah Beth Durst's beloved world of Renthia.

### Race the Sands
#### A Novel
In this epic standalone fantasy, the acclaimed author of the Queens of Renthia series introduces an imaginative new world in which a pair of strong and determined women risk their lives battling injustice, corruption, and deadly enemies in their quest to become monster racing champions.